PRAISE FOR

THE UNDEAD

"Dark, disturbing and hilarious. Not since Skipp and Spector's *Book of the Dead* has an anthology been compiled that so well represents the zombie genre. A must read for any true fan of horror, zombies, or just plain good writing."

—Dave Dreher, *Creature-Corner.com*

"Sporting some of the best horror writers in the field, along with a few up-and-comers, *The Undead* will leave you hungry for more. Buy it!"

—Steve Gerlach, author of *Rage* and *Lake Mountain*

"*The Undead* will strike you like a bullet to the brain. Fast and hard-hitting, these stories should fill the ravenous needs of any zombie fan."

—Jason Sizemore, *Apex Science Fiction and Horror Digest*

"Zombie fiction in its finest form: hardcore with loads of gore!"

—Geoff Bough, *Revenant Magazine*

"If you can't fly to Pittsburgh for the weekend, here's the next best thing... great fix for zombie freaks... just about every piece has a sharp new twist in it."

—Mark E. Rogers, author of *The Dead*

"A motley composition of post-apocalyptic morphine."

—John Bourne, author of *Day by Day Armageddon*

THE UNDEAD

Edited by D.L. Snell & Elijah Hall

Permuted Press
www.permutedpress.com
Mena, AR, US

A Permuted Press book / published by arrangement with the authors

Trade Paperback ISBN: 0-9765559-4-8
eBook ISBN: 0-9765559-5-6

Visit Permuted Press online at http://www.permutedpress.com

TABLE OF CONTENTS

Dear Publisher,

Attached you will find the Introduction to the zombie anthology "The Undead" as per the written contract between yourself and our client. We apologize that there will be no further revisions to this draft, as our client has been declared missing since shortly after the reanimation of the dead became a regional phenomenon.

We trust there will be no legal difficulties resulting from this matter. Thank you.

Sincerely,

Ad Gunn

The Law Offices
of Gunn and Troy

Introduction

by Travis Adkins

"I love zombies."

Couldn't be more unequivocal with that statement, could I?

Growing up in Smalltown, West Virginia, it was hard for me to find anyone else with similar interests, yet it never swayed me from expressing myself in ways that made others look upon me with a curious eye.

Take Halloween, for example. I loved (and still do) the very atmosphere of this holiday —from the overall smells of the season to the satisfying way the dead leaves crunch beneath your feet, and the way those leaves will swirl around you at the urging of a stiff breeze, (in the very same fashion you'd imagine a blob would devour a victim.) Last but not least, I love the way adults decorate their houses with orange and black streamers and whatnot, all the while trying to show an *'I'm only PRETENDING to care'* demeanor. And the sounds —let's not forget the sounds. Who could resist those prerecorded cassettes with the sounds of the wind blowing through a cemetery? And occasionally —much like the way someone would think they glimpsed Bigfoot through a grove of trees —occasionally you would hear the noise of a casket creaking open or —*better yet* —a gaspless moan.

Yeah, Halloween rocks.

I guess others might've just thought me lazy when they would see me in my costume, because it wasn't very ornate —just old

Herein you'll find wickedly clever tales like *Hotline* and *The Dead Life*. We also have the super eerie stories, like *Grinning Samuel* and *Donovan's Leg*. Or do you prefer tales of sentiment? Then take a gander at *Cold As He Wishes*, which explains to us the power of undying love, and *Only Begotten*, which shows us just how strong a mother/child relationship can be. Also worthy of mention here is *Ann at Twilight*, which chronicles a blind woman's struggle in the aftermath of the zombie apocalypse. Or maybe you want something hardcore? Then check out Andre Duza's *Like Chicken for Deadfucks*. Then we'll top it all off with one of my personal favorites, *Dead World* by Meghan Jurado, a story so unique I don't even dare attempt to categorize it.

Damn, this is good stuff. This is the anthology I've been waiting for my whole life —the perfect blend of Grade-A zombie goodness.

As I write this there is a full moon glowing through my window. My house is dark and outside I can hear the stillness of a West Virginia midnight. Some would call this the perfect inspiration. But suddenly there's a rapping —a shuffling in the grass. The crickets stop chirping and the fireflies are zipping away.

Now a breathless moan.

That's it. I'm calling the Zombie Hotline.

Don't wait up for me... Start reading!

T. ADKINS

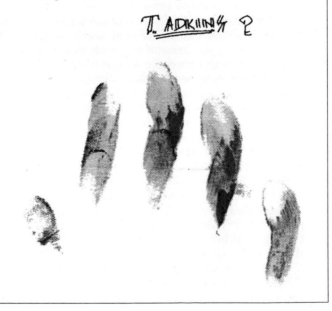

Chuy and the Fish

David Wellington

Rain came down so hard it was tough to tell the difference between the water and the air. It scoured the esplanade, a million soft explosions a second, and it battered the weeds that pushed up through the cracks in the parking lot asphalt. Chuy couldn't see five feet in front of him. He was on guard against dead people who might crawl up out of the channel and onto Governor's Island. But hell, man, not even the dead wanted to be out on a night like this. He stayed where it was safe and dry like a smart guy, under the covered doorway of an old officer's barracks. He wished he had a cigarette. Too bad there weren't anymore, not since the end of the world and all. His wife—she was gone now, and his little babies, too—she had always wanted him to quit. *Hell of a way for her to get her wish*, he thought, as the curl of her mouth swam up through his memory, the soft, soft hairs at the edges of her eyebrows—

Sound rolled up over him from the water. Sounds were coming up from the harbor all the time, but this one was different. A noise like something slapping metal. Like something hitting the railing. Chuy stared out into the murk. Nothing.

Chingadre, he thought. He needed to check this out. One time a dead guy had actually come up over the railing. His body was all bloated with gases, and he had floated across from NYC. They had lost three people that night before they even knew what was going on. When they finally shot the dead guy, he had lit up like a gas main going off and had knocked down one of the houses in Nolan Park. It had been bad, real bad, and Marisol, the

11

mayor of Governors Island, didn't want it happening again. Nothing for it.

Chuy stepped out into the rain and was instantly soaked.

He ran up the road a ways, water pouring down into his eyes so he had to blink it away. He scanned the street that ran around the edge of the island, studying the iron railing that kept foolish people from falling into the water. Nothing—just some garbage that had washed up against the railing. It looked like a white plastic bag, the kind you got at the grocery. Except there weren't any more groceries.

Not thinking much about it, he stepped closer for a better look. Maybe some garbage that had blown over in the wind from the city. The dead owned NYC now and they didn't do much cleaning. He squatted down and thought about getting dry again, sitting by a fire and maybe drinking some coffee. He had half a jar of instant hid away; he could afford to brew a cup if he was careful, sure.

It wasn't a bag. What it was, he didn't know. "Hey, hey, Harry," he called out. "Yo, big guy, come over here!"

Harry was patrolling a couple of blocks down. He had been a teacher up at CUNY before and knew a lot of things. Maybe he would recognize this. It looked kind of like a big, fleshy leaf, twice as long as his hand. It was all pulpy and shit, like the inside of a bad melon and it smelled like ass. Like cat piss, kind of, only a whole lot stronger. Dead-fish bad, but not the same, only kind of similar. Harry came splashing through the puddles and Chuy bent closer for a better look. It was attached to something, something long and thin that trailed down into the water.

He took the gun out of his belt—Desert Eagle, boy, all nickel-plated and deadly, nice one—and gently poked the thing with the end of the barrel. He didn't want to get that stink on his fingers. The flesh yielded okay. Bubbles squelched up when he applied real pressure. He frowned and turned around to look for Harry.

The fleshy thing moved on its rope—he saw it in his peripheral vision. It lifted up and slapped against his thigh. Chuy grunted in disgust, and then in pain. The underside of the thing was covered in tiny hooks that dug deep into him, tearing at him. "Hells no!" he shouted just when the thing yanked at him hard, pulling him by his leg, slamming him up against the railing.

"Harry! Harry!" he screamed. With a strength he couldn't understand, it tugged at him, trying to drag him down into the water. He wrapped his arms and his free leg around the railing, holding tight against the power that wanted to tear him loose. "Fucking bastard! Harry, get over here!"

Harry Cho slid to a stop a couple feet away and just stood there with his mouth open. His glasses were silvered with rain and his black hair was plastered down across his forehead. He was a short, skinny guy and he wasn't very strong. Dropping to the asphalt he grabbed Chuy around the waist and tried to pull him off the railing. "I don't want to tear it loose," Harry grunted. "It's stuck in there pretty well."

"Fuck that!" Chuy screamed. "Shoot this thing!" He could feel his skin peeling away underneath his pants. The ropy thing had twisted around his ankle and the bones there felt like they might pop. "Shoot it in the head!"

Harry unslung his M4 rifle and leaned over the railing. He shook his head, peering down into the choppy water. "I don't see any . . . I mean there's no . . ."

A second pulpy white thing, a twin to the first, batted at the railing a couple of times and made it ring. "Is that a tentacle?" Harry asked, but Chuy didn't care enough to answer. The club-end of the tentacle stroked the asphalt and then coiled around the railing and pulled. The whole island seemed to shudder as the thing on the other end of the tentacles strained and squeezed and dragged itself up out of the channel, great sheets of silver water sloshing off its back.

Eight thicker arms reared up to grab at the railing. The iron bent and squealed as the main body heaved upwards and into view. Chuy saw diaphanous fins, tattered with rot. He saw its long red and white body thick and heavy with muscles. He saw its beak, like a parrot's, only about ten times bigger. He saw an eye, the size of a manhole cover maybe, clouded with decay, and the eye saw *him*.

"*Orale, tu pinche pendejo!* Enough fucking playing!" Chuy screamed and he brought the Desert Eagle up to point right at that motherfucking yellow eye. He was no *cholo* gangsta (not good old funny guy Chuy; no, he had been a doorman in NYC), but at this range he thought he could score. He hit the safety with his thumb and then he blasted the dripping asshole, absolutely blasted it with three tight shots right in the pupil. The eye exploded, spraying him with a mess of jelly and stinking water. He spluttered—some of that shit went right in his mouth.

"An undead squid! Architeuthis?" Harry asked. He looked dazed. "Or is it—it couldn't be a Colossal. . . ." The ex-teacher brought his rifle around and fired a quick burst into its main body. Bullet holes appeared in a line down its back, big fist-sized holes that didn't bother the fucker at all. You could shoot a dead thing all day and it didn't feel it, not unless you got the head. Harry fired another burst at its head where all the tentacles attached: same result.

Rings of fire bit into Chuy's calf muscle, little round buzzsaws of pain. He bit the inside of his cheek as a wave of nausea and agony jittered through him. His hand twitched, but he couldn't let go of his pistol. No, that would be suicide. "Harry—*Christ!* Get some fucking backup!"

Harry nodded and let his rifle fall back on its strap. He twisted open a flare and tossed it high up into the air. Chuy looked up over at the towers on the ferry dock and saw the lights there flicker in acknowledgement. If he could just hold on—if he could just stay cool—help was on the way.

The railing groaned and the bolts that held it to the esplanade began to squeal.

"Where's its fucking brain?" Marisol demanded. "It's undead, right? You shoot it in the fucking brain and it fucking dies. Where's its brain?" She had a shotgun against her shoulder as she bent to stroke Chuy's hair. He was in a bad way. He'd lost a lot of blood and he could barely hold onto the railing. It had been maybe twenty-five minutes since the squid got hold of him. Gathered around him, the crowd had put dozens of rounds of ammunition into the asshole thing, but it only fought harder. It hadn't come up any farther onto land—it lacked the energy, looked like, to come crawling up any more—but it wouldn't let go, either. Its tentacle—one of the two big feeding tentacles, Harry called them—had wrapped around his leg so many times Chuy couldn't see his foot or his shin.

"That's what I'm telling you! It doesn't have one! It has long axons but they're spread out through the body. There's no central nervous system at all. Nothing to target." Harry looked away. "It has three hearts, if you care."

"I don't." Marisol knelt down next to Chuy. "We'll cut you loose, I promise."

Chuy nodded. They'd already tried that, with fire axes. The tentacle was so rubbery that the axes just bounced off. Marisol had sent somebody to look for a hacksaw.

The squid snapped its beak at Chuy's foot. It couldn't quite reach. It pulled again and he felt his skin coming loose. The pain was bright and hot and white, and it seared him. He screamed and Marisol clutched his head. Somebody came forward and tied a rope around him, anchoring him to the railing.

Nobody talked about chopping off his leg to get him free. There weren't any surgical tools on the island. Worse, there was no penicillin. People didn't survive that kind of injury any more. The tentacle had to go, or Chuy would.

He turned his face up to the sky and let rain collect in his mouth.

Someone set off a white flare and held it over his head. The sputtering light woke Chuy with a start, and his body shivered. He looked down and saw the fucking fish all lit up. It was as big as a school bus and it looked like chopped meat: they had done so much damage to it with their guns, but it wouldn't just die. "How long," he said, his throat dry and cracking.

Down on the rocks, Harry stepped close to the thing, keeping his head down, his hands out for balance. He had a hacksaw in one hand. He moved so slow, so quiet. He was coming up on the squid's blind side, on the side where Chuy had popped its eye. Maybe he thought the fish wouldn't notice when he started sawing through its arm.

"How long was I out?" Chuy croaked.

Somebody behind him—he couldn't see who—answered, "About an hour. Sleep if you can, guy. Ain't nothing for you to do right now."

"No jodas." Chuy tried to clear his throat but the phlegm wouldn't come. Down on the rocks, Harry stepped a little closer. He touched the hacksaw blade to the tentacle as if he was trying to brush off a speck of lint.

The squid's enormous body convulsed and the air filled with the stink of ammonia and dead flesh. Foul black fluid spurted from the holes in its back. Gallons more of it slapped Harry across the face, choking him, sending him flying on his back into the water. Ink—the fucker was squirting ink, Chuy realized. Harry thrashed in the water, the rain washing his glasses clean, but he couldn't seem to get his mouth clear. His arms windmilled and his legs kicked, but he couldn't get back to the rocks. Marisol leaned over the railing and threw him a bright orange life preserver. He grasped it in one hand and slowly got control of himself.

The squid rolled over, yanking Chuy savagely against the bars of the railing. He screeched like a dog, like one of those little dogs the white women used to carry in their purses in NYC.

Down in the water, Harry slid up onto a rock covered in green hairy seaweed. He couldn't quite get a grip. He was still trying when the squid's beak cut right into his ribcage. Harry didn't scream at all. He didn't have time.

Nobody spoke but they all looked, the way New Yorkers used to slow down on the highways to look at accidents. They couldn't turn away as the squid cut Harry into tiny pieces and swallowed them one by one, its whole mantle contracting as it sucked down the bloody chunks of meat.

In his dream, he was with his Isabel again, and she was laid out on the bed, smiling up at him. She was wearing a kind of nightie, only like one you get from Victoria's Secret. Her hair was pulled back in one big ponytail and was spread out across the pillows in ten thick tendrils. Those lips, man, they were like sugar. He jumped on top of her, felt her bones against his, and they smiled together. His gold cross pendant touched the skin above her breasts. It was so sweet, man, only why did she smell so bad? She smelled like something dead. He brought his mouth down and kissed her bony lips hard, so hard he could make her be alive again, like Sleeping Beauty.

His shivering had turned into real convulsions by the time the sky turned blue, the funny blue it gets right before dawn. The sea was a uniform and dull gray. The rain had stopped hours earlier, while he was unconscious.

"He's not tracking," somebody said.

He saw Marisol's face swimming before him. "It's shock, probably. Jesus. I've never seen anybody so pale. Do we just put him out of his misery?"

"Don't even say that. There's got to be a way to get him loose."

Marisol was used to making hard decisions. That was why they made her mayor. Chuy was pretty sure she would figure out what to do.

He saw pink clouds over Manhattan—so beautiful, buzzing with beauty—before he slipped away again.

Hot pain in his leg brought him up. The suckers on the feeding tentacles were rimmed with tiny hooks that tore the long muscles in his thigh. It had more of him than before. It was trying to bring him closer, to its beak. It must have gotten hungry again.

Chuy gritted his teeth. He felt foul—slimy with old sweat.

Something was happening.

He struggled to focus, to look around. He saw people running, some towards him, some away. He felt his leg being straightened, felt his foot being torn loose from his ankle and the pain was enormous, it was real big, but it wasn't like he'd felt before. Maybe he was getting used to it. He lifted his head, looked down at the squid.

It was rising up. Pulling itself up with its eight thick arms. He saw the dripping ugly wound where its eye had been, and he thought, You *serote*, I did that.

It was coming for him. The railing sighed and shook and then started to give way.

"Everybody get back!" Marisol shrieked. A bolt let go with an explosive noise, and a section of railing lifted up in the air, twisted. The squid dragged itself an inch closer. Chuy could see the beak, huge, hard, sharp—he looked over his shoulder and saw people edging away from him. So this was it, huh?

More bolts popped loose. Dust and rain shot out each time. The railing crimped back on itself. Chuy reached down and felt the knot of the rope holding him to the railing. Rain and seawater had soaked through it, made it as hard as a rock. He pushed his thumb into it, tried to wiggle it around.

The free feeding tentacle draped around Chuy's neck and arm. He tried to shrug it off, but it was too strong. Razor-sharp suckers sank into his back and he grimaced. He didn't feel the pain so much, but it made his body stop, just squeal to a stop like a taxi with bad brakes. When that passed, he tried to move his thumb again.

The knot started to come loose. "Somebody get me a grenade!" he shouted.

He'd had time to think about this. About how they were going to remember him. He kept working at the knot.

The squid heaved its body up onto the railing, its great big meaty mass. The iron cried out in distress. Tons it must weigh, the fucker. Whole tons. The railing broke under that weight and the squid started to slide, but it held on to his leg and his back. Its beak wallowed closer to him.

"A grenade!" he shouted again, and instantly it was there, hard and fist-sized and round. Somebody shoved it into his free hand and somebody else—they must have seen what he was doing—reached down and cut the rope with a combat knife. The only thing holding him to the railing then was his arm.

The squid rippled toward him. He could see its good eye now, yellow and black. Glassy. He saw the beak moving silently.

He let go of the railing. The squid pulled him hard and he went right through as it yanked him toward its beak. In the process, it shifted its center of gravity backward, toward the water.

It hit the foam with a splash that rushed across Chuy's chest and face, pummeling him. It was all he could do to keep a hold of his grenade. He fought—fought hard to retain consciousness.

"Good luck, *ese!*" he heard Marisol shout. Marisol was fine, he thought. It was good to have a fine woman cheering you on when you gave your all. Saltwater filled his nose and his eyes and made him choke, and then there was no more sound.

The squid took him down, fast. He felt pressure building up in his ears until they popped so hard blood spurted out of his head. He saw the light fading, the last rays of it reaching down from above but not quite reaching. He saw the seaweed on the rocks give way to gray algae, *colorless* algae, and then he saw the bottom and the dead men looking up at him.

They were little more than skeletons. Dead people who fell in the harbor and couldn't get out again. Exposed bone turned to rock, water-logged flesh turned white and fishy, their hands all missing knuckles and fingers, their feet rooted to the bottom muck. Their eyes were still human. He could see human desires and needs in those eyes. They were hungry. So hungry.

He wasn't going to be one of them.

The fish brought around its beak to nip off his foot, and he couldn't stop it. This was its world, and his lungs were bursting. He pulled the pin on the grenade and offered it up. Here you go, *pez pendejo*. Eat 'em up real good.

PALE MOONLIGHT

D.L. Snell

Crying, Nathan swung the axe. The beveled steel chopped into the stair. It squeaked against the wood as he wrenched it free and swung again and again and again.

Nathan didn't know that he was crying, didn't notice the hot, salty tears trickling through his thick beard. He was deaf to his own mutterings and numb to the snot stinging his left nostril. He was blind to the shaggy brown hair that tickled his dense and wiry eyebrows. He was too busy thinking about his father Jon, about how those . . . those *things* had slurped the intestines out of Jon's gut, how, beneath the pale light of a nearly-full moon, Nathan had pressed a gun to his own father's head, and—

"Arrrghh!"

Swinging with all his might, Nathan buried the axe into the stair. He tried to dislodge it, but it was caught in a stud.

Nathan cursed, spraying spittle and ropes of mucus. He slammed all his weight against the axe handle, pushing, face boiling red and teeth clenched. The axe began to move. Just a little.

He stopped with an exasperated splutter and wiped his sweaty brow on the back of his arm. He had rolled back the sleeves of his flannel shirt, so his arm hair came away from his forehead matted and wet.

Great. Just fucking great. He hadn't even demolished one step, let alone enough to keep those bastards out of the upper story, and now the goddamn axe was stuck.

Fighting the constipated aggravation that boiled in his chest, Dane slammed his body into the axe handle. The blade budged again. Another inch.

Then, a bad odor died in Nathan's nose. He stopped pushing against the axe and looked over his shoulder. He sniffed. Even through all the snot, he could smell rotting meat. And now that he was alert, he could hear something dragging across the concrete walkway outside. He could hear sluggish footsteps.

The gun he'd used on his father, a Smith & Wesson .38 special, was tucked in the waistband of his jeans. He tried to pull it out, but the hook-like hammer snagged the inside of his pants.

Nathan flinched as glass shattered in the parlor to his left. A wall blocked the room from view, but he could hear the window-pane shards crunch under a dozen feet. He could hear groans.

Nathan yanked on the gun. Something ripped, and the weapon sprang out. Its chamber echoed with a phantom gunshot, and its steel retained the pallid glow of last night's moon, the same moon that had formed cataracts on his father's staring eyes.

Shaking, cringing at the feel of the gun's oily wooden grip, Nathan leapt down the stairs onto the polished oak floor. The front door was straight ahead, with a patchwork rug at its foot. Nathan bounded toward it, glancing left into the parlor, his arm held out sideways to point the gun through the archway.

A pasty hand, veined with blue, shot out at his throat.

Nathan screamed and fired. The .38 shouted, bucked slightly, and the zombie's bloodshot eye disappeared. The ghoul stumbled back into the arms of its brethren. The others didn't try to catch it; they just trampled over its body, their groans muffled by the lingering gunshot.

As he reached for the door, Nathan's foot slid on the rug. His head hit the floor. It bounced, and a bright explosion blinded him temporarily.

Whimpering, he clambered to his feet and twisted the door-knob. Soon, he would burst out onto the porch, into the light of the newly risen moon, a nearly risen *full* moon.

Nathan yanked the door open.

Zombies crowded the porch. They groped and lurched forward.

Nathan stumbled back, feet tangling with the rumpled rug. He windmilled his arms to keep balance, but the weight of the gun bowled him over. He stubbed his tailbone on the floor.

The cannibal corpses seized his legs and started to drag him through the door. The intruders from the parlor were closing in, too. And the moon wasn't out yet.

With two shots, Nathan brained the duo clogging the doorway. He kicked their hands away, feeling fingers break beneath his Timberlands. Rolling into a crouch, he shot a parlor zombie in the collarbone, leaving a smoking hole in the thing's plaid shirt. The ghoul, beer-bellied and suffering male-pattern baldness, staggered back, but kept coming, pushed forward by the ones behind it.

Using his last bullet to deter the parlor zombies, Nathan strafed toward the kitchen, toward the back door, but corpses were already spilling out of the dining room. They seized the back of his vest and pulled. Nathan fought, knowing that most his extra bullets were in the vest pocket. But the zombies were surrounding him. Some were already snapping teeth at his face, and their breath was fetid because it didn't come from their lungs; it came from their bloated stomachs and intestines.

Managing to shrug out of the vest, Nathan pushed past a skinny female zombie that had her hair up in a bun. She swiped at him, but he dodged her, pounding up the stairs. Another zombie, this one a gas-pump attendant wearing a STIHL cap, snagged Nathan's ankle. Nathan fell and hit his head on a stair. He plunged his boot into the gas-pump attendant's face, breaking the twisted spine of the cadaver's nose. But the bastard clung, and more zombies were lurching up the staircase.

Nathan kicked again, shattering the attendant's nicotine-stained teeth. Then he smashed the ghoul's fingers between his boots. The attendant released him, and the other dead bodies reached forward. Nathan escaped their flailing hands and scrambled up the staircase. The zombies swatted at his heels.

At the top of the staircase there was a hallway, the oak floor carpeted with a strip of royal blue. The left wall was lined with dormer windows that overlooked the dark front yard. The right wall was lined with doorways.

Kicking open the second door, Nathan ducked into the darkness. An arm darted through the doorway and grazed his shirt collar. He slammed the door and the limb snapped, withdrew. Nathan shut the door and turned the lock with shaky hands. He flicked on the light switch, but the bulb popped and the light didn't come on.

Out in the hallway, zombies began to beat against the door. Their shadows moved in the light that leaked through the seams.

Eyes adjusting to the dark, Nathan moved to the nightstands beside the bed. A candle and matches stood on the nightstand's tabletop. Trying to light the wick, Nathan wasted three matches. When he got it right, candlelight flickered across the glass in a picture frame, illuminating the photograph within: though he was smiling and draping an arm around Nathan's mother, Jon's eyes were grave moons.

Nathan looked away, shuddering.

A zombie hit the door and its attack sounded like a distant gunshot.

Nathan dug into the pockets of his jeans. One pocket contained lint. The other held a single bullet.

Trying more than once to fling open the chamber, Nathan steadied his hand enough to slide the bullet into the .38. With the gun loaded, he tucked it in his waistband so he didn't have to touch it and remember his father—so he didn't have to remember the pale moonlight. He hunkered down behind the bed and tried to push it, but his face just flushed. He had forgotten that Jon had bolted all the heavy furniture to the floor. The dresser—which contained all Jon's socks, underwear, and t-shirts—was also secured.

Moaning, groaning, the zombies continued to pound on the door.

Nathan went to the only window and threw open the gossamer curtains. The candle made enough light that the glass reflected the bedroom. It also reflected Nathan's face, but he ignored his own sunken eyes; they were too much like his father's.

With a grunt, Nathan slid the window open.

In the yard below, zombies stopped crunching over mats of dead oak leaves and looked up. They moaned louder, gurgling, their useless lungs flatulating. Some were partially eaten, arms gnawed down to the bone and clothes blotted with russet blood. Others looked normal except for sallow skin, bruised purple in spots, except for torn shirts and missing shoes. But they all had one thing in common: they were all headed toward the house, toward Nathan.

Nathan ignored them and looked straight down, scanning the face of the house. The white siding, though overlapped, provided no handholds, no way to climb down, and the drop was nearly fifteen feet onto a brick patio; the overhang of the roof was too high up to reach, and the neighboring window, also too far away, led into a sardine can of the undead.

Nathan pulled his head back through the window and glanced over his shoulder toward the bedroom door. Something black jumped out at him. It was just the dresser's shadow, stretched into a tilting, two-dimensional skyscraper; the shadow recoiled only to leap again.

It sounded like the zombies were *kicking* the door now, slamming into it with all their weight. The door was shuddering. The doorjamb was splintering. And the *stink!* Flesh liquefying into seaweed-green rot. Bloated bodies belching green gasses.

Nathan only had one hope left.

He looked over the skeletal branches of the Oregon white oaks, and he searched the gangrene-soaked clouds for something that glowed like an incandescent bone. The moon had been nearly full last night when Nathan shot his father. Tonight, it would be *completely* full, and the shortage of bullets would no longer matter.

Behind him, the door bucked; it shifted back and forth. Nathan glanced back, then fixated on the sky again. And just as the clouds drifted past, Nathan saw it: the lunar skull, ghostly and round as a coin. It had just risen past the distant mountains.

At the mere sight, Nathan's hackles constricted and stood on end. His heart began to gallop, and his pupils dilated to the size of dimes. He felt his bones become restless beneath knotting muscles, and his beard began to itch.

The door lurched forward as zombies hammered it. There was one more crack, and the jamb gave way. The ghouls stumbled into the room.

Nathan's skeleton twisted, reconstructed. He screamed as his fingers went momentarily arthritic. He dropped the gun, and his fingernails protracted into claws. His pants, shirt, and shoes stretched against his bulging muscles, then ripped. His jaws and nose began to elongate into a snout, shoving knives of pain through his sinuses. His teeth grew into sharp canines. His eyes went black.

Unafraid, the zombies came forward and tore at his already ripped clothes. They dragged him down, and Nathan screamed, not from fear but from the pain of shifting bones. The cannibals sunk teeth into Nathan's rippling muscles, which were sprouting wiry, black hair. They piled over him, moaning and gnashing flesh.

Nathan's screams curdled, gurgled, and ceased altogether. The only sounds were hungry slurping and munching.

Then, a low growl. And a snarl.

Suddenly Nathan sprang up. He was a canine, covered with black hair. Zombies hit the wall, the bed, the closet door. One crashed into the window, shattering glass, and another bounced off the edge of the dresser.

Nathan shook off the clinging flesh-eaters and his skin mended over his wounds. Still, the creatures ambled forward, moaning. Nathan lashed out, severing arms, slashing faces. Entrails, runny from putrefaction, piled at his feet. A severed head bounced off the mattress and rolled, thumping into a corner. A bloated carcass toppled with half its skull clawed away. A dead woman fell with her face chewed off.

Nathan ravaged his way out of the house while zombies clung to him and bit away chunks of hairy flesh; their virus withered in Nathan's blood.

Outside, Nathan shook off the pests and stomped their heads to smithereens.

He looked up and he saw his father.

Jon was pale and bloated. The belly of his flannel shirt was ripped open to reveal the cave of his disemboweled gut, and a bullet hole blemished his forehead: Nathan's shot must've missed Jon's brain; then, after a pre-undead coma, Jon must've woke in his grave and clawed his way out.

With dirt still packed beneath his jagged fingernails, with dirt still caked to his shirt, Jon stretched out his arms and tottered forward. His moan was more of a chortle.

Snarling, Nathan slashed his claw through the air. But inches from Jon's sagging cheek, he stopped himself. He took a few steps back.

His father groaned, and the moon reflected in his dead eyes.

Feeling the burn of a single tear, Nathan shrugged away from newcomer zombies and loped across the yard. He howled as he crashed into the withering stalks of corn, and the moon watched over him; it was milky and pale, just like his father's dead and staring eye.

Hotline

Russell A. Calhoun

"How long have we been here?"

I looked up from my computer and stared across the office. Though his workstation was partially hidden in the shadows, I could still make out the scowl on Joe's face.

I was taken aback slightly, as Joe had not been a man of many words. In fact, in the past week, I remembered him saying barely more than a handful of sentences.

"How long have we been here?" he repeated, more to himself this time. A hint of exhaustion had crept into his voice.

I stared at the computer monitor, gathering my thoughts. Within the line of text, I caught a glimpse of my reflection, blurred and distorted on the phosphorous screen.

Christ! It seemed like an eternity since the first reports of zombiefied corpses started showing up on the evening news. But I knew it hadn't been *that* long. I tapped my stiff fingers against the desktop as I wandered through the maze of memories.

"About six months, I guess," I finally answered.

"Damn waste of a life if you ask me. How much longer must we exist this way? Tired, afraid . . . hungry."

I wished I had an answer for him. But I didn't, not a good one anyway. Not one he wanted to hear. I knew deep down in my gut that we were going to be here a long time.

The long fluorescent tube suspended above my desk flickered and buzzed like a wasp trapped inside a glass jar. The wastebasket next to my left leg emitted a sound of muffled scratching. I peered over its rubber lip. Between its blue walls laid our pet, Wormie, bits of yellowed newspaper clinging to his leathery gray flesh. His black, stumpy teeth tore into the rotting remains of the rat I had caught yesterday; scraps of rat flesh clung to the corners of his black lips.

Joe and Wormie had come into my life on the same rainy night. I had been ambling along the dark, glassy-wet streets on my nightly ritual to fill my ravenous stomach, which had been growing increasingly more difficult.

Above, the sky rumbled as if it, too, were hungry, hungry enough to swallow the earth. But I continued to walk. I rather like walking after a strong downpour, the way the air smells pure and the way it feels cool against my skin.

And how the streets are cleansed of the blood and gore. At least temporarily.

I ran into only five zombies that night, out like me, looking for food. They lumbered down the street, uncaring of the puddles of rainwater under their skeletal feet.

They didn't see me, but to be on the safe side I slipped into a darkened alleyway nestled between Harry's Hardware and a boarded-up antique shop.

I soon found that I wasn't alone.

In the alley, three teens were playing with a baby, little Wormie. At first, I just watched, hidden safely by the night's shadows. Wormie's left arm had already been crudely hacked from his body. It lay next to the squirming baby, rancid blood oozing from its jagged stump. One of the boys took his greasy knife and began to carve the flesh of the right arm. The other boys hooted and hollered.

Wormie snarled and tried to bite any body part that drifted too close to his clicking nubs.

Farther towards the back of the alley, the punks' rottweiler had its blood-soaked muzzle buried deep in the dead mother's vacated womb.

I had seen enough.

I retrieved the snub-nosed .22 from my leather jacket and squeezed the trigger. I always had lousy aim. The bullet whizzed past the nearest teen, missing his ear by a mere inch. It compacted on the hard asphalt.

The punk marched towards me, slashing his knife back and forth.

Swoosh. . .swoosh. . .SWOOSH!

Out of the corner of my eye, I saw a black shadow. A gunshot shattered the night's silence. Joe's bullet made contact, defacing the brick wall with brains and bone.

Two more squeezes of Joe's trigger finished the teens' night of games.

Two of the zombies I had seen earlier must have heard the commotion and had hobbled into the alley to investigate.

"Come with me," Joe said, tugging on my jacket sleeve.

I bent down to scoop up the baby.

"No. Leave it here."

I said nothing, but instead picked up the squirming bundle, careful to avoid its gnashing teeth.

Still gripping the pistol, Joe escorted me to an old abandoned warehouse near the east edge of the town, where he introduced me to the ragtag team he had assembled. There was Marty, a squat, scruffy man, his black hair always a tasseled mess. Marty was the communications and computer specialist.

Hank was the weapons expert. The way he stared at me, as well as his tremendous size, told me that he wasn't a man I should fuck with. The last man in the group was Doug, chief mechanic and driver, whose job it was to see that the rest of the rescue crew arrived at the scene in one piece.

Finally, Joe introduced me to Michelle, a sexy little thing with dazzling red hair. Her job is at the same time simple and arduous. Five guys alone can get pretty irritable cooped up by themselves. Michelle is a great stress reliever. There had been times that I thanked God for Michelle, like when I pulled the late shift, manning the phones. She would slink under my desk and gently tug down on my zipper, then coax out my member before slipping it between her slender lips.

Michelle's also one hell of a cook.

As he had done countless times in the past, Joe picked up the red phone receiver and listened intently for several seconds before placing it back on its cradle.

"Still working?" I asked, already half-knowing the answer.

He nodded, then said, "For now."

Soon after the cataclysm, the government set up an emergency phone system in fear that one day the local phone companies would fail. Marty had been able to hack into that system and provide us with unlimited phone service.

We hoped.

Suddenly, as if thinking about it made it real, the phone rang. The phone was actually *ringing!* Joe grabbed the receiver and began to speak.

"You've reached the Zombie Hotline. Please state your name, address, and the nature of your emergency." After two weeks without a call, he still remembered the spiel.

I picked up my phone, carefully muffling the mouthpiece with my free hand.

"My name is Dana Anderson at 1753 Johnsonville Lane. One of those goddamn zombies is trying to break into our house." She sounded hysterical.

"Calm down, madam. A team is being dispatched immediately. Please stay on the line until they arrive." With his left hand, Joe pecked the information into the database. In minutes, tires squealed and sirens wailed as our teammates headed to intercept the undead bastards.

In the phone, I heard whimpering. Joe must have heard it too.

"Is someone with you?" he asked.

"Just my daughter, Erin."

"How old is Erin?"

"She's fourteen." Dana began to sob. "Why did this have to happen? It's not fair. She shouldn't have to grow up in this world."

"Well, you just tell Erin that everything will be okay. Everything will be over soon."

"Thank you so much. With my husband gone, it keeps getting harder to survive."

As she spoke to Joe, I thought about what a lovely voice Dana had. It reminded me of Karen's voice. I still missed my wife and regretted having to put that slug through her brainpan. But she had turned into a zombie.

My arm still hurts from where she tasted me.

Gunshots exploded from the phone's receiver, then silence.

"It sounds like my boys have arrived. Why don't you let them in?"

"Yeah. Okay."

I heard a clatter as Dana laid the phone down, and several seconds later, the creaking of the hinges as Dana opened the door.

She shrieked. "Dear God, no. Run, Erin!" Her cries were drowned out by the grunts, followed by the familiar sounds of teeth tearing flesh. Dana tried to scream, but the warm blood flooding into her throat garbled it.

Joe and I hung up our phones.

Soon, the retrieval team would return with the day's catch.

"Hello, sweethearts," Michelle said as she wheeled out her clinking, stainless-steel cart, the half dozen chef knives gleaming under the florescent lights. She rolled up the Oriental rug that lay between my desk and Joe's, uncovering a paint spill of dried, rust-colored blood.

The tray is the closest thing we have to a kitchen table.

There are two breeds of zombies in the world. You have the bestial zombies, like my dear departed Karen, which use brute force to get their food. Then you have the more cerebral zombies, the zombies that were able to quickly evolve into thinking creatures, the zombies that retain their human thought processes. Zombies such as Joe and the rest of the team.

And myself.

The undead outnumber the living now, and the food supply grows short. It takes brains to eat nowadays.

Joe leaned out of the shadows, exposing more of his ghoulish, rotting head. "How long must we live this way?"

HOME

David Moody

I've been here hundreds of times before but it's never looked like this. Georgie and I used to drive up here on weekends to walk the dog over these hills. We'd let him off the lead and then walk and talk and watch him play for hours. That was long before the events that have since kept us apart. It all feels like a lifetime ago. Today, the green rolling landscape I remember is washed out and grey; everything is cold, lifeless and dead. I am alone, and the world is decaying around me. It's early in the morning, perhaps an hour before sunrise, and a layer of light mist clings to the ground. I can see figures moving all around me. They're everywhere. Shuffling. Staggering. Hundreds of the fucking things.

Just two hours now. One last push and I'll be home. I haven't been this close since it happened. Twenty-eight days ago—four weeks to the day—millions died and the world fell apart around me.

I'm beginning to feel scared. For days, I've struggled to get back here, but, now that I'm this close, I don't know if I can go through with it. Seeing what's left of Georgie and our home will hurt. It's been so long, and so much has happened since we were together. I don't know if I'll have the strength to walk through the front door. I don't know if I'll be able to stand the pain of remembering everything that's gone and all that I've lost.

I'm as nervous and scared now as I was when this nightmare began. I remember it as if it was only hours ago, not weeks. I was in a breakfast meeting with my lawyer and one of his staff members when it started. Jackson, the solicitor, was explaining some legal jargon to me when he stopped speaking mid-sentence.

He suddenly screwed up his face with pain. I asked him what was wrong, but he couldn't answer. His breathing became shallow and short, and he started to rasp and cough and splutter. He was choking, but I couldn't see why, and I was concentrating so hard on what was happening to him that I didn't notice the other man was choking too.

As Jackson's face paled and he began to scratch and claw at his throat, his colleague lurched forward and tried to grab me. Eyes bulging, he retched and showered me with blood and spittle. I recoiled, pushing my chair away from the table. Too scared to move, I stood with my back pressed against the wall and watched the two men as they choked to death. The room was silent in less than three minutes.

When I eventually plucked up the courage to get out and get help, I found the receptionist, who had greeted me less than an hour earlier, face down on her desk in a pool of sticky red-brown blood. The security guard at the door was dead too, as was everyone else I could see. It was the same when I finally dared to step out into the open—an endless layer of twisted human remains covered the ground in every direction. What had happened was inexplicable, its scale incomprehensible. In the space of just a few minutes, something—a germ, virus, or biological attack perhaps—had destroyed my world. Nothing moved. The silence was deafening.

My first instinct had been to stay where I was, to keep my head down and wait for something—anything—to happen. I slowly picked my way through the carpet of bodies back to the hotel. Each face was frozen in an expression of sudden, searing agony and gut-wrenching fear.

When I got back, the hotel was as silent and cold as everywhere else. I locked myself in my room and waited for hours until the solitude and claustrophobic fear finally became too much to stand. I needed explanations, but there was no one else left alive to ask for help. The television was dead, as was the radio and the telephone. Within hours, the power had died too. Desperate and terrified, I packed my few belongings, took a car from the parking garage and made a break for home. But I soon found that the hushed roads were impassable, blocked by the twisted and tangled wreckage of incalculable numbers of crashed vehicles and the mangled, bloody remains of their dead drivers and passengers. With my wife and my home still more than eighty miles away, I stopped the car and gave up.

It was early on the first Thursday, the third day, when the situation deteriorated again to the point where I questioned my sanity. I had been resting in the front bedroom of an empty terraced house when I looked out the window and saw the first of them staggering down the road. All the fear and nervousness I had previously felt instantly disappeared. At last, someone who might be able to tell me what had happened and who could answer some of the thousands of impossible questions I desperately needed to ask. I called out and banged on the window, but the person didn't respond. I sprinted out of the house and ran down the road after him. I grabbed hold of his arm and turned him to face me. As unbelievable as it seemed, I knew instantly that the thing in front of me was dead. Its eyes were clouded with a milky-white film, and its skin was pockmarked and bloodied. And it was cold to the touch. Leathery. Clammy. I let it go in disgust. The moment I released my grip, the damn thing shuffled away, this time moving back in the direction from which it had come. It couldn't see me. It didn't even seem to know I was there.

More bodies began to rise. Many were already staggering around on clumsy, unsteady feet whilst still more were slowly dragging themselves up from where they'd fallen days earlier.

A frantic search for food and water and safe shelter led me deeper into town. Avoiding the clumsy, mannequin-like bodies which roamed the streets, I barricaded myself in a large pub on the corner of two once busy roads. I removed eight corpses from the building (I herded them into the bar before forcing them out the front door), and I locked myself in an upstairs function room where I started to drink. Although it didn't make me drunk like it used to, the alcohol made me feel warm and took the very slightest edge off my fear.

I thought constantly about Georgie, about home, but I was too afraid to move. I knew that I should try to get to her, but for days I just sat there and waited like a chicken-shit. Every morning, I tried to force myself to move, but the thought of going back outside was unbearable. I didn't know what I'd find out there. Instead, I sat in isolation and watched the world decay.

As the days passed, the bodies themselves changed. Initially stiff, awkward and staccato, their movements slowly became more definite, purposeful and controlled. After four days, their senses began to return. They were starting to respond to what was happening around them. Late one afternoon, in a fit of frightened frustration, I hurled an empty beer bottle across the room. I missed the wall and smashed a window. Out of curiosity, I looked down into the street and saw that a large number of the corpses had turned toward the sudden noise and were beginning to walk towards the pub. During the hours which followed, I tried to keep quiet and out of sight, but my every movement seemed to make more of them aware of my presence. From every direction they came, and all that I could do was watch as a crowd of hundreds upon hundreds of the fucking things surrounded me. They followed each other like animals and soon their lumbering, decomposing shapes filled the streets as far as I could see.

A week went by, and the ferocity of the creatures outside increased. They began to fight with each other. They clawed and banged at the doors, but didn't yet have the strength to get inside. My options were hopelessly limited, but I knew that I had to do something. I could stay and hope that I could drink enough so that I didn't care when the bodies eventually broke through, or I could make a break for freedom and take my chances outside. I had nothing to lose. I thought about home and I thought about Georgie and I knew that I had to try to get back to her.

It wasn't much of a plan, but it was all that I had. I packed all my meager supplies and provisions into a rucksack. I made crates of crude bombs from liquor bottles. As the light began to fade at the end of the tenth day, I leaned out of the broken window at the front of the building, lit the booze-soaked rags which I had stuffed down the necks of the bottles, and then began to hurl them down into the rotting crowd. In minutes, I'd created more devastation and confusion than I ever would have imagined possible. There had been little rain for days. Tinder dry and packed tightly together, the repugnant bodies sparked almost instantly. Ignorant to the flames which quickly consumed them, the damn things continued to move about for as long as they were physically able, their every staggering step spreading the fire and destroying more of them. And the dancing orange light of the sudden inferno, the crackling and popping of flesh drew even more of the desperate cadavers to the scene.

I crept downstairs and waited by the back door. The building itself was soon alight. Doubled-up with hunger pangs (the world outside had suddenly become filled with the smell of roasted meat), I crouched down in the darkness and waited until the temperature in the building became too much to stand. When the flames began to lick at the door separating me from the rest of the pub, I pushed my way into the night and ran through the bodies. Their reactions were dull and slow, and my speed, strength, and the surprise of my sudden appearance meant that they offered virtually no resistance. In the silent, monochrome world, the confusion that I'd left behind offered enough of a distraction to camouflage my movements and render me temporarily invisible.

* * *

Since I've been on the move, I've learned to live like a shadow. My difficult journey home has been painfully long and slow. I move only at night under cover of darkness. If the bodies see or hear me they will come for me, and, as I've found to my cost on more than one occasion, once one of them has my scent countless others soon follow. I have avoided them as much as possible, but their numbers are vast and some contact has been inevitable. I'm getting better at dealing with them. The initial disgust and trepidation has now given way to hate and anger. Through necessity, I have become a cold and effective killer, although I'm not sure whether that's an accurate description of my newfound skill. I have to keep reminding myself that these bloody things are already dead.

Apart from the mass of bodies I managed to obliterate during my escape from the pub, the first corpse I intentionally disposed of had once been a priest. I came across the rancid, emaciated creature when I took shelter at dawn in a small village church. The building had appeared empty at first until I pushed my way into a narrow, shadowy storeroom at the far end of the grey-stone building. A rack of mops, brushes and brooms, which had fallen across the doorway, had blocked the only way in or out of the room. I forced my way inside and was immediately aware of shuffling movement ahead of me. A small window high on the wall to my left let a limited amount of light spill into the storeroom, allowing me to see the outline of the priest's body as it lunged and tripped towards me. The cadaver was weak and uncoordinated, and I instinctively threw it back across the room. It smashed into a shelf piled high with prayer and hymn books and then crumbled to the ground, the books crashing down atop it. I stared into its vacant, hollowed face as it dragged itself into the light again. The first body I had seen up close for several days, it was a fucking mess. Just a shadow of the man it had once been, the creature's skin appeared taut and translucent and it had an unnatural green-grey hue. Its cheeks and eye sockets were dark and sunken, and its mouth and chin were speckled with dribbles of dried blood. Its dog collar hung loose around its scrawny neck.

When the body charged at me again, I was knocked off-balance, but I managed to grab hold of its throat and keep it at a safe distance. Its limbs flailed around me as I looked deep into its cloudy, emotionless eyes. I used my free hand to feel around for a weapon. My outstretched fingers wrapped around a heavy and ornate candleholder. I gripped it tightly and, using the base, I bashed the priest's exposed skull. Stunned but undeterred, the body tripped and stumbled back before coming for me again. I hit it again and again until there was little left of the head other than a dark mass of blood, brain and shattered bone. I stood over the twitching remains of the cleric until it finally lay still.

I hid in the bell tower of the church and waited for the night to come.

* * *

It didn't take long to work out the rules.

Although they have become increasingly violent, these creatures are simple and predictable. I think that they are driven purely by instinct. Each one is little more than a fading memory of what it used to be. I quickly learnt that this reality is nothing like the trash horror movies I used to watch or the books I used to read. These things don't want to kill me so that they can feast on my flesh. In fact, I don't actually think they have any physical needs or desires—they don't eat, drink, sleep or even breathe as far as I can see. So why do they attack me, and why do I have to creep through the shadows in fear of them? It's a paradox, but the longer I think about it, the more convinced I am that they attack me out of fear. I think they try to attack me before I have the chance to destroy them.

Over the last few days and weeks, I have watched them steadily disintegrate and decay. Another bizarre irony—as their bodies have continued to weaken and become more fragile, their mental control seems to have returned. They respond violently to any perceived threat, as if they want to exist at all costs. Sometimes they fight between themselves, and I have hidden in the darkness and watched them tear at each other until almost all their rotten flesh has been stripped from their bones.

I know beyond doubt now that the brain remains the center of control. My second, third and fourth kills confirmed that. I had broken into an isolated house in search of food and fresh clothes and found myself face to face with what appeared to be the rotting remains of a typical family. I quickly disposed of the father with a short wooden fence post that I had been carrying as a makeshift weapon. I smacked the repulsive creature around the side of the head nearly to the point of decapitation.

The next body—the mother, I presumed—proved to be more troublesome. I pushed my way through a ground floor doorway and entered a large, square dining room. With sudden, unexpected speed, the body of the woman hurled itself at me from across the room. I held the picket out in front of me, and the wood plunged through the corpse's abdomen. I retched and struggled to keep control of my stomach as its putrefied organs slid out the hole in its back and slopped down onto the dusty cream-colored carpet. I pushed the body away, expecting it to collapse and crumble like the last one, but it didn't. Instead, it staggered after me, still impaled and struggling to move as I had obviously damaged its spine. As it lurched closer, I ran to the kitchen and grabbed the largest knife I could find. The body had managed to take a few more steps forward, but stopped immediately when I plunged the knife through its right temple. It was as if someone had flicked a switch. The body dropped to the ground like a bloodied rag-doll. In the silence which followed I could hear the third body thumping around upstairs. To prove my theory I ran up the stairs and disposed of a dead teenager in the same way as its mother with a single stab of the blade to the head.

It is wrong and unsettling, but I have to admit that I've grown to enjoy the kill. The reality is that this is the only pleasure left. It is the only time I have complete control. I haven't ever gone looking for sport, but I haven't avoided it either. I've kept a tally of kills along the way, and I have begun to pride myself on finding quicker, quieter and more effective ways to destroy the dead. I took a gun from a police station a week or so ago, but quickly got rid of it. A shot to the head will immediately take out a single body, but the resultant noise inevitably attracts thousands more of the damn things. Weapons now need to be silent and swift. I've tried clubs and axes, and whilst they've often been effective, real sustained effort is usually needed to get results. Fire is too visible and unpredictable, and so blades have become my weapons of choice. I now carry seventeen in all: buck knifes, sheath knives, Bowie knifes, scalpels and even pen knives. I carry two meat cleavers holstered like pistols, and I hold a machete drawn and ready at all times.

* * *

I've made steady progress so far today. I know this stretch of footpath well. It twists and turns, and it's not the most direct route home, but it's my best option this morning. Dawn is beginning to break. The light is getting stronger now and I'm starting to feel exposed and uncomfortable. I've not been out in daylight for weeks now. I've become used to the dark and the shelter it gives me.

This short stretch of path runs alongside a golf course. There seems to be an unusually high number of bodies around here. I think this was the seventh hole—a short but tough hole, from what I remember, with a raised tee and an undulating fairway. Many of the corpses appear to be trapped in the natural dip of the land here, and the once well-tended grass has been churned to mud beneath their clumsy feet. They can't get away. Stupid fucking things are stuck. Sometimes I almost feel privileged to rid the world of these pointless creatures. All that separates me from them is a strip of chain-link fence and tangled, patchy hedgerow. I keep quiet and take each step with care. It will be easier if I don't have to deal with them this morning.

The path arcs away to the left. There are two bodies up ahead of me now, and I know I have no choice but to get rid of them. The second seems to be following the first, and I wonder if there are any more behind. However many of them there are, I know that I'll have to deal with them quickly. It will take too long to go around them, and any sudden movement will alert any others in the shadows nearby. The safest and easiest option is to go straight at them and cut them both down.

Here's the first. It's seen me. It makes a sudden, lurching change in direction. Fixing me with its dull, misted eyes, it starts to come my way. Bloody hell, it's badly decayed—one of the worst I've seen. I can't even tell whether it used to be male or female. Most of its face has been eaten away, and its mottled, pock-marked skull is dotted with clumps of long, lank and greasy grey-blonde hair. It's dragging one foot behind it. In fact, its right ankle ends unexpectedly with a dirty stump, which it drags awkwardly through the mud, grass and gravel. The rags wrapped around the corpse look like they might once have been a uniform. Was this a police officer? A traffic warden perhaps? Whatever it used to be, its time is now up.

I've developed a two-cut technique for getting rid of corpses. It's safer than running headlong at them, swinging a blade through the air like a madman. A little bit of control makes all the difference. Usually, the bodies are already unsteady (this one certainly is), so I tend to use the first cut to stop their movement. The body is close enough now. I crouch down and swing the machete from right to left, severing both of its legs at knee level. With the corpse now flat on what's left of its stomach, I reverse the movement and, backhanded, slam the blade down through its neck before it has time to move. Easy. Kill number one hundred and thirty-eight. Number one hundred and thirty-nine proves to be slightly harder. I slip and bury the blade in the creature's pelvis, though I was aiming lower. No problem—with the corpse down on its knees, I lift the machete again and bring it down on top of its head. The skull splits like an egg.

I never think of the bodies as people anymore. There's no point. Whatever caused all of this has wiped out every trace of individuality and character from the rotting masses. Generally, they all behave the same—age, race, sex, class, religion and all other social differences are gone. There are no distinctions, there are only the dead, a single massive decaying population. Kill number twenty-six brought it home to me. Obviously the body of a very young child, it had attacked me with as much force and intent as the countless other adult creatures I had come across. I had hesitated for a split-second before the kill, but it was dead flesh and it needed to be destroyed. I took its head clean off with a hand axe and hardly gave it another moment's thought.

* * *

Distances that should take minutes to cover are now taking me hours. I'm working my way along a wide footpath which leads down into the heart of Stonemorton. I can see bodies everywhere. The earlier mist has lifted, and I can now see their slow stumbling shapes moving between houses and dragging themselves along otherwise empty streets. My already slow speed seems to have reduced now that it's getting light. Maybe I'm slowing down on purpose? The closer I get to home, the more nervous and unsure I feel. I try to concentrate and focus my thoughts on Georgie. All I want is to see her and be with her again; what's happened to the rest of the world is of no interest. I'm realistic about what I'm going to find—I haven't seen another living soul for four weeks, and I don't think for a second that I'll find her alive. But I've survived, haven't I? There is still some slight hope. My worst fear is that the house will be empty. I'll have to keep looking for her if she's not there. And I won't rest until we're together again.

Damn. Suddenly there are at least four bodies up ahead. The closer I get to the streets, the more of them there are. I can't be completely sure how many there are here because their awkward, gangly shapes merge and disappear into the background of gnarled, twisted trees. I'm not too worried about four. In fact, I'm pretty confident dealing with anything up to ten. All I have to do is take my time, keep calm, and try not to make more noise than necessary.

The nearest body has locked onto me and is lining itself up to be kill number one hundred and forty. Bloody hell, this is the tallest corpse I've seen. Even though its back is twisted into an uncomfortable stoop, it's still taller than me. I need to lower it to get a good shot at the brain. I swing the machete up between its legs and practically split it in two. It slumps at my feet, and I swipe its head clean off its shoulders before it has even hit the mud.

One hundred and forty-one. This one is more lively than most. I've come across a few like this from time to time. For some reason, bodies like this one are not as decayed, and for a split second, I start to wonder whether this might actually be a survivor. When it lunges at me with sudden, clumsy force, I know immediately that it is already dead. I lift up my blade and put it in the way of the creature's head. Still moving forward, it impales itself and falls limp.

My weapon is stuck, wedged tight in the skull of this fucking monstrosity. The next body is close now. Tugging at the machete with my right hand, I yank one of the meat cleavers out of its holster and swing it wildly at the shape stumbling towards me. I slice diagonally across the width of its torso, but it doesn't even seem to notice the damage. I let go of the machete (I'll go back for it when I'm done), and using both cleavers now, I attack the third body again. I strike with my left hand, cutting through the collarbone and forcing the body down. I aim the second cut at the base of the neck and smash through the spinal cord. I push the cadaver down into the gravel and stamp on its expressionless face until my boot does enough damage to permanently stop the bloody thing from moving. For a second, I feel like a fucking Kung-fu master.

With the first cleaver still buried in the shoulder of the last body, I'm now two weapons down with potential kill number one hundred and forty-three less than two meters away. This one is slower, and it's got less fight in it than the last few. Breathing heavily, I clench my fist and punch it square in the face. It wobbles for a second before dropping to the ground. I enjoy kills like that. My hand stings and is covered in all kinds of foul-smelling mess, but the sudden feeling of strength and superiority I have is immense.

I retrieve my two blades, clean them on a patch of grass and carry on.

* * *

In the distance, I can see the first few houses on the estate. I'm almost there now, and I'm beginning to wish that I wasn't. I've spent days on the move trying to get here—long, dark, lonely days filled with uncertainty and fear. Now that I'm here, there's a part of me that wants to turn around and go back. But I know that there's nowhere else to go, and I know I have to do this. I have to see it through.

I'm down at street level now, and I'm more exposed than ever. Christ, everything looks so different. It's only been a month or so since I was last here, but in that time, the world has been left to rot and disintegrate. The smell of death is everywhere, choking, smothering and suffocating everything. The once clear grey pavements are overgrown with green-brown moss and weeds. Everything is crumbling around me. I've walked down plenty of city streets like this since it happened, but this one feels different. I know this place. Huntingden Street. I used to drive this way to work, and the memories suddenly make everything a hundred times harder to handle.

Almost this entire side of the road has been burnt to the ground, and where there used to be a meandering row of thirty-some houses, now there are just empty, wasted shells. The destruction seems to have altered the whole landscape, and from where I'm standing, I now have a clear view all the way over to the red-brick wall that runs along the edge of the estate where Georgie and I used to live. It's so close now. I've been rehearsing this part of the journey for days. I'm going to work my way home by cutting through the back gardens of the houses along the way. I'm thinking that, behind the houses, I should be secure and enclosed, attract less attention. I'll be able to take my time. There will probably be bodies along the way, but they should be fewer in number than those roaming the main roads.

I'm crouching down behind a low wall in front of the remains of a burnt-out house. I need to get across the road and into the garden at the back of one of the houses opposite. The easiest way will be to go straight through—in through the front door and out through the back. Everything looks clear. I can't see any bodies. Apart from my knives, I'll leave my supplies here. I won't need any of it. I'm almost home now.

* * *

Slow going. Getting into the first garden was simple enough but moving between properties isn't as easy as I thought. I have to climb over fences nowhere near strong enough to support me. I could just break them down, but I can't afford to make too much noise. I don't want to start taking unnecessary chances now.

Garden number three. I can see the dead owner of this house trapped inside its property. It's leaning against the patio window, and when it sees me, it starts hammering pointlessly against the glass. From my position, mid-way down the lawn, the figure at the window looks painfully thin and skeletal. I can see another body shuffling through the shadows behind it.

Garden number four. Fucking hell, the owner of this house is outside. It's moving towards me before I've even made it over the fence, and the expression on what's left of its face is fucking terrifying. My heart's beating like it's going to explode. Jumping down, I steady myself and ready my machete. A few seconds wait, a single flash of the blade, and it's done. The cadaver keeps moving until it stumbles and falls. Its severed head lies at my feet, face down on the dew-soaked grass like a piece of rotten fruit. One hundred and forty-four.

Garden number five is clear, as is garden number six. I've now made it as far as the penultimate house. I sprint across the grass, scale the fence, and then jump down and run across the final strip of lawn. On the other side of the last brick wall is Partridge Road. The driveway of my estate is another hundred meters or so down to my right.

I throw myself over the top of the wall. When I land on the pavement, searing pains shoot up my legs. I trip and fall into the road. There are bodies here. A quick look up and down the road and I can see seven or eight of them already. They've all seen me. This isn't good. No time for technique now—I have to get rid of them as quickly as possible. I take the first two out almost instantly with the machete. I start to run towards the road into the estate, and I decapitate the third corpse as I pass it. I push another one out of the way (no time to go back and finish it off) and then chop the next one, which staggers into my path. I manage a single, brutal cut just above its waist, deep enough to hack through the spinal cord. It falls to the ground behind me, still moving but going nowhere. I count it as a kill. One hundred and forty-eight.

I can see the entrance to the estate clearly now. The rusted wrecks of two cars have almost completely blocked the mouth of the road. Good. The blockage here means that there shouldn't be too many bodies on the other side. Damn, there are still more coming for me on this side though. Christ, there are *loads* of the bloody things. Where the hell are they coming from?

I look up and down the road again, and all I can see is a mass of twisted, stumbling corpses. My arrival here must have created more of a disturbance than I thought. There are too many to deal with. Some are quicker than others, and the first few are already getting close. Too close.

I sprint towards the crashed cars as fast as I can, dropping my shoulder and barging several cadavers out of the way. I jump onto the crumpled bonnet of the first car and climb to its roof. The rabid dead don't have the strength or coordination to climb up after me. And even if they did, I'd just kick the fucking things down again.

I stand still for a few long seconds and catch my breath. Below me, the sea of decomposing faces grows, facial muscles withered and decayed, incapable of controlled expression. Nevertheless, the way they look up at me reveals a cold and savage intent. They hate me. If I had the time and energy, I'd show that the feeling is mutual. I'd jump into the crowd and rip every last one apart.

Still standing on the roof of the car, I slowly turn around.

Home.

Torrington Road stretches out ahead of me now, wild and overgrown but still reassuringly familiar. Just ahead and to my right is the entrance to Harlour Grove. Our road. Our house is at the end of the cul-de-sac.

I'd stay here for a while and try to compose myself if not for the bodies snapping and scratching at my feet. I jump down from the car, but turn back for a second—something's caught my eye. Now that I'm down, I recognize the car. I glance at the rear license plate. It's cracked and smashed, but I can still make out the last three letters: 'HAL'. This is Stan Isherwood's car. He lived four doors down from Georgie and me. And fucking hell, that thing in the front seat is what's left of Stan. What remains of the retired bank manager slams itself from side to side, trying desperately to get out, to get to me. It's held in place by its safety belt. Stupid bloody thing can't release the catch.

Without thinking, I crouch and peer through the grubby glass. My decomposing neighbor stops moving for a fraction of a second and looks straight back at me. Jesus Christ, there's not much left of him, but I can still see that it's Stan. He's wearing one of his trademark golf jumpers. The pastel colors of the fabric are mottled and dark, covered with dribbles of crusted blood and other bodily secretions. I jog away. It doesn't pose any threat to me. And I can't bring myself to kill Stan just for the sake of it.

From the shadows of a nearby house, a body emerges. Back to business as usual. I tighten the grip on the machete. The corpse lurches for me. Thankfully, no one I know. Or recognize, anyway. I swing at its head, and the blade sinks three quarters of the way into the skull, just above the cheekbone. Kill one hundred and forty-nine drops to the ground, and I clean my weapon on the back of my jeans.

I turn the corner, and I'm in Harlour Grove. I stop when I see our house, and I am filled with sudden emotion. Bloody hell, if I half-close my eyes, I can almost imagine that everything is normal. My heart is racing as I move towards our home. I can't wait to see her again. It's been too long.

A sudden noise behind me makes me spin around. There are another eight or nine bodies coming from several directions. At least six of them are behind me, staggering at a pathetically slow pace. Another two are ahead, one closing in from the right and the other coming from the general direction of the house next to ours. The adrenaline is really pumping now that I'm this close. I'll be back with Georgie in the next few minutes, and nothing is going to stop me. I don't even waste time with the machete now— I raise my fist and smash the nearest corpse in the face, rearranging what's left of its already mutilated features. It drops to the ground, my one hundred and fiftieth kill.

I'm about to do the same to the next body when I realize that I know her. This is what's left of Judith Landers, the lady who lived one door down. Her husband was a narrow-minded prick, but I always got on with Judith. Her face is bloated and discolored and she's lost an eye, but I can still see that it's her. She's still wearing the ragged remains of her work uniform. She used to work part-time on the checkout at the hardware store down the road toward Shenstone. Poor bitch.

As she reaches out for me, I instinctively raise the machete. But then I look into her face, and all I can see is what she used to be. She tries to grab hold of me, but one of her arms is broken. It flaps uselessly at her side. I push her away in the hope that she'll just turn round and disappear in the other direction, but she doesn't. She grabs at me again, and, again, I push her away. This time, her heavy legs give way. Her face smashes into the pavement, leaving a greasy, bloody stain. Undeterred, she drags herself up and comes at me for a third time. I know I don't have a choice, and I also know that there are now eleven more corpses around me, closing in fast. Judith was a short woman. I flash the blade level with my shoulders and take off the top third of her head. She drops to her knees and then falls forward, spilling the heavily decomposed contents of her skull onto my overgrown lawn.

I have carried the key to our house on a chain around my neck since the first day. With my hands numb and tingling, I pull it out from underneath my shirt and shove it quickly into the lock. I can hear dragging footsteps just a couple of meters behind me now. The lock is stiff, and I have to use all my strength to turn the key. Finally, it moves. The latch clicks and I push the door open. I fall into the house and slam the door shut just as the closest body crashes into the other side.

I'm almost too afraid to speak.

"Georgie?" I shout, and the sound of my voice echoes around the silent house. I haven't dared to speak for weeks; the noise seems strange. It makes me feel uncomfortable and exposed. "Georgie?"

Nothing. I take a couple of steps down the hallway. Where is she? I need to know what happened here so that I can—wait, what's that? Just inside the dining room, I can see Rufus, our dog. He's lying on his back, and it looks like he's been dead for some time. Poor bugger, he probably starved to death. I take another step forward, but then stop and look away. Something has attacked the dog. There's dried blood and pieces of him all over the place.

"Georgie?" I call out for a third time. I'm about to shout again when I hear it. Something's moving in the kitchen, and I pray that it's her.

I look up and see a shadow shifting at the far end of the hallway. It has to be Georgie. She's shuffling towards me, and I know that I'll be able to see her any second. I want to run to meet her, but I can't. My feet are frozen to the spot. The shadow lurches forward again, and she finally comes into view. The end of the hallway is dark, and for a moment I can only see her silhouette. There's no question that it's her—I recognize her height and the overall proportions of her body. She slowly turns towards me, pivoting around on her clumsy, cold feet, and begins to trip down the hall in my direction.

Every step she takes brings her closer to the light, which comes from the small window next to the front door and reveals her in more detail. I can see now that she's naked, and I find myself wondering what happened to make her lose her clothes. Another step and I can see that her once strong and beautiful hair is now lank and sparse. Another step and I can see that her usually flawless, perfect skin has been eaten away by decay. Another step forward and I can clearly see what's left of her face. Those sparkling eyes that I gazed into a thousand times are now cold and dry and look at me without the slightest hint or flicker of recognition or emotion. I clear my throat and try to speak.

"Georgie, are you . . .?" I stop when she launches herself at me.

Rather than recoil and fight, I try to catch her and pull her closer to me. It feels good to hold her again. She's weak and can offer no resistance when I wrap my arms around her and hold her tight. I press my face next to hers and try my best to ignore the repugnant smell. I try not to overreact when she moves, and I carefully tighten my grip. I can feel her greasy, rotting flesh coming away from her bones and dripping through my fingers. I don't want to let her go. This was how I wanted it to be. It's better this way. I had known all along that she would be dead. If she'd survived, she would probably have left the house, and I would never have been able to find her. I would never have stopped looking for her. We were meant to be together, Georgie and me. That's what I kept telling her, even when she stopped wanting to listen.

* * *

I've been back at home for a couple hours now. Apart from the dust and mildew and mould, the place looks pretty much the same. She didn't change much after I left. We're in the living room together now. I haven't been in here for almost a year. Since we split up, she didn't like me coming around. She never let me get any further than the hall, even when I came to collect my things. Said she'd call the police if she had to, but I always knew she wouldn't.

I've dragged the coffee table across the door now so that Georgie can't get out, and I've nailed a few planks across it, too, just to be sure. She's stopped attacking me now, and it's almost as if she's got used to having me around again. I tried to put a bathrobe around her to keep her warm, but she wouldn't keep still long enough. Even now, she's still moving, walking around the edge of the room, tripping over and crashing into things. Silly girl! And with our neighbors watching too! Seems like most of the corpses from around the estate have dragged themselves over here to see what's going on. I've counted more than twenty dead faces pressed against the window.

It's a shame that we couldn't have worked things out before she died. I know that I spent too much time at work, but I did it all for her. For us. She said that we'd grown apart and that I didn't excite her anymore. She said I was boring and dull. She said she wanted more adventure and spontaneity. Said that was what Matthew gave her. I tried to make her see that he was too young and that he was just stringing her along, but she didn't listen. So where is Matthew now? Where is he, with his fucking designer clothes, his city center apartment and his fucking flash car? I know exactly where he is—he's out there on the streets, rotting with the rest of the fucking masses.

And where am I? I'm home. I'm sitting in my armchair, drinking whiskey in my living room. I'm at home with my wife, and this is where I'm going to stay. I'm going to die here, and when I've gone, Georgie and I will rot together. We'll be here together until the very end.

I know it's what she would have wanted.

REAPERS AT THE DOOR

Eric S. Brown

Scott was torn from sleep by the blaring of alarm klaxons. His worst nightmare had suddenly become very real. The alarm could only mean one thing: the war had reached the Talon VIII station at last. He rolled out of bed, dragging on his uniform as he clumsily tried to open a com-link to the bridge. The attempt failed, and he guessed that no one up there was either able or had time to answer his hail.

Visions of Reaper war-pods filled his head. At this moment war-pods would be attaching themselves all over the station's hull and spilling their cargo of moving, violent, rotting flesh into the corridors. The Reapers didn't fight space battles. Their ships dropped out of nether-space already breaking up, spewing thousands upon thousands of boarding pods at the enemy target. Nor did the Reapers personally engage in combat. Only one out of a hundred pods contained a Reaper shock-troop. The rest were crammed full of dead humans, which the Reapers had acquired at the start of the war by using biological weapons without warning against the outer colonies. They possessed billions of human corpses, which, thanks to bio-manipulation, had become the perfect foot soldiers. The reanimated dead attacked anything that was alive and that wasn't a member of the Reaper race.

Scott knew the Talon's defensive systems would have thinned out the number of pods before they reached the station, but Talon VIII was from the Old Earth era and was mostly automated. Counting himself, the crew totaled twenty-three. From the second he had heard the alarm, Scott knew they were all as good as dead. The Reapers never sent less than five thousand boarders regardless of the target and its strength. They firmly believed in overkill rather than taking chances. Besides, the dead were expendable and easy to reanimate or replace.

Scott darted from his quarter and headed straight for the armory. Call it a human thing to do, but he didn't intend to sit around and wait for death to come to him. As he rounded the corner of the corridor, which led to the lifts on the lower level, a section of the corridor wall melted away in front of him, opening up into a Reaper war-pod. Stinking like spoiled meat, men and women poured out into his path. Their rotting flesh was a pale grayish color, but their eyes glowed orange and locked onto him with a feral rage.

He cursed loudly, spinning around to head back the way he had come with the shambling dead giving chase. Scott nearly ran head-on into the Talon's security chief, Heather. Her battle armor was tattered and blood leaked openly from claw and bite marks covering her body. "Get out of here!" she yelled at him. "Everybody else is either dead or cut off." She shoved a pulse rifle into his hands as he stared at her, amazed that she could even be standing, let alone barking orders. She moved past him, firing her own rifle at the approaching horde, which howled for the taste of his flesh. Scott snapped out of his shock as she screamed back at him. "Blow the damn core!" Then she vanished from sight as the wave of the dead washed over her.

Scott started running again, gripping the weapon in white knuckled hands, his boots pounding on the metal floor of the passage. A smile began to creep over his face. *Of course*, he thought, *the core*. He and his crewmates may be destined to die out here in the void aboard the Talon VIII, but at least he could take some Reapers and drones with him.

Scott skidded to a halt outside the blast doors to the main core. His fingers danced over the keypad, entering the access code. The huge doors dilated, and Scott found himself face to face with a real, living, breathing Reaper. The thing stood nearly nine feet tall and was all yellow scales and muscles. It hissed, spraying venom over his face and eyes. Scott cried out as he felt his eyes melting inside their sockets. His skin smoked where droplets of the saliva had made contact. A huge two-fingered hand and thumb closed around his neck, lifting him from the floor with the sound of cracking bone. The Reaper dropped Scott to the floor and stepped back as the dead approached. The Reaper flicked its forked tongue through the air. Things had gone very well, and its pets deserved a treat. It made no move to stop the dead as they converged on Scott and tore and ripped at his flesh with hungry teeth.

THE DIABOLICAL PLAN

Derek Gunn

Lieutenant Peter Fowler turned up the collar of his heavy watch coat as the cold wind whipped spray against his face. Strolling to the starboard side of the *HMS Swift*, he looked through his telescope to steal a final glance at their quarry before darkness descended and left them alone in its ebony embrace. The French frigate was still there, cutting through the swells like a knife and keeping the distance constant between them. Fowler looked up at the top gallants and sighed. The sails glistened as the soaked material caught the fading sunlight, but their beauty didn't help them on their desperate chase.

"She's still there, Captain," he shouted over the clamour on deck. One of His Majesty's frigates was always a hive of activity as crew raised and shortened sails in answer to the changing weather, as they set rigging or practised gun drill—anything to keep their two hundred complement busy on the long days at sea.

Today, however, there was more activity than normal. The Captain had ordered every piece of surplus baggage to be thrown over the side once night had fallen. Men lined the deck with anything not bolted to the floor—chairs, tables, even the Captain's desk—ready to cast the items overboard before running to repeat the process. Fowler raised an eyebrow when he saw a few men hacking the surgeon's blood-stained table into pieces so they could get it through the door and out onto the deck.

"Thank you, Mister Fowler," the Captain replied in his gruff, deep voice. "Carry on, Mister Winfield."

The second lieutenant delayed an instant, and the Captain glared at him. The man paled and then ran to the taffrail, shouting orders through his speaking trumpet.

"He is young yet," Lieutenant Fowler came to stand beside the Captain and nodded at the activity below. "It is an unusual order," he ventured, watching his superior for any indication of his stormy temper.

The Captain seemed to stiffen briefly. Then he relaxed and grinned.

"It is that, John, but if we don't catch him before he gets around the Cape, we will lose him. This is the only place we can be sure of his position come dawn."

Fowler nodded and saw the strain on his young Captain's face. Once again, he was thankful that he did not yet have his own command.

"Mister Flynn," the second lieutenant's shout found the midshipman ready and the fourteen year old turned to his crew and barked orders in a high-pitched, yet authoritative, tone. The men immediately pulled at one of the twelve-pound guns, manhandling the cannon backwards and then pushing the weapon along the deck to the entry port before tipping the gun over the edge.

As the gun displaced water and sprayed his men, Captain Thomas Butler wondered yet again if this was the best plan.

He had agonised over the decision for days now, but he was in command and could not ask anyone else to take the burden. Out here, he was closest to God, and all responsibility fell on him. He was gambling, not just his own life or his crew's, but possibly every soul in England.

He heard the splash of a second gun and wondered briefly what the Admiralty were going to say about dumping their expensive weaponry over the side. "Dead Men walking indeed," he imagined Sir John Powel's deep baritone as he ridiculed the young captain's report. His very success, if he were indeed successful, would ensure that there would not be any proof of the abomination in the hold of the ship in front of him. If he failed, then it would not matter.

He could very well lose his Captaincy, but he had witnessed the impossible. He had seen the French prisoner die, and then get back up. It hadn't taken long, merely an hour or so after death. The prisoner had been confined to sick bay and was fading fast. He had been left to the side while the surgeon had attended the other wounded from the skirmish. It already seemed a lifetime ago. His wound had been fatal and the doctor had pronounced him dead some time later.

Three crewmen were called to throw the body overboard, and it was while they struggled up onto the deck that Perkins had dropped the body with a scream of pain. His two shipmates laughed at him and other men teased him for his clumsiness. It wasn't until they saw the blood pumping from Perkins' arm that they stopped and went to help him.

The shouts for the doctor had attracted Butler's own attention, and with incredulity he had watched the dead man sit up and climb, somewhat drunkenly, to his feet. The men closest to the prisoner yelped in surprise and crossed themselves as they retreated across the deck. The doctor arrived on deck and went white as he saw the prisoner stagger towards him. Butler had seen the doctor stumble over a coil of rigging and fall heavily. The prisoner drew nearer, and Butler had shouted for the marines.

The doctor had continued to scramble away from the prisoner on his hands and knees, too frightened to regain his footing. The prisoner had remained silent the whole time, the pitch of the frigate sending him to and fro as if he had lost his sea legs.

The marines had arrived, three of them armed with muskets. A volley of shots sent the prisoner crashing back against the main mast. The Marine Captain had turned to help the doctor to his feet when a cry of warning snapped every head on the ship back to the main deck.

The crumpled figure of the prisoner had begun to move again. First his head lifted from his chin. Then his arms moved to the deck. The whole ship had looked on in shock as the Frenchman regained his feet and approached Perkins, who still lay whimpering on the deck with his arm held to his chest.

The Marine Captain bellowed an order and his men reloaded and took aim. Two rounds drove into the Frenchman's chest and he staggered, but didn't fall. The third man took an extra second to aim and the shot took the Frenchman between the eyes. The man crumpled and fell to the deck, unmoving. At least a half-hour passed before anyone approached the still form. The men wore thick coats when they lifted the body and threw it overboard.

The shock and fear had gripped the ship for the rest of the day, but what they had learned later provided more than enough resolve to catch and destroy the enemy ahead of them.

Perkins' death (the bite had festered and the fever had killed him yesterday) only fueled the crew's hatred and disgust for the frigate ahead. Nobody had wanted to wait and see if Perkins, too, would get up and attack his former shipmates, so they had beheaded his body and buried him with a quick service.

Butler watched the activity on deck.

"Do you think it will be enough, Captain?" Fowler came up beside his Captain and spoke in a low whisper.

"I pray it is, Mister Fowler. I pray it is."

They had chased the French frigate for four days and had slightly gained on her. They had spent a day and a half becalmed, with the frigate frustratingly close. The sun had baked down on the men, turning the wooden deck white in its merciless glare. Water had been rationed savagely, but the men had worked, driven relentlessly by their officers. Boredom was dangerous in a ship, especially when many of the crew had come from prisons, or were running from debt or the hangman; it was always hard to fill a ship's compliment, but especially so in times of peace when the press could not be used to conscript the unwary or the drunk.

"Those damned French," he cursed. "What has happened to honour?"

"I don't know, sir," Fowler replied, and the two men watched as the guns on the starboard side were thrown overboard one by one. Fowler ran through their armament in his head: twenty six twelve-pounders in all, along with four six-pounders on the quarterdeck, two nine-pounders, and two twenty-four-pound Carronades on the forecastle. All the guns were to be dumped, except for the Carronades and all the starboard-side twelve-pounders.

It was hoped that by dumping the guns at night, the French would not be alerted to their plan, allowing them to close on the frigate overnight. What they would do then was still locked away in the Captain's head. Fowler trusted his Captain, having been with him during three former skirmishes and one full blown battle, but disposing of so many of their armament unnerved him.

He contented himself to stand and await his Captain's needs.

Butler felt his first Lieutenant's comforting presence beside him and tuned out of the bustle of activity as he let the last few days replay in his mind. It was 1791 and an uneasy peace reigned. Signatures still held back a conflict that both sides knew, (and many eagerly anticipated), would soon engulf them all. At the end of the last war and the loss of the colonies, neither side had been able to claim victory and both countries were left burning with impatience. Like most of the Navy, Captain Butler had been beached at half-pay for the last year, his weekly visits to the Admiralty availing him nothing.

Finally he had been given a commission to accompany a merchant fleet to the East Indies. This was a new trade route, and the Admiralty had been forced to provide protection in the present climate of pirates and even some unproven stories of French attacks. Butler had been delighted to get back to sea, even if he was merely tagging along on a trade mission.

The first signs of trouble had been a French frigate and a Sloop when they had been a day from their destination. Butler had signaled the merchant ships to continue on to port and had gone to investigate. There really hadn't been anything suspicious about the two French ships, if he had been totally honest, but weeks of running at half his frigate's speed had dulled his crew; he wanted to get their edge back.

The French ships had moored off a small island about a day from the *Swift's* intended port. Butler had landed a party on the other side of the island to see what they were up to. He convinced himself that they were probably taking on water, but it was strange that they would do so when they were so close to port, even a port that only months ago would have given them a different kind of welcome. He was also curious about the strange contraptions they carried. Butler had been too far away to get a good look, but the French had certainly loaded something bulky into their launches before going ashore.

While his men were ashore, the sloop had come around the island and fired on them. The French frigate had come around the other side of the island in what should have been a devastating attack. Luckily for them, the Sloop advanced quicker than their sister frigate and had attacked thirty minutes too soon. Butler had engaged the Sloop, and though they had been damaged, he had managed to cripple the smaller ship and still turn in time to face the oncoming frigate.

The Captain of the frigate had obviously thought better of a sustained battle and veered off. The sloop had received a cannon ball below the water line and was now slowly sinking. Faced with being marooned on the island, they were quick to surrender. Butler had sent the wounded to sickbay and the healthy to work. Lieutenant Fowler had gone over in the jolly boat before the ship disappeared, and he had come back with despatches but little else.

The dispatches had been in French, of course, and Butler had put them aside to be delivered to the Admiralty. The Sloop's officers had been killed, except for their first Lieutenant who professed to know no English.

Butler had ordered them back to their merchant charges. It had been on their way that the incident with the French prisoner had occurred. After the incident, he had interrogated the French Lieutenant quite rigorously and it was then that they started to piece together the abominable French plan.

Butler shuddered as he remembered the sneer on the Frenchman's face as he had eventually broken and laid out the plan in surprisingly good English.

The French had discovered the Island recently, having laid anchor some months ago for water. They had been attacked by dead creatures almost immediately and sustained some injuries. They lost an entire ship to the dead on their return home, but their sister ship had returned home with a full account. This had been late in the war, and resources were too limited to take advantage of this knowledge at the time.

Someone had hatched a diabolical plan to go back to the island, capture some of these creatures and free them in England. Getting close to the land in peace time would be easy with most of the English ships in dock; the creatures would quickly spread their foul contagion across the entire country. Such a plague would spread through England's poverty stricken landscape like wildfire, and the cities, already filled to bursting with redundant soldiers, sailors and cripples, would have no chance at all. By the time the authorities actually accepted what was happening, the country would already be overrun. The French would wait until chaos had totally gripped the country, and then their largest fleet ever would sail for England, their victory assured.

Butler still couldn't believe the evil of the plan.

"That's the last of them, sir," Fowler reported, and Butler shook himself from his thoughts.

* * *

Up till now they had made slight gains, their keel being far newer than the French vessel and less encumbered by years of barnacles and other seaborne debris. Now that they had made the ship even lighter, Butler sensed a lightness to his ship, like a stallion suddenly freed of a training rein. He looked over at the master, Peter Moon. Even in the dull light from the half-moon above them, he could see the old man grin as he fought against the wheel.

"She be like a young buck, Cap'n," the man laughed, "But we better take her down a point in this light."

Butler nodded, and Fowler moved forward and shouted the necessary order. Butler was well pleased; at this speed, they should have made great gains by the morning, and their sudden appearance on their quarry's tail by dawn should allow them plenty of time to catch them before they rounded the Cape.

He squinted through the dark and could barely make out the topmen as they scampered up the ratlines to pull in the top gallants and control their speed in the darkness. There was little risk of reefs in this stretch of water, but only a madman would continue at full speed without adequate light.

Based on the last few nights, he knew that the French would reduce their speed also, seemingly content to keep their pursuer at a safe distance until they rounded the Cape and had the whole ocean to lose themselves in.

"Wind's pick'n up, Cap'n" the master noted, and Butler could hear the angry flapping of collapsed sails as the topmen struggled to control the material. The ship pitched more violently as the troughs undulated to the wind's command.

"Batten the hatches, Mister Fowler, if you please." Butler pulled his hat down tight as the wind picked up.

* * *

The storm hit in earnest around four in the morning and whipped and snatched at the *Swift*, lifting it high on troughs of agitated water before letting it crash down with bone shattering violence. Men, tied by rope to the masts, still worked the deck, their hunched figures bent into the driving wind as they slipped across rain and vomit. Butler remained on deck despite the screaming wind and numbing rain, and within an hour the wind had seemed to have blown itself out.

Despite the violence of the storm, Butler could now see brightness on the horizon that heralded the coming dawn and a promise of better weather.

"Deck there, sail on the starboard side," the call came from high above in the top gallants, and Butler rushed over with his telescope and scanned the horizon for the enemy. It was still dark, but the looming shape of the French frigate was easily visible against the lighter horizon.

We have caught them, by God, he thought, as he felt his heart thunder in his chest.

"Take her up a point, Mister Fowler," Butler bellowed, feeling the immediate response of the ship as the sails were unfurled. The enemy was only two hundred yards ahead of them now, but judging by the activity on their deck, they had just discovered their pursuer's position.

Fowler beamed. "We'll have them within the hour, Captain."

"Get the Carronade crews to announce us, if you will, Mister Fowler," the Captain grinned. "Let's see what they do. Mister Moon, make sure you keep them on our starboard side; we don't want them to know we are shy some gunnery."

"Aye, sir."

* * *

The explosion from the first cannon split the dawn like a peal of thunder and made everyone jump. The ball landed some way from the enemy on the port side, and the enemy moved to starboard as she began to come about.

"He's trying to show us his guns, sir," Fowler reported.

"Stay with him, Mister Moon, we'll only get one chance at this. Prepare the guns and run them out, Mister Fowler."

"Aye, sir." Fowler barked orders, and gun crews along the deck loaded the heavy shot in the sleek metal cannons and sprang back as the guns were pushed through the ports. Gun captains leaped forward, many of them sitting astride their charges as they aimed through the portholes.

The enemy ship got the first shots off, but their shots were hasty and most went wide or tore through the sails, mercifully missing any of the masts. As the ships drew closer, topmen replaced cut lines and rigging.

"Fire!"

Butler's command was passed on by Fowler, but the crews had heard the original order and leapt to their tasks. The guns belched their charges as one, and the thunder left ears ringing and noses twitching at the sharp reek of powder.

"Reload!"

Butler saw the cannon balls drive home into the enemy frigate. Men were tossed into the air, shredded and screaming in a maelstrom of splinters.

The French returned fire. Some of their starboard guns had been destroyed, but their volley struck home regardless. Butler's ship shuddered as the shot crashed through the ports and ploughed into the *Swift*, tearing gun crews to ribbons.

"They're trying to come behind us, sir," Fowler shouted over the screams of the wounded and the groans of tortured wood.

"Another volley." Butler judged the distance between the vessels. "Hard to starboard, Mister Moon. Bring us alongside. Boarders at the ready."

Fowler ran down to the main deck, gathering up uninjured crewmen. The marines stood on the forecastle and pumped shot after shot at the fast approaching French deck. Butler could see the Frenchmen run to repel the boarders.

The ships seemed to stand still as the seconds ticked away. Gun crews still loaded and fired, but their intermittent fire testified to how few of them remained in operation. Butler looked down over his own ruined deck, where bodies lay dead and dying, slick with blood. Their Mizzen mast suddenly cracked as a shot tore through the thick wood, and men rushed up the yards to cut the rigging lest the falling mast pull their sails with it.

The silence lasted another second, and then the boats bumped. Ripping his sword from his scabbard, Butler called on his men to follow him. He leaped onto the enemy deck and immediately began to hack at those around him. He was only vaguely aware that his men had followed him before the surge of bodies swallowed him up and he was lost in a blood-haze as he slashed again and again.

There was a sudden explosion above him, and he ducked instinctively. The shot from the small cannon on the forecastle buzzed over his head and tore a bloody swath through the men behind him. Englishmen and Frenchmen died as the pieces of shot tore through them with no regard for nationality.

The French began to push them back and Butler saw his men forced into a circle as the French began to turn the tide.

We are defeated, Butler thought desperately. *Surely God will not allow this diabolical plan to succeed?*

His men fought valiantly as their numbers began to dwindle. He looked up to see his own ship drift away as the lines were hacked, cutting off any hope of reinforcements.

He caught Fowler's eye before the French redoubled their efforts, sensing victory. All they could hope was that they had damaged the French enough that they could not reach England and deposit their vile cargo.

Suddenly, there was a scream over beyond their attackers. The sheer terror of the scream cut through the sounds of combat and was enough to give everyone pause. The Englishmen took the respite gratefully as they caught their breath and transferred bloody cutlasses from aching arms.

There was some confusion behind their attackers, but they could not see anything through the throng of bodies. Suddenly, their attackers dispersed in a rush, leaving the exhausted crew a clear view of the upper deck. The small band of survivors paled as they saw the cause of their sudden deliverance.

The dead creatures that had been held below had somehow been freed, probably by a stray cannon ball, and now tottered like drunken sailors across the deck. Their bodies were ravaged by age and decay, but there was not much room on the deck to avoid them. Men fell screaming as the creatures slashed and bit. Officers tried to rally their men and coordinate a defense, but the men were too terrified.

Some of them ran to the rigging and launched themselves up the ropes to get away from the horror, only to be picked off by Butler's marines on the deck of the *Swift*. Others launched themselves over the edge, crushed as Butler's ship finally re-gained enough control to come back alongside.

Butler saw two creatures approach his band of survivors. He paled as the stench of the creatures reached him, and he felt fear grip him. The first creature was mainly skeletal, with white bone protruding from emaciated flesh. Fresh blood ran down from its yellowed, broken teeth, and the eyes that stared at him were like pools of darkness.

"Mister Fowler," his voice croaked, and he had to cough to regain his composure. His first lieutenant appeared beside him, panting and bloodied.

"Take the men and get back aboard the *Swift* immediately. Leave me two men and prepare to burn this godless ship."

"But, sir—"

"Do as I say, Mister Fowler. We can not risk this abomination spreading. Go!"

Fowler reluctantly gathered the men, and Butler saw him bend low and whisper something to two of the biggest surviving crewmen.

Telling them to get me back alive or not at all, no doubt, Butler thought wryly, and then he launched himself at the first creature.

The creature was slow, but no matter how many times Butler hit the creature, it just kept coming. He tried to slash at its head, but the pitching of the ship kept his aim from taking the creature's head off. The two remaining crew joined him and together they hacked enough of the creature that it fell to the deck; it wasn't dead, but at least it was out of action while they dealt with the other lumbering atrocity. Men still ran about the deck, but now the recently dead had begun to join the fray.

The dead will soon outnumber the living, he thought, and looked around to see if the others had made it safely across. Suddenly, he felt an arm grip his shoulder, and he whirled around with his sword held high. He froze for a second as he recognized the uniform of a French Captain, its blank, dead face staring at him.

He stood frozen as the creature leaned towards him, and he felt drool drop on his throat as the creature sought his living flesh. His arm was caught on collapsed rigging above him, and he struggled against the dead creature's vice-like grip. It was no good; he was held fast. He offered up a prayer and closed his eyes.

At least Fowler will burn this hell ship, he thought.

Suddenly, the grip relaxed, and he opened his eyes to see the creature slip to the deck, half its skull ripped away. He looked dazedly around and saw the Marine Captain wave briefly before he reloaded and continued his shooting.

"Okay, men. We've done enough. Let's get back."

The men didn't need telling twice, and they vaulted over the rails and landed to a chorus of cheers from their own men.

"Mister Fowler, cut us loose."

The remaining French crew began to run towards them, trying to surrender, anything to get away from the horror that had taken their ship. The vessels grew farther apart, and they screamed for the English ship to come back. Fowler ordered his crewmen to throw their pitch-soaked flaming rags over to the French vessel and soon flames licked hungrily at sails and decking. The cries and wails of the remaining French crew soon died away as either the flames or the creatures found them at last.

"Poor devils," Fowler muttered, and then his face hardened as he remembered what they had planned for his own countrymen.

Butler looked at Fowler, and they shared a moment of understanding. No one would ever really know what had been achieved here; the story would be told in every ale house, to be sure, but no one would believe it. Butler smiled.

"Alright, Mister Fowler. Let's put the prisoners to work. Call the carpenter to repair that mast and call the good doctor, if he's sober."

Fowler grinned as the ship began to jump to life around them.

We will have to be careful and monitor our injured and dispose of our dead, but we have done it before, Butler thought as he walked wearily towards his cabin. He looked back at the flaming wreck of the French frigate as it began to slip under the surface. How any man could conceive such a plan was beyond him. He glared at the French flag, still flapping in the wind from the main mast.

He would return to England immediately and inform the Admiralty. They would know how best to deal with the island and the threat it posed. They would also know how to deal with the originators of the plan, and Butler suspected that the signature on the orders, locked away safely in his cabin, would sign their author's death warrant.

May he burn in hell, Butler cursed, and then he disappeared into his cabin.

* * *

The two men sat in silence as they stared into the flickering flames in the hearth before them. Outside, the wind snatched at trees, bending them almost double, and lashed rain at the window with such power that the drumming noise drowned out the wind's own mournful howl. The air was thick with cigar smoke, and an aide moved to refill their glasses in the gloom. The heavyset man (some would say portly, though never to his face) motioned for him to leave the decanter and then dismissed him with an impatient flick of his wrist.

"You've read the report?" the man asked. He gulped his brandy and looked over at his companion as he refilled his glass.

"I have," the second man replied, keeping his gaze firmly on the flames. His face was thin, almost gaunt in the pale firelight, and his eyes were hooded beneath full, dark eyebrows.

"And?" the other man shifted in his seat, impatient with his colleague's non-committal response.

"We were lucky," the thin man replied simply. "Such a plague would have taken far too strong a hold before we could have reacted."

"That's not what I meant, and you know it, Lewis." The other man's face grew red, either from anger or from too much brandy. "Would it work?"

Lewis continued to stare at the flames, and after what seemed an age, he turned his head to stare directly at the other man. "Yes," he said in a whisper, "I believe it would. We would have to use a less scrupulous Captain, of course."

"Don't worry about that," the other man snapped, spilling his drink on the arm of the chair and immediately refilling it. "I have arranged for our young hero to be sent to the West Indies; that should keep him out of mischief for a while. I have chosen a far more devious and evil bastard for this mission."

Lewis nodded.

"We will have to make arrangements to ensure that there is no trail back to us. What about the ship you are sending to the island?"

"I have already planted a few men in the crew," the portly man leaned towards his companion conspiratorially. "Once they have deposited their cargo, they will fan the flames of discontent among the crew. It shouldn't be too hard; mutiny is a fact of life, I'm afraid, especially with the way our good Captain treats his crew."

"As long as there are no survivors."

"There won't be."

"Well then," the thin man smiled and raised his glass. "Here's to the successful execution of the French stratagem."

The other man raised his glass in response. "Only this time we'll see how those bastards like a taste of their own plan.

Dead World

Meghan Jurado

Day 1.

Well, it happened. The world came down and my teeth dropped in. The holocaust sure was a big bang, maybe bigger than creation. When I saw that big bright light and heard that bang, I just dropped down on my knees and commenced to melt. Some people were screaming prayers while they melted, but as their lips melted away they were quieter.

I was dead. Dead and damn gooey.

Despite my new flesh consistency, I was able to rise back up on one knee and survey the barren wasteland of blackened buildings and crumbling streets. There were others still moving, some quietly vomiting up coils of intestine into glistening piles. Apparently the screamed prayers had not been received. Maybe Jesus was dead too.

We lurched to our feet for the most part, staring at each other. Most had sustained quite a bit of damage and were reeling around oozing. Some had it better than others—the gentleman to my left was in possession of a dangling nose. It was really quite gruesome.

Under the circumstances.

I don't think anyone quite knew what to do then. I'm sure most had expected to die and not come back, not die and stagger around stuffing their entrails back into their torso. One must make the best of everything, I suppose. I have decided to go east, away from the blast site. If there are survivors, that is where they would be.

I am also keeping this log to document my journey. It's not every day I die.

Day 2.

The first day of my death went pretty well. I didn't speak to anyone, as I am sure they would have been in a foul mood at best. I was not hungry or tired yet, and shuffled along east at a fairly steady pace. I was thirsty, however.

Walking in the sun is torture. My skin feels too warm all the time as it is, and the sun causes large blisters. Occasionally, one of the blisters will pop with an audible noise, and a yellow liquid will come seeping out. I am so thirsty I gaze at this discharge longingly.

Most of the clothes I had been wearing had burned away. I have been walking for a while, mostly nude. I came upon the remains of a small town and broke into a sporting goods store—if you can call walking into a big hole in the side of the building breaking in. There, I grabbed a roll of waterproof tape and set about wrapping my torso. I was unsure how many, if any, of my internal organs I needed, but the tape would at least keep them from trailing behind me, not to mention it would cover what was left of my breasts. I thought it best not to take any chances.

I also procured a backpack in which to carry supplies. I packed more tape and some other things that caught my eye—never know when you might need a screwdriver.

Found some hunting clothes that will do nicely. It's good to be wearing pants again, and the coat will keep the sun from burning my arms any more.

I think I will sleep here tonight and set back out tomorrow.

Day 3.

I have met other walking dead today. Some of them are quite civil, a little confused maybe. No one seems to be after brains, not that mine would be palatable. I am finally getting hungry though. What to try? Many of the walkers ask me about living survivors, but so far I have not seen a living person.

One walker I ran into was quite unpleasant: a grotesque corpse, too decayed to tell the sex, poked me in the belly with a sharp stick. It punctured my tape and fluid rushed out. It was quite inconvenient to try to get the tape to stick after it had become moist. I moved quickly away and patched it later.

Some of the living dead are unable to speak at all. I think their vocal cords might have melted. That must be very frustrating.

Day 4.

I don't know where I'm walking. I think I'm subconsciously seeking out the living. I don't know how welcome I will be if I find them. I have seen no sign of survivors (do I count as a survivor, I wonder?) since the day I died. I just keep heading east. I am getting very tired of walking, and my leg feels as if it's coming loose. Hoping to see a city soon. I have been wandering through wastelands for days.

Day 5.

I ate a dead crow today. I suppose I had to eat something sooner or later, and the crow was dead in the road, practically begging me to eat it. It was a compulsion I could not resist. After I had devoured all the meat and innards, I had pulled off its happy yellow feet and did a bit of the Charlie Chaplain with them. Found myself laughing for the first time in days. I think I will keep the feet in case I need a cheering up in the future.

I wonder where the crow ended up after I ate it. I don't know if I have a stomach anymore; I might have dropped it. At any rate, it was not very filling. Oh well.

Day 6.

Found a small village today—lots of dead people up and about, walking the streets, some even driving. Haven't seen a working car in days. Where I came from, vehicles either went wheels up or their vital components melted during the blast. The driving dead have poor coordination at best; between the deterioration of tendons, muscle, and eyesight (or the eyeball itself, I imagine), there are quite a few crashes, but hardly ever a fatality. Those who have working vehicles hoard them. I inquired about acquiring a car to ease the stress on my loose leg and got nothing but flat stares.

Everyone in town is talking about a "City of Living Men," about a three-day journey from here. Only a few citizens had been reduced to goo during the big meltdown. They have a doctor who is sewing parts back on and binding torsos; he's using cloth, which smells quite bad after a day or so, and it weeps almost constantly. Glad I used tape.

There has also been talk of the Doc finding a cure. I don't think a cure for dead will be a quick find.

It was nice, meeting a whole town of functioning living dead. Most were quite alert and coherent. I got the feeling that they had weeded out the more damaged members of society; there was a constant bonfire on the edge of town. Over the stench of everyone rotting (more dead = more stench. Looking forward to being on my own sooner rather than later!), I can smell burning flesh. Makes me feel almost hungry again.

Day 7.

A few people offered to travel with me. Not one has a car, so I don't think I want company just yet. I hear there are living people in or near the mountains. I feel a strange compulsion to seek them out.

I will leave tomorrow to find the living. If I succeed, I will return for the others.

Day 8.

Walked most of the day, but the mountains never seem to get any closer. Found a child's skull—so cute I'm going to keep it. For what, I couldn't tell you.

When in town, I had asked the Doc what we should be eating. He couldn't tell me either, and he had been working on that problem on his own. He has a town full of hungry people back there. They were starting to snap at each other.

Had to seriously tape up my leg today. Wrapped it from ankle to hip. I'm not sure what to do to stabilize it, as it seems to be an internal problem. I'm thinking about jamming a large stick through my hip to kind of pin the leg against it. Haven't found a big enough stick yet.

Tried to eat a rattlesnake today. I say "tried" because after I caught it, it bit me in the face a couple times and then slithered away. The venom seems to be rotting my face to soup where it struck. Stupid snake.

Saw a living dead fellow who was actually dead in the desert today. Someone seems to have shot him in the head. I wondered who had done it, or if the fellow had simply committed suicide. I didn't know we could do that. Something to keep in mind.

Day 9.

I'm going to have to start traveling at night. The sun is horribly hot, and it's giving me the feeling that I am cooking on my feet. It's certainly what I smell like.

The mountains loom ever closer. I see reflecting lights moving around during the day, and they seem to have fires at night: I can see the lights from here.

I tried to eat a dead body today. Found a just plain corpse, dead for only hours, out in the desert sun. Before I could think clearly, I had bitten into it and had devoured most of an arm before I stopped myself. My meal came right back up, but those initial bites really seemed natural. Apparently eating humans is still unacceptable, but I can't say I wouldn't recommend trying it.

I have seen other living dead that are heading for the living city. Sometimes I pass them, most times they pass me since my leg has become unreliable. None stop to chat.

Night 10.

Came up on the city today, but did not approach. Saw something terrible: the poor undead bloke in front of me got a bullet to the head from one of the living. I hit the dirt and played dead (played? Was? Who can tell anymore . . .), which was easy enough—the ground in front of the living habitat is littered with the corpses of those who had died twice.

Spent some time lying on the ground and wondering what to do. I certainly did not want to be shot in the head; I value what meager existence I have. I didn't walk all the way out here to do the living any harm. In fact, I had expected welcome. But the countless bodies of shot-down undead truly shocked and disturbed me. We as an undead people, I guess you would say, had risked life and limb (in my case, literally) to find others that had continued to exist after the blast only to be executed upon arrival, shot on sight.

My thoughts turned to those already on the way. They were walking to slaughter.

I decide to spend some time looking around before bugging out. I get up and move while the living are in other places.

The living wear radiation suits. I assume they are residing in or under the mountain. There are three of them to a jeep, all in yellow, all with guns. When I hear the tires, I flop to the ground, and they drive past, none the wiser. I do hate the stress all this duck and stand is putting on my leg; I have a noticeable sideways gait. I'm not sure how I'll manage if the leg comes off.

I have not found the entrance to the home of the living, but I have found many corpses. Hundreds of headshot undead litter the area around these mountains. The carnage is terrible. The fires that I observed from farther out are bonfires of the massacred. Crews come out, drag a few into a pile and douse them with gasoline. I almost got snagged for a roasting, but the yellow suit stopped one corpse over.

I will set out for the undead town tomorrow. There is nothing that can help me here.

Night 11.

I have found what we are meant to eat.

I was doing a final search of the living town when I came upon a yellow-suit man all alone. His back was to me, and he was standing in front of a rock face.

I was as quiet as I could be, and as luck would have it, he was whistling. I crept behind him, meaning to perhaps yank off his hood and give him a scare. Instead, I yanked off his hood and bit out his throat, surprising us both.

I don't know what came over me. One second I was fine, rational as could be, and the next I was tearing off the lips of someone I had never met. I didn't regain my senses until I had ripped his suit open and fed on his innards.

When I came to, I was covered in gore and was a little wary. I had no idea how long I had been sitting in the dirt, eating. I decided to leave for town right away.

Before I left, I looked at the rock face the yellow suit had been examining.

There was a keypad. On the keypad were these numbers: 107618

The keypad was on a door.

Night 12.

Walked most of the day as well. My head is spinning. I don't want to eat the living, but it seems I have no choice. And why shouldn't we eat a group of people that hates us so?

Caught a rattlesnake. Broke it in half, then stepped on it.

Night 13.

Almost back to the city. I felt wonderful the first two days out, but now I'm feeling drained. I think of the meat I left behind with real regret.

I think I should warn all the undead to stay away from the living city. I would hate for them to get shot. I wish I knew how many of the living were under the mountains. I was thinking of sending in a spy since I know the door code, but I have yet to meet a living dead that smells or looks like a living person. I should be back in town tomorrow. What should I tell them?

Night 14.

Well received in the city. Everyone wants to know how the trip went, and I have so far managed to avoid difficult questions. They want to go and talk with living people! They think that the living have a cure. They talk of being alive again.

I have to think it over carefully. I could just let them go. Most wouldn't make the trip, unless they all piled into a car. I'm sure a carload of the undead would be quite a surprise for the living! The others would be put out of their misery on arrival. But I myself am not entirely ready to lie down and die. Should I assume that they are?

I *could* take them there. Tell them to come in small groups, to fall when the jeeps go by and to avoid the yellow suits—to meet at a certain rock face. I have called a town meeting. To discuss options.

Night 15

Good turnout. Told them everything: about the living, the jeeps, the genocide of the undead. And what I found to eat, of course.

Not used to public speaking. I had to repeat myself a couple of times.

Some of them didn't believe me. About the living, the slaughter—any of it. And when I mentioned the tasty gentleman in the yellow suit, I actually met with *boos*. Some left the meeting at that point.

Others were clearly intrigued—and hungry. When I described my impromptu meal, a few of them drooled. Several were appalled that the living were killing the undead, and at one point, I had to wait for shouts to subdue into a kind of angry murmuring. Some of the more hotheaded members of the audience were ready to storm the gates.

There were those who were ambivalent. They felt safe where they were, and while they did believe the threat of the living, they were not hungry enough to risk invading the mountain. This group wanted a more live and let live policy. Or a live and let die policy, things being as they were.

In the end, there was a vote. Nothing complicated, just a show of hands. Of those that had not stormed out, a comfortable margin were in favor of heading out to the mountains. In search of food.

Day 16

Leading a party out to the mountains. We will drive as close as is safe, and then walk to better blend in. Three more parties follow over the next three days.

They all have the code to the keypad.

They also have guns. Just in case.

TWO CONFESSIONS

E. W. Norton

Capt. Eugene Bristol, Lakhnauti, India, June 8th, 1900

My Dearest Anne,

    I sincerely hope that you have opened this letter before opening the package that accompanied it, as you probably surmised by the large block letters spelling out "OPEN LETTER FIRST!" which I inscribed on both the package and the letter. In fact, if you are willing to adhere to my wishes completely, you will never actually open the package at all.

    I am sorry to have to make such a request. As I am well aware that you are, by nature, a rather curious sort, I know that restraining yourself from taking a peek inside a package from distant and exotic India will be quite difficult. However, please believe me when I tell you that the contents of that package are extremely dangerous.

    I am rather sick with worry to have sent the package to you at all. I would strongly prefer not to place you in harms way. However, I felt that it was imperative that the object within the package be sent to a place far removed from here.

    In fact, Major Thomas, my commander in the Thuggee and Dacoity Department of Her Majesty's Police contingent here in Lakhnauti, had actually ordered the item destroyed. As you now have the said item in hand, you can probably guess that I have obviously disobeyed a direct order. Thus, the story which I will relate in this letter will be something of a confession. . . .

* * *

Gregory Adams, Waysmouth College, Mass., USA, Oct. 18th, 2002

71

To whomever finds this letter,

To begin with, I would like to apologize to whomever finds this letter and the grisly scene in which it will be located. I am very sorry to have subjected you to the gruesome results of the events in which I have been caught up. Unfortunately, considering the horrific circumstance in which I find myself, I cannot see any way to avoid such an eventuality.

Please forward this letter to the Chapter House of the Phi Delta Kappa fraternity of Waysmouth College. I trust that my brethren there will be honorable enough to distribute this letter amongst my loved ones and other concerned parties.

As you may have realized by now, this is a suicide note. This note will, however, have to be quite lengthy. For I desperately want to explain to all those that I hold dear the series of events that led to this tragedy.

Due to the presence of my girlfriend Donna Tinley's body, I suppose it is rather plain that this letter will also contain something of a confession. . . .

* * *

Anne, I know that you are probably shocked that I would actually disobey a direct order. However, I simply could not help myself. I am unable to force myself to destroy the dangerous object contained within the package you hold.

Although I believe this object to undoubtedly be of purest evil, and also to be extremely hazardous, I could not force myself to burn an item which so plainly proves the existence of forces beyond the natural. To actually be in possession of a truly supernatural object is a development which I never could have foreseen in a thousand nights of dream-filled slumber.

I'm sure that you are skeptical that this item is truly magical. Hopefully, once I have related the entire tale surrounding the acquisition of this item, you will be somewhat more accepting of my assertions.

The whole affair began with the discovery of the murdered corpse of one of the Raj's closest advisors. . . .

* * *

Although, it is true that I will confess to some rather sordid acts in this letter, I will not actually be confessing to the murder of Donna. While it is true that I am partially responsible for her death, I did not purposefully murder her. Her death was a horrible accident. I did not intend to kill her and am not entirely sure how it happened.

Of course, I don't expect the authorities to believe such an assertion. So, completely unwilling to be arrested and branded as a murderer, I have chosen to take my own life. My only hope is that my loved ones will believe what I am about to relate. In order to ensure that my version of the story will be believed, I have decided to relate all the related events with complete veracity. I know that some parts of this story will be painful for members of my family to read, but I cannot risk altering portions that may later be discovered to be untrue.

The whole affair began when Donna developed an interest in the occult. . . .

* * *

The advisor to the Raj, who was named Lord Beauforte Kellman, had apparently been convinced by several recent acquaintances to join them on an excursion into some of the most untrodden sections of the Indian subcontinent. It seems that Lord Kellman had been indiscriminant in his choice of companions. Upon his failure to return in good time, an investigation into the backgrounds of his fellow travelers was launched. It was revealed that their identities had been completely fabricated. Moreover, there arose reason to believe that these men were involved with the Thuggee cult of Kali.

Such fears were confirmed when Lord Kellman's strangled cadaver was discovered in a secluded area, surrounded by the trappings typical of a Thuggee ritual. As you can imagine, the audacity of such an attack against a British Lord resulted in a massive mobilization of the colonial forces. As Lord Kellman's body had been discovered within our jurisdiction, it fell upon my department to spearhead the manhunt.

Previous to this incident, we had been under the impression that all activities associated with the Thuggee cult had been eradicated from our vicinity decades ago. After all, Sir William Henry Sleeman had started the campaign against this wicked brotherhood as far back as the 1830s. We had all but reconciled the Thuggees to a bygone chapter of history. In fact, there had even been a great deal of talk regarding the dissolution of my department.

Obviously, we had been somewhat premature in assuming that the cult was permanently thwarted. This new campaign against these villains made it apparent that they were still very much in existence, although they were definitely far from the strength they had enjoyed in the distant past.

One very peculiar incongruity which had struck many of the officers on this case was that the devotees of Kali would stage such a bold strike against British authority when they were obviously too weak to present an actual threat.

The answer to this conundrum became abhorrently clear when our inquiries finally led us to a hidden temple stronghold in the dense jungles of Hyderabad. . . .

* * *

Donna had always been sort of on the freaky end of the personality scale. She had a tendency to develop rather easily slaked thirsts for knowledge of the most bizarre varieties. Invariably, whenever one of these odd interests developed, I was conscripted as her chief researcher.

The most recent oddity to catch her fancy was tantra. This rather arcane practice of eastern sex magic has recently become quite popular, so, of course, she had to try it. As the subject involved sex, I certainly wasn't going to complain. I certainly wouldn't have wanted to give her any reason to look for some other assistant.

And so I soon found myself en route to a local new age shop. . . .

* * *

This clandestine temple of Kali was quite grotesque, being decorated largely in stylized skulls and engravings of gory sacrificial scenes. The temple was also fairly well fortified. The cultists had raised earthen bulwarks about the perimeter of the temple. I suspect that they feared we would be laying siege to their stronghold with heavy artillery.

Unfortunately, there were no artillery companies within the immediate vicinity. Thus, we did not have the option of simply flattening the evil fane via a barrage. We were, therefore, forced to surround the temple and keep the criminals trapped until we were reinforced by heavier fire power.

As we held our vigil around the heathen shrine, I was surprised to note that a group of about nine of the cultists emerged from the temple dressed in some variety of full ceremonial regalia. As this small cadre lined up along the earthen fortifications, another individual appeared from within the temple.

The sacramental robes which this last fellow wore were so extravagant, so heavily hung with precious ornamentation, that the robes of the first nine appeared rather ascetic by compari-

son. *This man most certainly had to be the head of the cult, their high priest.*

Of course, his ostentatious display of rank attracted the aim of every muzzle on our side of the structure. The priest did not seem at all concerned. In fact, he almost seemed to be moving in some sort of trance-like state.

As we looked on, we saw him approach the first of the other nine men. We were dumbfounded and truly aghast to see the high priest remove his sash, wrap it around the neck of the man, and viciously strangle him to death. . . .

* * *

The new age store was a fairly pleasant little place. Its atmosphere was thick with incense, and its walls bore a rather luxuriant growth of necklaces, fetishes, talismans, and other arcane accoutrements. Overall, the shop radiated an aura of calm and mystical charm. Unfortunately, as I scanned the room, I realized that this aura was disrupted by the presence of a certain disharmonious entity.

This entity went by the name of Cyrus Bristol. Cyrus was Waysmouth's foremost Goth freak. He wore the requisite jet black coif, bleach-white pallor, and ridiculous eye-shadow. He was one of Phi Delta Kappa's favorite punching bags. When I and my brothers happened to cross paths with the social misfit, we almost always took a moment or two to make some sort of gesture of disapproval. Most often, these gestures involved depositing Cyrus and all his belongings in the nearest trash bin. We always saw our little pranks as good, clean fun, but I suspect that Cyrus may not have felt the same way.

I wended my way through the maze of little tables and stands to the bookshelves that lined the rear of the shop, doing my best to ignore the presence of Mr. Bristol. As I perused the titles on display, an older lady approached, wearing a shawl and handkerchief tied over her hair. This lady was obviously the proprietor of the shop, as she offered to assist in locating whatever I was seeking.

I hemmed and hawed for a bit, not wanting to confide that I was seeking a book on sex magic. Finally, I told her that I was just looking.

As the woman retreated to another section of the shop, I was surprised to find Cyrus standing at my elbow. I was about to tell him to get away from me when I noticed he had a book which he was apparently holding up for me to view.

"This would be what you want," Cyrus said. "This is the best book they have on Tantra here, at least for your purposes. Its all about sex magic, none of the other bits of Tantra that westerners prefer to ignore."

I gingerly took the book from his grasp and flipped through the pages. To my untrained eye, it appeared that the Goth was being sincere in his book review. The manual even had a large number of helpful, and rather stimulating, illustrations.

I thanked him in a rather hesitant manner, not at all sure why he was being helpful. As I turned to go he added, "Of course, if you really want to do effective magic via that method, you're going to need a special tool. . . ."

Personally, I have never needed any sort of tool in bed to please Donna. I was about to turn around and flatten the freak when I noticed that he was holding out something quite different than what had popped into my mind.

"This is a special tantric scarf," he said. "Just wrap this around your lady's neck before you begin and she'll experience some *real* magic. . . ."

* * *

We all watched in shock as the unholy priest proceeded to throttle all nine of his apparently willing victims. All of my comrades seemed to be frozen; they were unable to take action, completely stunned.

As the priest finished off the last of his visible followers, I felt an incredible rage building within me. Without really even thinking, I took aim and fired. My shot found a home within the skull of the evil cleric.

A cheer went up from our line as the wretch went down in a spray of blood and other less identifiable fluids. Surely, the loss of their high priest would completely demoralize any surviving members of the cult within the wicked edifice. It seemed that a ridiculously easy victory would be ours. . . .

* * *

"How much is that thing?" I asked. I looked around for a display of similar scarves, but I saw none in evidence.

"They don't sell these here," Cyrus replied. "This is mine. But, as I always try to help out fellow delvers into the arcane, I'll let you borrow it for awhile. Trust me, this thing makes all the difference. My great-grandfather sent it back from India when he was stationed there about a hundred years ago."

I was understandably skeptical. First of all, this guy had absolutely no reason to be helping me out; second of all, this piece of cloth did not look like it was that old.

"Yeah, right," I said. "Like they did sex magic in India a hundred years ago. . . ."

"Ah, you do know that Tantra comes from India, right?" Cyrus looked taken aback and slightly amused. "Tantra is one of the most ancient forms of magic known. The Indians were probably doing sex magic way back when your ancestors were hiding in the hills from Roman invaders."

Noticing that the lady who ran the shop had again come rather near, I gestured to her and asked her if she thought the scarf actually looked like some sort of Tantric item.

The lady examined the scarf closely, her eyes plainly showing a great deal of personal interest in the specimen. Finally she announced that the scarf bore symbols that were definitely related to Tantra. She also admitted that she wasn't sure exactly in what sort of Tantric practice the scarf was meant to be employed. She then gave a cryptic warning about not all Tantra being sex magic.

I was rather embarrassed that it had been so plain to her that I was interested in sex magic. Wanting to get out of her shop, I just thanked Cyrus for the scarf and told him I would give it back later in the week. I couldn't imagine why he was being so friendly. Finally I decided that maybe he was just hoping his actions might result in fewer visits to the nearest trash can. Heck, if this thing worked like he said it did, I figured I might even tell the guys from the frat to lay off the freak.

With the book and the scarf in hand, I set off towards my girlfriend's dorm. I figured that she would be pleased with my successful acquisition of the items she had desired. It looked like I was going to get lucky tonight. . . .

* * *

Our men continued to wait for some action from anyone remaining in the temple. We were in rather good spirits, having eliminated their leader. Unfortunately, our high morale was doomed to vanish all too soon.

As I watched the temple for signs of movement, I was startled to catch a glimpse of something shifting around in the area where the mad priest had recently strangled his followers. Had one of them survived the garroting? Soon, it became apparent that one of them had. Although it seemed that the extended period of oxygen deprivation may have caused some brain damage, for the man stood up and began to walk right at us.

We held our fire at first, thinking that maybe he was trying to surrender. As he came closer, I noticed more movement behind him. All of the strangulation victims were coming to their feet. It seemed that their high priest was surprisingly incompetent at strangling. This was rather odd, considering that strangulation was basically a holy rite for these black-guards.

The first Thug was coming quite close, so we yelled at him to stop and raise his hands. We were surprised to find our orders ignored. We repeated our demands, but the cultist kept coming. Finally, we fired a warning shot.

I was startled to note that the follower of Kali didn't even flinch when the shot was fired. I also realized that the fellow had a distinctly inexpressive facial expression. His features couldn't have made him appear less interested than if he had been dead.

As the cultist reached our lines, we were forced to fire on him. To our dismay, our bullets did little more than momentarily impede the man's juggernaut-like advance. In moments, the Thug had lunged forward and wrapped his hands around the throat of one of my fellow officers. The cultist's face was, unbelievably, still devoid of expression.

The Thug was already riddled with bullets. At this point, he probably contained more lead than he did flesh and bone. As his hands crushed our man's throat, we began to hack at the cultist with bayonets and bash him with the butts of our rifles. All to no effect.

The other eight were almost upon us. We began to panic: it seemed like we were doomed. . . .

* * *

Donna was definitely intrigued with both the book and the scarf. We looked through the book a bit, but couldn't find anything to do with a neck scarf. Finally, I suggested that perhaps it was used for something similar to auto-erotic asphyxiation. Supposedly, some people believed that oxygen deprivation enhanced orgasms.

Donna thought it sounded dangerous, but as it was dangerous in a kinky way, this apparently served only to excite her. She decided that we were going to start practicing our new method of arcanum immediately.

After disrobing and assuming one of the easier positions suggested in the instruction book, I began to tie the piece of cloth around her neck. Since she wanted to try erotic-asphyxiation, I made sure it was a little tight, but only a little.

However, as I tried to tie a knot in the scarf, I was horrified to see my hands moving of their own volition. My mind reeled madly as I was forced to watch my hands use the scarf to strangle Donna. I strove to exert some sort of control over my actions, but I was too weak.

Now, Donna is lying on the floor beside the bed, dead. I have no sane defense against a murder charge. I can either kill myself now, or go through the hell of waiting for the state to do it for me eventually. I appear to be doomed. . . .

* * *

As the other eight cultists attacked, we broke ranks and began to scatter, running in all directions. In a blind panic, I unwittingly rushed right towards the temple. I did not manage to overcome my horror until I had crossed the earthen bulwarks.

I turned to look back at the melee which I had just fled. The nine unstoppable cultists had each slaughtered one of my men, effortlessly crushing their throats with inhuman strength.

Sergeant Patel had ended up near me, just on the other side of the earthen fortifications. He was a native Indian and had always impressed me as being a little too superstitious. Of course, having seen the horrors which were besetting my unit, I was ready to give greater credence to his peculiar beliefs.

I saw that one of the monstrous cultists was approaching the sergeant from behind. I tried to yell to him and warn him of the danger. However, I don't believe he heard me; he was screaming something about the cultists being ridden by Rakshasas. Apparently, my complete lack of comprehension was plain on my face. He thought for a second and then yelled that the cultists were zombies. He then went on to babble something about having to kill them with magic.

He had climbed the bulwark and managed to reach me at exactly the same time that the Thug zombie managed to lunge forward and grasp him. Sergeant Patel and the monster began to struggle, Patel desperately attempting to keep the thing's hands from his windpipe.

I beat at the creature's head with the butt of my rifle, but the thing didn't appear to feel it at all. In desperation, I began to look around for something a bit more substantial with which to strike at the Thug. As I scanned the area, once again near panic, my eye happened upon the high priest's scarf.

At a loss for any other effective act, my fevered mind came to the conclusion that if the sash put the cultists down once, maybe it could do it again. Apparently, luck lay with the fevered that day, for as I put the sash about the thing's neck, it suddenly closed about its throat with incredible force. Within moments, I was relieved and delighted to see the cultist once again lying dead on the ground.

Having finally found a way to kill these beasts, we were eventually able to lay them all to rest. Unfortunately, our losses were grievous.

When we entered the temple, we found it empty. It appeared that the last few members of the Thuggee cult had decided to throw themselves against us in a necromantic suicide attack.

This is how the sash within the package you hold came into my possession. The thing is obviously some sort of unholy artifact of great power. Please place it under lock and key and avoid any temptation to examine or inspect the item.

I'm not at all sure why I chose to preserve it. I have no clue as to what kind of use I could put it. For now, I think it will be best to treat it as a special family heirloom. Perhaps one of our descendants will be wise enough to find a proper use of the horrid cloth.

Eternally Yours,
Eugene

* * *

Cyrus Bristol was obviously not merely making a ploy at obtaining mercy. It has become horribly obvious that this situation is the result of an act of revenge on his part.

That is my story. I don't expect the police to believe it, but I pray that my family will. In moments, I plan to kill myself. I only hope that my afterlife will not be as terribly and foolishly mismanaged as my life has been.

Oh my god! Donna just moved! She's not dead! She's getting up! Thank god, the nightmare is over, I'm saved!

13 Ways of Looking at the Living Dead

Eric Pape

"I was of three minds
 Like a tree
 In which there are three blackbirds"—Wallace Stevens

1.

Darkness, whittled down by streetlights and ambient moonlight, spreads through oaks and willows, the preferred foliage for tombstones and crypts. Kelly runs through the cemetery, stumbling over vandalized tombstones and decaying bouquets. She runs in a sort of sideways, skipping tumble, looking back over her shoulder at the darkness. We cannot see through the darkness. We cannot see the things she flees.

Kelly wears tight denim shorts over long, oyster-pale legs. Her shorts cut into the skin of her hips, revealing almond crescents as she escapes. Her belly quivers over her waistband, and on closer examination, a light trail of down fades into the top of her shorts. She wears a shiny black satin bra. She runs barefoot.

Kelly has that fairy look, the pale skin and light hair, her tiny, swollen lips and a nose so small it's nearly absent. Her large blue eyes animate the trembling of her lips. Her eyebrows, thick and darkly shocking under the fair hair, almost meet in the middle. Silver rings inscribe the pointed edges of her ears, her hair is molded short, and her bangs stick in the sweat on her high forehead.

Even as she flees, Kelly bubbles with life. Life shivers along her skin and glows from her eyes. Life ruffles her hair and causes her toes to curl. Kelly's life bursts from every pore, every follicle, from the way her fingernails bite into the meaty part of her palms to how her tongue folds over her bottom lip when she concentrates on the darkness.

Sounds emerge from the shadows. Not voices, not roars, nor growls nor screeches, only a low shuffle in the leaf litter and over the lawn. A moan perhaps, so low in tone it might be the wind, or maybe it's cars on a freeway far in the distance. These sounds strike panic in Kelly. Now she's running practically backwards, her legs pumping and her belly seething. She breathes hard. She fails to see the oak, so intent on avoiding the shadows. The thick limbs arch from the trunk to the ground, the result of some trauma a few tree rings back. Sucker branches grow perpendicular to the curving angles of the bark.

A naked branch snags the back of Kelly's bra, and now she runs topless. Her breasts wobble, small, just enough subcutaneous fat to allow bounce and wiggle. Kelly seems not to notice. She stops, listens, much like a rabbit pausing in its headlong flight. She hears something she does not like, and she turns full around to run full out.

Kelly enters the most populated part of the cemetery; the tombstones like thick stubble. She runs gracefully now, no longer in conflict over whether she should watch behind her or reach her goal. The dull sounds from the shadows grow louder. Kelly leaps over one of the few clean white graves on which the epitaph is legible. Her back arches in the full of the leap, her legs spread wide, front knee to her chest, back foot to her hip. Her arc carries her directly over the stone, three feet over the stone, and she is an antelope fully in flight. She knows the wolves are far behind her, and her leap carries that confidence.

Just as she reaches the height of her jump, the turf breaks below her. First, fingers, puckered with maggots, then a hand like a cheese Danish, glazed with shiny fluids. An entire arm crashes from the scattered mud, and the hand clutches Kelly midair. Kelly doesn't even have time to scream before she vanishes into the disturbed earth. The darkness thickens.

2.

The dead move slow and stiff. They fail to animate. The dead lack; it is in their nature to be missing. So they slowly overcome the victim, shambling in overwhelming numbers, to rip into the soft animated flesh for which they feel home sick. The dead are nostalgic.

This is why they crave the brains of the living: to crack into a skull and scrape the bone clean of matter, not only in their hunger for the soft gray tissue (so much like chocolate pudding), but to consume, to devour the life they find inside. The dead embody flesh without the animation of intelligence. They move without direction, without the puppetry of all but the most negligible of electronic impulses. Nothing leads them but a hunger for animation.

The craving for flesh has interesting consequences. They leak a lot. Fluids seep from every orifice and from orifices newly created by rot or violence. Thick liquids pool at their shuffling feet. Eyelids ooze humors. They leave a wet track behind. You never see the dry dead, the fleshless, skeletal, dusty dead. Rather, you see the various stages of decay, the newly bloody to the bloated and syrupy. You wonder what happened to the dead that have lost flesh. You can only speculate that the dead desire to continue the flesh, and when gone, the flesh no longer has the capacity to be jealous.

Why then can the dead only be killed by a shot, or a blow, to the brain? If they desire brains, desire animation, how can they be stripped of movement by the loss of their useless intelligence? Or is there something else trapped within the confines of their skulls?

3.

Earlier, in the disquieting hours of the morning, at a laboratory located in uncomfortable proximity to a large cemetery, Dr. Roderick closes his eyes and lets out a long, slow breath. He's tired. He's worked too hard for too long. Though the laboratory gleams spotless, a raw smell pervades every corner of the white room. *Why do I keep at it,* Dr Roderick wonders, *what drives me to this work?* He thinks of his wife and begins to twist the simple gold band around his finger. He pulls off the ring, and puts it in his mouth, to taste the sweat and the cold metal. He bites down just a bit on the smooth edges, and then pulls it from his mouth. Slick with his saliva, it slips through his fingers and pings on the tile floor. He hears it bounce and knows he has to find it.

Scrambling on his hands and knees, he's so tired that he can hardly see straight. Strange lights flash in his peripheral vision.

He finds the ring under one of the gurneys and realizes he must complete his work as he slips the gold band back onto his finger. He pushes himself to his full six feet two inches and brushes the dust from his stained apron. He pulls back a crisp white sheet to reveal the pale cadaver below.

First body, first formula, he reminds himself. He pulls an old-fashioned brass syringe from a bulging apron pocket. The fluid inside glows green, fluorescent; it moves like a mayonnaise jar full of fireflies. With the needle against the dead vein in the arm, he presses the plunger. For a second, nothing happens, and then the air is filled with the smell of moss, of leaf litter and decaying pine needles. The odor fades and the body remains limp on the gurney. He makes a note in his journal.

Dr. Roderick moves to another gurney. He pulls out a Technicolor multi-syringe, the kind they use in military movies, a needle-gun, loaded with amber fluids in various stages of yellow: piss yellow, citrus yellow, linseed yellow, and Dijon yellow. He hauls the corpse to its belly, exposing dark flaccid buttocks. He shoots the fluids in the left cheek and waits. The corpse exudes a yellow gas, completely odorless. Dr. Roderick coughs into his latex gloves as the gas fades into the ventilation ducts. *Interesting effect,* he thinks as he describes the reaction in his journal.

Dr. Roderick moves to the next body. From the inexhaustible supply of syringes in his apron pocket, he pulls a stainless steel beauty, with retractable needle and clear glass vial. Very, very tiny bubbles play in the clarity of the fluid. *This stuff,* he thinks, *looks like expensive and pretentious mineral water.* He presses the needle to the carcasses' neck and shoots the clear, carbonated fluid into the jugular. Dr. Roderick waits a full three minutes. The corpse seems then to clarify, the blotchy colors of death fade into a clear, brilliant peach, just a bit rosy on the cheeks, with glossy red lips. *He looks more alive than I do,* Dr. Roderick thinks, but the body never animates.

After making his note, Dr. Roderick shuffles to the last body. So tired. The pressure builds behind his eyeballs and the blood rushes in his ears. His hands shake. The last gurney sits next to a rusted and stained sink. The drain is stopped up and a concoction of dark brown and dull green fills the sink halfway to the brim. There is a thick skin of long dead suds adhering to the sides of the sink. On the gurney next to the body, Dr Roderick sees the broken hammer, the rusted railroad spike, and an ancient rubber syringe, the kind used to baste turkeys. He pulls back the sheet on the last body to reveal a stinking hulk. He hammers the railroad spike into its chest, grabs the rubber syringe and fills it with liquid from the sink. He shoves the rubber syringe into the gaping wound and squeezes the rubber head.

The wound sucks at the syringe, the skin puckering. The bloody, ragged edges of the puncture climb the plastic cylinder like lips, the dead chest now like a heaving mouth, pumping fluid to swallow. The eyes flutter.

It's done, thinks Dr. Roderick, *it's finally finished. I can stop now. I can go home and I can rest and have a snack and cuddle with my wife and see my kids again. I think I'll stop on the way home and pick up some ice cream.* Dr. Roderick doesn't have time to think about anything else before he's pulled to the gurney, where the jaw full of broken teeth is waiting for him.

4.

Let's examine the language. We call them the living dead, but what does that mean? It seems, of course, an oxymoron, something like, to paraphrase George Carlin, jumbo shrimp and military intelligence. They seem, in fact, a paradox, something that cannot be, the living and the dead.

Notice that the phrase is in the present tense and exhibits an existing state. These are neither the *live* dead nor the *lived* dead. By *living*, these dead currently give all the indications of a life being lived. But the word *dead* is final. *Dead* signals a condition that cannot be changed and cannot be mitigated. By living dead, we mean they live in the continuous state of a final condition. In this they are like alcoholics and AIDS patients. Alcoholics suffer from a progressive disease that never ends. They get a daily reprieve. Aids patients live with AIDS, searching not for a cure so much as a method for continuing to live with AIDS as long as possible. Zombies have a daily reprieve from the condition of death and live with their deaths as long as they can.

The living dead then, are constantly between life and death, not alive but dead and not in a state of death but seeming to be alive. It follows that their victims are inordinately a part of an in-between demographic—the teenager.

In comparison, the idea of the undead is a double negative. If you are undead, you are not dead and you are not alive. You are, in fact, a vacancy. Vampires are so much sexier than zombies because they are empty.

Finally, let's look at the word *zombie*. *Zombie* is an exotic word, almost funny. It references voodoo and Haiti, powdery substances, and Scooby Doo episodes. But it is also a descriptive term used to denote a lack of consciousness. "I was like a zombie last night," we often say, and we mean that we were walking around without being conscious of what we were doing. "I had a Zombie," which means that I had a powerful cocktail designed to make me unconscious as soon as possible. To be incognizant, unaware, doing stuff but unaware I am doing it. Zombies, then, operate as unconscious urges, that vast and unknowable realm of appetite and disorder. Further, they function as an excuse for that condition, in that "I cannot help but eat your brain, because I am a zombie."

If every dream is a wish, then to dream of zombies is to dream of an appetite without responsibility.

5.

We watch from behind barricaded windows as the living dead shamble through deserted streets. We're not sure whether to be terrified or amused. Vast herds of the dead fill in the spaces between buildings. They flow like stuttering particles of light from a broken strobe, around turned-over autos, still flashing ambulances, streetlights, and sidewalk benches.

A zombie shuffles and bumps into another zombie. The second zombie stumbles and disappears briefly in the crowd of sliding feet. It reappears, lacking an arm, which is picked up by a third zombie who uses it to clear a path for itself, sweeping the oozing limb back and forth like a scythe.

Two zombies butt heads; they fall back dizzy. Their jaws fall off. Both zombies duck down to pick up the bottom half of their faces, butt heads yet again, and rise with the wrong jaws. They force the mismatched teeth and chins under their noses. Black skin merges with white skin and a full beard becomes an Abraham Lincoln anachronism.

We load shotguns. We try and talk about ordinary things, such as the unseasonably moist heat and the way the Dog Star seems to glow just a little bit brighter than usual. In the atmosphere, in the crackling electrical silence between conversations, eyes widen and upper lips twitch. We pace a lot. We pull at our hair and we twist earlobes and stroke chins. We can't seem to keep the waistlines of our pants in the right place. We run to the toilet to be sick.

When the banging on the front door begins, we throw more furniture on the threshold, mostly steel case office stuff in that avocado shade someone thought was cheerful. There's about seventeen of us sheltered in this red brick turn-of-the-century warehouse. From all parts of the city, we have gathered here, perhaps the last survivors, or the first victims. We don't know. All the phones are down and the emergency radio network stopped broadcasting an hour ago.

Dusty and rusted-out machinery litters the corners of the warehouse. Broken glass glitters under lantern light. Some bleary-eyed children nest on a stinking purple-green sofa, folded into each other like sleeping puppies. The racket at the door grows louder, and now it's coming from the windows too. Dead hands grasp at the edges of warped boards. We run from window to window, from the cheap hollow-core office door to the aluminum truck entry in the back. We build up the barricades with whatever we have, until finally we use our own bodies.

We fail to secure the skylight. The first zombies splattered on impact with the cement floor. The others that followed used the writhing mass of still living limbs and torsos as a cushion, picking themselves up from the gore and heading our way. We use the last of our shells and rounds. We beat them with two-by-fours and muddy shovels. The zombies fall like spiders now from the ceiling. We keep fighting.

6.

What's so scary about zombies, you ask? They fall apart if you bump into them hard, they move so slow that my grandmother could escape them with her walker, they don't even have enough brains to come up with a good military strategy. . . . Not much of a threat, are they? This is what you ask.

Yes, but zombies don't just hunt you down and kill you. That would too easy to avoid, as you say. No, the problem is, you see, that the living dead are *contagious*. Their saliva functions as a powerful agent of contagion. One bite infects and one bite kills. Those infected rise again to carry the virus further.

The living dead work together to spread their condition. They are the perfect viral life form. As they are on the microscopic level, they are on the human level. They form a perfect, continuous consciousness, the microscopic directing the macroscopic. Each zombie represents a huge, shambling germ, spreading the disease, being the disease. Zombies are viruses, which carry the virus that created them.

This is why you fear them, the zombies. We are half-baked in comparison. Do you know what your micro-organisms are doing tonight?

7.

He wakes and doesn't know why. He had been dreaming, his skull full of darkness. What was it? He couldn't remember. If he could hurt, he'd feel agony. His muscle fibers scrape against each other like straining wires, and his skin is as dry as a salted slug. His throat bleeds and his eyes adhere to dry sockets. He knows this, can sense that some corner of this mind acknowledges that there should be pain, but the nerves just under his skin are incapable of carrying the message.

He searches his mind for something to think about. A part of him realizes he should wonder more at his singular condition. He is dead, isn't he? But, for some reason, he can't seem to get too excited about this. He tries to remember darkness, or even the time before, but can only recall with any certainty the moment of this wakening. Somewhere, though, somewhere deep within him, he can feel a hunger steadily growing.

The hunger pulls at his guts. Though his skin sloughs off in several sections, he can only feel the hunger. He knows that he is not hungry for just anything, but can't recall his hunger's goal. Something soft, something delicate, a subtle flavor he can almost taste in the back of this throat. It sends thrills throughout the surface of his tongue.

Now, his hunger overcomes him. He aches with it. His hunger fills him with a vacancy. Though he cannot feel the rotting of his fingers, he can feel his stomach itch, can feel it grow tender, feel it shrink into itself, like a tightened knot.

He groans and shuffles. He senses others that are like him and moves to join them. Perhaps they will know what substance will satisfy him. He finds them and they bump and stumble together. Now, they suffer together and their suffering feels better for it. They are together in their urges. The aches in his stomach spread to his chest, filling his useless lungs. It spreads to his throat. His Adam's apple is like a rusty ball bearing. It spreads to his head, and his head fills with agony. Every curl on his cerebellum is allergic, every neuron shorting out. He smells brain.

Brain, he realizes, is the substance he craves. He can smell it in the live ones, in the space between their ears. He knows it will make him whole, satisfy his pain. Why should they have it? Why should they be allowed to keep it? We need it more. I need it more. It's the only thing I need, the only thing that will make me whole, make me stop missing, missing what, missing what the brain carries.

He can smell it underneath the floorboards, the brain like a meaty grapefruit. The little girl screams when he rips apart the wood flooring to find the little oubliette where the girl hides. She is six years old and very scared, with hair in rows and a bow as bright as a birthday balloon. He uses ragged fingers to rip the scream from her throat, because he doesn't want the others to hear. He wants this one to himself. Her brain in his gullet sends shivers through every pore. He can feel his lungs fill, can feel the bright taste of fresh water. He can feel sunlight and being safe under blankets. He can smell mother's coconut hair, and feel father's beard tickle his belly. The shivers stop, and he moans, and he searches for more.

8.

As seen from the clouds, there appear to be maggots in the carcass of the Midwest. Throughout the old rust belt, from Philadelphia in the east to as far as St Louis in the west, wriggling pale figures surge from mutilated soil, from the guts of America.

Streets empty of the living. The streetlights out, the freeways vacant, the shopping malls transformed into hilltop fortresses. The dead inhabit this emptiness; they cling to the darkened fractures of urban habitats.

With so many maggots here, so many worms and beetles, I have tried in vain to find a space for life. I have looked to the daylight and found suppuration, looked to morning and found a bacterial stench. Just as I have always suspected, our history will waste us.

9.

"Tonight, we're gathered to discuss the religious implications of the ongoing living dead crisis. Cemeteries throughout the Midwest are emptying and their tenants rising in search of victims. Because of the ongoing nature of this crisis, we really don't know what the death toll is. We apologize to our viewers, but reports from the area are sketchy at best.

"But tonight, we have three representatives here of religious orders: Reverend Whitehead of the Northeast Baptist Ministry, Father Tom Connell of the Pittsburgh archdiocese, and Rabbi Ben Scholem, of the Reformed Indianapolis Synagogue. Gentlemen, welcome to the show.

"By telephone connection, we will also be talking to Mike Begin, a Navajo Shaman based in Gallup, Mew Mexico, to listen to his unique perspective. But first, Reverend, you've been quoted as saying that this ongoing crisis represents the first in a series of events leading up to the apocalypse. Will you explain your views?"

"Of course, Tina. We know that the Book of Revelation describes what will happen before the Second Coming of Our Savior and we also know that some of those events are pretty traumatic and unreal. What could be more traumatic and unreal than the rise of the dead? John specifically addresses the rising of the unsaved dead in an army that will—"

"Excuse me Reverend, I'm sorry to interrupt, but we have breaking news from the frontlines in Philadelphia, where reportedly the worst outbreak has occurred. Let's go to Sean Hallinan in Philadelphia."

"Good evening Tina. I'm here in front of the Liberty Bell in this most American of cities. Reports are coming in from all over the Midwest and parts of the Northeast that the armies of the dead are falling back. Our early reports say that crop-dusting aircraft are spraying the dead with some form of chemical release. Some reports suggest that the chemicals used are greenish in color, and others have reported that the chemicals smell like, quote, lemon polish.

"Wait, Tina. Can you hear that? It sounds as if there are planes flying above to the southeast. I can see searchlights scanning the sky. Over, there! It looks as if there are three or four small, prop-driven aircraft circling an area about a quarter of a mile from where we are. I'm not able to identify any chemical spray at this point, but, yes, it does smell like lemon polish. And perhaps . . . *mineral water?* Tina, we're going to attempt to get closer to the spraying. We'll update you when we can. Sean Hallinan, CMM from Philadelphia."

10.

Zombie love: Zombie 1 leans over an oozing skull, dishes up a handful of jelly. Brain spills from purple-black lips. Zombie 2 leans over to lick the stuff from Zombie 1's pus covered chin. Takes a piece of jaw, crunches it and grins. Their tongues meet. Planes overhead, the drone covers spreading gas, which seeps into their pores as they slurp. Pink health grows from their eyes. Rot and wounds vanish. With blood still flowing from their full red lips and smelling sweet as a bottle of liquid detergent, they stroll off hand in hand, under a chemically colored sunset.

11.

Dear Vince: I think it's over now. I wouldn't have believed it a week ago, but the worst seems to have passed. I can still hear the dusters outside, but the engines seem rarer now, more like a mopping up than a battle. I suppose you wonder how we came up with what the papers are calling a "miraculous cure" for the zombies. You should be, after all, since it was your foundation that paid for the original research.

Your man Dr Roderick did not realize what he had. He was so concerned about the creation of life in the dead that his success, the triumph that led to his untimely death, stopped his work. His unbending concentration blinded him to the truth and probably killed him. A few of us here in the operation center have already realized the underlying cause for his single-mindedness. What did you do with his wife and kids, Vince?

What he didn't see was that his failures were actually the cure for the condition he manufactured. Roderick made four formulas, but only one of them could give life to the dead. The others, he abandoned as useless. It turns out that the three failed formulas individually act as an inoculation against some of the more disturbing symptoms of being dead. We have synthesized these other formulas, refined them into a gaseous form and are now using crop dusting aircraft to spread the concoction around.

What's the worst thing about being dead, Vince? You look like shit, you smell bad, and you can't stop the processes of decomposition. One of the formulas, which we're calling in the lab the green goddess, acts as a powerful odor inhibitor. It stops the spread of the bacteria that cause the odors. Another formula, yellow fever, completely inhibits the process of decomposition. It may even stop the process of aging. Finally, we also use a formula we call super-Perrier to clean up the appearance of the living dead. We're still not sure how the hell that works. We think that Roderick may have begun some early experiments with nanotechnology.

We're not killing them, Vince; we're not even curing them. We're just cleaning them up, giving them a makeover. They'll never be terribly intelligent, but they won't be that much stupider than average. Your bizarre fantasy of creating a military force out of the living dead seems not to have been fruitful. In fact, Vince, look around you. In another couple of days, there will be the living dead all around you, surrounding you on every side. And you won't even say, "I had not thought death had undone so many."

Rather, you will not even know the difference. The dead will be among us; they'll be our employees, our children, spouses and bosses. They'll be washing your car, auditing your taxes, reading the evening news. They'll be in front you in the check-out line, next to you on the subway, in that car honking at you for not using your turn signals. We'll never be able to tell the dead from the living again. In fact, you might say, that these days the living are indistinguishable from the dead.

12.

Not far from here, in a laboratory tucked under some ivy-covered building, the night janitor Peter shuffles his mop back and forth over sickly green tiles. The bristles catch on broken grout lines, but Peter doesn't notice. Peter thinks of the water. He dips his mop in the suds and dark grease, and he thinks of the bubbles forming as he carefully lifts his mop. The bubbles are dark. They roil when he twirls the mop head. They undulate and shake. So dark, almost burgundy with the dirt. They remind Peter of something. Something he needs, but he can no longer remember what he needs or why he needs it. He stops. He leans over the bucket and dips a perfectly healthy and normal index finger in the filthy liquid. He brings his finger to his lips, opens his mouth, and sucks deeply at the grease.

13.

These fragments I have shored against my ruins. . . . I've collected these scraps, these little pictures of the time when the living dead walked the earth. I had hoped to understand what happened. I had hoped that there would be some message, some lesson here, some way of never letting this happen again. These pieces, from published reports, letters and first hand Interviews, remain only fragments. The bigger picture remains obscure.

I was one of those who finally located Dr Roderick's laboratory and his work. Roderick was the first victim, and one of the first to take the cure. He's a night janitor at the University of Chicago now. In his lab, we are still cleaning his blood and brains from the masonry walls. What did Roderick learn from his research?

Is it that we're so afraid of dying that we keep looking for ways to overcome death? If so, this will happen again. Why are we afraid of dying? Do we fear extinction, emptiness? I don't believe so. Failed suicides report extinction as their aim. No, we don't fear death so much as we fear justice. We fear retribution, and we're not even sure why.

The pathetic zombies that Roderick created are a pale simulacrum of death, a wind-up jack-in-the-box designed to startle children. The real living dead move swiftly, not slowly at all. They race from victim to victim, to suck the life from every experience of sunlight and warm feelings. The dead move in memories and regrets. They paint the sky with their color.

GRINNING SAMUEL

David Dunwoody

The air was musty and stale, choking Ryland with every ragged breath. Seated on a rickety old chair before a table coated with dust, he imagined he was in the waiting room of a mausoleum. He'd been here two hours. Seemed the Reaper was overbooked today.

Before him yawned the mouth of a maze, a series of catacombs cut deep into the earth. A bitter cold whispered at him from the blackness, further constricting his lungs. In contrast was the warmth of klieg lights on his back; his long face was made longer in shadows cast sharply upon the table.

On second thought, this seemed less a mausoleum than a television studio. Backlit like a late-night host, Ryland crossed one leg over the other and tapped his gold wristwatch and waited on his guest. Flanked by the klieg lights at Ryland's rear, his audience sat, a huddled contingency wearing insect-like nightvision helmets, hugging their M4 carbines, which would punctuate his words like a laugh track if the guest wasn't being cooperative.

The hush in the entrance of the catacombs was as palpable as the mold in the air. His men's breath, filtered through their helmets, was inaudible. Ryland coughed on a mote of dust. The sound cracked and echoed like a rifle report. Then the hush returned.

The hush was anticipation.

Something shifted in the catacombs. Ryland straightened up a bit, as a formality; although what was shuffling through the dirt towards the klieg lights likely couldn't see him. Not because of the lighting but because its eyes, Samuel's eyes, had long crumbled from their sockets. Still, Samuel always found his way to the table. Sometimes Samuel found his way to other things as well.

He was attired in a soiled and worn shirt from the colonial era that had once been white, but was now a dingy brown; the same with his loose-fitting trousers. Samuel never requested new clothing. He probably only wore these threadbare threads out of habit. If they finally fell from his shoulders, revealing his emaciated husk of a frame, he'd likely not react.

Everyone always noticed his hands first. Ryland's gunmen heard the rusty creaking of Samuel's metal fingers, crude constructs tethered to his wrists with wire, fitted over what remained of his original appendages with an intricate system of antique clock parts housed within the palms. The mechanical hands flexed continuously as Samuel plodded along.

Once interest in the fidgety hands had waned, there was nowhere else to look but his face: brown flesh-paper so fragile thin, stretched over an angular skull; the holes where eyes and nose had once been to serve purposes now fulfilled by other means; and the jaws, another mechanism, screwed into the bone and affixed with steel teeth. Ryland stared in wonder, imagining Samuel seated somewhere deep in the catacombs, working with his mechanical hands to build his razorblade smile.

"Grinning Samuel" was his full moniker, Samuel not being his real name, (no one knew what that was). He settled in a chair opposite from Ryland and placed a small burlap sack in front of him. He stared, eyeless, at the living.

He was uncommonly picky, and any transaction came with certain rules of conduct. Some had been established from the get-go while others were learned at great cost. Most important was the invisible line running down the middle of the table, separating Ryland from Samuel, a line of principle as effective as an electric fence. No one crossed that line. This cardinal rule had been established when Ryland's predecessor had reached out to grab that little burlap sack.

In the ensuing melee, all the gunmen had swarmed past the now-screaming-and-bleeding liaison with every intention of dismembering Samuel. And he'd killed every single one of them. Every one. The liaison had watched and died as blood jetted from the stump of his wrist. Watched and died while the blind, smiling Samuel had stuffed the gunmen's remains into his stainless-steel maw. He didn't feed often, yet he still thrived down here, in these catacombs beneath a defunct Protestant parish, a walking testament to the potency of the earth around him . . . the earth contained in that burlap sack.

Opening a briefcase, Ryland turned it towards Samuel. This was the transaction. He slid the case to the center of the table, just shy of that invisible line, and the zombie's mechanical fingers rummaged through its contents. Watch gears, springs, miniature coils and screws. Although whatever it was that infused this accursed earth had kept Samuel from rotting away entirely, he still needed to maintain his most-used joints, his limbs, his appendages, those terrible jaws. They creaked as he fingered a brass cog.

Seemed like it'd be so easy right now to snatch the burlap purse with its pound of dirt and to riddle Samuel with bullets, throwing the table in his face, cutting him to ribbons with automatic fire, to finally storm the catacombs. Ryland felt his own fingers jumping anxiously in his lap, but he forced himself to picture his predecessor, dying on the earthen floor beside this very chair, dying on his back in a shitty paste of dirt and blood.

Ryland was jarred back to reality as Samuel pushed the sack across the table. His sightless, metallic jack-o-lantern visage turned slowly from side to side, as if surveying the firing squad flanked by klieg lights. Ryland, never certain whether the after-dead could still hear, mumbled thanks and took the sack. For the first time, he addressed his team. "Fall back."

They did, except for Goldhammer, who came forward with a HAZMAT container the size of a lunchbox. Samuel sat quietly as Ryland took a handful of soil from the sack and, like a drug buyer testing the product, sprinkled the dirt over the dark mass in the container. "What's his name?" He asked Goldhammer, who replied through his bug helmet, "Pancake." Ryland smiled wryly and stroked the ball of black fur. Now, he felt a rhythmic movement beneath his fingertips; the kitten shuddered, shifted. It was in an advanced state of decay and had been broken beyond repair by a parade of freeway traffic, so there was little for it to do now but purr.

"Dirt's good," Goldhammer called back to the others. Another container was brought forth to receive the sack's contents. Ryland closed the HAZMAT lunchbox over the cat. It muttered weakly with dead vocal cords. He smiled again. The sack was returned to the table beside the briefcase, both for Samuel to keep. Taking one in each metal fist, the zombie stood up.

The lunchbox jerked in Ryland's hands, and even before the black blur flew past his face and down the tunnel, he knew; even as his legs pumped against his will, sending him past the table and over that invisible line in futile pursuit, he knew. God-damned crippled cat!

A clutch of mechanical fingers took root in the center of Ryland's chest.

Pulled off his feet by Grinning Samuel and out of reality by the numbing terror in his veins, Ryland heard dimly the patter of bullets against Samuel's back. Goldhammer, like a double-jointed ballet dancer, pirouetted off the table and drove a boot into the afterdead's defunct groin. While his legs jackknifed through the air, he planted his M4 against Samuel's temple and got off a good quarter-second burst of fire before the zombie punched through his body armor and yanked out a streaming handful of guts. A spurting, slopping mess that cushioned the soldier's fall immediately followed it.

Ryland had been thrown clear of the battle and had crashed into the dirt; having been tossed deeper into the catacombs, he saw Samuel as a hulking silhouette against the lights, swaying under a barrage of gunfire. Ryland felt bullets zipping overhead and pressed his face into the earth, tasting that accursed dirt for which Goldhammer had just died.

Died. . . . Christ.

The government had accumulated a half-ton of soil from the parish over the past three decades, and had been burying bodies in it, clocking their resurrection and administering tests of strength, endurance, and aptitude. What little intelligence Samuel exhibited was rare in afterdead (except those who stayed near their Source, of course); they usually came up sputtering the last of their blood and bile and clamoring for the nearest warm body, abandoning all higher faculties in the lust for living flesh. Indeed, such was the case with Sergeant Goldhammer, who sat up beside the besieged Samuel and fixed his bug-like gaze on Ryland. His exposed viscera was caked with soil, his back to the other men—but surely they realized what he'd become. . . .

Goldhammer made a wet noise inside his helmet. Ryland heard it over the gunfire.

Pawing through his own innards, the dead soldier came at his former commander. Former as of thirty seconds ago. Yes, he was fresh undead, and there was still some basic military proto-col embedded in that brain of his, wasn't there, so Ryland threw his hand out (wrist broken, he felt) and screamed, "Stop!"Gold-hammer did, crouching on all fours with a rope of intestine dragging between his legs. He cocked his head and was the perfect picture of a sick dog. He was trying to recognize the word and why it had halted him in his tracks. Ryland could see the gears turning, like the gears in Grinning Samuel's jaw, and at that moment, Samuel ripped into the firing squad; the hail of bullets was reduced to a drizzle.

Goldhammer pounced. Ryland pivoted on his broken wrist with a blinding snap of pain and caught his aggressor with a boot heel between the glassy bug eyes. Goldhammer grunted, batted the leg aside. They wrestled there on the ground with Ryland kicking himself farther and farther down the tunnel, all the while aware that Samuel would soon be finished with the others.

Backpedaling on his hands and hindquarters, he disturbed a pile of pebbles—no, gears, the strewn contents of the briefcase! Ryland closed his good hand around a fistful of them, and, with a half-hearted cry, he hurled them into Goldhammer's face. Relatively pointless but still an amusing precursor to Samuel's hand sweeping down like a wrecking ball and crushing Gold-hammer's skull against the wall. The soldier crumpled to clear a path for the grinning afterdead. Samuel's steel maw was painted with liquid rust from the insides of Ryland's men. The zombie knew right where his prey was, and Ryland's situation hit rock bottom as the damaged klieg lights faded out.

"STOP!!" He shrieked. "STOOOOOOOOOOP!!!" He now knew for certain that Samuel could still hear by the way that his pace quickened. A barely discernable silhouette in the faint remnants of light, Grinning Samuel's grasping fingers squealed as he drew closer. Ryland's back struck a wall. He waited for those fingers to find his heart.

His broken wrist was jerked into the air. He screamed, imagining that his entire arm had been ripped off. But it hadn't been. Samuel wasn't even moving now.

With his breath caught in his throat, Ryland just sat and listened in the dark.

And then he heard it.Tick-tock, tick-tock.

His wrist twisted a little. He bit into his lip while Samuel traced the band of his gold wristwatch. The pair remained motionless in the shadows for what seemed like an eternity, but Ryland counted the ticks and tocks and knew it was less then a minute. Finally, in spite of both terror and logic, he stammored, "It's a Rolex."

The watch left his wrist, and his intact arm dropped into his moist lap. Samuel could be heard shuffling off into the catacombs, down beneath the parish churchyard where the mystery of his unlife dwelled. The tick-tock, tick-tock gradually ceased.

Ryland sucked icy air into his lungs and sat there for what really did seem like an eternity. There were a few dull spots of light down the tunnel. There, he'd have to confront the remains of his slaughtered team; but Samuel would have done quite a number on them, and none would be getting back up. He pushed his ankles through the dirt until the circulation returned to them; he tried to stand. He was still a bit shaky, wrist throbbing like mad. Goddamn, it was getting colder by the second. He took another breath, sat back down, and listened to the silence.

Then he heard something new . . .

Meow.

Ryland smiled again and reached a blind hand into the darkness.

Ann at Twilight

Brent Zirnheld

When the dead had risen to eat the living, Ann's nice little world crumbled around her. One of the first to die had been her husband, Lamont. He'd never gotten a proper burial, nor had Ann been able to touch him one last time. In fact, he'd never been buried, but shot in the head and left on the streets of Knoxville, Tennessee for rats, cats, birds, and dogs—that is if the living dead had left anything behind after they had gotten their fill.

"Pity you can't see what a beautiful day it is," Jeb said. "Damn fine day. Blue sky, white puffy clouds, green trees. Damn pity."

Ann listened from the truck's passenger seat. To her, a beautiful day was the warmth of the sun on her skin and the songs of birds. She'd never been able to see a beautiful day, blind since birth. Living in the dark, she'd been particularly challenged when it came to life in this new Dark Age.

After Lamont's death and the general collapse of society, Ann had depended on the kindness of strangers. She'd met an ex-cop named Glen who'd been a Godsend. Unlike most of those who wanted to survive, he hadn't let her blindness deter him; he and his brother Tom had rescued her from the squalor that had become Knoxville and took her with them when they left, despite the liability that having a blind woman created.

Unfortunately, Glen was killed halfway through Arkansas, and Tom blamed Ann for the loss. He'd raped her and traded her for two rifles, ten gallons of gas, and several boxes of ammunition.

That was two weeks ago. Once Ann was healed enough from Tom's brutal attack, she'd been put on the market again. Two hours later, Jeb arrived with a truckload of reefer, and Ann had switched owners.

Maybe it wouldn't have been so bad if she'd been bought by someone who would actually protect her and give a damn about her well being, but Jeb was part of a white supremacist clan. And he'd only made it too clear what her new role would be once she was taken back to the ranch.

"Oh, well it *was* a beautiful day. Lookie what I see out there. Ha, ha, you can't look, can you? Well, let me describe 'im to you," Jeb said, slowing down the truck.

The vehicle shifted to the right. As it slowed, it left solid pavement and crunched gravel on the road's shoulder.

"He's a big 'un. Hobblin' this way like he's got a snowball's chance in hell of catching anything going by on this road. Best of all, he's a nigger just like you. Nice to know another one's dead. I'll be damned if he's gonna be around much longer to put the bite on someone, though."

Jeb pulled something Ann assumed was a rifle from the rack behind her head. Part of it struck her in the left ear as he jerked it free.

"Is he in a meadow?" Ann asked, rubbing her ear. "How far away is he?"

"Oh, she speaks!" Jeb said.

She heard a mechanical sound as he did something to the gun, readying it for firing.

"What's distance to *you?*" Jeb asked. "He's way out there in the open. How the hell can I describe it? A hundred yards maybe, does that help? Far enough away to be a good challenge to hit from this range."

"What time is it?" Ann asked.

Jeb laughed. She was afraid he wouldn't tell her, but he blurted with a chuckle, "Five-thirty. You got a hot date? Oh, of course you do. First with me then with Ed, then with Steve, then with Ralph, then with John, then with Rick and maybe we'll even let little Joe have some of that fine pussy." Jeb laughed harder. "Yeah, you got yerself several hot dates tonight."

Seven of them, Ann counted, including little Joe. At least seven, anyway; Jeb could have forgotten to list some of them.

"Don't you guys have girlfriends?" she asked.

"We got us some other women, but they get old after awhile. It'll be extra good to have somethin' new to liven things up for a little while. Especially somethin' we don't mind roughin' up."

Ann kept silent. It wasn't her habit of talking back to those who could strike her with impunity. Besides, she had to figure out how the other women played into it. Were they captives or willing partners?

Jeb opened the door. Ann heard his feet hit the pavement. He left his door open.

Ann waited. The left side of the truck dipped ever so slightly. He was leaning on the front of the truck.

Holding her breath, Ann reached forward. Her fingers touched the dashboard. With the tips of her fingers, she sought the glove compartment's release. While she'd opened glove boxes before, she hadn't so much as touched this one, so there was no telling what kind of release mechanism she'd be dealing with.

Trying to keep her back straight, Ann hoped Jeb wasn't paying attention to her while he was outside the vehicle. There was no way to know. If he caught her, he'd tie her hands and she'd get no further chances. This was likely her only opportunity to find a weapon, so it would have to be worth the risk. Once he returned to the truck, she'd better have a weapon to use, or there would be no stopping him. He'd take her to his clan's ranch, and she'd be their toy until they grew tired of her—or until she broke.

Her fingers found the latch. It was round with an upraised surface. A knob? She twisted.

The rifle exploded, startling her. The glove compartment's door hit her knees.

"Dammit!" Jeb yelled.

Her heart seized and she froze in place.

But then he prepped his gun for a second shot.

Abandoning subtlety, Ann reached into the open box and found a gun. Two of them.

Second shot.

"Yes!" Jeb exclaimed.

Ann quickly withdrew the nearest gun. It was a revolver, she could tell by the swell on each side. With her left hand, she closed the box, praying it would stay shut. It did.

She put the gun beside her right leg, but it was possible he might still see it, so she lowered it between the seat and the door. It was very heavy. There was no way she'd drop it, though. Not a chance. This gun was her salvation—the only way she'd be able to escape this sicko.

Jeb hopped into the truck. Slammed the door.

"Shoulda seen that! Knocked 'im backward three whole feet before he went down on 'is back."

The weapon struck Ann in the side of the head again as he put it back from where it came. His giggle signaled that this time he'd struck her on purpose. Behind her head, the rifle bumped her once more before sliding into the rack.

"Oh, well if that don't beat shit, there's another dead nig," Jeb said, his sour breath passing across Ann's face.

Ann wondered if Jeb was staring through the window at the dead man. Which direction? The same direction as the other dead man? The same general vicinity?

"Spooky sucker. Just standing there. Should I put 'im out of his misery or just let 'im wander around?"

"Where is he?"

"Too far to hit. Maybe this one's still alive. He's just standing there. Hard to tell these days. I liked the dead back in the beginning before they learned to get sneaky. Used ta be, you'd just sit there with a rifle and pick them off one by one until they were gone or you was out of ammo. Then they started learnin' to play dead, or crawl, or hide, or sneak around. The worst ones pretend to be alive. Like this one. Dead sucker's waving at us."

"Maybe he's not dead," Ann said. It was habit to keep Jeb talking, but he was such a heavy nose breather that she knew exactly where he was when he didn't speak.

Ann felt the sun on her chest and chin, the rays soaking into her blouse and exposed skin from her neck to her forehead. They were definitely facing west from what she could assume, given the time of day. The sun could be coming from the side, but Ann doubted it as her whole face was feeling the sun's warmth.

"He's dead alright. Missin' one of his arms, I think. Front of his shirt's covered with blood like he's been eatin' himself a good meal. Startin' to walk this way."

There was silence as Ann wondered what Jeb would do. From his voice, she knew that the dead man was in the field to her right. If she ran, she'd be going straight for him unless she stayed on the road. She could hardly stay on the road, though. Someone who knew Jeb and his friends could happen along.

"Screw it. I gotta be gettin' you back to the boys. Me and Rick will have ta come out here tomorrow and see where those dead folk are comin' from. Gonna have us some fun with you tonight and I can't hardly wait."

Jeb grabbed her left breast and squeezed. He knew just where her nipple was, too.

"Ow!" she exclaimed, jerking away.

Jeb laughed and touched her cheek. "Don't tell the boys, but I think yer kinda cute in your own darkie way."

He started the truck.

Balancing the gun against the side of the seat, Ann slid her fingers downward to grip its handle and slide a finger through the trigger guard. With her middle finger, she felt for a safety, but didn't find one readily so she took the chance.

Reaching for the door handle with her left hand, Ann pressed her right wrist against her left shoulder to steady her aim. She squeezed the trigger. It was a tough one to squeeze, very tight, so she added pressure.

"Damn bitch!" Jeb yelled, opening his door.

The hammer fell on an empty chamber. Jeb had left the first hole empty as his "safety." She squeezed again. The gun bucked in her hand and filled the truck's cab with an explosive report that made Ann's ears ring louder than they ever had.

She squeezed the trigger again.

Then she opened her door and turned her body. Deaf now, she slid off the seat, knees bent slightly as she braced for contact with the ground. Her feet landed at an angle, pitching her forward. Throwing out her arms, she braced for impact. It came quickly, her knees and hands landing on gravel that poked into them, especially the fingers of her right hand that were smashed between gravel and the gun's handle. She didn't let go of the gun, though.

Immediately, Ann scrambled forward. She moved in the direction she thought would take her to the rear and away from the truck. Toward the field. Maybe. The fall had disoriented her somewhat. She could feel gravel and plants beneath her feet, but heard only ringing in her ears.

"You damned cunt!" Jeb screamed, his voice sounding farther away than what it was. She could still tell he was behind her and to the right.

Her heart sank. Not only was he still alive, her only method of sensing his location was going haywire from the gunshot. Her ears would be ringing for at least the next few minutes—the next few minutes being the most crucial moments of her life.

"I'll kill you!" Jeb screamed. Then he cried out in agony. "Cunt!"

He screamed again, a howl of pain. She'd hit him at least once, though how bad was anyone's guess.

Ann continued moving as fast as she could, expecting a bullet to strike her in the back at any moment. She might be heading in the general direction of the dead man who would eat her flesh if given the opportunity, but there was no way to know.

Still armed, she was thankful she hadn't dropped the gun. It was a useless weapon against Jeb at the moment, but it might come in handy should she walk into the arms of the dead.

Ears still ringing, she trudged onward, her feet moving forward as fast as she dared. She didn't have a cane or a stick of any kind, so she had to walk very carefully, keeping her balance on the rear leg until she had firm footing for the leg she was throwing forward. If her forward foot struck an obstruction, it wouldn't knock her off-balance.

How far from the truck was she? How hurt was Jeb? She expected a bullet to come at any time. She ducked her head and hunched forward to make herself a smaller target. Of course, Jeb might just come after her hoping to grab her gun arm before she could shoot him. Did he dare?

Ann tilted her weight forward to her right foot and kicked her left foot out to take the next step. The top of her shoe struck something. She lifted the gun.

Jeb fired his rifle.

She felt nothing. Had she been hit? Evidently not or she would have felt the impact. She knew you could get shot and not necessarily feel it, but Jeb's rifle had supposedly pitched a dead man backwards, so she knew it had punch to it.

Reaching forward, she felt nothing. Lifting her hand, she found a wire. Barbed wire. It was a barbed wire fence.

Stooping, Ann felt the weeds. They were almost knee-high.

Jeb fired his gun again. A loud thump as the bullet struck something solid, just to her left. She heard what might be the sound of vibrating wire.

Quickly, Ann moved along the fence, feeling it with her left hand. She came to a fence post. If she could get over the fence, she might be able to make her escape by crawling through the high weeds.

—Provided she cleared the fence before getting shot.

Ann stuck the gun in her front pocket, shoving it so hard she heard seams rip. Putting her left hand on top of the post, she grabbed the top wire with her right hand. She lifted her left foot to the first wire, then onto the second. The only way to climb a barbed wire fence safely was near a fence post since the brackets more steadily held the wires—something Glen had taught her.

In the distance, Jeb screamed. He hurled vile obscenities at her, or his situation, and she prayed he would continue because when he yelled she knew he wasn't aiming that big gun at her, or if he was, he wasn't doing it with much accuracy.

Ann threw her left leg over the fence as the wires bobbed and wiggled beneath her. The post was her only solid support.

Then Jeb fired again. Her left arm buckled when it was struck. Ann leaned toward the side of the fence she wanted to be on and then pushed as she fell. She struck the ground on her right side. Luckily, she didn't break anything in the fall.

Ann instinctively grabbed her left forearm. It was wet with blood. Pain radiated from the spot where she'd been struck. She put her right hand in her left to see if she could still use the left hand. Tightening her grip was painful and she could only flex her middle finger, index finger, and thumb. At least the radius or ulna didn't seem to be broken.

Withdrawing the gun from her pocket, Ann lashed out with her left foot, swinging it left and right until it struck the fence post. Reoriented, she began crawling deeper into the field.

"You ain't gettin' away!" Jeb yelled. "You hear me?"

He was coming. She could barely hear him on the gravel, hobbling as if he had a bad leg. As bad as his aim had been, her first instinct was that she'd shot him in the arm. Maybe she'd hit a thigh.

The ringing in her ears had died some, enough to hear him behind her, climbing the fence.

Panicked, Ann stood straight and ran. It was dangerous—she cursed herself for attempting something so reckless—but with each footfall that she didn't collide with something or lose her balance, Ann was farther from Jeb.

Her left foot landed sooner than she expected, and her balance was hopelessly lost.

A gunshot echoed through the field as she fell to the rough weeds, scratching her face.

"Ha, ha! Got you, you bitch!"

Ann stayed still. Her breathing was labored. For obvious reasons, she didn't do much running, so she was winded easily.

Had she been hit? She didn't feel anything.

Her instinct was to get up and run, or at the very least, crawl, but she held back. Jeb thought she was down, maybe she should stay that way. If he thought he could take her back alive, he'd do so; otherwise, he'd have a lot of reefer to answer for. That meant he'd come to get her, provided he wasn't wounded too badly.

Pressing into her thigh was the gun. She slid her hand over and retrieved it, keeping a tight grip on the handle and placing her finger on the trigger.

"I hope yer still alive!" Jeb yelled. "Ow, dammit!"

She heard him fall in the weeds behind her. But he was close. Really close.

When he reached her, he poked her in the ass with what was probably the barrel of his rifle.

"Hey!"

He poked the barrel into the wound on her left arm, but she'd figured the move was coming, and she'd braced herself for the explosion of pain that nearly made her flinch.

"What the hell you starin' at, you dead fucker?" Jeb exclaimed. "Come and get it, then!" Jeb tossed his rifle to the side. Ann heard it hit ground to her left, at least a few feet away.

Then he knelt beside her and rolled her over. She raised the gun and fired twice. The third time she pulled the trigger, nothing happened.

His weight fell onto her lower legs, but it wasn't enough to pin her to the spot. She frantically crawled in the direction of his rifle. Her left arm was useless for supporting her weight; she used it to feel the ground in front of her.

Behind her, Jeb screamed bloody murder. She knew from the squeal that she'd gotten him good this time.

Her left hand found the rifle's stock. She shoved the empty revolver into her pants' pocket.

"Oh Gawd," Jeb screamed. "Finish me! For Christ's sake, *finish me!*"

Ann stood, bringing up the rifle with her right hand. The rifle was heavy, and her left arm was too weak to help support the weapon.

"Please, dear God, please! You gut shot me!"

The way Jeb was carrying on, Ann assumed it was plenty painful for him. Good.

"How many shells are left in this?" she asked.

"Two . . . three . . ." He blurted, making a sound akin to gagging.

"Where's the dead guy?"

"He's coming!" Jeb screamed. "Kill me, pleeeeease!"

"Which direction?"

"Yer blind! Stupid bitch, how ya gonna hit 'im?" He punctuated the statement with a long moan.

Ann thought better of letting Jeb know how stupid he was for letting a "blind, stupid bitch" give him a fatal gut shot: gloating wouldn't secure his cooperation.

"Which direction is he?"

"Shoot me and I'll tell you," Jeb said, obviously not thinking clearly.

Ann tried to think. Her left arm was throbbing, she'd lost track of her bearings, and Jeb was moaning and complaining and cursing so loud and so often that she couldn't hear the approach of the dead man. It would be easier to shoot Jeb and shut him up, but then Ann would have five minutes of ringing ears as the dead man hobbled closer.

"Guide me to the truck. Why should we both die?"

"Just kill me. Please!"

"How close is he?"

"Kill meeeeeeeeeeee!"

Ann gritted her teeth. The rifle would do her no good if the dead guy reached her. It wasn't a close-quarters weapon. She had to make it to the truck in time to reload the revolver.

"How close is he?" Ann asked.

"I ain't tellin' you! Fuck you! Let 'im eat you if he's gonna eat me!"

Ann started stepping forward. Slowly. "Am I heading toward the truck?" she asked.

"No!" Jeb yelled. He laughed, but cried out in pain and then moaned for a good long time.

He was probably lying to her. Maybe she was headed in the right direction and he wanted to confuse her.

"I'm alive! You'd rather see me get killed than help me? You'd rather help the dead?"

"Yer a nigger! The less of you there are when society gets restarted, the better!"

Which way to go, which way to go?

"Please help me!" Ann exclaimed. "Please!"

This wasn't fair. It just wasn't fair! Why'd she have to be blind *and* black? Why not one or the other? She'd never asked for any of this!

No, no, no, that was silly thinking. Neither was her fault. Her blackness wasn't what was preventing Jeb from helping her—that was his choice and his choice alone.

"Go straight!" Jeb yelled. "The direction yer facin'! He's almost to ya!"

"Straight? Walk this way? And I'll get to the fence?"

"Y-yeah!"

Ann thought about it.

Briefly.

She turned and walked the opposite direction, sweeping the rifle's barrel back and forth in front of her.

"No! The other way! Stupid bitch, yer goin' right toward 'im!"

Ann kept moving, undeterred in her conviction that Jeb would rather see her die than live. He'd probably intended to walk her into the path of the dead man so as to have the satisfaction of watching her die first.

"Ha, ha, that's what I hate about you people! Yer so fuckin' dumb!" Jeb screamed. "I told you that knowin' you'd go the opposite direction!" He laughed. The laughing turned to a gag and a moan.

Ann swept the rifle in a wide arc. She tucked her left arm against her abdomen and held it there, hoping it had stopped bleeding.

"I hate you!" Jeb yelled. "I hate you! I hope you rot in hell! Yer blind! How long can you last out here? Huh? It should be you here, not meeeee!"

The barrel of the rifle struck something. She stopped and raised the weapon.

Jeb screamed. His cries were strained, as if he were struggling against something. He continued to sob, pleading for God to take him.

"How . . . loooong . . . can . . . you . . . laaaaaaaaaaasssssssssgkkllch."

Ann lurched forward and grabbed the fencepost. She threw the rifle to the other side. Then she climbed, mostly with her good arm. The left was just about useless.

Jeb's cries ended as he was consumed. Depending on how much of him was left, soon he'd be rising into his second life.

Ann pushed away from the fence and landed on the rifle. She fell to her buttocks, but grabbed the rifle and then stood. Keeping her left arm against her, she put her back to the fence and then started forward, hoping to reach the road. From there, the truck should be to her right, depending on whether or not she'd reached the fence near the point where she'd first climbed over.

In the back of her mind, she wondered what she'd do once she reached the truck. Jeb's fellow clansmen would come looking for him sooner or later. There were dead people in the field, so she was pretty much in deep shit no matter what.

The revolver was in her back pocket. Another was in the truck. A small gun would keep her fate in her own hands. There were fates worse than death and she'd be damned if she'd allow herself to be a fuck toy for a bunch of bigots before taking her own life.

Picking up a handful of gravel, Ann squared herself and heaved the rocks to her left. She heard them scatter on pavement and land in weeds. Another handful the other direction clattered on metal.

She grabbed the rifle from the ground and started in the direction of the truck.

The sound of the engine of another vehicle slowly grew more audible. Some kind of motorbike. She turned her head to the left and right, but couldn't tell from which direction it was coming.

Ann hurried along the roadside, not wanting to be defenseless when the person arrived. At this point, she had to assume it would be foe, not friend.

Sweeping the rifle outward, Ann was in the act of swinging it back toward the left when she struck the rear of the truck with her left knee. She fell to the ground, wincing in pain.

The motorbike was coming from the west. The very direction Jeb had been traveling.

Ann rushed alongside the truck and slammed into the partially open door. She stepped backward, dropping the rifle. Throwing the door wide, Ann grabbed for the dashboard. Her right hand fumbled along its front until she found the twist knob.

The motorbike stopped near the truck as the glove box door fell open. Ann found the gun, another revolver, and withdrew it from the box.

"Jeb?" a young kid called.

The driver's side door opened.

Ann aimed the gun.

"Don't kill me!" the boy exclaimed.

Ann couldn't pull the trigger.

"How old are you?" she asked.

"Thirteen, ma'am."

"What's your name?"

"Joe."

He was one of them. Jeb had mentioned him. Little Joe. And Joe had called for Jeb, proving the connection to Jeb and his clan.

Ann fell against the seat, exhausted.

"Where's Jeb?" Joe asked.

"Out in the field. Getting chewed on."

"Oh."

"You don't sound too upset about that, Joe."

"Jeb teased and hit me a lot. Never liked him much."

"What about the others? How do they treat you?"

"They'll treat me a lot better if I bring you back."

"You're not going to take me back. How many women do they keep locked up?"

"They got about five, but ain't none of 'em pretty as you."

"But I'm black, doesn't that bother them?"

"That was Jeb's thing. Him and Ed used to be in the Klan."

So it wasn't really about race after all, it was about having concubines. Ann had heard a lot of that was going around. Amazing how far removed from normalcy things had become, as if there'd been a thin line between civilization and savagery before the dead had returned.

"Hey, you're blind aren't you?"

"Yes," Ann said. "Can you drive this truck, Joe?"

"Sure can."

"Can you drive me away from your friends? If they get a hold of me, they'll do bad things to me. That isn't right, you know that, don't you?"

"I know."

"Why don't you drive me to Memphis?"

"Ed and Steve would kill me if I did that."

"They're not your friends if they hurt you and teach you women are nothing but toys."

"They're all I've got now that my parents are gone. Besides, they don't treat all women bad. They're good to Jessie. Maybe they'll be nice to you."

Ann sighed. "Can you at least not mention me when you go back?"

"I can't leave you out here, lady. There's eight dead people in that field headed this way. You'll get eaten for sure."

"There's a fence."

"Not fifteen feet away from the front of this truck is a huge hole in the fence. They'll get out. Besides, I've seen 'em climb fences before. They use to not be able to climb and stuff, but they can do that now."

"I'll take my chances."

Ann stood. She swept out her foot until she found the rifle.

"I'll take you to Memphis," Joe said.

"Really? I'll kill you if you're lying to me, Joe."

"I'm not lying. Really. I promise, I'll take you to Memphis."

"Let's go then. I'm trusting you."

"Let me park my bike first. It's too heavy to put in the back of the truck."

Ann put the rifle in the seat, barrel to the floorboard. Then she climbed inside. She wasn't sure if she could trust the kid, but what choice did she have?

"How close are they?" Ann called.

"Halfway through the field. Couple of 'em are headed Jeb's way, but the rest are coming this way. And one of them is fast."

Joe parked his bike then he hopped into the truck and started it.

"I'll just turn around and head the other direction," he told her. "You know, toward Memphis."

"Please, Joe," Ann said. "I'm trusting you. Your friends will rape me and probably end up killing me. I can't let that happen, do you understand? I've come too far to give up now and I'll kill you if I have to. Don't misjudge me because I'm blind. Look at Jeb."

"I understand. That's why I'm taking you to Memphis."

The truck started forward. Joe swung it left, and the tires crunched gravel when the truck reached the other side of the road. He kept the truck in a tight circle and Ann felt the vehicle begin the second half of the route that would have them facing west again.

Joe let the truck sit idling for a moment as he said, "All set to go to Memphis."

"So we're not going back to your friends?" Ann asked, feeling the sun on her face again.

"No, ma'am," he answered, and Ann was able to get a fix on his head. This time the gun's first chamber was loaded. A loud crack filled the cab and Joe's body came falling onto Ann, blood gushing from the wound. The truck rolled forward.

Lurching toward the steering column, Ann felt for the gear-shift selector. She found it and jerked it all the way up. The truck came to a hard stop.

Gunpowder and the coppery scent of blood filled the cab. Ringing filled her ears as she reloaded the empty chamber.

She opened the door and slipped out.

Leaving the heavy rifle, Ann headed down the road toward the east. Her left foot crunched gravel, and her right foot touched solid pavement as she used foot placement to keep herself heading more or less along the road.

As the ringing in her ears subsided, she could hear them behind her. One had taken to the pavement with his bad leg, dragging it behind him as he hobbled. The fast one was in the gravel. Others were alongside the road, the sound of their feet making a light hissing sound as they passed through the tall weeds.

She didn't know if she'd have the energy to outpace them. She was already pretty damned tired.

A cool breeze blew against her sweaty face. The sun's rays weren't as strong on her back any longer. It was almost nightfall.

Ann kept a good, tight grip on the revolver. She'd probably need it real soon since she'd always been told the dead came out in full force at night. However, it was still the scum that came out during the day that she feared most.

The Last Living Man

Kevin L. Donihe

His legs are twin machines. He holds no control over them. They scissor back and forth, back and forth. Sometimes he imagines the sound of gears churning and pistons pumping beneath his skin. He doesn't need to think before running, not anymore. He is a machine, and running is his default.

The last living man runs down streets clogged with cars. Those who once drove them now clamor in the distance. He runs through dark tunnels where the echo of his feet sounds like *them*. He's been running forever. Standing still is just a dream dreamt while running.

His breath exits in short, staccato bursts. It ravages his lungs, but masks the rasping sounds behind him. He once considered driving a stick through his eardrums; he heard the dead even when they were nowhere near. Finally, he got past this. He's gotten past many things.

He's gotten past the memory of brown and twisted creatures smashing through doors and windows to plow green teeth into his wife. He remembers the wet smack as her body was chewed and chewed and chewed and chewed.

And he remembers her resurrection, and how wide and toothy her mouth had been.

But he's gotten past those memories too, much like he's gotten past seeing the death of his world. The last living man no longer needs to be with his own kind. He doesn't need company or conversation. He is an island floating in an ocean of decay, his past life just another running dream. In this knowledge, he finds cold comfort.

A sharp and sudden pain lances his chest. He's thirty-six, but the stress of near-constant running has put years on his heart. The pain once frightened him, but he has found a way to change fear into fuel, to sharpen pain into a spear that goads him.

But even that spear feels duller now. *Everything* feels duller. The world is washed in shades of gray that will never brighten. Night will never change into day. Perhaps it's time to end the game. Perhaps he should have never started playing in the first place. It would have been easier that way. *Quicker.*

He stops, turns to face the dead, and closes his eyes. The world tilts and sways under his feet. It feels like he's still running. No matter. It won't feel that way for long, not once green teeth and clacking jaws end the running forever.

The last living man waits.

Where are the dirty claws? Where are the green teeth that will end this game? He finds himself wanting them, almost sad that they've yet to deliver him from a world of running.

He opens his eyes after minutes seem to pass.

The dead, he sees, have halted in front of him. They stand in ragged rows that extend for miles. *A field of rotten scarecrows,* he thinks and wants to laugh.

Confused, he stares at the phalanx. In the past, all he managed were quick glances over his shoulder. He never lingered on faces. Instead, he looked down at slouching suits and dirty dresses. Didn't have to see their eyes that way. It wasn't so bad, without the eyes. They were all so hollow and empty, like those of dead fish. He couldn't look at them without first feeling horror, then revulsion.

The dead stand before him, still motionless, still swaying. His feet tell him to run, that the dead remain interested in playing the game. So—heart pounding, chest tightening—the last living man obeys. Days seem to pass before he stops near a collapsed and flaming bridge. Perhaps the dead are now tired of the game, too. No such luck. Again, they halt, slack-jawed and swaying.

Suddenly, he understands. Terror fades, and then vanishes completely. For the first time, the dead seem pathetic, worthy of pity. These are not conquerors; these are slaves without masters. The last living man realizes *he* is their sole purpose, that he turns the gears that maintain their existence. He is the crux and the pivot. Nothing will pull them along once there's no one left to chase.

He stares deep into their eyes, deeper than he ever imagined he could. He sees more than just stark emptiness. He sees a definite longing in those pits and, buried even deeper, a rudimentary need that, perhaps, might be love.

The last living man draws his first deep breath in ages. He unleashes it in a slow sigh before beaconing the dead with a forward sweep of his hand.

"Come here."

They continue to stand, swaying, watching.

"Come here," he reiterates, this time more urgently.

They approach, hesitantly at first. In time, they surround him. Hands tug at his filthy t-shirt and brush against his face. These are no longer the hands of killers. These are the hands of *supplicants*. A woman—a windswept skeleton with yellow parchment skin—reaches over and places a crown of hastily woven grass atop his head. A man—hollow eyed and reeking of death—bows before him; a knee bone protrudes from tattered slacks. Others attempt to hoist him atop shoulders, forgetting how decay has abused their bodies.

His mind spins. He wonders how many years will pass before they craft the crude tools of ritual from urban trash. How many years until they create tribal drums stretched taut with degraded skin. How long before they scrape together old newspapers and street refuse to collect in a new Bible, a Bible to be forgotten as soon as decay renders the last corpse formless and immobile, a Bible as ephemeral as quicksilver on a hot city street.

He pulls himself from his thoughts. Miles upon miles of the dead have taken the lead of the first supplicant. Millions bow before him—the desire to worship something, *anything*—still rattling through their brains, an instinct that will never slouch away.

The last living man cackles at the sight, and thus gives his coronation speech.

Only Begotten

Rebecca Lloyd

"Come to me," she croons, kneeling and holding out her arms. The small figure in the corner fixes its flat, milky eyes on her for a moment, then loses interest and goes back to chewing on its thumb. Blood drips on her hand-knotted cream wool carpet, puddling darkly. She feels her belly twist up a little with anger, but breathes it away, knowing that her sweet little boy can't help it. She beckons again. "Come."

It glances over and slowly pulls the mangled thumb from its mouth. She smiles; it blinks, whimpers faintly, and starts crawling. Stiff with morning cold, it drags itself clumsily toward her, leaving little reddish smears in its wake. She coos encouragement, trying not to dwell on what cleaning the carpet will cost her. When it comes near enough, she bundles the squirming form into her arms, ignoring the clamminess of its skin.

She's already taken off her beige silk blouse, not wanting to alarm the dry-cleaner with more stains. She tucks her baby against her bare shoulder, wincing only slightly as she feels it set its mouth around her scab-covered collarbone. It's teething, chewing on everything and making a mess; babies do at this age. The newly cut points leave little nipped-out gouges; it hungrily laps up the blood and bits of flesh. She keeps a smile of contentment pasted across her lips as it nurses.

Its hunger has grown more demanding since it first started cutting teeth; it worries at her like a small dog, letting out little growls of frustration at the meager meal that flows from her barely-pierced skin. "There, there," she soothes, rocking it. "I'll have something better for you soon."

She is fifty and has been trying to have a baby for the last ten years. Doctors counseled her after the first four miscarriages to settle for adoption, but she wouldn't have it. Only a child of her own blood would do. Even after cancer took her husband, she kept trying, with sperm they had banked just after his diagnosis. But her miracle boy almost didn't make it, despite all her efforts: the fertility specialists, the hormone treatments . . . almost a quarter of a million dollars laid out for one child. At eight months along, she went into contractions that all the drugs in the world couldn't stop, and what came out was blue and still and responded neither to the doctor's slap nor to the crash-cart team's best efforts.

She's been pulling in six figures since she was thirty-five, and when they told her that her miracle boy was stillborn, she refused to stand for it. Legs still half-numb from the epidural, she snatched the quarter-million-dollar corpse from one of the nurses and walked right out of the hospital with it. Rocking it. Cooing to it. Waiting for it to move—for it *must* move, it *had* to move. She had never been the sort to admit defeat; she ended up standing in the parking lot, shaking the body and screaming at it to wake up.

When it twitched and opened its moonstone-colored eyes, she knew with a surge of triumphant joy that she had done the right thing. She went home that night with her son in her arms, ready to devote the rest of her life to him.

It took a bit of time, but her late husband's lawyer handled the complications that she left in her wake at the hospital.

As with any preemie, her baby has special needs. It doesn't like sunlight, and so the shades are always drawn. It's wary of strangers, and so she doesn't have friends over much anymore. (She does not miss them; they always had something snotty to say about her little boy.) And then there is the matter of its dietary needs.

Breast milk did the job for a little while, but her child did not thrive no matter how greedily he drank. He vomited up cow's milk, formula, even plain water; he sucked both her breasts dry but still seemed hungry. When his skin started turning grey in patches, she took him to a pediatrician. The screaming argument that ensued only served to convince her that she alone should see to her son's welfare.

A day later, while making a cabbage rose out of a tomato to garnish her dinner, she discovered what her baby really needs purely by accident. The sharp little paring knife sliced her fingertip—nothing serious, but as the first drops of blood welled, he started whimpering for them. Fortunately, she's a quick study, and within minutes had him slurping from her greedily. A week of feedings after that, his skin was a healthier tone, and it had stopped flaking off at the joints.

Now, her hands are as scabbed as her shoulders, and she knows he needs more than she can give—but how he's grown! Soon enough, he will be walking. That will make providing food that much easier—especially once he grows strong enough to help her handle the details.

She's decided to start with this week's gardener. He's a day laborer, and though she speaks almost no Spanish, she knows he's suspicious of her and her baby. Just yesterday, he gave her the ugliest look when she brought her little one out for some air. Perhaps he was simply curious about all the dark swaddling . . . but she can't take chances. Besides, she can hardly be expected to nourish a growing boy on her own.

The mess can be minimized by doing it outside. That means keeping the gardener on until after dark, which will make him suspicious. But illegals are desperate for money; a big enough wad waved in front of him will earn his trust fast enough. Provided that she hides what's left of the body thoroughly, no one will miss him. And for a while at least, her little boy will have plenty to eat.

His teeth scoop out a bigger shred of skin than she is used to, and she gasps and nearly drops him—dislodging his mouth from her flesh in the process. He immediately whimpers and starts mewling. "Oh no, no, it's all right, don't cry. Mommy's sorry." She holds his head and gently guides him back to the wound.

Undead Prometheus

Rob Morganbesser

The pounding at the door of the small home he'd slipped into let him know that they had found him again. Their puny minds thought of anything bipedal that was not dead as their prey. Once again he would have to kill a few to prove that he was not. He sat in an overstuffed chair, surrounded by desiccated corpses, likely those of the family that had lived here. They might have been on the run and besieged here, decided that suicide was the best escape. Each had a neat, dried-out hole in the center of the head. Where once the brains had sat, that few pounds of matter that had made each person an individual, now nested roaches, all scraping every bit of tissue from the corpses. Survival is an instinct in every living creature.

A window on the door, hastily barricaded with a large china closet shattered to bits, made a tinkling noise as the last crystal shards of the window tumbled down in the space between the closet and the door. Other hands scrabbled at the door, the owners of the hands no longer intelligent enough to turn a knob.

The man rose to his feet, his head brushing a chandelier. He was nearly seven feet tall, his body gaunt and well muscled. He'd traveled across most of the world in his long life, had seen the Czar's Cossacks ride into villages, leaving nothing alive. He'd seen the result of Stalin's pogroms, the rise and fall of the Nazi eagles. He had seen death in every one of its myriad ways, or so he had thought.

Then this had happened. For some reason that science had not calculated, the recent dead had risen from their slabs and deathbeds to attack and devour the living. After a few months of the government trying to keep order, the forces of civilization had shattered like the window his attackers had just broken. In his long life, the survivor—and he was the *ultimate* survivor—had never seen such horror. In a way, it amused him to see the civilization of those people who had conquered so many diseases and who had solved so many scientific mysteries fall apart because the dead rose. He'd saved some of the living, had brought them to outposts run by governors who understood that, to survive, a more brutal civilization was needed. A civilization in which everyone chose between work and exile, a certain doom: few could live alone in these dangerous times.

The survivor could. He was strong, and these creatures, as many as they were, gained nothing but his hatred. Hatred had been one of the first things he had ever learned, a simple emotion yet strong. Would he have this reservoir of hate if his father had not rejected him? He thought not. But for as much as he hated— hated the people who shunned him before civilization collapsed, hated those who now recognized him for his strength and abilities—he also loved. He loved the great masters of music, the artists of the Renaissance, the great literature he had taught himself to read. He was a creature of many passions, both dark and light.

Now he could feel that passion growing within his chest. With every beat of his heart, he felt his hatred for the creatures outside growing. All he wanted, all he had wanted since his father had rejected him so many years past, was to be left alone. Obviously, these foul creatures with their fetid breath and unending hunger could not understand this. He had killed thousands of them, shouting "Leave me be!" Then he had finally understood that they could not learn. They were the lowest of the low, eaters of human flesh, hunters of children. They were a plague on the earth, an earth that had created them out of the toxins man had spilled into the earth; air and waters had caused them to rise. They would remain alive until the earth could purify itself of these toxins. That might take centuries.

The survivor tilted his head. What was that sound? Closing his eyes—one blue, the other brown, a sight that gained him odd looks—he listened.

There from a distance was a high shrill yell, the yell of someone in absolute terror. That was why he had left the protected zone of Saint Louis and plodded his way to this small town. People from this area had managed to make radio contact with one of the outposts, but its governor had enough problems. Unless the survivors were scientists, teachers, doctors or dentists—someone who could contribute to the new society—he had no rescue team to spare.

Rising to his feet, the survivor checked his auto-shotgun he'd taken—with the governor's permission—from the outpost's supplies. On full auto, the weapon could decimate several creatures at a time. There were few alive who could handle the weapon on full auto. To him, it was like a toy.

Striding to the door, he shoved the china closet aside, toppling it with one hand. Grasping the door through its mail slot, he wrenched it off its hinges and threw it out at the jabbering ghouls. It struck two, knocking them backwards. This was a small group, perhaps twenty-five. *Good*, he thought. *I can work my anger off on them*. Stepping onto the porch, he raised his weapon and fired. Set for three-round bursts, the 12-gauge bucked in his great, large knuckled hands. The first of the ghouls were blown back, their heads torn from their shoulders in bloody gobbets. Others were blown in half, torsos flying one way, legs another.

Finally, the weapon clicked empty. With a roar of anger, he waded into the living dead, great fists pumping up and down. One ghoul fell, its head crushed down into its shoulders; another's face was shattered, shards of nose and cheekbones driven into its brain. One of the creatures stood there dumbly, unaccustomed to being attacked. Usually, the food went down screaming, not fighting. Before it could retaliate, he grabbed it by its tattered coverall, lifted and threw it against a car, breaking its back.

With a look of disdain, he moved off, thick fingers reloading his weapon, the ghouls he'd destroyed forgotten. The irate person—a woman he guessed from the pitch—was still screaming. It sounded like anger rather than fear.

Well, if she kept from being bitten, she'd have nothing to fear. At least for a while.

* * *

Bridgett Conolly was trapped on the porch. Why had she listened to Jimmy? He couldn't think his way out of a plastic bag. True, their food had been running low. True, the outpost wasn't that far off; outposts had moats filled with spikes or water and were constantly patrolled. The zombies might be numerous, but they were far from nimble. Once one fell into a moat, it was easy pickings for guards. Retractable bridges kept zombies out. When more room was needed, a new moat was built. Once the area was cleaned out, it became part of the outpost.

Bridgett and Jimmy had headed toward one of these outposts, but they'd run out of gas here in Podunkville. The sound of the car had brought ghouls in droves. Bridgett and Jimmy had run, looking for a place to hole up. Jimmy had been dragged down, the creatures setting their teeth in him, tearing him to bits. Bridgett hadn't even looked back; she had climbed up a small ladder onto this porch and had been trapped. The windows were barred, and the house was too far from another to jump. All she'd been able to do was pull the ladder up. Now her only option seemed to be jump down and run for it, which was not really an option since they'd be on her the minute she hit the ground. She could also put her gun in her mouth and blow out her own brains. Better that than sitting here until dehydration drove her insane.

Bridgett screamed at the creatures. Though it meant nothing to them, it gave her some small feeling of comfort.

Then she heard gunfire. Below her, ghouls began exploding. The creatures were staggering under the barrage of a heavy caliber weapon. The small gang that had treed her was gone in moments, only a few moaning parts left.

The tallest man that Bridgett had seen in years calmly stalked down the middle of the street, reloading his weapon. A ghoul staggered out of the darkness of early dawn and moved toward him. Without missing a beat, the man brought a fist up and down, crushing the zombie's head. Brains spewed out of its cracked skull like a spilled carton of cottage cheese. Bridgett stared. She'd never seen such strength! And his demeanor—how could he just walk out there like he was on a Sunday stroll?

As the ghoul collapsed, the man reached into a pocket of his duster, removed a plastic flask and threw it to her.

"Drink, then climb down. We have to get out of here. More of them are coming."

Bridgett swallowed the water, which was, even though flat and metallic, the best she'd ever tasted. She jumped down and ran to the man. His face was heavily scarred as if he'd been in a horrible auto accident, and his eyes were two different colors.

"Can you drive?" His voice was rough, as if he didn't speak often.

"Yes," she replied. "I have a car, but no gas."

He looked back over his shoulder to where the growing light of dawn revealed more creatures. "Take me to your car."

It was a jet-black hummer, civilian issue. She and Jimmy had found it when they fled from Kansas City. It ate gas, but could drive over ghouls with little problem. As they neared it, the scarred man said, "Get in. Put it in neutral."

Bridgett was going to protest, but the look on the scarred face, which was mutilated worse than she had originally seen, told her to obey. She got in, but he stayed, walking around to the back of the hummer. As Bridgett slid the gearshift into neutral, the scarred man began to push. The vehicle moved slowly at first, then picked up speed. The slow, shambling things were left behind as Bridgett, amazed at the man's strength, steered.

* * *

When Bridgett saw the chain link fence, she braked. Her savior came around, unlocked the sliding gate, then pushed the Humvee through and closed them. Once the gate was locked, he motioned to Bridgett to come out of the car.

"Wow!" She exclaimed. "How much weight do you lift? I've never seen anything like that!"

He didn't answer. "We'll put fuel in your vehicle and eat. Tomorrow we can head for the outpost. Come with me."

As they walked, Bridgett stuck out her hand. "I'm Bridgett Conolly. I was a pre-Med student at Kansas State when the world came apart."

The scar-faced man stopped and took her hand gently. His flesh felt odd. It was cold and rough with a slight clamminess to it. Bridgett shook it but was glad when he let go.

"Do you have a name?" she asked.

The scar-faced man gave her a half smile. So curious! She reminded him of another from long ago. "I was never given one, so I use my father's name."

Bridgett shook her head, short red hair going in all directions. "Your father never gave you a name?"

"He was more of a creator than a mere father." The man sighed. He hated telling anyone this, but some believed even when they were awed by the information.

"My name is Frankenstein. Victor Frankenstein." He looked up at the sky, ignoring the woman's look of amazement. "We're safe in here, we'll stay until daylight. Sometimes a helicopter comes."

Inside the lone building protected by the fence, the man who called himself Victor Frankenstein began preparing food. Bridgett sat quietly staring at the man. In the light of the propane lamps, the scars on his hands and face cast deep shadows. His skin was lighter than hers, almost albino, but not the dull green of the ghouls, who were rotting away even as they caused their terror.

"So," Bridgett said, voice wavering. "You're not really like Frankenstein's monster, right? What happened? You survive some car crash and the doc did a bad job of putting you back together?"

He smiled mirthlessly. "If it makes you more comfortable, call me Victor." He put a plate of canned stew in front of her. His own plate held twice the amount. "I'm sorry there's no bread." He sat and began spooning the food into the jagged gash of his mouth. After seeing that she wasn't eating, he put his spoon down. "It's impolite to stare at the dinner table."

With a start, Bridgett began eating. The stew was warm and filling if somewhat bland. Her eyes kept flickering to her companion, who ate in a business-like way: spooning, chewing, and swallowing. If he enjoyed the meal, his face didn't show it.

After a few more moments of uncomfortable silence, Bridgett said, "You were really created from the bodies of the dead?"

Victor put his spoon down, his meal almost done. "You can see that those creatures out there, the once dead, have risen to devour the living, yet find me unbelievable?"

Bridgett shrugged. "It's just that—I've seen the movies. I read the book. You don't look anything like that."

Victor sighed. "The movies. That damned Shelley woman. I should have been more forceful in my warning to her. She made a travesty out of what had been an amazing accomplishment."

Bridgett's eyes widened. "You knew Mary Shelley?"

Victor pushed his plate away. "I have known many great people and some not so great." He flexed his large hands. "In 1923, I could have crushed Adolf Hitler's skull. I was as close to him as I was to you. But for years I stayed hidden, keeping away from human affairs, seeking only to be left alone."

"Then why come out now?"

Victor's two different colored eyes glazed for a moment as he stared into the propane lamp. "I feel more kinship with humans than I do the dead."

Bridgett's heart ached from the sadness in Victor's words. He was certainly more intelligent than most of the people she'd met.

"Thank you," she said in a low voice.

He looked at her, lank dark hair nearly hanging in his eyes. "Don't thank me until I've gotten you to an outpost." He looked out the dirty window where a smattering of raindrops had appeared on the glass. As the rain increased, he said, "Will you keep my secret? I've told very few over the years."

"Why tell me?"

Victor stood and went to the window. The small building they were in was drafty and indefensible. If the fence didn't hold, neither would the building. "You remind me of someone I knew many years ago. She accepted me, horrible as I appear, for she could see beyond my crude flesh." He smiled sadly, thinking of the Duchess D'Orly, who had been his friend and sheltered him during the 1850's when revolution had swept through France again. He'd kept her safe from the radicals. He remembered standing in front of her estate, arms in gore up to the elbows, crushing bones and tearing flesh until the revolutionaries ran off screaming. That had been the last time they'd threatened her.

A flash of lightning illuminated the yard near the Hummer. Victor tensed; he could see shapes out there. Only two or three, but that was too many.

"Do you have a weapon?" he asked.

Bridgett patted the .357 semi-automatic pistol, which hung from her belt. "Yep. I know how to use it, too." Jimmy had taught her to shoot when they were in the hills, hiding. She hadn't thought of Jimmy since she'd met Victor. She didn't want to remember how Jimmy's flesh was peeled from his face, how he hadn't even had time to scream before the creatures devoured him.

"Wait here." Victor stalked toward the door.

"Why? What's going on?"

Victor lifted his shotgun, checked its load. "Some of them are inside the fence. Lock the door behind me."

Without a further word, he stalked out into the rain. Lightning flashed, letting him see that the gate was secure and that there were no holes in the fence. Still, there were three of them, each more worn and rotted than the next. Victor slowed and watched them. One had no eyes, following the others by sound. All were dressed in tattered coveralls. Perhaps they had been trapped here. Soon they would be free. Victor let his shotgun hang on its tether. These three would be done silently.

The first ghoul, a savage-looking specimen whose wrists bore razor cuts, tottered forward.

Raising his arms, Victor brought his fists together on each side of its head, shattering the skull like a cheap plate. The zombie collapsed, maggot-infested brain destroyed, danger ended. The second came from Victor's left, grabbing him by the arm. Quickly, he grabbed it by the throat and squeezed. Victor's fingers dug into the flesh like putty. Closing his large hand, he popped the creature's head from its shoulders. The blind zombie turned its head stupidly back and forth. One blow from Victor's fist and it collapsed, its potential for threat ended forever.

Making a round of the perimeter, Victor found a small storage building, far in the back of the fuel compound. Its door was open. Inside lay a note addressed to whoever might find it. Trapped by the ghouls outside the fence, with no food or water, the men had chosen to kill themselves. They must not have known about the reactivation of the brain. When this place had been taken over for the use of the helicopters and stocked with food, the men had been overlooked, trapped again, doomed to wander and rot. *No matter*, thought Victor, *they had gone on to their final reward*. Closing the door, he made his way back to Bridgett.

* * *

"Aren't you afraid I'll tell who you are?" Bridgett asked, watching him take off his sodden coat and shirt, hanging them to dry. Victor was heavily muscled. The scars of his creation were present everywhere, as if someone had used Victor for an anatomy lesson.

"If someone told you they had discovered Frankenstein's creation, would you believe it? I can tell by looking at you that you still don't believe it." Victor sat at the small table, his pale flesh glowing oddly in the propane light. "You humans couldn't even believe it when the dead were at your doors, killing you."

Bridgett nodded sadly. "True."

Victor lifted his hand and flexed it. "The Baron was a brilliant man, centuries before his time. I wonder, had religion not been shoved down his throat, would he have ever done what he did?"

"Is the book real?"

Her curiosity reminded Victor of the Baron as well. His burning need to know had led him to the act of creation. Was his life a gift or a curse? He'd been asking that same question for decades.

"Some is true. Wollenscraft was a friend of the Frankenstein family. Before the Baron ran away, after he discovered I still lived, he told her everything. I met her once; it was from her I discovered that he had fled into the northern wastes."

Bridgett touched Victor's hand. He appeared not to notice as she ran a finger along his cool, rough flesh. "So you were lost in the north?"

Victor rose and peered out the window. "Yes. We were buried in a cave, in a glacier. He died. I slept. When a part of my prison broke free and drifted south I woke and decided to explore. All I ever found of the Baron was his head. It was withered and mummified. I brought it back to Europe and buried it in his family's mausoleum."

Bridgett yawned, the events of the day taking their toll on her. "I can't imagine the things you've seen."

Victor's eyes were hidden in shadow as he replied. "Mostly cruelty and evil deeds. Men are more monstrous than I could ever be, even were I the terror from the films."

"Perhaps we'll be better," Bridgett said. "Those of us that survive the ghouls, that is."

Victor laughed, a sharp harsh noise. "Those who have the survival instinct are not usually the kind ones."

* * *

Victor woke Bridgett by moving about their shelter. When she opened her eyes, he said, "It's time to go." Bridgett jumped to her feet, strapping on her pistol belt then pulling on her coat. She had dreamed strangely, visions of man-made creatures battling the undead, all of whom had Jimmy's face. "Are the outposts really safe?" she asked.

Victor turned from where he was opening the door. "Safer than here."

Bridgett followed him out. Several ghouls stood at the gate. One had no arms, and the flesh on its face had been peeled off. Another with an outlandish Mohawk, jingling with body piercings, was snarling and trying to bite through the chain securing the gate. The hope Bridgett felt faded from her green eyes. "We're dead. We'll never get past them." Even as she spoke, more of the creatures were tottering toward their haven. Soon they would crowd the gates, making any attempt at escape futile.

Victor turned to look at her, his different colored eyes flat and emotionless. "Start the vehicle. We'll get out."

As Bridgett complied, Victor entered one of the other sheds. He came out dragging eight propane tanks, the kind once used for barbecues. He'd tied the canisters together. Walking up to the gates, taunting the ghouls with his size, he tossed one end of the rope, tied in a neat loop, over part of the fence. Tightening the line he brought the propane tanks up to the middle of the gate. Turning away from the ghouls, who were clamoring for a bite of his ancient flesh, he stopped and gave them the finger. Inside the Hummer, Bridgett laughed out loud. That was the last thing she'd expected to see her companion do.

Pulling back the fabric that protected the Hummer's interior from the rain, Victor stowed it in the cargo area. Sitting in the passenger side, he leaned to the side, auto-shotgun in one hand. "Start moving forward. After I blow the gate, drive fast." He hated to forfeit this safe zone, but it was a small price to pay since most of the supplies had been used up.

Bridgett nodded. "You got it boss!"

Victor set his shotgun to single shot and aimed at the propane tanks. He pulled the trigger once, and the tanks exploded in a ball of fire, blowing the gates back fifteen feet. Ghouls disintegrated in the blast. Those that weren't atomized fell back, some burning. Bridgett stomped the gas, and the Hummer peeled out, running over a few crippled ghouls. As soon as they were on the far side of the small town, she glanced at Victor. "Say, you're a couple of centuries old and you don't know how to drive?"

Victor stared at her. "I never bothered to learn. Not many vehicles are made for someone of my size."

* * *

They drove along the highway toward the Saint Louis safe zone. The road was beginning to show signs of neglect. Potholes were forming, railings had rusted and had fallen away, and road signs were fading. Bridgett concentrated on driving, but she was still amazed that she was sitting next to a legend. Myth. Fable. She wasn't sure if any of them were the right word to use. She, like many others, had grown up with movies about the Frankenstein monster. But he wasn't really a monster at all. Monstrous in appearance perhaps with his pale skin, odd colored eyes, and thin white lines of scars on virtually every piece of exposed flesh. His dark hair was thin and lank. But she had a feeling that he was an honorable being, a man of his word. On impulse, she reached over and patted one of his large hands.

He started and stared at her. "Why did you do that?"

Bridgett smiled at him. "Everyone needs a pat or a hug once in a while. Think of it as a thank you for saving me."

Brooding, he replied, "But I haven't saved you yet."

* * *

The sky darkened and out of the west came forks of lightning and blasts of thunder. At each blast, Victor looked up, his eyes glowing oddly in the minute blasts of light. Drops of rain appeared on the windshield. Bridgett turned on the hummer's heater and windshield wipers. The drops quickly became a torrent, the rain sluicing off the windshield, the wipers barely able to keep up.

"Perhaps we should stop," said Victor. He was looking ahead, where the beams of the headlights were barely piercing the darkness.

"Good idea, but I'll keep the engine running." Bridgett slowed, staying in the middle of the road, allowing the vehicle to come to a stop. She put it in park and turned to face Victor.

"Do you have any idea why this has happened to the world?"

He shook his large head, eyes hidden in the dim light of the dashboard. "Perhaps the creator is annoyed at humanity's intrusions in his domain."

Bridgett shut the headlights off. If the rain stopped suddenly, as spring storms were wont to do, they would serve as a beacon to any unfriendly things—not all of them dead.

"What's your first memory?"

Victor was usually annoyed at questions and sought not to answer them, but his companion's were so open, her curiosity so refreshing, he felt it would be wrong not to answer.

"Pain. My rebirth was painful. The Baron was hoping that I would have my previous memories, but this was not to be. When the brain is starved of oxygen, whatever holds our memory fails and the memories, the personality of the person, is gone."

"Wow! You were like a newborn baby!"

"Yes, for lack of a better way of saying it. But I was an abandoned baby. Many times I've wondered if the dead eat the living because they are in pain, or are jealous that they feel nothing. Perhaps that is why they attack me, even though my flesh is not appealing to them."

Bridgett stared at him. "How do you know that?"

Victor smiled in his sad way, only the right side of his mouth rising. Pulling back his left sleeve he showed her the teeth marks. "Early on one of them got close enough to take a taste. He spit out what he'd taken, but it takes me a long while to heal."

"Do you know what happens to one of us when we get bitten?"

"You die. Horribly and slowly, always aware each time you fall asleep that perhaps the next time you wake, it will be as an empty vessel, filled with nothing but endless hunger. I've seen it many times."

Bridgett crossed her arms. "You make it sound so simple."

"It is," he replied. "Mankind is facing its greatest challenge. The dead are prevailing. Whoever survives to conquer them will make the race stronger, if anyone survives."

"So," Bridgett asked, her voice strained. "Why do you rescue us?"

Victor drew in a deep breath. "I do it so I can get supplies, a safe place to rest for a while. Because I would not want to see the light of humanity fade from the world."

"Do you sleep?"

Victor wondered if she would ever stop asking questions. But at least the ones she asked weren't the foolish ones people had asked in the past. Things like, do your scars hurt? How does it feel to be made of dead flesh? In truth, Victor considered himself a miracle of science. The Baron had, working with the primitive tools of his time, reconstructed a being, reattached limbs, organs, miles of veins and arteries, then given that creation life. If only the Baron could have seen beyond the act of creation, to assume responsibility for his creation. What would the Baron have thought of the ghouls? Could he have figured out why the dead had risen? He was a genius far in advance of his years.

"I rarely sleep. I have vitality beyond normal human beings."

Bridgett glanced at him. "Do you consider yourself human?"

Victor felt a slow pulse of anger grow inside him. This was one of the more foolish questions she had asked. "I was created from human beings, so I am human. Perhaps more than human since I am superior in strength and endurance."

"Do you think that if you died, you'd come back as one of them?"

That was something Victor had not considered. "I don't know if I can die. I've been frozen and returned to life. I have suffered injuries that would kill someone like you instantly. If I were to die and come back, I think I would be very dangerous as a zombie."

This caused Bridgett to fall silent.

* * *

"Slow down," commanded Victor, who had not spoken for miles.

"What's wrong?"

"There's something in the road ahead."

Bridgett stared ahead. She could see only the gloom of on-coming twilight, but she slowed down. As they moved closer to whatever Victor saw, he let out an explosive breath: "Looters."

"Looters?" She had heard rumors of them. Gangs of roving humans, living off the land, they killed anyone who was in their way. Dead or living, all were their enemies. Some governors had authorized their militias to shoot looters on sight, even though some occasionally joined outposts and were productive.

"Don't stop," Victor said. "But keep an eye out."

Ahead of them, a small motor home lay on its side, spirals of smoke rising slowly from it. A few ghouls were hovering around it, some holding bones that glistened with bits of meat. A body, mutilated beyond recognition, had been hung from a telephone pole. It had been crucified and skinned. The muscles reflected the dull light of twilight as the sightless head moved back and forth. Hanging just out of reach of the ghouls, a large spike had been driven through the body's chest. It was impossible to tell the corpse's sex. Beneath it, several ghouls were struggling with parts of its skin in a bizarre tug of war. Bridgett felt her throat constrict as she realized that the body had revived. It would now hang there until it rotted enough to fall off.

Victor ignored the corpse, having seen hundreds of thou-sands of them in his long life. "They were probably trying to reach Saint Louis. The crucified one either tried to fight, or was a looter with a conscience. The dead must have arrived later since the looters had time to do that."

"Can we go?" Bridgett was barely keeping herself from throwing up. In a world where horrors were commonplace, the skinned corpse was almost too horrible for her to bear.

"Yes, but drive carefully and keep a good lookout. The loot-ers may still be about."

Bridgett stepped on the accelerator, glad to be leaving this horrible sight behind her. "With all the things going on, we can still find the time to kill one another! Maybe we don't deserve to survive!"

Victor, hands curled around his auto-shotgun, shook his head. "I gave up being amazed or dismayed at humanity's capacity for violence long ago."

Bridgett felt embarrassed at the way this being, this creation of one her kind, simply dismissed the violent acts he'd seen. Had he become jaded in his long life, attuned to the horror of the world? She'd seen many people die, mostly at the hands of the ghouls, but she hoped she would never get used to it.

"You will," Victor said, as if he were reading her mind. "If you don't get used to the sights around you, you'll go mad."

* * *

They drove until Bridgett nodded off in the driver's seat. When the car suddenly swerved, Victor steadied the wheel. "Pull off the road. I'm going to refill the tank. Lock the door. If anything happens to me, drive away quickly."

As soon as the vehicle slowed to a stop, Victor was out of the car, his weapon ready. Bridgett locked the door and sat there, shivering even in the warmth of a summer evening. She jumped a bit as an image went across her eyes. Screaming she tugged at her pistol when the window next to her shattered. She heard someone screaming, then there was a sharp pain in her head and she heard nothing else.

* * *

Bridgett awoke to angry voices.

"I don't know what the fuck it was! Benny jumped the big bastard and got his fucking arms pulled from their sockets."

Bridgett lay still. She was in some kind of house or shack, the rough floorboards uncomfortable. She could taste blood in her mouth, a gift from whoever had knocked her unconscious. She tried to move, but a rope bound her. Lying still, she listened to her captors.

"So where is this big guy? This tough guy?"

"We left him for the ghouls, man. He didn't only whack Benny, he wasted Julio too. Hit the fucker so hard in the face that his brains came out his ears."

"You are so full of shit." The sound of a slap followed, and the scrabble of feet. "If you weren't my asshole of a brother, I'd stake you out for the ghouls like that camper geek."

Bridgett felt her blood run cold. These were the looters. How did they find us? They had to have been hiding or following. Bastards.

"Wake up!" A hand grabbed her by the hair and rolled her over. In a fit of anger, the looter tore off her blouse, leaving her topless.

Bridgett opened her eyes. Three men loomed over her, all nasty looking and worse smelling. They hadn't shaved or bathed in months, it seemed. One of them had his hand on his groin. "She's a fine looking frail, Flea. You did good this time." The speaker leaned close to her. "Your boyfriend's dead, sweetheart. You got two choices: make us happy and we'll take you along, make us unhappy and we'll do what we want and leave you for the ghouls."

The other one, hand still on his groin, smiled nastily. "Yeah sweetheart, what's it gonna be? Take some advice, listen to Dirk."

Bridgett smiled sweetly, then brought her foot up into Flea's testicles. Flea's face went white as, with barely a whimper, he slumped to the ground.

Dirk grabbed Bridgett by the hair. "Bad decision there, frail. He's an idiot, but he's my brother."

Bridgett barely saw the fist coming. It smashed into her nose, knocking her unconscious again.

* * *

Victor woke to the early morning sun in his eyes. It had been years since he'd been knocked unconscious. That had happened in a landslide in the Rocky Mountains. Rising to his feet, he stopped and looked around. The dead had arrived. One of the two men he'd killed was back, armless and no threat. His head was buried in the innards of the man whose face Victor had crushed. Victor listened carefully. A shrill scream was cutting the air, a woman's scream.

Bridgett.

Looking around, Victor saw his shotgun, trampled into the mud. He grabbed the weapon and pulled his bag out of the backseat of the now wrecked car. Victor didn't know why the looters had wrecked the vehicle, nor did he care.

Victor studied the ground around the Hummer. Decades spent in the near primeval forests of Europe had taught him tracking skills that were unparalleled in this day and age. Moving off, he followed the sounds of torment.

* * *

Bridgett lay on the floor, a puddle of blood spreading out from the various wounds the looters had inflicted on her. Her nose was broken, blood flowing from it, making it hard to breathe. One eye was swollen shut, and they'd made several shallow slices on her. It had all started with Flea's attempt to rape her. Dirk had egged him on, daring him to do it. Bridgett had laughed when he'd dropped his pants, and the three of them had beaten her. Now she wished she would die; it would be a release. Did the dead have any memory from before when they came back? She hoped so. Because if she did die, she could come back and wreak vengeance on these fuckers.

A fourth looter came in through the front door, his place as watchman taken by Flea, who'd spent his anger and his lust. Bridgett could feel it drying on her abused stomach.

"We've got deaders coming, Dirk. We should finish up and move on."

Dirk, who'd done things to Bridgett she'd never thought possible, smiled. "I think one more time, then I'm gonna scalp her fine red hair, keep it as a souvenir."

Bridgett thought she'd spent all her tears, but now they flowed quick and warm. She hoped he'd at least kill her before doing such a thing, but she knew he wouldn't.

Dirk was beginning to kneel between her legs when the door came crashing in. Flea fell backwards, bleeding from a dozen wounds. Behind him came the filth encrusted, rotting, hungry dead.

* * *

Victor crashed through the woods, unheeding of the scratches that branches left on him, ignoring the occasional sounds of the dead. He may have killed several; he may have killed none. His mind was set on rescuing Bridgett.

As Victor entered the clearing near a small house, he could hear the sounds of gunfire. A group of the undead crowded the doorway, trying to claw past each other. Victor raised the auto-shotgun. Fire erupted from the bore of the weapon, the heavy slugs smashing into the ghouls. They were a small group, not more than thirty. Victor advanced as he fired, blowing the ghouls away from the door. Heads exploded in fountains of curdled brains. Others were broken in half, a threat to no one. From inside came the sounds of fire and corpses falling. Victor's gun ran dry. Angry beyond thought, he let it fall, the sling holding it as he advanced.

A few ghouls turned to snarl at him. He snarled back, large fists coming up. One ghoul, a hideously injured male, slumped to the ground, head beaten off its shoulders. Victor kicked it aside like chaff. He grabbed another, a female this time, her tattered bikini bottom still hanging on though she had no weight left on her hips. Victor broke her back over his knee and tossed her away.

What Victor saw when he entered the small house was horror. Flea had been devoured, leaving only his head, reanimated, eyes blinking. Leek had been dismembered, and his head was missing. Twelve ghouls, all shot through their heads or decapitated by bullets, lay about the room.

Then Victor saw Bridgett. She lay in the middle of the room, her stomach torn open, one of her eyes gone. Bites to her arms, legs and neck were bleeding, showing she was still alive. Victor came near, unsure of what to say or do. That she was still alive amazed him, proved how strong her spirit was. For only the second time in his long, long life, he shed bitter tears.

Dirk rose from behind the barricade of bookshelves he'd thrown down. Before he could move, Victor reached out and grabbed him by the neck. Dirk struggled for a moment then tried to bring out his gun.

That was a mistake.

Victor brought up one great fist and slammed it into the looter's head. He went limp instantly. Victor dropped him and turned to Bridgett.

"Knew you'd come." She hissed it, her throat damaged from the ghoul's attack.

Victor covered her ravaged lower half with a small throw rug. "Don't speak. I'll take you out of here."

"No." She shook her head feebly. "I'm dead. Please ..." Her voice faded; her eye rolled back as the last of her breath escaped. Victor wiped away the tears and rose to his feet. Pulling Dirk out of his barricade, he took the man's pistol and placed it against Bridgett's forehead. "I pray the creator has taken you to a better place." The gun roared. Victor turned on Dirk, who was moaning slightly.

* * *

Dirk awoke to pain and heat. He was outside. Turning his head, he could see that the house was in flames, a thick spiral of dark smoke rising into the afternoon sky. A shadow fell across his vision. It was the huge guy who'd knocked him out. He held something in each hand. Dirk stared a moment, then felt himself go cold.

In Victor's right hand were Dirk's hands. In his left, Dirk's feet.

"You won't die," Victor rumbled. "Not for a while. I cauterized the wounds. Soon the dead will come. Then you'll die."

Victor turned and ambled off. Behind him, Dirk started to laugh as the first of the dead began to come out of the woods. "You'll die too, man. No one can survive on their own! No one!"

Victor wasn't listening. He had a long journey back to the outpost. As he walked the long miles, he wondered if humanity would survive the plague of the dead.

And he wondered if he really cared anymore.

HELL AND BACK

Vince Churchill

Richard glanced through the sheer curtain at the neighboring homes. Uninterested in their manicured lawns and expensive cars, his attention skipped to and from each front door. He shook his head, jaw clenching. Nearly all the homes had some sort of red rag or blood-colored garment marking their entrances. The super flu bug had spread faster and was hitting harder than anyone could have predicted, overwhelming the city's emergency services. Ambulances and fire trucks now simply patrolled, administering assistance the best they could to red-flagged homes. Richard pulled the curtain closed and stepped away from the window, not sure if he was more upset about the number of red markers or the fact there had been no response to them. So much for being a taxpayer on the Westside.

Seemingly everyone had the flu. During his last few healthy days, he'd driven into work only to put in a couple of useless hours in a nearly deserted office. The companies he did business with were equally stricken. The healthy and the sick alike had been urged to stay indoors in an attempt to slow the contagion. Los Angeles traffic was at an all-time low, God finally answering his prayers for a solution to all the freeway congestion. Of course, he never realized just how many people would have to fall ill or die in order for it to happen.

Be careful what you wish for.

Richard wiped at the bead of sweat nearing the corner of his eye. While his other symptoms were hardly a bother, his fever continued its slow climb, causing a numbing headache and bone deep chills. He glanced back at his sleeping wife. She was curled up under the covers, the heat of her own high fever plastering her hair against her pale skin. Over-the-counter medicines only seemed to delay the bug, but slowly, surely, he and Claire were succumbing to the virus. Miraculously neither of the kids had gotten as much as a sniffle. Thank goodness for small blessings.

He wished he could do more to ensure their safety. Sheer luck would only carry them so far.

Getting the kids to their grandparents was impossible. With martial law on the verge of being declared, travel was extremely limited and neither he nor his wife was in any shape to venture out. Even under normal circumstances, the kids were just a bit too young to travel a great distance alone. Hopefully they could beat the odds and not get sick, and continue to take care of themselves until either he or Claire got back on their feet. The best they could do at the moment was continue to keep the kids isolated in their room and only let them pop out to scamper to the bathroom or to fix peanut butter and jelly sandwiches and microwave pizza. Even in their room they wore their small paper medical masks. Taking all precautions the last couple of days as his wife's condition worsened, Richard spoke to them only through their closed door. Their giggling response to his bad knock-knock jokes made him feel better than any of the medicine he'd taken.

Sitting in their family room, the light from the television danced across the walls like the flickering reflection of a campfire. Richard stared at the screen. His bloodshot eyes strained in the evening darkness, the throbbing pulse in his head and lack of sleep undermining his ability to focus. His head felt like a cement block hanging from a thread, and several times his chin bobbed to his chest before jerking back up. Soon, just keeping his eyes open was a challenge. He struggled to pay attention to a nationally broadcast program regarding the flu virus and some type of mutated strain. . . .

The television screen blurred with his vision, but even as he faded in and out of consciousness, words and snippets of information clung to his mind, fighting to stir his awareness.

Suddenly, he was on his feet, struggling to get to his children, to protect them . . . somehow . . . lock them away in their room . . . the program on the television . . . couldn't be real . . . make sure the kids stayed safe . . . this had to be a hoax. Or a nightmare.

He staggered toward the stairs, his rubbery legs threatening to collapse with each step. His body felt as if it had been doused with gasoline and set ablaze. He glanced at his hands, half expecting to see actual flames. He was almost disappointed there were none. The family room began to spin, and he reached out for something on which to steady himself. Richard took another wobbling step, and everything went black in the instant before the floor rushed up to greet him.

Kaleidoscope images and sensory glimmers flashed off in his mind, flickering for a split second before being swallowed up into the darkest pit of unconsciousness.

Shattering glass. A blooming crystal rose of destruction. A flash of incomplete sound.
Silence.
A cornered tabby cat hissing a warning.
Slate black.
A terrified shriek. A human siren of fear and pain.
Then sheer nothingness.
Dead world.

Richard was slumped on the floor, the world blurring and swirling in dizzying shades of red and black. He couldn't feel the thick shag carpet beneath him. He couldn't think straight. It was as if at the snap of someone's fingers Richard had awakened from a deep hypnotic trance. He was staring at his hands, the very first image of the just-turned-on television program playing oddly before his eyes. His brain would not allow him to blink. The simple sight of his hands demanded his full attention. His thawing mind wouldn't allow for any other action or thought.
Noise . . . pounding . . . coming from somewhere. . . .
His fingers were gnarled like the roots of an ancient tree. Fingernails were missing, the ends of his fingers ragged and raw. Knuckles were swollen, the flesh split open like tiny melons. His fingers seemed frozen, some pointed in absurd angles, but there was no agony. Both hands were covered in dark drying syrup. Looking at the mutilation of his flesh was like watching a movie through someone else's eyes. It was just images.
The pinkie finger on his right hand was gone. A ragged hole remained in its place. The wound wept, but there was no pain. There was no anxiety. There was nothing. He felt hollow. He

couldn't think enough to feel or wonder or decide or cry out. He was just there, hardly feeling the floor, merely floating beneath the disorienting red and black waves of a mysterious sensory flood.

Dead world.

When he awoke the second time, his vision pulsed from ebbing blur to sudden vividness. The scarlet and black tinting was gone, but the rhythmic indecision of his sight, combined with the throbbing in his head, made his stomach twist and revolt. His hands still floated before his eyes as twin blood-soaked ghosts determined to haunt his every waking moment. Even the singular sight of his hands jumping in and out of focus rocketed the searing contents of his stomach up the back of his throat. Vomit gushed down the front of him. The eruption sent another lancing pain through his skull, causing his head to sag enough to see the bloody puke in which he'd covered himself. Startled by the violent ejection but still feeling oddly distant from himself, Richard forced his head up and leaned it against the wall. Slowly, his sight eased back to normal. Coughing, he closed his eyes, trying to quiet his headache. When the feverish tremble passed through his body, his first clear thought assembled itself.

The super flu.

His stomach convulsed again, twisting like a wrung-out dishtowel. Only clear drool slipped free from his mouth. Another strong shiver and he could feel the fever and the chills warring inside his system.

Fragments of thoughts and memories started to drift through his mind like the glowing wind-tossed embers of an autumn bonfire. He'd gotten sick. . . . He squinted for a second, but closed his eyes again, still disoriented. He tried to concentrate through the pain and nausea.

A killer flu had decimated China, then the Far East, then it had jumped the Pacific Ocean. . . . God . . . that's why . . . he was on the floor . . . getting sick all over himself.

The super flu . . . strange words circled and swirled and repeated themselves in his mind. He fought to decipher them. There were gaps, missing bits. He recognized words but couldn't explain them, couldn't quite give the phrase the full definition it warranted. But there was no doubt he was sick. So he sat, seeking as much comfort as he could in the calming darkness behind his closed eyes. Feverish flashes passed through him like small electrical jolts. Time was of no consequence.

His eyes jumped open. Sunshine was still knifing through the gloom. The upstairs hallway stretched out before him in silence. A thought leaped to the forefront.

His family—the kids. Oh God, where were they? Where was everyone?

The debilitating flu symptoms had eased. He tried to pick himself up off the floor but sensed that his body was paying little attention to his mental commands. His hands were tingling, working to re-establish feeling. Soon, that feeling was all over his body, the sharp, glistening needle-prick pain of nerves re-awakening, almost a relief from his migraine. He grimaced, glancing down at himself. He was dressed in his *get well* clothes, a pair of matching worn flannel pajamas he wore whenever he was under the weather. They reminded him of a pair of favorite pajamas he'd had when he was a small boy. Well worn, they were as comfortable as hell. Right now, they looked long past ruined. He could feel the cool seep of his vomit soaking through the fabric, and looking closer, he could see the pajama top was already splattered in dried droplets of . . . of . . .

He jerked his attention away from the sight of himself before his mind settled into answers he wasn't yet ready for. Instead, he took in his comfortable surroundings.

He was seated awkwardly on the floor of the upstairs hall-way, down at the end by the stairs. A bright sliver of light sliced through the drapes at the end of the hall, providing the only light in an otherwise gloomy corridor. He called out, his voice dry and cracked as if he hadn't spoken for days. His words were slurred.

"Honey? Christopher? Nina?" Silence drew itself into an agonizing length. He tried to move again but only managed to tip himself over, grunting as his shoulder met the floor. His legs, splayed out stiff and straight, trembled and shook, though thankfully didn't cause him any more pain. His eyes darted to and fro, a feeling of helplessness settling on him like frost. As he lay, his eyes flittered over the floor and walls, suddenly locking on something. He squinted, wishing there was more light. In moments, his eyes adjusted, the sight causing his mouth to drop open.

There was a long smear down the wall, almost as if done by an old paintbrush. The closest end stopped not far from where he lay. Even without the benefit of better lighting, he instantly knew it was blood. He was almost frightened by his own desperate cries.

"Claire! Claire! Oh God baby—" His body rocked on the carpet but it didn't respond enough to propel him to his feet or scoot him toward the bedrooms and bath. Frustrated and growing panicked, he threw himself over and over against the prison bars of his own body. Agonizing in the apathetic response of his urgings, his head sagged to the floor, weary and gasping from the effort.

His memories continued to thaw, a slow seep of the mind. Then suddenly, coming to him drop by drop was a tidal wave, slamming into his brain from every side and every sense. Images of the recent past battered their way into his consciousness. He laid still, his mind working to absorb all the input while also dealing with the horrific things now in his head. He stared down the floor of the hallway toward the bedrooms of his family, the sight blurring . . .

The television had shown the world slowly starting to crumble. In the United States and Europe, the bug had quickly grown to epidemic proportions, the mutating strain defying the world's scientific and health communities. Death tolls soared to record numbers. Religious organizations began to preach plague and Revelations. Then all hell really broke loose.

He felt the first tear slide down his face, the truth echoing in his head, refusing to be ignored.

While the super flu was stealing the lives of infants and young children with a malignant efficiency, the virus was having a different, more prolonged effect on healthy teenagers and adults. Newspapers and programs reported that instead of adult lungs drowning during the pneumonia phase, the extreme fevers drove infected brains into comas, resulting in a ghastly state where the victim awoke but functioned only on the most primitive level, driven by violent impulses and a hunger, an unnatural hunger. . . .

Larger cities like New York, Chicago, and Los Angeles were forced to declare martial law in response to the virus' new monstrous effect. The general public was instructed to stock food and water, stay indoors and avoid contact with others until the emergency had passed and an antidote had been isolated. Extreme caution had been advised. The flu was capable of changing anyone into a lethal enemy, even a loved and trusted pet.

The name popped into his mind. He blinked.

The Romero Flu. The Romero Flu.

His chest hitched, and he started sobbing. His eyes focused on the bloody gash where his pinkie finger used to be. Pain began to creep into his consciousness, and his slowly reassembling memory didn't slow its advance.

The Romero Flu, nicknamed after the creator of those cult zombie movies about the dead rising up and . . . and . . .

Oh, Jesus.

He stared beyond the bloody absence of his finger, down the hall, following the dark smear. The other end of it started outside the threshold of his bedroom.

His scream burst from his throat like a severed artery, and he squirmed his way to his hands and knees, using the wall as he crawled slowly into the gloom.

"Claire! Claire! It's me!"

From downstairs, there was desperate pounding at the front door.

"Oh God . . . Claire . . . Nina . . . Christopher—Jesus, oh God, please no. . . ." The more that came back to his mind, the more he was driven to see the truth of what had happened when he'd finally succumbed to his fever, sometime after he'd crawled under the blankets piled on the bed he and his wife shared, drawing his wife's burning and sweat-soaked body against his. He remembered whispering into her glistening, unconscious face, telling her it was going to be all right, that she and the kids would be all right. He recalled that he hadn't been able to reassure her without coughing wildly himself. He had lain under the hot, damp sheets with her for a while until, unable to sleep, he'd barely made it downstairs to watch the television. Normal feeling was creeping back into his legs and he was able to unfold himself into a staggering crouch, fighting the urge to fall with every step as he followed the telltale smear.

With only a few more steps to go, he fell. As his body crumpled to the floor, the memories of what he'd done to his wife exploded into his mind. An instant later, he heard the front door slam open, announcing the arrival of unwanted guests. There were guttural moans and growls, shuffling movement.

Tears streaking down his face, Richard dug into the plush carpet with his ruined hand, clawing forward, driven to acknowledge the fate of a family he knew had not survived the false safety of their own home. He sobbed as the atrocities he committed upon his wife flashed through his mind, each image more sickening than the one before. Body shaking, he retched again and again. He vaguely heard movement from the stairs as he curled his body into a tight ball, fighting not to remember, wanting it all to stop. Lord knows he hadn't meant to do all those inhuman things. He loved his wife and children.

The flu had made him into a monster.

Laying just a stride's length from the closed door of his children's room, he stared pleading, eyes welling with tears. From the floor, he couldn't quite reach the door. The doorknob itself seemed a million miles away.

Suddenly, there was a flutter of shadows from under the crease of the threshold. He heard vague movement.

"Daddy?"

Richard closed his eyes, a flare of emotion overwhelming him. He forced himself to speak, his voice half a croak.

"Yes, yes, its daddy . . ."

Quiet sobbing followed. There was more movement from the other side of the door.

"Don't—don't open it," Nina said. Fear carried her voice as much as the air. "Remember, he said he was sick—and that he might hurt us."

His son whispered back. "I'm hungry. The pizza is all gone."

"It's . . . it's alright now honey," Richard whispered. "I'm alright, baby. Daddy's feeling better, and I promise I'm not going to hurt you." There was a long pause.

"Where's Mom?"

The last of Richard's strength drained into the floor. He closed his eyes and rested his head. The lie came out as easily as the vomit.

"Your Mom is sleeping. She's still not feeling too well."

Richard had become the enemy the television programs and the newspapers and the radio shows had warned his family about. But somehow he had returned. Somehow he had survived Romero, somehow he had beaten the virus, though not before the devastation of his own family. He didn't notice the shadows of those that had climbed the stairs, searching.

"I'm unlocking the door," Christopher spoke from the other side.

"Wait!" his sister cried out. An odd thought struck Richard as he heard the lock release with a snap. Perhaps he was the key to an antidote. . . .

There wasn't even time for a warning.

A cloud of putrid odors assaulted his nostrils as the first zombies fell upon him, tearing at his soiled clothing to get to his fever cooked flesh. He wondered if he would actually die, or if he'd become re-infected and rise again from the plague of 2005. His last glance saw the kid's door crack open, then forced wide as a shambling tangle of legs moved around him.

The sheer number of attackers overwhelmed his feeble struggle. Inhuman snarls filled the air but couldn't drown out the terrible screams of his children. Yellowed teeth snapped and ravaged his flesh. Fingernails ripped at his eyes and violated his abdomen. A flash of pain as pure as God erupted, erasing his remaining thoughts.

His screams fell on dead ears.

The Dead Life

Mike Watt

"Henry! There are zombies in the basement!"

It was a common complaint. The dead had been returning for over four years. At first, it was a frightening phenomenon, one almost too terrible to comprehend. As recently deceased loved ones resumed walking, people began to openly panic, looking to the church for answers, demanding government intervention and investigation as the dead continued to multiply. The zombies shambled, their motor skills virtually non-existent. But they bit people, and these bites became infected; the infection raced to your brain and heart, causing fever, extreme paralyzing sickness, and ultimately death. But then, soon, you were back on your feet again. The media dubbed it "The Infestation," which was as good a name as any.

Gradually, as the sight of staring, bloated, rotting corpses began to be commonplace, the fear subsided. Zombies were slow, off-balance, stupid. If you ran, they tended to abandon chase once they lost sight of you. The only time they became worrisome was when they traveled in packs—which was rare and unlikely.

On the other hand, there was the smell, and the fear of disease, especially a few weeks after the initial rising; the corpse became too rotten to move, and it just laid there, in a messy, undulating heap in the yard, and even the dog wouldn't go near it. And the zombies smelled worse after rain.

What was worse, people were dealing with them on their own. Gun-happy homeowners turned to extermination, and were causing more accidental deaths by shooting away at anything that came near their houses. Postal workers grew more disgruntled by the day.

It took months of public outcry before the Federal Government finally stepped in. There was no progress towards a cure, and it was still a mystery as to why Mr. Jones returned but Mrs. Jones didn't. It was a random infection with no known catalyst. But thanks to Presidential decree, there came NOE: The National Organization of Exterminators, the federal office of zombie control and removal.

This made most people happy, knowing their tax dollars were finally put to work for something. Private individuals who had been offering their services in the same area, however, were not so happy; they considered NOE yet another example of the government creating a monopoly to edge out the small businessman. After protest upon protest, these private exterminators were placated less than a year later by the Exterminators' Privatization Act.

Even less pleased and never placated were the Society for the Preservation of the Undead Individual, but they were a small, radical group, constantly and publicly shouted down by the larger Living Rights Movement, a much higher-profile citizens' group.

Now, the zombie infestation, which had seemed so terrible in the past, quickly evolved into nothing more than a nuisance. Zombies were still about, of course, and they got into everything, but they were manageable. In most cases, single zombies were deterred from your doorstep with a broom to the nose, and if there were more groaning about, you had your choice of NOE, or the slightly higher-priced private exterminators, who arrived quicker and who worked faster. And, as always, the cliché had been proving true and appropriate for the past four years: life went on.

* * *

"Henry!" In the front room, Bernice Dobbs shouted for her husband once again.

Henry, who was in his den in the back of the house, heard her perfectly. He didn't get up from his chair to answer her. He was busy watching last night's taped episode of *The Dead of Night with Necro-Phil*. The film viewing was for his church group; they were trying to decide whether or not television's top-rated television show was worth boycotting.

Necro-Phil, the host, was a green, bug-eyed zombie puppet with a slick Elvis-pompadour and a voluptuous human female co-host in a skull-print micro-bikini, which seemed to be her only function on the show. Necro-Phil was offensive in just about every conceivable way. He was abusive, not only towards his guests, but his audience; he made tasteless jokes about sex and death—mostly sex—and the worst of these offenses, Henry was writing down, to show the group. Henry, for one, was shocked, had been for twenty or twenty-five episodes, and he, for one, would vote for the boycott. At his wife's third bellow, however, he paused the tape.

"Yes, dear?"

"Henry," she cried, quite anxiously. "There are zombies in the basement!"

"Yes, dear?" Henry replied, with a different inflection relaying concern.

"Henry," she said, adopting an explanatory tone, "There are zombies in the basement on my day to host the women's auxiliary luncheon."

"Yes, dear," he said, to convey his understanding of the urgency.

"Henry," Bernice began, taking a stand against the injustices of the world. "There are zombies in our basement, and I have made a soufflé. With all their banging around down there, groaning, doing God knows what to the new paint, they are going to make my soufflé fall. I do not want my soufflé to fall, and I do not want there to be zombies in our basement when the women's auxiliary arrives."

Henry stopped the tape. "Well," he said, thinking a moment. "We'd best call NOE."

Henry hung up the phone and looked at his wife, who was wringing her hands alternately in the direction of the kitchen, then the basement door, then back at her husband. "NOE can't be here until five o'clock this evening," he told her, his voice tinged with regret.

She looked at him, her eyes turned icy. "Henry," she began, patience dripping from her words. "Blanche MacGillicutty is coming. *Blanche MacGillicutty*. This is the first time she's been out since she got her new hip!"

"I don't think that would be as impressive to them as it is to me, dear. Five o'clock seemed pretty firm on their end."

Bernice's patience finally broke, and she shoved her husband aside as she lunged for the phone book. "Oh, get out of my way, Henry. Go back to your television. Honestly, if I want anything done around here, I have do it myself. I guess I'll just have to call a private exterminator." Her fingers were walking with what could be considered a violent step through the hapless Yellow Pages.

"Liable to be expensive," Henry said. That got him the look again.

"Henry," Bernice said. "It's *Blanche MacGillicutty*."

With a final whip of a page, her eyes fell upon an ad in the upper right hand corner of the page:

"Sr. Mary Bliss. From the Order of Our Lady of Perpetual Motion. Spiritual Enlightenment. Marriage Counseling. Extermination by Appointment. Reasonable Rates."

"There," Bernice said, triumphantly stabbing out the number. "I'm sure a religious woman can have this place cleaned out in no time."

The order of Our Lady of Perpetual Motion was formed towards the end of the period when Women's Liberation was considered a cute notion, and on the cusp of the period when it became dangerous to consider liberation anything less than a deadly serious right that must be supported. The founder, Sr. Barbara Loudin, was not a nun, but was religious in many ways, mostly about her own independence and her upwardly mobile attitude. She would conquer the man's world of business if she had to kill every man to do it. And since many men in the world have a deep-seated, inexplicable and inherent fear of nuns anyway, she decided to use that to her advantage.

Since its foundation so many years ago, the Order has provided countless young women with the strength and support necessary to take advantage of all that the business world had to offer. They encountered little resistance from the male dominated society. Or, at least, no man would dare give them any lip while they were actually in the room. Every self-appointed sister carried a mean-looking ruler in those days, mostly for show, but it did a world of good.

Over the years, the Order has grown, with branches in virtually every major city in the country. And it was a local chapter founded by a local celebrity that Bernice Dobbs called that day.

The phone rang and was answered by Sr. Agnes, junior sister and shareholder.

"Our Lady of Perpetual Motion, Sr. Agnes speaking. How may I direct your call?"

"Yes, hello," Bernice said, a little taken aback by the beatific voice on the other end of the line. "I need an exterminator right away."

"I'm sorry, but Sr. Mary is in a counseling session at the moment. If you will give me your name and number, I'm sure she can get back to you later today."

"Isn't there someone else there who can do the job?" Bernice pled. "It really is important to get this done as soon as possible."

There was a pause on the line as Sr. Agnes considered the request. "If you will hold for just a moment, I'll see when Sr. Bliss will be available." And with that, Sr. Agnes touched a delicate finger to the "Hold" button and then turned to the intercom.

Sr. Mary Bliss wasn't the average member of the Order, if there was such a thing. Among the many impressive articles on her resume, she was a political activist, who fought against NOE at its inception, putting pressure on the government to privatize extermination. Though that was an important achievement, she was better known as a published author and celebrated marriage counselor. Her book was the basis of her controversial counseling methods and was aptly titled *You Should Always Hurt the One You Love*. Sr. Bliss was an advocate of monogamy, but held very deeply that discipline was an essential ingredient to the bondage of marriage. And she often taught these services to young couples who had trouble in their union. Her fees were modest and her sessions were quite popular, though the cost was the least of the incentives.

At the very moment Bernice was calling, Sr. Bliss was in the middle of one such session. A newly-married couple in their mid-twenties were shackled to the wall in her private chambers. She was just about to instruct the wife in the importance of good house-keeping with a riding crop (before lecturing the husband in the area of tender affection with horse-hair flail), when the intercom above her desk buzzed urgently.

Sr. Bliss paused mid-swing. "Excuse me for one moment," she said, and turned from the breathless wife, who was now reconsidering her previously narrow view of counseling. Sr. Bliss touched a button on the intercom. "Yes?"

"I'm terribly sorry to interrupt you, Sister Mary," said Sr. Agnes. "But there is a woman calling who is requesting an extermination."

Sr. Bliss tapped her palm with the doubled end of the riding crop, weighing her options. "Did she say if it was an emergency?"

"Yes, Sister, she did."

"Hmm." And there was a pause as Sr. Bliss thought further. Extermination was very seldom a matter of life and limb, but it was higher profile, better for business, and was more apt to bring in repeat business, as well as references. Married couples who visit her for sessions, more often than not, treat it like a jealous, joyous secret, and rarely recommend her to friends, no matter how many times they come back themselves (often resorting to invented marital stress, just to have something to talk about; good therapy can be addictive). Finally, she made her decision. "Get her address, and tell her I'll be there within the hour."

"Yes, Sister."

Turning back to her clients, Sr. Bliss continued tapping her palm with the crop. The couple stared at her over their out-stretched shoulders, eyes wide with anticipation. She smiled. "I've decided to give you some time to yourselves, for silent contemplation on the joys of marriage itself. For no charge, of course," she added. "But I'll return soon, and we will resume the session where we left off. Any questions?"

As they were gagged, there were none.

* * *

Simon MacForman had issues.

With women mostly. But also with NOE. And then there were his issues with people in general, but that was only because he was naturally anti-social.

Women bothered him because they mystified him. They did weird things he didn't understand. Like have careers. Why couldn't they just be happy serving their husbands? Making them food and ironing and all that natural women stuff? And why did they get so angry when he asked questions like that?

His problems with NOE ran deeper, and he'd expounded on his hatred of the group during his many guest spots on *The Dead of Night with Necro-Phil*. MacForman had been a member of NOE—one of the charter members, the first to join up when the organization was formed—and he had been speedily rising through the ranks of the special paramilitary unit. Unlike most government organizations, when first founded, NOE was considered a godsend, its officers superheroes. The popular recruitment commercial featured Nation Commander Jackie Sawyer swinging in through a plate glass window and stomping zombie butt left and right with a mixture of kung fu and heavy artillery, rescuing the helpless, grateful teenage girl and her puppy from the hordes of vicious undead. If that didn't sum up America, MacForman didn't know what did.

So in the beginning, NOE officers were treated like celebrities. MacForman was treated no differently, beloved in his hometown where he was once considered a violently dangerous hooligan. And when STUDZ™ Magazine singled him out to be their centerfold and Man of the Year, he was flattered, though by no means surprised; he accepted without hesitation. The photo spread was very tasteful, he thought. His spiked g-string covered his essentials (though he considered his hanging the NOE badge where he had a stroke of artistic genius), and there were only two beautiful naked girls at his feet, nothing he considered offensive.

NOE thought otherwise.

His dismissal from the force was a media event. There was outrage on both sides, the viewpoints equally and strongly drawn. There were his detractors on one side, demanding that he be dragged behind a patrol car through all the neighborhoods that he'd shamed with his vulgar heathen pictorial, and on the other side were those MacForman deemed the "healthy thinkers," who felt that he should be vilified, that NOE should not only apologize on national television, but that MacForman should replace that über-bitch Jackie Sawyer as National Captain.

Unfortunately, there weren't as many "healthy thinkers" in the world, and amidst a week of headlines, Simon MacForman was summarily discharged from the National Organization of Exterminators, the Living Strike Force.

It was a conspiracy, of course, as MacForman would explain to anyone who would listen, usually on the Necro-Phil show. He'd seen things at NOE. Things he couldn't explain. Things that hadn't made sense in the beginning. Such as their penchant for cleaning out a particular house, to which they would get called back a week later to clean out family members who had recently turned into zombies. Most people dismissed his speculations as paranoid, and MacForman was perfectly willing to give them that, but it still made him wonder if NOE was keeping themselves in business by seeding neighborhoods with zombies, or in some way creating them.

After a while, his novelty wore off, but not his crusade. He was determined to ruin NOE by jumping their claims. He had a scanner in his car—"car" in the loosest sense of the word: a roundish purple Geo dubbed "the Grape of Wrath"—and whenever a call came over the NOE band, he'd race to the sight, clean it out and leave just before the strike force arrived, which wasn't difficult, as NOE gave clients a waiting period whether they were busy or not, the lazy bastards.

This particular day was a slow one, so he was biding his time tapping Sr. Bliss' phone. She was a favorite target of his, mainly because she got the best calls, those from the wealthier clients who needed discreet exterminations and who would pay handsomely for the caution. There was very little money in jumping NOE's claims, as they were a public service provided by tax dollars. Jumping Sr. Bliss' calls paid the bills.

Jotting down the Dobbs' address, he hit the ignition, the Geo roared to life, and he sped towards the ritzy part of town.

MacForman and Sr. Bliss arrived at the same time. The front wheel of her Honda Nighthawk stopped within inches of the front bumper of the Grape of Wrath. A growl escaped her throat as she tore off her helmet and went right for him. She had her crossbow up and ready just as he drew his .45. They were at a standstill, but she didn't care.

"This was *my* call, MacForman!" He'd done this to her before. Too many times to count. The heathen was a thorn in her side.

The ex-official exterminator glowered down at her; the chains on his jacket jingled lightly as he twitched. "No it's not! I tapped it fair and square!"

She glared at him, then lowered her weapon and pointed behind him. "Look out! NOE!"

MacForman spun around, pistol ready. "Where?"

But Sr. Bliss was up the steps and ringing the bell before MacForman had time to react. Holstering as he ran, he almost killed himself twice, arriving at the door just as it opened.

Bernice looked out at the odd pair on her porch. Ordinarily, if such an unsightly duo had appeared at her door, her first instinct would be to call the cops. Then boil some oil. She was hard-pressed to decide which of the two disturbed her more: the small woman dressed in a black leather jumpsuit, or the monster beside her with the leather jacket and mohawk. The pair smiled at her.

"Exterminator," they sang in unison.

"Oh, dear," Bernice said, reconsidering the boiling oil. "I wasn't expecting two of you."

Sr. Bliss shot MacForman a withering glance. "Neither was I." She completely failed to prevent MacForman from stepping forward.

"Simon MacForman, ma'am. At your service. Now that I'm here, you can kiss those zombies goodbye . . . well, not literally, that'd be gross."

As it was, Bernice was a hair away from a nervous breakdown. She was certain her soufflé had already fallen, and only God knew how many zombies were down there. With all the racket, it sounded like a marching band falling down a flight of steps. Her nerves were completely frazzled, and now *this*. "I'm sorry, I called a Sr. Mary—?"

Sr. Bliss stepped forward, taking her cue, elbowing MacForman back. "That would be me. Sr. Mary Bliss. The Order of Our Lady of Perpetual Motion." Her voice dropped to a whisper, and she leaned in close to the old woman. "Don't let him in, ma'am. He was kicked off NOE for posing for pornographic pictures."

"Hey!" Simon was still very proud of those pictures. "My moral standing has nothing to do with my awe-inspiring ability to kill zombies!"

Sr. Bliss was undeterred. "Ma'am, I must warn you that this man is a thief and a fornicator and will only serve to bleed you dry."

"Oh, yeah. Don't listen to her! You know she . . . she showers in the nude! The *nude*!"

There was a dreadful crash from the basement, and suddenly Bernice didn't care who came, as long as they got those horrible, smelly things out of her basement. "Come in, come in. I don't care how much it costs, I need those things disposed of. I'm having very important company over soon. Can you both be fast and discreet?"

Sr. Bliss took Bernice's hand. "You have my word, ma'am. And God's." She stepped inside.

Simon followed. "Mine, too," he said.

Bernice closed the door.

As soon as the unkempt exterminators were inside, Bernice led them to the basement. They stepped through, and she closed the door quickly behind them. No telling what might happen, she thought, one of those things loose in the house. Although at that point, she was unclear as to whether *things* referred to the zombies or the exterminators.

On the landing, the pair peered into the dim basement, searching for their prey. They didn't have to search long. The basement was filled to capacity with the undead. They were shoulder to rotting shoulder, bumping together and moaning like an early-morning commuter crowd on a narrow subway platform. At the sound of the closing door, the teeming corpses turned their heads to stare up at the pair on the stairs.

MacForman drew his .45; Bliss removed a twin pair of sai from her belt. "Here's where I start earning your paycheck," Simon said. "Aim for the brain!" He leapt off the stairs and into the rotting mass beneath.

Oozing, rotting flesh and brackish blood began to fly as he opened fire. Sr. Bliss calmly descended the stairs and began her own method of extermination.

"This is the third time you've done this to me!" she said, driving the point of her sai through a zombie's forehead. It made a neat crunch as it exited through the back of the skull.

"What?" MacForman demanded, bringing a wicked dagger down through the top of a rotting head.

"Tapping my phone! Jumping my calls! Next thing I know, you'll be doing marriage counseling out of your car."

"Look, I leave all the kinky stuff to you, don't I? Why begrudge me the exterminations?"

"Because they're *my calls!*"

"Well, you get all the best ones. People think you're all holy and shit. That religion thing's quite a racket, you know that, Mary?"

"That's Sister Bliss to you, you heathen!" She whirled around, and in one impressive motion, side-kicked a zombie into two others, taking them down. She took her time, punching through the skulls with her sai, destroying their brains. Like her other occupations, Sr. Bliss practiced extermination with finesse.

Across the room, as he hacked and slashed and ripped, McForman slid around in piles of innards and pools of blood, like a new-born calf trying to gain its footing for the first time. No style, Sr. Bliss decided, and not for the first time.

Upstairs, Bernice paced anxiously in front of the closed cellar door. The crashing and banging and gunshots drifting up through the floor sent her into a whole new conniption of hand wringing. Then a new sound pierced the house, filling her with a panic she'd never felt before.

It was her front door bell.

"Oh, no!" She gasped. "The Woman's Auxiliary!"

Calmly sliding another steel-tipped bolt into her crossbow, Sr. Bliss drew back the string and took careful aim. A zombie shambled towards her, arms outstretched, a low moan escaping from its cavernous mouth filled with brown, rotting teeth. She squeezed the trigger, sending the bolt through the zombie's milky left eye.

McForman glared at her as she shot him a satisfied smile. Reaching into his jacket, he withdrew a nickel-plated .357 Magnum. He was standing in a ring of zombies, the space between himself and the undead quickly diminishing as they closed in, moaning, drooling. Returning her supercilious glance, he raised the pistol and fired, moving in a tight circle. Six skulls exploded as the shells ripped through the bone. Five corpses fell to the concrete floor; the sixth teetered on its gray mottled feet before toppling over, revealing a headless seventh corpse, which had been standing directly behind it. It, too, joined its comrades in the messy pile on the floor.

McForman smiled at her. "Well?"

"Eh," she dismissed him and returned to her own work. The piles were much neater on her side of the basement. However, there were still plenty of zombies for the two of them to contend with, as the undead continued pouring in.

A large crash disrupted the uncomfortable silence in Bernice's sitting room. Five women, all in their golden years, smiled uneasily at each other, not sipping their tea, not nibbling a single pristine lady lock. Bernice wanted to crawl under the rug and die.

"So, Blanche," she smiled sickly. "How's the hip?"

* * *

"How big is this fucking basement?" McForman's dagger was lodged in the jawbone of a still-moving zombie. He'd slipped on a kidney and mis-delivered the uppercut blow. The zombie was still grasping for him as he struggled to dislodge his blade.

Across the room, Sr. Bliss sat on the washer, reloading her crossbow, holding a zombie at bay with the toe of her boot pressed to its scarred and disintegrating chest. Its arms flailed as it struggled to reach her. Stifling a yawn, she raised her bow and squeezed the trigger. The bolt passed straight through with a satisfying *punch*, coming to rest in the cement wall across the room.

McForman was starting to hate her.

"Watch the spray, Simon," she said, examining her long crimson nails. "The walls look like they've just been painted."

"Lousy woman," he muttered under his breath. He gave a final wrenching tug and the dagger came loose; the jaw skittered across the floor. With the dagger free, he was able to finally deliver the deathblow to the skull, sending the zombie back to the land of the truly non-moving dead.

Catlike, Sr. Bliss slid from the washing machine and stood coolly, taking out a remaining trio of shamblers, her back to the gore-covered heathen. MacForman growled and slammed another clip into his .45. The sudden motion, combined with the slick conditions beneath his boots, caused his feet to fly out from under him. His face turned into a comical mask of surprise as he flipped backwards and landed with a heavy crash on the wet floor. "Ugh," was his assessment of the situation. He didn't even attempt to regain his dignity; the fall hurt.

As expected, Sr. Bliss glanced over her shoulder at her prone rival, a slight smile on her porcelain face. Simon was tempted to shoot her, but she turned her dark brown eyes away from him, and he suddenly felt weird about shooting her in the back. He struggled to get to his feet, but with all the innards beneath him, it was like wrestling in cold oatmeal—not that he'd know anything about that, of course.

That's when the thing crawled out from under the stairs: a zombie—no, *half* a zombie. It was cut off at the middle, obviously run over by a truck or similar vehicle capable of severing a body in two. Its eyes were milky, teeth rotting. It opened its mouth, let out a hiss, and began to crawl towards Sr. Bliss. Her back was toward both Simon and it, and it was moving fast.

Simon raised his hand to finish it—he'd help her, but he'd be damned if he was going to warn her (that made sense to his oddly-wired brain)—only his hand was empty. The .45 lay in a pile of brains a few feet away. An inarticulate growl escaped his lips as he reached for his gun, but the zombie was gaining ground on the sister. Simon found some leverage in the corpses around him and lunged forward, his hand closing around the end of intestine that the zombie was dragging behind him.

"C'mere, you!" He yanked back on the organ. The zombie didn't slide back with it. Instead, the intestine gave, and a foot more slid out of the body cavity as Simon fell back from the unexpected slack. "Hey!" He began grabbing the intestine hand over hand, but more lengths spilled from the body. Simon felt like he was unraveling a sweater, remembering with dismay that there was something like fifteen miles of intestine in the human body. Screw this, he decided, yanking intestine and reaching for his gun.

At the other end of the innard, the zombie was suddenly aware that it was somewhat snagged. It looked back at Simon, intestine hanging off his shoulders and covering his lap. The zombie hissed at him and the exterminator glared back. "Oh, shut up," he muttered as his hand finally closed around the .45. Swinging forward, fighting through the gut-pile, Simon aimed at the half-zombie.

A crossbow bolt exploded through its skull from behind. The half-zombie collapsed to the floor, its insides stretching clear across the length of the basement. Rage welled up inside MacForman, his arm trembling, the outstretched pistol vibrating in his hand. This was precisely the reason it didn't pay to try to do anything nice for anyone.

He was coated, absolutely *coated* with stale blood and gore and bits of brain. Ordinarily, he would have been proud of a job well done. But Sr. Bliss was standing over him, looking smug and pleased with herself. She was completely clean. Not a spot, not a speck of bone marred her pristine leather jumpsuit. Her grin stretched from ear to ear.

The grin faltered as she glanced down. "Oh," she said, bending at the waist, giving him a teasing glimpse at her ample cleavage. Tearing a scrap of cloth from a dead zombie's shirt, she quickly wiped away a dime-sized spot of blood from the toe of her polished thigh-high boot. Righting herself, she nodded. "That's better."

Just then, a clot of gore struck her in the face, clotting her hair. Simon smiled up at her with a toothy grin.

And clouds came over her smiling face. Her dark eyes narrowed, ruby lips parted revealing tiny white, sharp teeth. Simon's grin disappeared.

"Now wait a minute—" was all he had time for before she leapt on him.

"Yes, thank you. I'm so glad you came. I'll bring the recipe next week. Oh certainly. I'm terribly sorry for the noise. Yes, the soufflé was a tragedy. Oh well, there's always next time. Yes of course. Why, thank you. Goodnight."

With a lunge, Bernice slammed the door behind the last of her exiting guests, leaning against it with a sigh. The meeting had gone horribly. She'd never live this down. The humiliation was too much to bear. They must think she was the filthiest house-keeper, to attract zombies like that. Then to call such low, common gutter trash to clean them out. Oh, she could never show her face at her bridge club again.

But downstairs, all was silent. Bernice held her breath as she listened. No moaning, no crashing, none of that dreadful cursing. Just quiet.

She sighed, daring a smile. Finally, she heard clomping foot-steps coming up the basement stairs. As the door flew open, her smile vanished completely as her mind refused to comprehend what she was seeing now.

"Clean as a fucking whistle," MacForman announced.

A nightmare. Her worst fears imagined. The pair of them, red from head to toe. Red dripping from their clothes, caking their boots. Standing in her hallway. *On her white angora carpet!*

"My carpet!" it was a low whisper, between outrage and in-comprehension. The terror welled up inside her. First the humiliation, now *this!* "My carpet! Henry!!!"

Simon had a sneaking suspicion he wasn't going to get paid.

Donovan's Leg

Eric Shapiro

Stop thinking. Your thoughts are going haywire. There's no forward momentum. Stop it. Hold still. Meditate. Clear yourself.

No use. My mind's on a conveyor belt to hell. I'm all the way out here in the desert, far from all forms of technology, yet my body's producing enough electricity to power a whole city. The electricity knows its way around. It finds my fingertips and back teeth and every last hair on my body.

This is panic. A wire of black energy runs through me. The sun doesn't help much. Before I got out of my car, the radio said it was 115 degrees. This is not the earth. I don't know what planet I'm on. Scratch that; I *do* know. Welcome to Planet Arizona.

I left California because I had debts. There were men coming after me. Knocking on my door in the middle of the night. They wouldn't have killed me; these aren't *that* kind of men. But they're not to be reckoned with, either. They would've broken my arms, cut my nose off, made me ugly (which is not to say I've ever been handsome). So, seeing as these men have never been all that mobile, I decided to head east. New York? Boston? I would figure that part out later.

Now I'll never figure that part out. Oh, fuck. Don't wander down that tangent. You *may not* die out here. Look around the inside of your head. Try to find some optimism.

Christ, I've never been optimistic before; how could I start now?

Shut up. Fuck that. You are optimistic. That's why you gambled. You saw *possibilities*.

But you lost, you piece of shit. You fucking lost over and over again, and you had to run away like a lowlife scum. And now you're gonna lay out here on the sand and get eaten alive. Unless you die of shock first.

Shit. Don't say that. Cool your head. Think. *Do* something. Do people actually die of shock, or is that just a rare occurrence?

Fuck you; you know it's not a rare occurrence. Nobody ever told you it's a rare occurrence. You're making that shit up, you fucking liar. So many lies have passed through your teeth, it's amazing that they're not broken.

Maybe I should kill myself. Take matters into my own hands. Do I have a sharp object on me? No, of course not. I never carry anything on me, except for my sorry, empty wallet. Your only option is to snap your own neck. What would be worse: snapping your own neck, or getting eaten by the Indian? The first choice would make you a quitter, the second choice would make you a submissive victim.

This is all Shannon's fault. Word got around that I was leaving town, and she called me over for one last fuck. I shouldn't have gone. I didn't even feel like it. Shannon's sexy and all, but I haven't really been getting hard lately, what with the collectors knocking down my door. Anyway, I went and fucked her. She begged me not to leave. Both of us cried. I said, "So long," and headed for the door. Then she said the magic goddamn words: "Don't forget to bring water. It gets hot out there in the desert."

So I lined my passenger seat with six liter-bottles of spring water. Shannon was right, of course. My throat got real dry real fast. But then, less than twenty minutes after the deejay said, "115 degrees," my bladder started struggling. Next thing I knew, the liquid had filled up my dick.

I pulled over onto the first wide piece of shoulder I found. The traffic was nonexistent; it's Wednesday afternoon. Nonetheless, I didn't want my manhood hanging out too close to the freeway. Something uncivil about that. So I took a little walk, maybe forty or fifty yards into the desert. My pores got all leaky. I'm overdue for a haircut, so sweat dripped from my scalp onto my forehead, making annoying puddles on top of my eyebrows. Had to piss fast. But before a squirt of liquid left my body, I looked over my shoulder and saw the Indian.

My bladder sighed. I zipped up and turned around. The Indian was midway between the interstate and me. He was making some intense eye contact. My heartbeat skipped. I said, "Sorry, sir, I had to use the bathroom."

The words came out without thought. They were a product of my unconscious mind. Why did I apologize? Why did I even address him?

The guy looked ancient. Well, maybe not ancient, but definitely not current. He wore feathers and moccasins and white paint on his face. His black hair hung down to below his knees. He seemed preternaturally calm, as if the modern world had never laid its hands on him.

I made a mistake. I approached him. Worst thing I've ever done. Probably one of the last things I'll ever do. I didn't know what I intended to say to him. Some primal curiosity made me want to figure him out, especially since he'd failed to answer me. I got within five feet of the Indian before I turned around and ran.

I hadn't run so fast since high school gym class. My speed was so aggressive that my heels hit the ground before my toes did. The Indian's face molested my mind: white paint, no mouth; dark pink pupils.

While I ran across the desert, I looked over my shoulder to check him out. He was not running. He didn't seem to be moving at all. *Maybe* he had progressed one or two steps. I stopped short. My sneakers scraped against the sand. The hot air offended my lungs. I bent over at the waist and tried to catch a good breath or two. Upon looking at my pants, I noticed that I'd wet myself. Desperate scumbag that I am, I thought of wiping my hand against my dripping crotch and licking the piss. My tongue was dry and hard like a toad's back.

That's when my brain started getting soft. Back in the car, I was nice and sharp, but now my head was turning into sludge. "Fucking idiot," I called myself. It was stupid to run away from him. I should've circled around him and gone back to my car. Whatever; it's not my fault. My instincts had taken over.

I looked at him. He was a dot in the distance. My car was an even smaller dot behind him.

Think. Don't fuck up. My chest was burning; I needed lots of water. The guy didn't seem to be a runner. But then again, how had he appeared behind me from out of nowhere?

You can't over-calculate this; you're not a scientist. Come on, shithead, act before you think. Otherwise you'll be toast out here.

So—retard that I am—I ran back toward the Indian. My intention was to make a wide pass on his left and fly into my car.

My chest turned to stone as I ran. I had hot coals where my lungs belonged. Do this right, I told myself. This will not be the end of your life. While running to my car, I couldn't make out the Indian's expression. From this distance, he seemed curious, as though I was a zoo exhibit. His posture indicated patience and composure. But his eyes—his stirring, colorful eyes—had indicated anything but.

When I tripped, somehow I knew that my leg would break before it did. It happened so fast that my mind's understanding ran ahead of my body's experience. The snap brought giant icicles to mind. Despite the weather, my blood went cold.

The break is high, between my knee and my hip. This is no modest fracture we're dealing with. I'm up against an honest-to-God break. The only things holding my leg together are flesh, veins, and muscles. The only thing holding my mind together is the fact that I'm still alive.

The Indian has been approaching me for over an hour now. He takes a step, then waits for a minute or so, then takes another step. This seems to be his natural speed. I have no clue how he snuck up on me before. He's less than twenty yards away from me, and I can make out his face pretty well. As it turns out, he does have a mouth. It's just obscured by bulbous lip tumors. The tumors, like the rest of his face, are painted white, but they stand out because of their shine.

I screamed for the first few minutes after I fell. My pain and fear and regret blended into a pretty impressive howl. But there's no echoes in the desert. Only dim, judgmental silence. The thick air was pleased to prevent my shrieks from traveling too far. That ruled out any hope of a motorist coming to my rescue. And the Indian didn't seem daunted by my sound. I wonder if he has ears behind his hair.

My screaming stopped when a new emotion overcame me. Despite the fact that I've been alive for twenty-seven years, this emotion was foreign to me before now. Dread. Crushed ice piping through my veins. Fire burning out my skull.

Christ, Donovan. You're a fucking pussy. All your life, you've admired the nobility and heroism of movie characters and historical figures, but when reality calls you out onto the playing field, you fail every fucking time. Be resourceful, you slave. Instead of pondering your own dread, why don't you do something? The Indian is slow. He's giving you time to think.

I try to move. High-pitched bells toll from my leg. My knee-cap quakes. I grunt, pick up some sand, and throw it at the Indian. Half of the sand flies back in my face. Half of what flies back in my face ends up in my mouth. The Indian pauses. Through moist eyes, I take note of his chest. Something seems to have sliced it. An axe or a carving knife. The wound isn't fresh. In my non-expert opinion, I would guess that the wound is older than my great-grandparents are.

"You fuck! Leave me the fuck alone, you son of a bitch!"

My nervous system is uncoiling.

"I'll fucking crush your skull if you come over here!"

There's an idea. Is there enough adrenaline left in my system for me to fight? Or will the pain bring me down? Part of me wants him to hurry up. I'm eager to test the fighting idea before I forget I had it.

The Indian pauses again. I can really see him now. He'll be on me in ten more paces. From the looks of him, he seems to be thinking. Not with much complexity; more like with a grave single-mindedness.

His mouth drops open. The blackness behind his teeth is dark and oily. It looks as if he has no tongue. But then a drop of beige saliva falls from his lower lip. My whole torso contracts.

The Indian is hungry.

I'll have to fight him when he comes. Despite my torment, I can't go out without a fight. Think of all your heroes. This is your last chance to do something right. Concentrate now, you fucking bastard. Preserve a positive mindset. You will fight. You will fight, and you will win. Snap the fucker's neck. That's right, asshole; instead of snapping *your* neck, snap *his* neck. Bury him in the sand. Spit on his dead fucking corpse.

That's when I remind myself that the Indian is dead already.

You piece of shit. How dumb could you be, hatching a plot to kill a dead man? You're not gonna put up a fight. Let's be honest: this guy's gonna have you for lunch. And you know what, shithead? You probably deserve it.

Nine more paces.

Cold As He Wishes

C.M. Shevlin

It all started with a girl. No, wait a minute. That's not entirely true. It all started with a dog. But since everything comes around to the girl eventually, I might as well begin with her. So . . . Sheila. She was always too good for me. Everybody said so. Too pretty, too clever, too funny, too . . . *everything*. The two of us together never made any sort of sense except to me. We met at St Jude's, somewhere I should've never been in the first place. But I had every one fooled into thinking I was pretty smart, paid attention in class most of the time, and everyone at home had high hopes, especially when the teacher put me down to sit the scholarship exam for the local grammar school.

But two days before the exam, my dog Winston died in his sleep. I really loved that animal, I mean really. He wasn't any-body's idea of a prizewinner—a sheepdog crossed with some mysterious other. He'd been crippled with arthritis for the last year and was occasionally incontinent, so in a way it was a release for him. Of course, I was eleven and didn't see it like that—completely gutted I was. My mum promised me anything— puppies, money, *anything*—to settle me down enough to take the exam. Nothing worked. Finally, she turned to my granddad and demanded, "Isn't there anything you could say to him?" Grand-dad just shook his head and went on filling his pipe.

I lay awake for ages that night on the sofa bed; I had been sleeping there since Granddad had moved into our terrace house in Cavendish Street. Dwelling on the unfairness of it all, I was staring at the ceiling when the stairs creaked. Quickly, I rolled over and faked sleep, but my granddad shook me, holding his fingers to his lips, "Shhhh. Get dressed, come with me, Chris."

It was a warm night, so I just shoved my feet into trainers and pulled a jacket over my pajamas. Granddad carried two spades. Together, we walked to the patch of wasteland down the road where we'd buried Winston. I'd left his favorite ball atop his grave but it was lying yards away, already punctured and torn. I picked it up, blinking back the tears.

I kicked the ball away. "So why are we here?"

Granddad tossed me the other spade and said, "Dig." He'd been in the army more than twenty years ago, so when he said, "Dig," I dug, the spade easily turning over the dry earth. We unwrapped Winston's canvas body bag, and Granddad grunted as he bent down and picked up a handful of the dirt that had covered the carcass. He scattered it in a circle. Taking a knife from his pocket, he slit his palm and walked the circle again, shaking blood onto the earth. Painfully he bent and used the knife to smear blood onto the dog's mouth.

"Granda," I said, finding my voice, "What're you doing?"

He ignored me.

Pressing a hand to the small of his back, Granddad straightened. He took a deep breath and held the knife in front of him. In a cracked but resonant voice that contrasted with his matter-of-fact words, Granddad called out, "Time to get up, boy. Blood and earth calls you, we command you."

"Granda . . ." I whined, by this time close to peeing where I stood. There was a sudden twitch in the dog's body, like a violent tic. I jumped back. After another convulsion, Winston turned onto his front. He began to make efforts to get to his feet, his eyes rolling and his mouth tightly closed, strings of saliva dripping on the canvas beneath him.

"What?" I asked in an awed whisper. "Is that really Winston, Granda? Is it?"

He shrugged. "Something like him, anyhow. Here," he handed me the knife. "Feed him your blood, or he'll slip back again. Just a bit mind you, don't let him catch you in a grip."

I gripped the handle and resolutely cut down into my palm, which immediately began to stain with blood. I held it out, shaking. "Here boy, here Wins—"

My grandfather's hand clamped down on my shoulder. "Don't use his name. Call him something else . . . or just 'boy.'

"Why?"

"If you use his name, he might remember who he is. And he mightn't be that happy about it."

My forehead creased in confusion, but I turned back to the dog, which was dragging himself towards my hands and the droplets of blood. I squeezed the cut, and the drops quivered and fell into Winston's mouth. He swallowed and, energized, got to his feet, fixing me with an empty stare.

We headed back home, Granddad's handkerchief knotted around my hand. Winston shambled awkwardly behind us, still slowed by his arthritis. I was hardly able to believe what had happened.

"Granda?

"Hmmm?"

"Would that work on humans?"

"It could do. But it's not done."

"But why? I mean, if it could work . . ."

He grabbed my upper arms and gave me a couple of shakes. "It's not done, do you hear me? Never! Don't even think about it!"

"No, Granda. I won't, Granda." I twisted out of his painful grip.

He released me and wagged his finger. "Remember what I said, now." He started to shuffle away, but stopped. Without looking back, he said, "Don't ever do it, Christopher. But . . . if you do . . . give 'em plenty of raw meat and they'll last maybe a few weeks. And when they start getting that look in their eye, put them back and put them back fast, before the hunger gets too strong. Or else you'll wish you had. Put 'em back the same way as you woke 'em up, but use salt instead of the blood."

Next morning, my mum's lips got all tight when she saw Winston, but she didn't say anything. I took the entrance exam and passed with flying colors. I had my dog back so everything was great again. Although it wasn't the same. He still followed me everywhere, but when I stroked him he didn't lick me or roll onto his back, begging for more. And he never took his eyes off me, just stared. Not with devotion or hatred or even hunger really. Just . . . a waiting stare. So when I woke a week later to find him gone, I didn't make as much fuss as you might think. Anyhow, school started soon after, and then there were new classes, new teachers, and Sheila.

Yeah, we're back to her. I used to sit for whole periods, just mesmerized by her long shining fall of hair right in front of my desk, so close I could have run my fingers through it. It took me a whole year to pluck up the courage to talk to her, but when I did we got on really well. We'd read the same books, we felt the same about different stuff—or mostly, she'd tell me what she felt about things, and I'd nod and smile. Everybody started coupling up about second year, so it was pretty natural for us to do the same. But we stayed together, all the way through junior school and the exams, which I managed to scrape through with her help.

Hard to believe maybe, but I never even thought once of Winston. Even when I was sixteen and Granda died, I just sat beside Sheila at the funeral as she stroked my arm, and I thought of the sex we'd have that evening if I could get Auntie Flo to stay with Mum. I thought we'd be together forever. I can see now that was incredibly naïve. What are the odds of marrying your junior school girlfriend anyway? Who'd even want to? Except me of course. Beside the point anyway. Like I said, Sheila was clever. She was headed straight for a university, and even with her help, I miserably failed finals. We promised we'd stay together—call, write, visit at weekends—but well, yeah, you know what happened. She met someone else at school. She wrote me a letter to tell me we'd always be friends, blah blah blah.

When I eventually emerged from the walking coma caused by *that* little note, I messed around for a couple of years, worked in a video store, drove taxis. Had fuck all luck with women really. Even the ones who were distinctly not in my league (which I felt had been raised by going out with Sheila) sharply rejected me. Bastard. Selfish tosser. Those were things I heard quite a bit. Or from the psychology diploma student I dated for a while, "emotionally unavailable." That takes us up to a night about a year ago.

I'd been out on a drinking binge with some mates from Blockbuster where I'd struck out at least ten times. My best mate Ian and I walked home, singing and generally making arses of ourselves. I must have taken a detour somewhere because when I woke up in the early hours of the morning, I was in the graveyard lying over what seemed to be a pretty fresh grave. The economical wooden cross read "Josephine Hamilton. Born 12th February 1980 Died 13th February 2004 aged 24 years. Beloved daughter and sister."

Well that blows, I thought, *day after your birthday*. Sort of like someone went "Alright, I'll give you twenty-four years. But not one day more." 13th February. That was yesterday.

Flopping onto my back to stare up at the sky, it took a minute for the notion to percolate through my booze sodden mind. I like to think it would have seemed appalling had I been in my right senses. But right then, I was thinking, *Well why the hell not? Just try it and see. Probably won't work anyway. . . .'*

If I'd encountered any obstacles at all, chances are good that I would have abandoned the idea right away. But the night watchman was nowhere to be seen, and his shed nearby contained the necessary implements: a spade and a penknife. I was so sloshed I didn't wonder about state the corpse, about how long the woman had been dead. Thankfully when I opened the coffin and took a fascinated and repelled glance inside, Josephine Hamilton was as fresh as her grave. I was shaking at this point, just as I had all those years ago. But I'd come this far and something inside me had to know if it was even doable.

"I'll put her right back," I said, "if it works. Which it won't." I copied everything I'd seen my grandfather do that night—the circle of earth, the circle of blood, the blood on the lips. Then the words, which I felt more than a little stupid saying, I don't mind telling you: "Come on, time to get up, girl. Blood and earth calls you, and I command you."

Nothing happened. I exhaled a long breath, sneakily relieved like when Granddad had taken Winston in the night to put him back into his grave. The horror of what I had just done hit me, and I felt stomach acid rise in my throat. I turned away and vomited. Finally, I wiped my mouth on my sleeve and turned around, steeling myself to cover the coffin and fill in the grave.

Josephine Hamilton's head and shoulders were up out of the coffin, and her white hands gripped the sides as if to pull her to a sitting position. I froze, then continued to retch, even though there was nothing left to come up.

Experiencing a nearly uncontrollable urge to run, I backed away. What had Granddad said? If I didn't feed her, she'd just slip back. But she was watching me with that familiar flat stare and still trying to hoist herself out of the coffin. I had the sickening feeling that if I didn't give her what she wanted, she'd drag herself out and follow me until I did, that I'd hear a scratching at my door later. I cut my hand and held it above her mouth only to snatch it away just as she swiped for it. Once her tongue darted out to taste the blood on her lips though, she was able to pull herself up and step out of the coffin in one fluid motion, watching me all the while.

So what would you have done? Like I believe you. Like hell you would have put her back. You'd have been afraid but intrigued, just like I was. I took her home, after filling in the grave again. I left her sitting at the kitchen table, and I barricaded myself in the bedroom. God knows how I slept, but I did. When I woke with a hangover, it seemed obvious that it must have all been a dream. Except when I stumbled to the toilet, there was Josephine Hamilton, deceased, sitting in a beam of morning sunlight in my flat.

Don't get me wrong, it was still creepy the way her eyes followed me without her head ever moving, but in the daytime, she really didn't seem that frightening. Just a pretty girl with short brown hair and chocolate eyes, a little on the plump side, but definitely attractive.

Forgetting my need to pee, I sat down with a thump opposite her and said to myself, "Now what am I going to do with you?"

Her head lifted a fraction and her mouth stretched into a sweet smile. "I don't know," she said.

My mouth dropped open. I looked into her eyes, still perfectly flat. "You can talk."

She looked back at me, seemingly unoffended, but without response.

I leaned forward a little and said, "Jo—" and suddenly remembered my granddad's advice about Winston: "If you use his name, he might remember who he is," he had said. "And he mightn't be that happy about what you've done." I finished, "-anna. Joanna. That's your name."

She raised no objection. "I'm very hungry," she said, her voice as flat as her eyes.

"Sure you are, well you would be . . . why wouldn't you be?" I could feel myself begin to gabble. "I'll get you something to eat."

At the fridge, I pulled out the roast my mum had left. She was to come over and cook it the next day, so it was still red bloody and raw. I set it down in front of Josephine/Joanna, and for a split second I thought I saw disappointment in those expressionless eyes, but she began to tear at it with frantic fingers. When she was done, I tentatively dabbed at her mouth and chin with a cloth to remove the traces of blood and the gobbets of meat.

She followed me about the house for the rest of the day, until I told her to stop, after which she just sat. I headed out that night, and, surrendering to an impulse, I took her with me. I was expecting it to be a disaster. I *deserved* it to be a disaster. Imagine my surprise when she was a hit with my mates. She smiled a lot, she laughed when others laughed, she was pretty—yeah, I got a lot of envious glances. Slowly I began to enjoy myself as I realized this could be a relationship in which I had complete control. Jo would never leave me, and I could dispose of her whenever I got bored.

I kissed her outside the pub that night, and it wasn't unpleasant. She was cold, colder than a normal girl even in November, and my lips felt a little numb when I pulled away. But she made all the right movements with her lips then, and back at my flat, she made all the right moves with the rest of her body. I learned early on to send her to bed with an electric blanket a half an hour before joining her.

So for a few weeks, things were good for me. But several things upset the balance of what was the most secure relationship I had ever had. Firstly, it got harder to satisfy her appetite for raw meat. Also, her complexion began to grow sallow, and her flesh took on an unpleasant consistency. When I touched it, it was as if the different layers would slide over each other. And sometimes when she moved, I could hear a sloshing sound, which I began to imagine was the liquefaction of her internal organs. But it was when I woke up one night to find her standing over me with hunger in her eyes that I knew it was time to put her back. I took her to the graveyard with a tin of table salt and knife in my pocket. I was more than a little nervous about this as I hadn't seen my granddad perform this part of the ritual. Together we dug up her grave again, exposing the coffin. I opened it and ordered her inside.

She turned and looked at me. "I don't want to."

She looked so forlorn, and something like human emotion appeared for the first time in her eyes. I almost weakened, but the hunger that sharpened the bones of her face persuaded me.

"Get into the coffin," I repeated, and she obeyed.

It went just like my grandfather had said it would—the earth, the salt, the words. When the last spadeful of dirt had been thrown in, I said "Goodbye, Josephine," before walking away.

It didn't end there. I started scanning the obituaries, which unfortunately don't come with pictures attached. Sometimes I had to travel all around the countryside. Still, I wasn't overly fussy. Blondes, redheads, brunettes—an endless procession of perfectly biddable women entered my life and left it again just as easily. My friends couldn't believe my luck.

"But where do you find them?" Ian asked. "I never see you pulling."

And you wouldn't want to, I thought dryly to myself, remembering my last raising, where the subject had seemed to have a little trouble getting out of the coffin, even with me pulling her for dear life. It was only when I moved the blanket that I discovered the article about the industrial accident she had suffered. The obituary had neglected to mention the amputations. I put her back again pretty quick, I can tell you. There are some things you can't explain away down at the pub.

It was Carol—no wait a minute, it was Jeannie, that's right— that I was with when I bumped into Sheila. She was coming out of the shopping centre, loaded down with Christmas shopping. For a few seconds, I forgot who—what—was beside me. It was Sheila's pointed glances towards my companion that prompted me to make introductions. Jeannie smiled because that's what I'd told her to do when I introduced her to strangers. "Nice to meet you," she said. That encounter knocked me for six. Coming up on seven years, and I still wasn't over Sheila. I guess everyone has one person they never get over. Of course, I realize that not everyone substitutes that person with a series of zombies.

A Sunday morning two weeks afterwards, I got a telephone call. Jeannie—naturally, that wasn't her real name, but I always liked that sitcom, you know the one with Barbara Eden—anyway, she answered it and said in her perfectly flat voice, "Just a minute, please," and she handed the receiver to me.

"Chris?" an unfamiliar female voice asked.

"Yeah, can I help you?"

"Chris, it's Kathy," she said with a little catch in her voice. I came awake with a start. Kathy was Sheila's best friend, still is, though they're not as close as they used to be what with her going away to the university and all. Kathy and I kept in touch on and off; we always did get on well, and occasionally she had news of Sheila. Plus I figured that we had something in common, having been left behind by the same person.

"It's Sheila. . . ." It sounded like she was crying. "There was an accident—she was on her way to the airport and . . . oh God, Chris, she's dead."

I think I said all the right things then, asked all the right questions, but I'd been lying on the bed quite sometime before anything started to make sense. Sheila dead? My mind started racing, ticking overtime. She wasn't dead, couldn't be dead. But I wasn't really thinking about the senseless tragedy of it all, oh no. I was thinking, *Finally, she's in my league.*

It wasn't long before I said bye-bye to Jeannie and hello again to Sheila. When I called her out of the coffin, I did what I hadn't done with any of the others. I bent and guided my hand to her lips and let her take more than a few drops of blood. When her teeth began to tear the flesh, I took it away, and she let me. Slowly, her eyes slid to meet mine, and my heart began to speed up. Somewhere in the dull brown was a hint of something familiar, maybe a hint of recognition.

"Sheila?" I asked, but didn't get an answer.

Since then, I've broken all the rules that I made for myself. I feed her raw meat like I did with the others, but occasionally I let her take a mouthful of flesh from me. Never more than a bite. I like to think she's being careful, that maybe she remembers me. Once, before sinking her teeth into the soft tissue on my arm, she said once in a confused voice "Chris?" But it's been three weeks.

One day soon, what she takes from me won't be enough, and she won't stop at a few bites. I know this and in a sick way, I don't care. There's no way I could put her back. She needs me. *Me.* Sheila dragged me to see a play in London once when we were still going out. Wasn't really my cup of tea, but I do remember something one of the characters had said. He said it was no good trying to fool yourself about love, that if you didn't realize that it took muscle and guts, you'd better give up on the whole idea. Of course, he probably didn't mean it literally. I do.

DEATH ROW

James Reilly

There were three of us on death row: me, Pastor, and Svelski; the guards had long gone.

Pastor sat with his back to the bars and took a long drag off his cigarette. He didn't pay much mind to the dead thing on the floor outside his cell. Hell, even the blood on his hands didn't faze him, although I suppose nothing much did these days.

It started a week ago. We'd only gotten the story in bits and pieces from panicked guards and workers on their way out of the jail—out of the city. They left us a few cases of canned fruit, bottles of Coke, and water, and they even set up a television right outside my cell. They wished us luck and left.

After all, we were on death row for a reason.

There were reports about a disease that made people *change*. The news was flooded with images of riots and mass evacuations. It was chaos out there.

After a day or so, all of the networks had switched to the emergency broadcast signal, except a local access one that ran a continuous loop of bible quotes.

Seemed a little late for that.

Today was the first time we'd actually seen one.

There were slow and clumsy footsteps in the hallway. I figured it was someone else who got left behind. Pastor pressed his face to the bars and looked down the hall.

"Hey!" he yelled. "Down here!"

There was no reply, but the footsteps kept coming. I could see him now, too. He was a short, heavy guy in a gray suit. His left arm hung limply by his side.

"Hey," I said, "You alright man?"

Pastor shook his head. "This ain't right at all."

"Yeah, whatever," Svelski muttered, and then yelled to the man in his grating, nasally tone. "Hey, get us the fuck out of here! We got rights, you know!"

Hiram Svelski was a Brooklyn boy, thin, dark, and as greasy as a Greek pizza. He wasn't a hardcore criminal, just a white-collar schmuck who had wanted out of his marriage but had wanted to avoid alimony and child support. He had burned down his house while his wife and three kids slept inside.

In the hall, the man kept coming, and as he got closer, as I got a better look at him, at his *face*, a prickling sensation ran up my spine.

The man looked up at me. He bared his teeth and let out a deep, guttural moan. I stepped away from the bars, certain he would charge at me, but instead, he lunged toward Pastor, plunging his arms through the bars and grabbing him by the overalls.

"Hey!" Pastor cried as he grabbed at the thing's hands. "What the fu—?" He let out a howl as the man dug his fingers into Pastor's flesh. I could see the blood slowly spread across the orange sleeves of Pastor's overalls. Pastor jerked violently to one side, and I could hear the bones in the thing's arms snap. Pastor reached around and clasped his hands over the back of its head, pulled it toward him, and anchored his feet against the base of the bars.

"Kick its ass, Pastor!!" Svelski yelled. "Kick its fuckin' ass!"

Pastor leaned back and pulled the thing's head through the bars, eliciting a sickening series of grunts, cracks and snaps as its skull caved in. Once he was satisfied that it was dead, Pastor stood back and looked at his blood-soaked hands.

I could see by his expression that this wasn't the first time he'd seen them like that.

Pastor scowled and wiped his hands across his chest. He seemed more inconvenienced than horrified as he lifted his leg, pressed his foot against the thing's face and kicked it loose from the bars.

The corpse fell into a heap outside his cell.

"Okay," Svelski said, staring down at the body, "So what the fuck was that? It's . . . it's just a fuckin' guy."

I knelt at the bars. "Certainly looked that way, didn't it?" Twisted toward me, the thing's face was a pale blue and covered in a web of darker blue veins.

"Ain't no man," Pastor said, still catching his breath. "Maybe he was once, but he ain't no more."

Pastor fell against his bunk and sat down. He started rubbing at his arms where the thing had dug in its nails.

"You all right?" I asked.

"Yeah," Pastor said. "Peachy." He threw his legs up on the bunk and leaned against the bars, turning his back to me. As Pastor lit up a cigarette, Svelski ran to the front of his cell and pressed his face through the bars.

"Hey, you got another one o' those?" Svelski asked.

Pastor didn't bother answering.

I pulled one from my pack and tossed it across the hall. The cigarette landed a few inches from Svelski's cell. "There," I said. I still had a few packs from the carton that my uncle had brought me just before this thing started, and with the way things were going, I'd probably starve to death before I ran out.

"Good man, Steve-O," Svelski said. He knelt down and reached out for the cigarette, pausing as he looked at the body that lay a few feet away.

"It's dead, Svelski," I said.

Svelski grimaced and grabbed for the cigarette. "Smells somethin' fierce, don't it?"

"Smells like a dead man oughta," Pastor said, still scratching at his arms. "I looked into that thing's eyes. There was nothin' there. I seen a person's eyes when life be leavin' 'em. In that thing? There was nothing at all."

Still staring down at the body, I repeated what I'd heard on the news. "They said that's what happened when you got sick. They said it was like everything that made you human, you just lost it."

"So what was he then, if he wasn't no man?" Svelski asked, rolling the cigarette between his fingers.

I shrugged. "I know as much as you do, man."

Pastor said nothing. He just sat there with his back to us, still scratching at his arms.

Just then, a loud buzz emanated from the speakers as the cellblock lights shut down one by one.

Ka-CHUNK Ka-CHUNK Ka-CHUNK

It was an automated evening on death row. Save for the amber glow of the exit signs, the hall was pure indigo.

"So that's it then, eh?" Svelski lit his cigarette. "I mean, this is really it." Dancing shadows cast across his angular face as he took a puff and laughed.

"I don't know," I said, feeling my way back to my bunk. "I don't know what to think."

"'Course you know," Pastor said from the darkness.

"Oh, *here* we go," Svelski muttered.

"This is the reckoning, people," Pastor's booming voice sounding weary and weaker than usual. "And God tellin' us we done fucked up all he given us and now he gon' wipe the slate clean."

"Why does everything gotta be about God with you, Pastor?" Svelski asked.

"'Cause everything *is* about God, little man. And the quicker you realize that, the quicker you can be makin' your peace with him. I know I have."

"What, an' you're goin' to heaven, right? Fucking stupid nigger, you're a convicted murderer! You're frying like the rest of us, am I right Steve-O?"

"Shut up, Svelski," I said. I could only see the head of his cigarette bobbing around in the darkness. It wasn't that I disagreed with him. Me and God, we parted ways a long time ago. I was just sick of hearing his voice, that nasally whine, the way he called me Steve-O.

"What? I'm wrong? You think this big dumb African's gonna be sproutin' wings and shit now 'cause he found God on death row? Be-for-fuckin' real."

I heard the creak of Svelski's bedsprings as he slipped into his bunk, and I watched the head of his cigarette fall to the floor. It laid there, its glow almost reassuring as I drifted off to sleep.

* * *

I knelt beside her and brought the statue down upon her head, again and again and again and again. With every blow, she looked less and less like my Lisa. Her face was distorted, mutilated, like raw meat.

Like clay.

I was molding her.

I was changing her.

I was erasing her from my world.

In my dreams, I'd shatter her bones, turn her teeth to powder.

And when I slept, I'd hear her scream.

And scream.

And scream.

* * *

I awoke to the sound of Svelski's high-pitched shrieks and tumbled out of my cot, falling to my knees just in front of the bars. I'd somehow slept through the night: the cellblock was once again fully illuminated by buzzing fluorescents. As my eyes adjusted, I saw Pastor lying on his back in the middle of his cell, his arms splayed, scratched nearly raw. Blood trickled from the corners of his mouth and eyes, and he wasn't breathing, at least as far as I could tell.

Svelski cried, "He's fuckin' dead, man! He's fuckin' dead!"

"Just . . . just calm down. Just calm the fuck down."

"Calm down?" Svelski shrieked. "What if . . . what if it was that thing? Man, I mean, what if it's spreading in here now?"

I shook my head. "No, no . . . if it was in the air. . ." I thought about it a second. *Was* it in the air? Then I looked at Pastor's arms. "No. Pastor, he got scratched. The thing, it scratched him up."

Svelksi seemed to calm a little. His grip on the bars loosened, and the color came back to his knuckles.

"Yeah," he said. "That's right. That's right. He touched it. He *touched* the fucking thing. I mean, we're okay then, right? We're okay?"

"Yeah," I said, but how was I supposed to know? "I think we're okay."

Just then, I noticed Pastor's fingers move. At least I thought I did. Was it my eyes still adjusting to the light?

Pastor's fingers twitched again.

"Svelski . . ." I whispered as calmly as possible.

Pastor's fingers wiggled some more.

"Svelski . . ."

"What?"

He grabbed the bars again and squeezed his rat face through, twisting his head as far as the bars would allow. "What . . . what are you lookin' at?"

Pastor's fingers were no longer moving. Maybe it *was* my eyes?

Then, suddenly, Pastor's fists clenched.

I fell backward.

"What are you *lookin'* at, man?"

Pastor convulsed wildly.

"Ah shit!" Svelski yelled. "Ah Shit shit shit!"

As Pastor's arms and legs flailed against the cot and bars, orange foam spewed from his mouth and nose. He hissed and spit and let out a moan that was deep and pained and unearthly. And, in one sudden move, Pastor flipped from his back to his haunches, his hands on the floor in front of him, his teeth bared in a snarl and his eyes . . . dear God, his *eyes*.

Svelski flew back across his cell and hunkered in the corner, blocking his ears with balled-up fists and rocking back and forth like a scared child. "Oh Jesus Christ, no!"

Pastor stared straight at me. He snorted, and a cloud of red and orange mist burst from his nose, followed by a thick strand of bloody mucous that dripped to the floor. He cried out again and charged, slamming into the bars. He pushed his arms through and clawed at the air, knocking over the stacks of canned fruit and soda cans. They crashed to the ground and rolled in all directions.

"Kill him!" Svelski cried. *"Kill* him!"

"How the fuck am I supposed to do that?"

"I don't know, just—oh god! What the fuck?" Svelski covered his head in his hands and kicked at his cot. "What the fuck is he?"

And the question hung in my head. What *was* he? *Who* was he? He certainly wasn't Pastor anymore. Pastor was dead. This thing . . .

This thing was just hungry.

* * *

I could still hear Svelski sobbing, just as he had been all day. He calmed down just about the same time that the Pastor thing realized it wasn't getting out of its cage.

I watched the thing all day. When the lights buzzed out for the night, I could still see the glow of its eyes, fiery orange, almost ethereal. The thing didn't close them for a second. Hell, it didn't even blink.

As I sat there, staring at Pastor, there was a loud bang in the hallway: metal on metal, like cell doors slamming shut.

"What was that?" Svelski whispered.

"No idea. Maybe . . . I dunno . . . maybe help?" I didn't believe it, but wanted to.

KaCHUNK!

Another bang, followed by the unmistakable sound of shattered glass; whatever was here, it was getting closer.

"Oh fuck. It's another one of those things!" Svelski said.

"We don't know that," I said, even though, deep down, I was just as sure as he was. "Be cool."

"Fuck, fuck, fuck, fuck," Svelski whispered. I couldn't see him, but I could tell by the sound of his voice that he'd moved toward the back of his cell again. I looked over at the Pastor-thing; it was still standing there, its eyes still glowing back at me. At least I knew where *he* was.

Down the far end of the cellblock, something banged against the doors. There was a rhythm to it now, slow and steady, but growing louder and harder. Then a brittle cracking sound, the rattle of glass raining onto the tile floor.

Now I could hear *them*.

"Jesus Christ, Steve. You hear that?" Svelski's voice sounded pinched, nervous. "Steve?"

"Shhhhh!" I hissed.

They were scratching on the door, fumbling at the latch. Something gave. The door creaked as it swung open. They were in.

I moved to the edge of my cell, pressed my face between the bars, and peered down the hallway toward the shuffling footsteps, the grunts, the deep moaning. My heart sank in my chest, and a wave of panic washed over me. I fell back across my cell, slammed hard into the cold brick wall, and froze. The shuffling and moaning all but drowned out the desperate prayers from Svelski's cell as the things drew nearer. The air was thick with the heady aroma of dirty laundry and desert road kill.

Now they stood before us, eyes like those of the Pastor-thing, dozens of them, hanging there like a swarm of fireflies in the darkness. While I couldn't see it, I could feel their arms plunging between the bars of my cell, disturbing the air as they flailed about, groping for purchase. Svelski's prayers had given way to shrieks, but I could barely hear him now above the grunts and moans.

They were louder now, more urgent.

They were in a frenzy.

I don't know how long I stood there, pressed up against the wall, but my muscles ached and my mind worked feverishly, preparing for what I would see come morning.

When the lights finally did buzz back on, what stood before me was much more horrific than my imagination could conjure. Men, women, and children . . .

At least, they used to be. . . .

Their faces were swollen and bruised. Chunks of flesh were missing from some. Entire limbs were missing from others. One of them was nothing more than a torso, its lower half a ragged mess of bloodied tissue, organs, and bone. It slithered across the floor, using its hands to propel it, leaving a snail's trail of blood in its wake.

These were the faces of the dead.

Yet here they stood.

"Svelski?" I yelled, feeling my way along the wall.

There was no reply. I pictured him cowering under his bunk, praying, eyes shut tight.

"Svelski? You hear me?" I couldn't see him through the things in the hallway. I looked at my cot and carefully stepped up on it. The mattress sank under my weight, and I felt my body shift forward. I threw myself back, smacking my skull against the brick wall. The pain shot straight through to the back of my eyes, but I managed to keep my balance. Had I fallen, it'd have been right into the waiting arms of the things outside my cell.

I could see him now. His face was pale as a winter moon, his head tilted back slightly, a gaping slice across his neck. Svelski still clutched the bloodied peel-top from a can of fruit cocktail in one hand. The other rested in his blood-soaked lap.

When the first gunshot rang out, I nearly fell forward again. There was another shot, and another as the things turned away from my cell and shambled down the hall.

I heard a voice.

"Get the one on the left, Wally."

Another shot rang out, followed by the sound of blood and bone splashing across the tile floor. I scurried to the front of my cell and tried to look down the hall, but couldn't see past the sea of dead that shuffled toward the gunfire.

"Hey!" I cried. "Hey, I'm down here!"

"Whoa, we got a live one down there, Tucker."

"Just hang on, there, fella. We're comin!"

There were several more shots, followed by the wet sound of bodies dropping to the floor.

"Sheeeeeit! Did you see that fucker blow?"

"Get back you jagoffs." It was another voice, deeper, clearly the one in charge. "We ain't got time for this chicken shit."

The cellblock filled with the deafening roar of an automatic rifle. Bullets whizzed past, ricocheting off the concrete and tile and brick. I dove into the corner of my cell, instinctively wrapping my arms around my head until, mercifully, the gunfire ceased. In the silence, the last shells tinkled to the floor, and a high-pitched ringing deafened my ears. As I stood, I saw three men step into view: a middle-age man in a flannel coat and a Yankees hat, a teenager with a pierced lip and jet black hair, and a big man wearing fatigues. The patch on his shirt said Tucker, and he cradled an M-16.

"Take care o' that one," Tucker said, nodding toward Pastor's cell. The teenager smiled and leveraged a double-barreled shotgun right under the thing's nose. I blocked my ears as I watched the contents of the Pastor-thing's skull splash against the baby blue wall of the cell. The thing dropped to the floor, and the teenager grinned back at Tucker.

"Righteous," he said.

Tucker shook his head and looked back at me.

"This thing need a key?" he asked, gesturing toward the door of my cell.

"No . . . uh . . . down the hall. There's a guard room. I think it's the . . . uh . . . the orange lever. It unlocks all of them," I said.

Tucker nodded and looked at the middle-aged man, who stood there for a moment, but finally sighed and walked down the hall, muttering under his breath. After a few seconds, the doors buzzed and Tucker swung my cell door open. As I stepped out, he aimed the M-16 at my chest.

"We ain't gonna get any trouble from you, right?"

I held up my hands. "No. No trouble at all."

Tucker gave me a long look and then lowered his gun. He looked back at the other two. "Alright, let's make sure the rest of this place is clear and meet up with the others."

"What about this one?" the teenager asked, pointing at Svelski.

The middle-aged man shrugged. "He looks plenty dead to me."

Tucker took a deep breath and let it out slowly. "Better safe than sorry," he said.

The teenager grinned and swung open the door to Svelski's cell.

Tucker grabbed my shoulder, and we started down the hallway. A single shot rang out behind us.

The other two caught up to us as we stepped through the emergency exit and started down the stairs. I heard scattered gunfire in the distance as we walked through the prison lobby.

"So what the hell's going on out there?" I asked Tucker.

He smiled wryly and stepped in front of me. "Oh, it's hell, alright," he said as he swung the tinted glass doors open.

And then, as I saw the bodies and the chaos and the black plumes of smoke rising into the gray sky as the city burned around us, I understood why they came for me, for a killer on death row. Things had changed now.

And then I remembered something Pastor had said: *"This is the reckoning, people."*

There was no time for right and wrong.

There was no room for good and evil.

There was simply war, a war between the living and the dead.

And the dead were winning.

The living needed every man they could get.

EXISTENCE

John Hubbard

What you are about to read is real. It really happened, or in my case, it is really happening. Most stories have the benefit of a controlled plot, along with a beginning and an end. My story does not. I have no idea how it all began and there is no end . . . yet. In that aspect, you may view what you are about to read as an episode or chapter or an incident report. But it is real. Of that I am certain. Here is my hell.

My wife and three-year-old son left for the Piggly Wiggly at 3 PM. Three hours later, when my family still had not returned, I got out of bed and walked into the kitchen. I tried calling Linda's cell phone, but a cold, digital voice told me that all the circuits were busy. It wasn't like Linda to take so long. Tyler would need to eat soon, and if they had decided to go to Linda's parents she definitely would have called because she was in our only car, a 1998 Ford Explorer. I worked from home, as a service manager for Bell South and we didn't really need another car. But at times like this, it could be a minor annoyance to be stuck without transportation.

I hung up the phone and decided to make some coffee. As I ran the water in the sink to fill up the reservoir, I looked out across the yard to the barn. The side door, which hadn't been left open in the three years since my son's birth, was now thrown wide, and the lock was hanging as if someone had pried it off. A barn is no place for a small child; if not seen to, it can turn into a treacherous madhouse of tetanus, splinters and long falls from the hayloft. Linda and I decided from day one that the barn would remain locked when not in use. And not four hours ago, I had locked the barn myself.

We live on one hundred and seventy acres in southern Georgia. To someone from New York, this would seem like a small country, but in reality the deep south views a one-hundred-and-seventy-acre farm as a blip. If we had to actually farm the land to survive, we'd go broke in a week. The farm was bought in the late 1800's by my great grandfather. Ever since then, it has been used as a recreational tract for my family. I grew up hunting in the woods and fishing in the seven-acre pond. I inherited the farm in 1991 when my father died, and Linda and I had moved down from Atlanta in 1992 to become transplants. It was only two hours away from the big city by car, but it felt like two centuries away in terms of quality of life. We were happy here. We were safe. We'd never been robbed or bothered, and our nearest neighbors were a half mile down the road. When I saw the barn door open, I knew something was wrong.

I went out to the barn. False bravery or stupidity filled my head. Nobody fucked with my property. The door had actually *not* been jimmied. Rather it looked like something had clawed or chewed its way in. There were sticky, brown and purple splotches on the white paint that looked like plum sauce. Inside, there was nothing but silence. I opened the door wider and reached to the right to switch on the light. Someone grabbed my hand.

"Don't turn it on, John. You'll just attract more of them."

I turned it on anyway, yanking my hand away from the grasp. It was my neighbor Lucious Royal. He went by the moniker "Lucky," which he was anything but. Twice divorced, he lived two farms over on a six-hundred-acre spread he'd inherited from his father. He was broke-ass poor and some judge had given him custody of his two boys, eight-year-old Delmar and fourteen-year-old Chuck. The six hundred acres he lived on had once been twenty-three hundred, but he had sold it off in parcels every few years, like clockwork, so that he'd have enough money to get by. He looked like he had been run over by a tractor.

"Lucky, what the hell happened to you?" I asked. "And why are you in my barn?"

"John," he said, "I killed a zombie. Just like in the movies. The un-fucking-dead."

I would have figured him to be drunk or on drugs as soon as he said *zombie*, but you should have seen him. His shirt was ripped down the front, and part of his scalp was torn. His left ear was completely gone. The blood covering his head had mostly congealed into the consistency of blackberry jam. He was leaning up against the wall, wheezing, and I could tell he was scared to death. Oh yeah, he was carrying a shotgun as well.

"John," he repeated, uttering my name like it pained him to talk, "I chased one in here. All the way down from my place. I thought it was some peeping tom. Saw him looking in my living room window. Ran outside with the shotgun, but the fucker just stood there. Circling out of the light. I shot up in the air to spook him, and he ran out the drive and headed this way. He tore up your door like a hot knife thru butter. Oh god, man. This is fucked. I killed it John. You understand? I killed a zombie. But it ain't just a zombie. It's a fucking Dietrich Dalrymple zombie."

Dietrich Dalrymple was a peculiar man who still lived with his parents. In his late 30's, he was heavy but not obese, and he worked for Talbot County as a middle school bus driver. If the undead were really taking over rural southern Georgia, they couldn't have picked a worse candidate to propagate their species.

"Lucky, did you shoot Dietrich the bus driver? What exactly are you saying?"

"He's dead John. I shot him. He's in the corner of the barn. He's not Dietrich anymore. Don't get too close to him."

I went forward, through the small office area, into the main barn. The halogens were still warming up, but there was enough light to see that there was, or what appeared to be, a body in the corner of my barn. I grabbed the rusty pitchfork that was hanging on a hook. I held it in front of me as I approached the prone figure.

It was Dietrich all right, or what had once been Dietrich. He/it was unmoving. The whole body splayed out on the floor like it had fallen out of an airplane and had just struck earth. The skin, where I could see it, was covered in pustules like the worst type of textbook acne. The hands, forearms, neck and face were infested with chicken-pox-type lesions that oozed what looked to be pus mixed with Vaseline. The body looked wet, like some kind of plague or Ebola victim. I was staring at this monstrosity for a few seconds when his/its eyes opened and turned to look at me.

The pupils were dilated and fixed. They eclipsed the entire iris. It was like looking into the soulless depths of a black hole. No beginning or end. Just the hollow nothingness like the depths of space. What had once been a bus driver pushed himself up on infected arms and grinned:

"Hey, John boy. How's it hanging?"

When he spoke, I could see pieces of what could only have been Lucky Royal's ear and scalp. They hung in shreds, stuck between Dietrich's teeth like moist pieces of a mango. He looked like a sloppy eater at some gruesome deep-south barbecue festival.

"Stay the fuck put, Dietrich. Don't move. I don't know what the hell is going on with you and Lucky, but you just stay down for a minute."

As I spoke, he stood up not six feet away. I could see burn marks in his torso. Lucky must have got him good with the shotgun from close range. Also, his legs were ruined. He stood on splintered bone. His right foot and sneaker were behind him against the wall, disconnected from his leg. His left leg had holes in the shinbone and a good chunk missing from the knee. All behind him, the barn wall was splintered and gouged. Lucky had really let him have it. How I could have slept through this melee was beyond me. But what was even more fucked up was how this goddamned *thing* was standing up. It should have been dead.

Dietrich walked towards me, grinning with pieces of my neighbor stuck between the teeth of his lower jaw. It was a ventriloquist dummy's grin, insincere and vacant. I wanted to stick him with the pitchfork but was worried that the fork might stick in the body and then I'd be defenseless. Instead, I lowered my shoulder and slammed into him. Because of his wasted legs, he toppled over easily and fell where he had lain before.

"You can knock me over, John, but you'll never stop all of us. I'll be up again sooner or later."

I was betting on sooner. I backed out of the main barn into the office. I wanted to go back and get Lucky's shotgun in case that thing came at me again. When I stepped into the room, I was met with a scene from some kind of George Romero movie. Lucky's youngest son Delmar was in the office too. He was covered with the same type of rotten complexion that Dietrich had been infected with. Delmar was down on his hands and knees, tearing the meaty part of his daddy's hip off with his mouth. He was feasting on Lucky's thigh meat like it was a piece of KFC. He snarled at me, his young face covered with gore.

"Mine," he said.

I freaked at that point. This was no unexplainable altercation between neighbor and local bus driver. This was an actual type of Zombie occurrence. It didn't matter whether or not the infected were actually the walking dead or victims of some type of horrific disease. They were here, and they ate the living.

I stabbed at Delmar as fast as I could. I caught him vertically through the neck and collarbone area and pinned him against the barn. The eight year old screamed. He seemed more angry than hurt as he tore at the prongs, trying desperately to unstick the fork from the wood behind him. I looked down at Lucky. In my unprofessional opinion, he wasn't going to make it. In fact, his skin was already turning more gruesome near his missing ear and scalp. It was red and swollen with lesions, which grew upward and caused the skin to slough away and split. He was beginning to change.

I ran from the barn back towards the cabin. Before I climbed up the steps, I caught a glimpse of a slight glow down the driveway, towards the road. I couldn't actually see a light because of the trees, but there was a glow where there should have only been darkness. I decided to sprint down the driveway and see what it was. I'm not sure why I didn't return directly to the cabin, but I didn't and I'll never forgive myself.

I ran past the pond on my right. Its floating dock bobbed out in the middle. Underneath the half moon, the water looked like spilled blood, cold and vacant. After the pond, the drive snaked through a patch of woods for about six hundred yards. It wasn't any quieter than any other normal night. I could hear frogs and owls and other night sounds.

At the head of the driveway, I saw what I had feared: our family car, half in the road, half in the drive, engine off, headlights on. I went to the driver's-side door and just stared. Linda was dead. Her body was in the road, only one arm remained in the driver's seat, detached from her torso, still gripping the bottle of mace on her key chain. I recognized her clothes and her engagement ring. I knew it was my wife, even though her head was missing. Her body had been picked at. Some thing, or a group of things, had feasted on my wife's body. There were bloody prints all over the hood and the driver's side of the car. Some looked to still be wet, and some looked to be dry and solidifying. I stumbled towards the trunk of the car and tried to throw up. I hadn't eaten since breakfast, so my tank was a little empty. All the fear and uncertainty came out of me in the form of mucus, saliva and dry heaves.

Once I had gained my bearings a little, I looked in the back of the car. Tyler was not in his baby seat. The nylon straps that had once held him safe had been severed. They looked like rats had chewed threw them. My baby was gone.

My baby was gone.

I had to make some decisions. Should I take the car and go for help, or go back to the house, lock up and call for the police? Would the police even come? Should I look for Tyler? Oh god, I couldn't decide. While contemplating, I heard a noise a few feet away, behind me, in the woods. It sounded like somebody or something had shifted from one foot to the other. I was being watched.

"Da Da?" the voice came.

I can't tell you how hopeful I was. It was my boy. Alive and well.

"Tyler, is that you? It's Da Da."

"Da Da." A statement. No longer a question.

I could make out his little form about six feet in front of me, his shadow a small blotch, slightly darker than the surrounding area. I took a step to him, arms outstretched, and that's when it came.

"Da Da!" it screamed as it launched itself at my leg.

The thing that had once been my son latched onto my leg, below the ankle. It sank its little teeth into my shin and started to chew. It didn't hurt at first, I was too shocked. I felt the force of the attack but didn't really grasp the entire situation until the little abomination began to slurp.

I kicked it loose, grabbed it, and flung it onto the hood of the car. It looked at me, the same blank eyes I had seen on Dietrich. Tyler's body wasn't in bad shape. I could see no wounds clearly. His skin, however, was horrific. Like the others, he almost resembled a burn victim dipped in oil. He was rotting. He was no longer my son. I turned and ran for the cabin.

In the background, I heard the singsong voice of a little boy: "Da Da, let's play."

As I came back to the front of the cabin and climbed the stairs to the back door, I sensed shapes to my right. I turned, door half open, and saw Lucky and his son Delmar, rubbing his shoulder where I had stuck him, standing in the glow of the bug light at the far end of the porch.

"Howdy neighbor," Lucky said. Delmar stood next to him silently, glaring at me hungrily. "Care to join us for a stroll?"

The skin over their entire bodies was ruined. Their features seemed to be melting off them. They were becoming walking and talking bodies of putrefaction and gore.

"Stay the fuck away, Lucky." I was halfway in the door, defenseless, but I couldn't tear my eyes away from the surreal pair. At this moment, another form materialized from the barn. It was, of course, the zombie version of Dietrich Dalrymple.

"We won't be coming any closer, John Boy. Don't need to. You got the fever already." He nodded his head downwards, towards my raw-looking leg. "We'll just wait out here, enjoying the night. You'll be joining us soon enough."

I left them there, standing in my yard, Dietrich propped up against my barn on his ruined, splintered femurs, Lucky and Delmar standing side by side, staring blankly towards nothing at all. I backed into the house and locked the door. I climbed the stairs to my bedroom and locked the door.

I sat on the bed. My leg was hurting, but there was nothing I could do. I'm not a doctor, and a nice cleansing bubble bath didn't feel like the right thing to do at that moment. I looked at the shin in horror. It had started to fester. A pus-like material was bubbling out of my leg like rancid EZ Cheeze. The skin around the teeth marks was starting to swell, and what looked like varicose veins, or spider veins, had encircled the infected area.

It was starting.

I was physically and emotionally drained, yet I was getting hungry. I couldn't exactly put my finger on what I was craving, but I was becoming more ravenous by the moment. My mouth was dry, and I caught myself just staring off into space. If this was just like the movies, I was probably changing already. In fact, now I know that I was definitely changing. Or more honestly that I *am* changing as I speak.

I thought of the gun in the closet, the razors underneath the bathroom sink, even the assorted pills that Linda and I had lying around in the bathroom closet. But was suicide the answer? I didn't think so, and I still don't. I don't think it would matter. I would probably still rise again as one of those things.

Even now, I can feel the effect of what Dietrich called *the fever*. Its tendrils, hot and pulsating, massage my brain like small epileptic signals. It hurts, but the pain is hypnotic. I go away for moments at a time. When I come back to myself, I am scared but also satisfied. I fear that, sometime soon, I will not come back to myself at all. Maybe it isn't so bad. But I know it is. Deep down, I know.

I am scared to death of what lurks outside in the night. I want it all to go away. I can't stand another encounter with those things. But what I am even more scared of is that, at any moment, I may walk downstairs, on something other than my own free will, unlock the kitchen door, and invite the darkness into me and become one with my nightmare.

I will try to exist as myself for a little while longer, for as long as I can, until the fever takes me. But I will lose in the end. . . . You all will.

GRAVEYARD SLOT

Cavan Scott

Hilda settled herself into her favorite comfy chair. It had been a long day. Gingerly, she flexed the swollen toes beneath her slippers, flinching at the sharp pain of cramped muscle. She had been longing for this sit down all day. In the seat beside her, Bert grunted and scrabbled for the remote control.

"Oh Bert," Hilda croaked. "How's about a cup of tea?"

"You know where the kitchen is," came the gruff reply. "I'll have a coffee."

"Really Bert, I've been on my feet for hours! Is it too much to ask—"

"Yes," Bert cut her off. "At the moment it is."

"Well, that's charming it is. I slave all day . . ."

The TV blared on, kicking in at that volume only old folk can stand: somewhere between deafening and the sound of Armageddon.

"Sorry." Bert grinned, displaying a row of yellowing, ragged teeth. "Can't hear you. You'll have to speak up!"

The din from the set smothered Hilda's most unladylike response. Moaning loudly to her unsympathetic audience, she struggled back to her feet, feeling her back creak ominously as she did. Before turning for the kitchen, she glanced over half-moon glasses at the television screen.

"Oh Bert, you're not watching *that* show are you."

Bert ignored her, transfixed by the boob-tube.

"It's disgusting, that's what it is."

"What're you saying now woman?"

"Disgusting! You should know better at your age."

Bert dismissed her with a wave of his liver-spotted hand. "Ah, what do you know? It's the best thing on the box by miles. All the guys down the Retreat watch it. Now, leave me in peace, will you?"

Hilda's eyes rolled heavenward as she shuffled from the room, just as the first blood of the episode speckled the screen.

"Hey-hey, they've got themselves a gusher!" Bert cried excitingly before shouting over his shoulder to his wife. "Hilda, don't forget to put sugar in mine."

Sarah's tongue explored the inside of her mouth. She had no idea why this was important (after all she had bigger concerns than her dental plan), but somehow the action seemed to make sense. Start small and work up. If you can work out what's broken in there, you can move bone by bone through your ravished body, cataloguing every fracture and tear. The tip of her tongue met recently ripped gum. One, two . . . God, three teeth lost. No wonder her mouth tasted like she'd been gargling with Type O. No time to worry about what had happened to the missing molars, though. Nope, now she had to work on bigger problems. Like how to open her eyes.

The harsh light streaming from the hole above singed her retina as she cautiously took her first glance at her new world. Up there, in the realm of birdsong and lush fresh grass, the day was beginning to wane. Down here, in the cavern she now occupied, darkness was swarming in from every corner. Ignoring her own cry as she carefully pushed herself up, she took in her surroundings. Her arm complained as she grunted into a sitting position, but at least it wasn't the sharp agony of bone grating bone. She remembered the harsh punishment from deep within her flesh when she'd tumbled from the climbing frame as a kid. This was nothing like it. She was bruised, sure, but nothing seemed to have snapped. Miracles *do* happen, she thought grimly as she gazed up to the rocky ceiling. There was no worried father to haul her into his arms this time, and she'd sure as hell fallen from more than just a climbing frame. The yawning gash in the rock above must have been fifteen feet up or thereabouts.

As she rubbed her pounding arm, Sarah tried to piece it all together. She had been walking. Yeah, that was it. But where? Oh, of course. Back from seeing Tony. Back from their—what was a nice way of putting it—their rendezvous. Just walking through the fields at the bottom of old Owen's farm when . . .

The ground. That had been it. The ground beneath her feet had been there one minute and gone the next. She remembered falling and then . . . nothing. The lump on her head was enough to inform her why the rest was a little hazy.

But where was she? Her eyes narrowed as she peered into the skin-chilling gloom beyond the shard of light that spotlighted her battered and bloody form.

"Well done, Sarah," she said aloud. "What a marvelous hole you've discovered."

Around her, cavern walls rose to the remnants of her entrance. They were ragged, but somehow they looked unnatural. Whatever this place was, it was manmade. A mine? At least that would explain why the ground had swallowed her whole. She'd grown up with stories of folk tumbling into old shafts, weakened by the onslaught of time. Never thought she'd end up as one of those tales herself.

Her ankle smarted, but it held as she finally got to her feet, brushing crud off her jeans. Yeah, manmade for sure. The old wooden boxes in the corner of the cave proved that at least. Limping slightly, she moved over to them. Decades of dust kicked up as she lifted one of the warped lids. Empty.

Sarah wasn't sure what she'd expected to find. Shovels. Picks maybe. Anything that would help her out of here. There was no point in shouting for assistance. She'd been all alone as she'd tramped through the long grass. That was the whole point. "No one can risk seeing us together," Tony had explained one day, as if speaking to a child. "If she found out . . ."

Sarah hated when he talked to her like that. She wasn't stupid. Well, she was stupid enough to be fooling around with him, but . . .

This wasn't helping. There was an escape to be had. Sarah started to run through the alternatives.

Plan A: Climb back out.

This of course could lead to a whole lot of slipping and dashing out one's brains on the rocks beneath. Nope, she'd been lucky enough to keep her grey matter in her skull thus far; there was no need to tempt fate. So then, back to the proverbial drawing board.

Plan B: Wander into the dark corridors that led off from the cavern and try to find an exit.

Sarah stared at the nearest doorway, which had been clouded before her eyes had adjusted to the shade. The pitch-black murkiness stared back. She'd be venturing into the unknown, blundering around blind until she either tumbled down a pothole to dash the aforementioned brain, or until she walked into a very hard and immovable dead-end.

Not the best of options. Next?

Plan C: Begin digging through the wall with a nail file until she tunneled her way to freedom.

Promising. That could work. If she were indeed the female equivalent of James Bond and actually possessed a nail file. Absently, Sarah patted her pockets. Something bulged against her backside. What was this? Of course. Her wonderful cheap lighter, bought at the drug store for a sneaky post-coital cigarette. Sordid affairs be praised. At least something about her grubby little encounter with Tony would prove beneficial today. The flame burst from the red plastic at one flick of the dial. She had fire, and where there was fire, there was light. No darker than dark corridors to traverse any more. Plan B was open for modification and possible success. Granted she could still get lost in a labyrinth of creaking, twisted passages, but hey, it was worth a shot. If Tony hadn't had swiped the last of her Marlboros, she would have had a victory smoke to celebrate her impending salvation. Ah well, there was no more time to lose. She'd better get moving before—

The noise was deafening in the confines of the cave. Sarah froze, hair standing to attention from the bottom of her spine to the nape of her neck. Someone else was down here. For a second, she stood there, ears straining for any other signs of life. There was nothing. What had it been? Could a gust of wind have knocked something over? It had sounded like a billy-can or something hitting the deck. If it had been a breeze, she should head in that direction; the wind must have come from somewhere. But what if it wasn't a breeze? What if a human hand had brushed by the can? She hadn't considered the other forms of danger that could be lurking in the shadows. Someone might be living down here, someone who wouldn't take too kindly to her little visit. And what if it wasn't even human? Had there been stories of wild animals living down here after the miners had moved out? She was sure she could recall something. Wolves? Was that it? Or bears? Good god, what would she do if she came face to face with a grizzled grizzly down here? Have both her arms pulled off and her skull split open by its maw, of course.

Still there was nothing. Not a howl nor a growl. Just silence.

"Hello? Is anyone there?"

She almost jumped at the sudden voice until she realized it was her own. What the hell did she think she was doing? She might as well be yelling out 'Hello there. Slightly scuffed thirty-one-year-old woman here, ready for you to ravish / maul / break into little pieces (delete as appropriate).' As her echo ricocheted from the cavern walls, she relaxed. There was obviously no one else down here. In fact, if there was, it wouldn't probably be such a bad thing. They could at least point her in the right direction.

But there was no need to take unreasonable risks. Shivering slightly in the chill, Sarah spun on her sneakered heel and strode purposely in the opposite direction. Laughing slightly at her own nerves, she called out to the phantom noise.

"Catch you later, Mr. Lonely Hermit of the Mines. Bye, rabid wolf. Sorry to be an inconv—"

The hand that clasped around her mouth tasted of stale sweat and earth.

Hilda slammed the mug of coffee beside her husband, who did nothing except fart a thanks back at her. Forty-seven years of marriage, she thought, and this is what you end up with. At least before he retired he was out from under her feet every day. At least she never had to watch trash like this back then.

"Isn't there anything else on, Bert?" she ventured, knowing fully well what the answer would be. "That Dick Van-Dyke show you like is on the other side."

Bert slurped his java.

"You never used to miss an episode of that."

"Enough of the nagging," Bert snapped. "I haven't watched that show for years, and you know it. A load of old crap watched by old people in old people's homes."

Well, we could arrange to have you shipped to one so you could tune in, Hilda thought to herself, smiling at the wickedness of the idea.

"Now, we're watching this, and that's that."

Hilda sighed in defeat as she poked around her chair for her knitting needles.

Her training kicked in as soon as the arms snaked around her. Sarah could hear her instructor even now: "If you choose to fight back, girls, you have to commit one hundred percent and be as fierce as possible. Believe in yourself and channel your fear into anger." Fear was something she seemed to have with lashings to spare today, so channeling it should prove no problem. With a shout, she brought her heel down hard on the arch of her attacker's foot, satisfied to hear his surprised grunt. Then her elbow came back, ploughing into his gut. The second she felt his grip loosen, she turned, grabbing his arm as she spun. His body crashed to the floor, where it lay still for a second before Sarah buried her toe in his groin. Okay, so that wasn't particularly necessary, but *god*, did it feel good. Now if she'd remembered her instructor correctly, she should have been making for the hills about now, but the sight of her attacker made her pause.

"Jeez, lady," he whined. "There was no need for that."

"Wasn't there?" she shot back angrily.

The lad couldn't be more than eighteen. He'd obviously been down here for a few days. His hair was matted, and his skin was smeared with grime. Perhaps he'd fallen through the weak earth, too. Who knew? This wasn't the time to find out, though. She was far too irate for that.

"Oh I'm sorry," Sarah said. "I thought you'd crept up behind me and shoved your greasy palm over my mouth. Now where I come from, that's reason enough."

The kid groaned as he began to lower his knees from his chest. Maybe she hadn't needed to kick him that hard.

"I was just trying to shut you up, that's all."

"Shut me up? What the hell are you talking about? Why should you care if I shout the roof down? And what are you doing down here anyway, you little pervert?"

Again, that last comment was probably unnecessary. Who said he was a pervert? In the cold light from above, he looked normal enough, a little on the skinny side, but an average Joe for sure. Still, it had added the right effect. And there was nothing that said he *wasn't* some kind of deviant, which meant a kick in the sacks was just desserts.

Carefully, he swung his legs around and got to his feet, slightly hunched from the dull thud that was no doubt throbbing through his nether regions.

"For the same reason as you, of course," he spat. "Why would anyone be down here?"

"A good question!"

"And as for why I wanted to shut you up," the boy replied, "I didn't want you to alert them to our presence."

Sarah shook her head in frustration and confusion. Could today get any worse? *They?* Who are you talking about, kid?"

The boy's lanky arm came up as his face fell. Slowly, not really wanting to see what was behind her, Sarah turned in the direction of his gesture.

"Them," he intoned, pointed at the shuffling zombies that glared at them from the shadows.

No one knew what caused the outbreak. Some said it was radiation. Some said it was a crashed meteor affecting the earth. Some said it was the wrath of God. But whatever it was, the dead had decided that they'd spent enough time rotting in their graves and had clawed their way to the surface. At first, the wild stories of zombies had been dismissed as urban legends, but soon there were too many of them to belittle. In panic, the populace fled from the cities, leaving the manmade canyons to the undead. The ghouls squabbled over the flesh of those idiots who refused to leave their homes or shops, and the streets quite literally became a ghost town. Sarah remembered her elder brothers boasting that they had driven into town one day to play chicken with the zoms, but she knew they were full of bullshit. There was no way they'd go anywhere near the ghouls. They'd have pissed their pants just thinking about it.

And as soon as it began, the crisis was over. Reports of new resurrections dwindled over time, and army helicopters had napalmed the infested cities. The President had said it was the only way, and they'd believed him. Even if they hadn't, the bombs did the trick. The zoms were scorched from the face of the earth, and the dead stayed dead. It didn't stop people from decapitating anyone who passed away, of course, but there was nothing wrong in playing it safe. Her brothers had tried to scare her by describing how Dad had sliced off Grandpa's head with a shovel when a heart attack had finished the old soul. But they needn't have bothered. She'd been terrified enough back then. They all were. But that was then, as the old saying went. In twenty years, there hadn't been a single resurrection as far as she knew. Life had returned to normal. There were no more zombies.

"Shit."

Sarah could have hoped for a more sophisticated comment to slip past her suddenly dry lips, but it was not to be. Stunned by what her own eyes were seeing, she tried again.

"Shit."

Nope, all intelligent dialogue had left the building, leaving the basics of vocabulary behind. And could you blame her? No more zombies. The anchormen had promised, grim-faced but with an air of victory on the six o'clock news. Every reanimated corpse had been destroyed. People could return to the burnt husks of their homes and start again. The monsters weren't coming back. Not this time.

"Shit."

The glassy stare of zombie number one proved that they were liars. The maggots in the cheek of zombie number two screamed that the monsters *had* come back. The hungry groan that escaped from their ragged throats hinted that this wasn't the time for starting anew. Instead, it was time for running, screaming, dying.

Never taking her eyes off the rotting duo, Sarah asked, "What's your name, kid?"

"What?"

"I said *what's your name?*"

"Tim."

"Tim. Are you as petrified as me right now?" She didn't bother to look for the nod of his head. "Okay, well this is what I'm going to suggest . . ."

Zombie number one took the first tentative step forward, slipping slightly on some loose soil. It stumbled with a snarl, but never took its eyes off the prize.

"In a second, when the moment is right . . ."

Zombie number two cocked its head at the sound of Sarah's voice, a stream of bloody drool spilling from the hole where its bottom jaw had once sat.

". . . we run for our lives. Is that clear?"

"Wow, great plan. Must have taken a lot of thought!"

Sarah's shot the kid a withering look. Was this really the time for sarcasm?

Zombie number one lurched forward, its arms stretching out. If she had not known that it wanted to chow down on her innards, Sarah would have found such an uneven gait hilarious. But there was nothing laughable about their situation. She'd seen what these bastards could do. Images of Pete flashed into her mind, lying there as the schoolgirl zombie plucked another intestine from a hole in his belly.

"Well, Einstein, unless you've got a better scheme hidden up your sleeve, I suggest you shut the—"

Zombie number two bellowed, barging number one out of the way as it steamrolled forward. If she'd had the chance, Sarah would have cursed herself for believing the old wives' tale that these things could only blunder along at a snail's pace. Olympic gold it wasn't, but the bitch sure could move. As the banshee lurched closer, filling the chamber with its vile stench, Sarah grabbed Tim's arm.

"Come on."

Tim didn't answer but stood his ground. As Sarah gawped in horror, the creature was suddenly upon him, pushing the lad to the floor. His hand flashed up and closed tightly around its neck, fingers punching through paper-thin skin and tissue. Sarah gagged as inky black ooze dripped down his arm and speckled his face, but she wasn't about to watch an innocent kid get eaten alive. Not again. Not like Pete.

Pushing aside her revulsion, she jumped forward, grabbing the ghoul by its shoulders. The bone within the loose flesh shifted beneath her hands as she yanked it off Tim. The zombie wailed, flailing as Sarah lost her footing and pulled it with her to the floor. Ignoring the complaints of her already bruised body, she shoved the corpse aside and rolled free, avoiding the clutching arms as the creature twisted to ensnare her. A booted foot slammed down on its back as Sarah's head snapped up. Tim stood over them, pinning the horror down as he swung the gun up in his hand and cracked off a single shot. Thick, black brain matter spurted across the cavern floor. The zombie immediately fell still beneath his weight.

"What the hell . . ." Sarah began before her eyes welled with renewed terror.

Zombie number one's hand came down like a vice on Tim's shoulder, the kid gasping with a sudden cocktail of surprise, anger, and fear. It was over too soon. Rancid teeth tore through the side of his neck, muscle shredding as the zombie pulled the bite free. Tim twisted, one hand shooting up to the hemorrhaging wound while the other swung around to take aim. The gun's report echoed around the cave as the bullet tore through the creature's shoulder. It stumbled back a couple steps before righting itself, gore tumbling from its lolling mouth. The second shot took off the top of its head. White eyes glared with frustrating desire before the putrid frame crashed to the floor.

For a moment, they stood there in silence, staring at the horrific duo sprawled at their feet. Then Tim's knees gave out, and he crashed into the ooze-soaked floor with a sigh.

Bert smacked his lips together. "How about some supper?"
Hilda sniffed in annoyance. "Bert, I've only just sat down."
"And?"
"And you know where the kitchen is."
Bert grunted as he considered this for a second. Finally, he settled back into his chair. Maybe he wasn't so peckish after all.

Sarah paced back and forth as Tim stirred. This wasn't good. This wasn't good at all.
"And what the hell was that?" she asked.
"Excuse me?"
Sarah crossed her arms and glared at him. "Well, one minute we're getting ready to take to the hills, and the next you're popping caps in undead ass."
Tim flinched as he sat up, tenderly feeling the raw wound. His head sank forward, defeated, blood trickling through grime-encrusted fingers. "It doesn't matter any more," he muttered.
"It doesn't matter? *Doesn't matter?* Didn't you think to mention the fact that you were—what's the appropriate phrase? Ah yes, 'packing heat'?" Wrinkling her nose, she glanced down at the gun where Tim had dropped it. "Where'd you get it from anyway?"
"What are you, lady? My social worker?"
"Well, excuse me for not liking guns. It's not unusual, you know. I just have a little tiny problem with the way they go bang just before people splatter all over the wall."
"You didn't seem to mind when I was shelling zoms."
"That's not the point," she snapped back, unable to deliver a wittier response to such a matter-of-fact observation.
Tim's fading eyes glared back at her. "Isn't it?"
Stalemate.
Sarah blew out a long, slow breath. What were they doing bickering like a couple of kids in the playground? They had more important things to worry about. Like the fact that a chunk of Tim's flesh had ended up on a zom's taste buds. That was a situation that demanded action. Once again, she eyed the pistol. As if he could read her thoughts, Tim suddenly piped up.

"Ruger P-85. 9mm short-recoil double-action semi-automatic. Introduced during the '80s. 15-round magazine. 4.5 inch barrel. Fixed sights."

Whoa! Had the kid swallowed a gun catalogue?

"I'm impressed. You sure as hell know your firearms."

Tim shrugged, spilling another dark stream from his neck. He seemed to have forgotten the pain, the color waning from his face by the second. It wouldn't be long now.

"Not really. Never even held one before the training day. Just remembered wh . . ." He broke off, swaying slightly.

Sarah started to move stealthily toward the fallen weapon.

"I just remembered what they told me."

"Who told you, Tim?" She had to keep him talking. "Who gave you the gun?"

Tim coughed, splattering foul sludge against his own knees.

"The producers, of course. Who do you think?"

"Ha-ha!" Bert cried. "Did you see that, Hilda? The lad's done for, good and proper."

Hilda tutted, not taking her eyes away from her knitting needles. Bert had changed since they'd subscribed to that damned cable channel.

"Zom TV!" the leaflet had exclaimed. "The only channel to show you what every other station is too scared to broadcast!"

Typical yanks, she'd thought. Hadn't they seen enough horror in their lifetime without glorifying it on the box? But Bert couldn't get enough. And if he wasn't watching the stupid program—*Graveyard Slot*, or whatever it was called—he was lapping up what the papers were saying about the idiots who were playing the game.

No, it wasn't her idea of entertainment. She'd rather listen to *Parky* on Radio 2.

Hilda swore as she dropped a stitch.

"Yup," Bert muttered beside her. "He's a goner that one. Won't be long before he's a zom!"

Sarah let her head fall back against the cold roughness of the stone wall. Her brain had heard what Tim had said, but somehow couldn't compute anything so stupid. He had to be lying or delusional. Maybe both.

"Let me get this right . . ."

Tim groaned. "Lady, I'm feeling kinda whoozy here. Can you keep it down?"

No way, buster, Sarah thought. In a minute you'll be just another reanimated cadaver waiting to tuck into a helping of my brains, with a freshly torn spleen on the side. The least you could do is listen to your future lunch.

"Not all the zombies are dead."

"They're all dead, lady. That's the general idea of rising from the grave." His laugh was weak, lacking the energy of the jibe that fueled it.

Sarah didn't bother to fire back a retort. There wasn't time for another infantile argument. "And some moron has been storing them here in this mine . . ."

"Yeah."

". . . for use in some kind of TV show!"

"Top of the class, lady. Top of the class."

Sarah sat there for a second, letting it all sink in. Her eyes inattentively wandered around the chamber, resting on the massive mirrored surface inset into one of the walls. The sun had shifted now, and the light streaming through the hole in the roof had only recently brought it to her attention. For a second, she wondered why anyone would put a mirror in a mine, but her current priority was why someone would flood the same mine with legions of the undead.

"And you," this was the bit that still confused her, "actually volunteered for this?"

A tired and mournful sigh passed over Tim's parched lips. "They offered us money, okay? A million bucks to spend a week down here."

"With those things."

"Yeah, with those things. I realize to a genius like yourself such a course of action may seem dumb, but a million bucks, lady! Imagine that. They armed us to the teeth and set us out here."

In the distance, the plaintive wail of their deceased neighbors grew. They'd picked up the scent.

"You know the funny thing, lady? I really thought I'd make it. I've always grown up on the bad side of the track. Had to fight for everything I ever owned. I thought this would be a walk in the park compared to what I've got through before."

The uncanny whine became louder still. Sarah's hand rested on the gun that lay by her side. She still couldn't take it in. People actually watched this. They sat with their TV dinners and gawped as contestants were torn apart. Who were the ghouls here? The shuffling, rotten husks, or the producers pointing their cameras at the action and watching the ratings roll in. Bastards.

Suddenly it clicked.

"They're behind there, aren't they Tim?"

She may have looked calm as she pointed to the glass, but inside she was reaching boiling point. Tim may have asked for this, but she hadn't. What had started as a pleasant day of infidelity and heartache had ended in a trip to hell and back. She didn't want the prize money. She just wanted out.

Tim didn't answer. He was babbling now, his fevered brain finally giving up the ghost.

"It's the mirror. That's where they are. Watching us right now."

Something in the next chamber cried out as it trudged forwards.

"Don't care anymore. Gonna be one soon anyway."

"Shut up Tim." Sarah began pulling herself to her feet.

"Gonna be a zom. Gonna want to eat."

"Shut the fuck up!"

"And you're gonna be one too."

"Now I *know* you're crazy, kid. There's no way I'm going to let one of those things get within three feet of me. No, I'm going to get out of here alive and then take this sick little operation to the cleaners. They're going to regret the day I tumbled into their set."

Tim giggled childishly. It would be the last time he would ever laugh. "Big talk from someone who's already infected, lady. Don't believe me? Then look at your hands."

Brow furrowed, Sarah glanced down at her battered palms. The blood from her fall had clogged into tiny black rivulets across her skin. She heard the last rattle of breath slip from Tim's ravaged lungs and saw the shambling shadows of the zombies out of the corner of her eyes, but couldn't respond to either. She was recalling the shoulders of the thrashing creature she'd wrestled earlier, the mush of infected blood erupting from the brittle skin and washing over her own hands, seeping into every cut and graze.

Beside her, Tim's corpse twitched as dead muscles strained to move.

Christopher Lock snatched up the telephone at the first ring. "Lock here." His jaw tightened as he listened carefully. "Are you sure?"

Whoever was at the other end of the line obviously was.

"Okay, go to commercial break."

He slammed the receiver back down on its cradle.

"Bad news?" ventured the plump Asian girl by his side. Chris just stared through the one-way mirror at Sarah as she, in turn, stared at her hands.

"We have to try and get her out of there. The public's going crazy—the website forums have gone nuts apparently—but the suits are worried. She never signed a disclaimer. If she's injured, or infected . . ."

"I don't think there's much *if* about it!"

"Exactly. Her family could have us up against the wall by the end of the show. *Graveyard Slot* will be axed sooner that you can say *Baywatch Nights*." Chris massaged the bridge of his nose. "Lynda, you'd better phone security. Get them to round up the remaining contestants. How many have we got left?"

The girl checked her PDA.

"Three: Karl Owen, Richard Jacques and Laura Delaney."

"Okay, show's over. Let's get them out."

Defeated, the producer turned to leave, patting the cameramen on the shoulder as he passed. It was going to be a long night. Heads would roll, and he guessed his would be the first on the block.

"Er, Chris?"

He needed a coffee. Or maybe something stronger.

"Not now, Lynda. Just get it done."

"I know, Chris, but I think you'd better see this."

Sarah's knees felt like they were filling up with Jell-o. Beside her, the creature that used to be Tim wavered on the spot, but she knew it wouldn't attack. Zom's never struck one of their own. What was the point? Why would they want to chew through carrion? There was no pleasure in that.

She could sense the newcomers behind her, drawing closer.

"Wait for it, guys," she called over her shoulder to her mephitic brothers. "I'm about to serve up a peach of a feast."

Her vision began to blur as she raised the gun towards the mirror. They wanted action. She'd give 'em action all right. More action than they knew what to do with.

"Can you hear me behind there?" she yelled. Tim's remains cocked its head. "I'd just like to thank you for proving to me that my life could actually get worse. You see, I was having a pretty guilty and self-loathing time before all this, but I think that, in a few hours time, my little fling will seem like small fry compared to the unquenchable lust for human flesh. Not that I'll care by then. In fact, if I am going to become of them . . ."

She flicked her mousy hair in the direction of the zombies.

". . . then I hope I choose your brains for supping."

Her stomach cramped, adding to the tears that ran down her mottled cheeks. It was getting harder to breathe too, but as long as she had breath she'd tell these cocks what she thought of them.

"But I guess you think you're safe in there, don't you? Never thought anyone would turn one of your pop-guns back on you, eh?"

The zombies were beside her now, flanking her in her blind face off. Of course they had no idea who she was addressing, but the sheer anger in her voice was exciting them. Something was happening. They didn't know what, but they wanted part of it.

"Well, my friends," Sarah continued, fighting the nausea that threatened to overcome her, "You never reckoned on me dropping by. Big mistake. *Huge* mistake. If you ask me, it's about time you stepped on this side of the cameras."

Her first bullet ploughed into the mirror.

The cameraman had already fled his post. Christopher cursed under his breath. Damn them from taking him off-air. This was first class TV, the stuff of legends. And now no one would see it. Lynda shifted uncomfortably.

"Are you sure that glass will hold?" she whimpered as Sarah fired another slug into the shield between them and the hungry zombies. Cobwebbing cracks snaked from the impact points. The creatures' increasing snarls rumbled through the speaker system.

Chris shrugged arrogantly. "So I believe." He peered through the mirror, his arms folded over his chest. "My god, Lynda. Look at her. You can almost see the poor girl fighting the change. It's fascinating."

A third bullet smacked into the glass, which shifted in its frame.

"Absolutely fascinating."

Sarah cursed the glass. She should have guessed. No one in their right minds would lock them down here with the likes of them—with the likes of us, she corrected herself—without taking precautions. Was it worth wasting any more ammo? There was only one other use for it now, and Sarah was trying her hardest not to think about that option.

Tim lurched forward, its hand raised to the glass. Dead fingers probed the cracks, cutting themselves painlessly against the sharp edges. Then slowly, purposefully, it pushed its face against the mirror. What the hell was it doing? Surely in death, Tim hadn't suddenly become the vainest of all zombies, obsessed with its own reflection?

No. The realization of what it was doing hit Sarah so hard she nearly swooned: it was smelling what stood behind the scarred glass. It had picked up the odor of fresh human flesh. And if Tim had twigged what was going on, then it wouldn't take long for her esurient companions to do the same. A smile played on her lips. It was time to join the pack.

Christopher stood inches away from Tim's face, ogling its unseeing eyes as the other zombies threw themselves at the glass. Startled, Chris jumped back as the pane bulged and twisted under dead weight. Behind the zoms, Sarah grinned like an avenging angel. Slowly, her shaking hand came up, and another bullet smashed into the mirror. With an ear-spitting crack, it finally gave, pouring shards and famished demons into the camera room. Lynda screamed as the glass tore into her skin and eyes, but was silenced by the dull fingernails of the first ghoul scratching at the wounds. She twitched as its jaws tightened around her flabby neck.

The glass crunched under Sarah's feet as she calmly stepped into the room. *What a day*, she thought, as she looked down at Tim, who was happily cracking the producer's head open with Lynda's PDA. Sarah supposed that the man's cries probably sounded terrible, but she couldn't really hear anything anymore, save for that annoying buzz emanating from deep within her pulsating skull. As black dots danced in the corners of her vision, she watched a third zombie pitch its way out of the room to find more tasty morsels. Justice had been done, a bloodied eye for an eye. Slowly, she brought the gun to her temple and stared directly into the lens of the camera. She would have liked to offer some witty one-liner to the millions out there, but her throat had closed, and she'd lost the ability to speak. So instead she just pulled the trigger one last time.

Hilda glanced up from her knitting. "I don't think it's coming back on, dear."

Bert peered in vain as the *Graveyard Slot* logo emblazoned the TV screen. Hilda chuckled.

For a moment, the room was filled with the clackity-clack of her knitting needles and the musak flowing from the set. Bert huffed and reached for the remote.

"I think you're right, woman. Bloody stupid machine."

He shot another look at the screen, as if giving it the chance to show the program again, before jabbing a stocky digit down on the button. Dick Van-Dyke's cheerful face replaced the logo, and Bert settled back into his cushions. "You don't fancy putting the kettle on, do you Hilda?" he asked mindlessly. "I'd kill for a cup of tea."

The Project

Pasquale J. Morrone

The breaking waves shoved his limp body onto the beach. At first Alex thought he was alone, but several minutes later he thought he heard a voice calling out. Maybe it was birds or the splashing of the surf. With the thundering waves that crashed and rumbled into the nearby rocks, it was a wonder he heard anything else.

Farther up the beach lay another survivor. Alex wasn't sure who it was, but it didn't matter. One thing he *was* sure about: he wasn't alone here, wherever here was.

Alex lay there for what seemed like hours, breathing deep and digging his fingers into the wet sand. When the fatigue finally subsided, he was able to rise slowly to his knees and examine his surroundings. Considering that he had just escaped from a crash in a company plane, he realized he was lucky in one instance. Twenty feet away were jagged rocks, which he would have slammed against, crushing his already pained torso had he been that much closer.

As he pulled himself to his feet, the pain in his right shoulder emanated down the arm, numbing his fingers. Nonetheless, he worked his way down the beach toward the figure lying on its belly. Before he was halfway there, his companion rolled over on his back, his chest rising and falling with quick breaths. Alex could now make out the features of his colleague, Marshal, and he dropped back down to his knees, cupping the aching shoulder with his left hand. Once again he looked around; fear, pain, and bewilderment took turns at distorting his features.

As far as he could tell, the island was small. Several hundred feet of sand shoreline encompassed a bevy of dense trees and thick foliage, which in turn surrounded a mountain of black rock. Alex turned his attention back to the man on the beach; once again he picked himself up, wincing as he staggered to him.

"Marshal, are you okay?"

The other man remained silent for a moment. He finally turned his body to one side, keeping his neck stiff.

"Marshal, it's Alex. You hurt anywhere?"

"My neck. I think I did something to my neck." He blinked continuously, rolling his eyes around. "You?"

"My shoulder. I don't think it's broken, but it hurts like hell."

"Any . . . anyone else?"

"No. Not on this side of the island, anyway. We need to get to some cover and out of the sun." Alex leaned closer. "Can you bend your legs?"

Marshal slowly drew his knees up and down. "Yeah. Yeah, I think I'll be fine if you can lift my shoulders."

They managed to work their way into the cover of trees. Several hours later, a cooler breeze replaced the warmer one, their semi-dry clothes making them shiver as the sun dipped behind them. In the crown of a fallen tree, both men drew their legs up to their chests, waiting out the night. There were questions galore, but questions would have to wait; pain found its way to new places in their bodies, and they could only think of the worst. With no medical attention, God only knew what internal injuries either of them might have.

For both men, sleep was intermittently interrupted by some form of a water-related nightmare. They would jolt upright and cry out in pain at the involuntary movement. The morning found them with their eyes sealed shut by dried tears and sand. But it brought with it a warm, light rain and fresh water.

"What the hell happened?" Alex asked.

"I don't know. Your guess is just as good as mine. We were fine—and then all of a sudden—all hell broke loose."

Alex cupped his hand over his shoulder, moving it up and down. "I can't remember anyone mentioning any trouble during the flight. The sky was clear. How could this happen? This is a fucking nightmare!"

"You think they know what happened?" Marshal asked.

"They?"

"The FAA, or whatever. Do you think they saw us go off the radar? You know, the little bleep—just up and disappear?"

Alex stared at the sand a moment. He finally said, "I don't know how it works. Even if they did see us go off the screen, I don't know whether they knew our position or not."

"This is our cemetery, Alex. And that back there," he pointed his thumb to the mountain of rock, "is our headstone."

"How's your neck?"

"Huh? Oh, it's stiff, but it doesn't seem to hurt as much."

"Good. I'm going to get some wood together and try to build a fire."

Marshal couldn't help but laugh in spite of their situation.

"What? We could use it as a signal fire. It'll keep us warm at night, too."

"No, I'm sorry. I wasn't laughing at you. I . . . I just thought of something funny in spite of this shit. We at least won't have to talk to a volleyball."

"That's about as funny as a turd in a punch-bowl, Marshal." Alex held his shoulder and laughed. "It's been quite some time since I played Boy Scout." His stomach began to rumble as he walked around, gathering dry twigs.

"What about the project?"

Alex dropped the kindling and knelt. "Gone. All went in the big drink."

Marshal watched as his friend vigorously slid one piece of wood over another, favoring his right shoulder. The dried grass eventually began to smolder and finally burst into a small flame. Alex threw small branches atop the flame and brought it to a reasonable-sized campfire.

"I need to make a confession, Alex."

"A confession? 'Bout what?"

Marshal stayed silent. For a long moment, he just stared out to sea.

"You were saying?" Alex asked, leaning against the fallen tree.

"The project. The others—they were . . . Christ!"

"They were . . . go on."

"Shooting up. They were shooting up with it. Nancy tried it first, then got Richard to try it." He paused for a moment. "I don't know about Ed."

"Fuck! Goddamn it, Marshal! The serum was . . ." he groaned, searching for a word, "*Tentative*. The FDA didn't even know about it, nobody did. It worked on the laboratory mice, but it was a small amount, and you saw how anxious the mice became."

"Hey, relax. I didn't try any of it. They said it felt sort of like morphine, except not so potent."

Alex grasped a handful of sand and flung it toward the surf. "I guess it doesn't matter now, does it? Maybe that's what happened. They might have been high on the serum when we took off."

"Okay, since I'm on a confessional spree here, I'll tell you my part in it."

At first Alex could only look at him, then: "What, there's more?"

"The kids have these domesticated rats. Well, the male took sick and I had to remove him from the cage. I was afraid he'd infect the rest of them, or injure the babies. I didn't want my kids to see that."

"Oh, tell me you didn't? You took that shit home with you? Marshal, how the hell could you know that stuff wouldn't be a potential threat?"

"I didn't, okay! I gave the male a shot. I mean, he looked like he had some kind of flesh-eating virus. Isn't that what we worked so hard at?"

"I have to think for a moment," Alex said, getting to his feet.

"Alex? Look, I know I should have . . ." He watched his friend disappear around a group of rocks.

It was several hours before Alex returned. Marshal woke to find his friend staring off into the horizon. The fire had been reduced to white-hot ashes, which burst into a flame when he tossed on several dry branches. He then followed Alex's gaze into the water and locked his eyes on something floating. Marshal pulled himself to his feet and walked towards Alex.

"I found the other two, Nancy and Richard," Alex said. "This one must be Ed."

"Where?"

"About fifty yards from those rocks. It's not a pretty sight. I'm going to need your help in getting them buried. We'll have to find something to dig with."

Marshal nodded. "Sure."

Alex moved as far as he dared into the water, toward the rocks. The waves had subsided, but were still strong enough to cause injury if he were to be caught off guard. Ed's legs spun toward him, and Alex was able to grab a foot. Marshal waited on the beach and helped him tug the dead man's body onto the sand, away from the surf.

"Jesus, I—" Marshal turned and dropped to his knees, regurgitating yellow bile.

They found a pair of flat rocks and began to scoop up the sand. When the hole was at least two feet deep and five feet long, filling with water fast, they tucked Ed's body in and covered it up. From there, they moved to Nancy and Richard.

Fish and crabs had ravaged Richard's body, leaving small pock-like craters in his waterlogged skin, but Nancy's was far worse. One of her eyes was missing along with most of her upper lip and part of her nose. Her front teeth protruded, giving the appearance of a morbid smile. In an hour, they had all three bodies under the sand.

"It's a hell of a time to bring this up," Marshal said, moving back toward the fire with Alex, "But I'm starving."

"I'm so hungry, I can eat the ass out of a rotten dog," Alex added.

"Any animals on this place? Rabbits, maybe?"

Alex shook his head. "How would they get here, swim?"

"Coconuts then, I guess."

"Unless we can get a few of those crabs."

The sun was well past zenith by the time they gave up attempts to spear fish and capture crabs; they settled for knocking down coconuts. Alex stared into the fire a few moments; his friend's voice brought him back to reality.

"How pissed are you at me?"

Alex tilted his head. "It's water over the dam. And as far as our friends, they fucked up and died, and, as you can see, left us to do the same. I *did* manage to find some shelter over on the far side of those rocks. In the brush a ways, there's a cluster of rocks with a huge split in the center. I nosed around in it a bit. It'll be enough for the two of us to keep out of the weather."

The western horizon was blood red when they finally made torches and started a new fire in the shelter of the rocks. And it was in the nick of time: once again, it started to rain, this time with lightning. Both men had gathered large groups of leaves and had made makeshift beds. It was early in this part of the world, but their unsatisfied hunger was assuaged only by sleep. They woke in the late morning and walked around the island, searching. For what, neither man knew. But it had to be something other than sand, saltwater, and coconuts.

"There's not even any birds," Marshal said.

"Too far from any other land. I thought I heard birds when I heard you yelling the other day. There's no other living souls here, but . . ."

"What?" Marshall asked. "What's the matter?"

"The matter is—we didn't walk there. See? Or did you?"

Footprints were scattered over the sand. They appeared to walk right into a tree, which stood in a little grove. At the tree's base, it looked like there had been some type of scuffle.

Alex moved closer to the trees and inspected the area. There were two sets of prints: one set was larger than the other, and one of them was wearing a single shoe. Alex continued to trace the prints back to their source. The footprints zigzagged, like drunkards leaving a beach party.

"What in the hell?" Alex stopped and pointed.

"Mary, mother of God," Marshal whispered.

Alex ran . . . ran to the other side of the rocks. As he rounded them, he could only stand and stare, his chest heaving, his brain screaming for more oxygen.

"Animals, Alex. Animals dug them up. I told you there were . . . animals." Marshal stared at the empty grave.

"We've got to get back to the shelter," Alex said. "We have to find out what the hell is going on." He stumbled away from the rocks.

"The smell. It was the smell that drew them to the bodies. It was the sm—"

"There's no fucking animals, Marshal. Where's their tracks? Next, you'll try to tell me that—maybe the crabs dragged them away!"

"I'm not going back in that cave."

"Why? Why, Marshal?" Alex's grip was vice-like.

Marshal's face became contorted. He lowered his head, his shoulders heaving up and down. Alex released his grip and stepped back.

"The rat, it—was stiff. It was dead, Alex. I ran as fast as I could to get something to put him in. Anything, so the kids wouldn't see what happened." He ran his fingers through his hair. "I came back with several plastic grocery bags, but I knew they weren't going to work. When I got back there, it was tearing at the metal bars. Tearing at them with its teeth all bloody and broken. It was ripping its own teeth out trying to get at the cage, trying to get at its mate and babies.

"Reanimation," Alex said.

"W . . . What?"

Alex sagged against the rocks. "Not only of the infected flesh, but of the whole body. Not just resuscitation, but more like a resurrection."

"I didn't know, Alex. I didn't know."

"What did you do with the rat?" Marshal shook his head and shrugged. "I used some old burlap bags I had in the garage. I got it into the doubled-up bags with some rocks and threw the damned thing into the river."

Behind them, on the other side of the rocks, something groaned. Nancy staggered toward them. Her empty eye socket held an opaque gray flesh that hung down on her cheek. She hissed, spewing a brown filth from a partially devoured nose and from a mouth that was now totally void of lips. Farther down the beach, another figure swayed and stumbled its way toward them; it had one arm.

"It kills and then reanimates the dead tissue," Alex said, grabbing Marshal's arm and pulling him along toward the other side of the island. "We discovered it, and we also have isolated it. Right here with us."

"We've become the animals, Alex." Marshal was out of breath and terrified. "We've become the hunted!" Richard, the man who was once their assistant, came out of the brush from the direction of the shelter, carrying a severed arm. He, too, groaned and hissed, tearing flesh from the dead appendage.

There was an old saying. Alex thought about it as they ran. He had no idea why it just popped into his head, but it did. He knew it was only a matter of time. They had to sleep at some point, but they knew sleep was now a lost cause. He thought again, *You can run, but you can't hide.*

* * *

Six months later, a seaplane made its way toward the beach. The cove was calm, and the wind was warm, carrying with it the sweet smells of decaying coconut and palm. *It was perfect*, the director thought, as his crew scattered for a better look.

"I knew I saw this place," the director said. "It's perfect."

The producer and director of photography both agreed. It was perfect for their newest horror flick, *Zombie Island*.

"Hey," one of the crew yelled, emerging from the brush. "I found some prints back there. It looks like someone else was here, and not too long ago. I also found a cave back there. Smells kind of dank, but that might add some atmosphere."

"It's getting dark," the producer said. "Let's play campers. It's much safer than trying to make it back to the mainland. Show us that cave."

The director joined the two. "Yes, I'd like to see this place at night."

* * *

The old man rocked back and forth, watching the traffic outside his window, honking and squealing brakes.

SNAP!

"Gotcha, ya fucka!"

The dragging sound was faint at first. The old man watched the doorway leading into the kitchen. Then it came around the corner. The Rat. The rat in the trap, its head under the steel bar, its eyes bugging out, blood red. It dragged the contraption across the wooden floor. It looked at the old man, watching him with its swollen, beady little eyes. It dragged its teeth across the blond wood, digging and grinding them into the red pattern.

"Traps ain't good no mo," the old man said. "Gotta cut off yo head, too." He lifted the heavy butcher knife from the oil stove.

"Damnedest thing I ever did see."

LIKE CHICKEN
FOR DEADFUCKS

Andre Duza

June 2015

Anonymous man awoke to pinpricks of white-hot pain. Having no recollection of his surroundings, of how he got there, or even of himself, he fell hard against the warm leather seat cushion, his fingertips massaging his clammy brow in small circles, as if to initiate recall.

A quick survey of the area returned bits and pieces of information. It was the dead of night, he had been asleep, or unconscious, in the passenger seat of someone's car (for how long he had no idea), sitting idle in the rear section of the 24-hour Megamart's vast parking lot, back where the dumpsters lined up to gobble refuse next to a trio of loading docks.

Brachiosaur-necked lampposts laid bright eyes on the lot-markers (X, in this case) blinking faintly in effigy of shoddy workmanship from nineteen-inch screens mounted on each side, and halfway down its neck.

A door, facing Anonymous man (from now on he was going to go by X; being a black man [somehow he just knew] it seemed strangely appropriate that he adopt the lane marker [X] as his temporary identity) from one hundred feet away, past a few scattered cars, and patches of dried blood, looked to have been left open by the skinny Wigger clothed in store colors who had just went back inside after his smoke break. He had spent the bulk of his break taunting the zombies behind the electrified fence and laughing at the ever-malfunctioning parking-lot guides.

Lot Escorts they were called, holographic companions (they came in all races, genders, and physical types) that, for $125 a month, would escort the client to his or her car should they forget where they parked, or in case it was dark. If there was trouble, the escort reacted by speaking in a commanding tone, something along the lines of,

"Step away from the customer!"

or,

"Stop, or I will alert the authorities!"

There was talk of a *"Classic Hollywood"* series coming in a year or two.

To X, the whole place looked infected with pesky apparitions hailing from all walks of life, appearing and disappearing, some lingering longer than others, some stuck in perpetual stutter, some going through their normal routine and making small-talk with the empty air next to them as they walked to an empty spot, waved, then vanished.

One had walked right up to X's window: a fat, overly ac-commodating woman. He didn't see her until she was right up on him. He turned, and there she was. She looked right at him, past him, and waved. Something about her fake sincerity gave him chills.

Like many businesses, the Megamart's parking lot was sur-rounded by 15ft. electrified, concertina wire fencing topped with a coil of barbed wire that came to life like a chainsaw smile when touched.

On the other side, hundreds of full-blown zombies stood back, perusing the live menu with slack-jawed intensity, zeroing in on the meaty parts. Thanks to the malfunctioning escorts, they were riled up, their collective moan upgraded to a deep-throated growl and seasoned with frustration. 800,000 volts reacted with lively bursts of electric-blue admonishment to the touch of cold dead limbs and digits, of the few who refused to be denied. Small fires here and there awarded those who could hold on to the fence the longest.

At the entrance, double-reinforced scaffolding erected in the shape of a twenty-five-foot watchtower lined with giant flood-lights, housed three glorified rent-a-cops who took turns picking off zombies who wandered too close to the steady pageant of vehicles going in and out. It was mostly people restocking canned goods and various foods that boasted of prolonged shelf lives. There really wasn't any other reason to come outside these days.

Instead of jump-starting his memory, the lack of cohesive relevance sent X spiraling into phobic territory. He let his head fall forward, his brow smacking the dash with a thud. He repeated it again and again.

Suddenly, the click-clack of footsteps approaching from the rear—*real* footsteps. There was a distinct difference.

Through the fogged windows, X noticed a police officer who was approaching to investigate, nightstick twirling in his hand with reticent authority. He walked right through an escort dressed in a military uniform.

X also noticed that the back seats had been pushed down as if someone had forced their way in through the trunk of the car. It gave him his first real clue as to how he might have made it past the guard-tower around front.

The officer was close enough now that X could see the letters on his nametag: Officer D. Mira.

X quickly deferred to the rearview, as if he just now realized that it existed. He was thrown for a loop by what he saw looking back at him.

Half jumping, half falling, X sprung from the car, from whatever it was in the rearview mirror, and in turn, sent Officer Mira back into a defensive crouch, his service revolver now in place of his baton.

"Don't move!'"

Somewhere deep inside his own mind, X was pinned down by unseen hands that taunted and teased him with prolonged periods of sight, sound, and sensation, sans the ability to respond and react voluntarily.

Via his actions, X seemed to comply to the officer's demands without hesitation; however, he was frozen in residual shock-waves of mule-kick reflex action and fleet-footed understanding of a second tenant who occupied his inner space and of the ghastly warped thing in the rearview, pock-marked with bullet holes (hundreds at least) and exaggerated to devilish proportions.

Like everyone else these days, the thought of becoming a zombie had crossed X's mind at some point, creeping up with icy fingers sharpened to a point, replacing the fear of death itself as the motive for nonsensical countermeasures, like fanatical commitment to religion, and the acquisition of unnecessary things to clog the wheels of logic.

He'd seen people turn after being bitten. Akin to an erosive virus, it was a slow, excruciating process that started with nausea, fever, chills, violent mood swings, and dementia, none of which he had yet experienced.

His subconscious suggested that it might be demonic possession. Before Jesus, and the zombies, he would've laughed at that.

"Who . . . er, what *the fuck* are you?" Mira barked, maintaining shaky composure that started and ended with the handgun that he held out in front of him, elbows locked straight. "And how did you do . . . what you did?"

"I . . . I don't know," X said, his hands upturned, arms spread, beckoning, his mangled visage waxing innocent as if he expected some give in Mira's stance. "I don't remember anything before waking up in the car."

X took a step forward.

"I SAID DON'T FUCKING MOVE!" Mira sunk deeper into his ready-stance. "I suppose you don't remember killing those cops back in the bus station, then?"

Watching X with experienced eyes, slightly reddened due to fatigue, but sharp as a hawk's, Mira leaned his head to speak into the communicator on his lapel: "This is Mira. I'm in row X of the Megamart parking lot on Lansdowne and Garrett road. I've got our cop-killer. I repeat, *I've got our cop-killer*. Send back-up." His eyes rolled up and down X's gruesome body. "Fuck it, send a meat-wagon too. He's in bad shape now, but that's nothing compared to what he'll look like when I'm done with him."

"Mira," a voice blared from his lapel, "This is Drake. Are you out of your mind? This mutherfucker just took out twelve of us *by himself*! Just hold tight 'til we get there."

"Yeah! No shit," Mira barked back. "Two of 'em were good friends of mine . . . yours too, Drake."

"Don't you dare, Officer!" exclaimed another voice from the lapel, this one tainted with an accent that bore some distant relation to police-speak.

His gun still pointed at X, who stood with his arms in the air, eyes reading disbelief as he surveyed himself from the feet up, Mira considered doing the right thing and waiting for back-up. He played out the scenario in his head and found little satisfaction in the outcome. He wasn't dumb enough to actually believe in the system. Especially not now.

"Who the hell is this?" Mira replied, speaking to his lapel.

"This is Detective Makane, Officer. Now you listen to me. I understand your anger, but this case is bigger than that. You do anything to keep me from questioning that asshole and I'll—"

"Do what you have to, Mira!" Sergeant Brooks interrupted. "Just don't take your eyes off that scum. I'm on my way."

"Stay outta this, Sergeant!" Makane demanded. "You and your men have no idea what you're dealing with."

"I'm sorry, Detective. It's not usually my style to step on someone else's toes, but this guy took down twelve of my men."

"Thirteen, actually," X teased in a voice vastly different from, yet equally genuine to, the one that had resonated from his diaphragm only moments ago. With its distinctly feminine cadence and deep Appalachian drawl, it made Mira's hands tremble and constrict around the butt of his gun when he realized that it sprung from this teenage boy who stood before him. Mira put him at seventeen or eighteen years at most.

"Wh . . . what did you say?"

"Goddammit officer!" Kane yelled via the lapel-receiver. "Just get out of there. *Now!*"

"I said that I killed thirteen little piggies, you dumb cunt. You forgot to count yourself."

Mira had only begun to squeeze the trigger when hundreds of what looked like bullets punched free from X's torso, legs, and face. They zipped to a livid hover at either side of X's head and shoulders. Pulsating with aggression and taunting with half-lunging feigns, the swarm restlessly awaited their cue from X, who was clearly caught in some kind of trance.

Mira fired three times. In retrospect, it seemed like a stupid move, what with the bullets—which they clearly were, bullets—hovering in a sentient mass all around this kid.

X buckled and tensed in an orgasmic flutter as Mira's shots hit him. The most it did was energize him.

Turning to face Mira, X lurched and coughed. With his tongue, he fished something small and round up from his throat. The object had a deadened glow and was streaked with red. X rolled the object between his teeth and spit it at him.

Mira cried out when his own recycled bullet bit him in the gut and dug into his soul. It was the worst pain he had ever experienced.

He pulled his hand away from his stomach and watched the dark stain in his uniform expand. Dying was the last thing Officer D. Mira expected to happen today when he woke up. In fact, he awoke looking forward to using his new vibro-shock baton to crack some zombie skulls.

Mira did his best to ignore the pain and react as he was trained. It was all he knew.

He lifted his gun and pointed.

X, who was still entranced, had plenty of time to react. Pain chased Mira's body in a weird path, which it traveled at a pause-and-go pace, on its way to a full stand. It was almost comical how long it took.

Mira was fading, swaying to a seductive song called creeping death. He managed to squeeze the trigger one last time, half involuntarily.

The brutish verve of hundreds of bullets pounded Mira from every angle as he spun away and danced into the dark uncertainty. His last thought, that there might be no afterlife, worked with his relaxing muscles to guide his last meal out into his underwear.

Mira's own slug hadn't even left the barrel before he expired, on his feet, dancing to the beat of lead projectiles. He crumbled to the ground when they were done with him, nerves twitching, electrons firing Hail Marys.

Weaving in and out of the mother-mass, the living-lead chased each other into braided formations upon their return to their host-body (X), who accepted their heavy-handed homecoming with open arms.

Just like that, X awoke from the trance.

Now that he was himself again, and armed with selective recognizance (waking in the car, the escorts, the approaching cop, waking just a second ago to a burning sensation all over his body), X was able to deduce that he was most likely responsible for whatever had happened to the police officer (Mira) who lay broken at his feet. And he was instantly reminded of the bigger threat.

FUCKING ZOMBIES. . . .

They were everywhere. Their collective moan, so pervasive that it drove a few folks to suicide, was hypnotic at times. X could see in their eyes how bad they wanted to come through the fence and eat his ass. They seemed to look at him differently than they did the escorts, as if they knew.

Vying for the top spot in the background din, the haunting wail of police sirens bounced from building to building and out into the open where X stood searching for somewhere to hide. Around front, the rent-a-cops in the tower (he could see the top ten feet from where he stood) had their hands full with a faction of zombies that had begun to rock the tower to get at them. Still, the front gates were locked, the fences all around him humming with current. X was trapped.

Forgetting, for the moment, his brief collection of memories, X focused on his best option (blending in with the late-night shoppers in the Megamart), and took off running toward the back of the building. The stockroom door gave when he turned the knob.

The stockroom was damp and cold. The generator's un-abashed rattle drowned out any noise, so once he realized that he was alone in the room, he hurried to the door on the other side and teased it open to a crack.

As usual this time of night, the store was fairly empty, which seemed to give the music more room to reveal the overhead speakers' poor quality.

What X could see from the back corner of the store encour-aged him to further explore Megamart as a potential pit-stop: an extremely overweight single mother dressed in ill-fitting designer knock-offs and large gold earrings with the words 'Bad Girl' written in cursive on the gaudy triangular frames, and her obnoxious young son who she ignored completely, except when he wandered out of her sight and she yelled out his name "DARIUS!" at the top of her lungs; zit-faced employees stocking shelves and talking smack about the store hottie (a fine, young brown-skinned thing) who sat facing a large monitor keying in irregular items up in the manager's booth that was situated high above the colorfully stocked aisles at the back like some adminis-trative watchtower; a group of college students complete with the obligatory stoners (two of them) who snickered at shit like 'butt shank portion,' 'turkey necks,' and store substitutes for popular brand name products, 'Mega-tussin,' and 'Mega-jock itch cream'; and the broken-down security drone resting among two older models that didn't work either in their station a few feet from him.

X had not yet seen himself since the last blackout, and his appearance was suspiciously left out of his recent memory. So he maintained a crouch as he made his way to the nearest empty isle (Tools and Hardware) and fell on his ass between two columns of stacked boxes marked Sure-Grip.

He tried to steady his breathing, to escape reality by losing himself in the holographic celebrity spokesman that stood before a pyramid of stacked socket-sets and a state-of-the-art riding lawn mower that could hover six inches off the ground and cut grass with lasers. Then there were the animated mascots that touted products from their respective packages, talking over each other with repetitive sales-pitches that eventually bled into one voice that X was pretty sure instructed him to "KILL THEM ALL! You can start with that fine young thing up in the manager's booth. I bet her shit even smells like roses."

Voices in his head were one thing, but these were external. Could it have been a personalized ad via retinal scan, or facial-recognition software built into the package itself? Tools and Hardware weren't usually known to use profanity and sexual references as part of their repertoire, though. That was left to the porn section, which was over in aisle seven.

"If it's Meleeza you're worried about, she'll never know, not unless you dig her up and tell her."

The voice was clear this time, deep and gravel-pitched, yet feminine, and made all the more peculiar coming from the mouth of a praying mantis in a tool belt looming from a flat-screen angled down above the Mantis Tools alcove in the middle of the aisle.

With it came total recall. X remembered the following:

His name; Jason Williamson . . . and another: Boring.

The rush of heat that seemed to leap from his girlfriend Meleeza's body into his as she died in his arms only a week ago. . .

How, in complete concert with aggression, anger, and hatred, the sentient heat made him feel for the split second before he vomited all over her and after he came in his own pants as a result. . .

The days that followed, wrought with drastic mood swings and bouts of violent sickness. . .

The confrontation with the police in the bus station where he gained his bullet-down guise. Up to that point, he had been possessed in the classical sense.

How good it felt to break that security guard's fucking neck and toss him to the ground like he was a child when, in fact, he was much bigger than Jason. Sensing that something was wrong with him, Jason was trying to leave town before he lashed out at his mother or anyone else close to him like the new tenant in his body was trying to convince him to do.

Worst of all, Jason remembered how he looked and exactly how painful being shot repeatedly was.

Listening over the choir of hucksters, Jason scrutinized every sound and labored to understand the source of the voices coming from the next aisle. In any case, he knew that he couldn't stay where he was for long without being seen.

Lifting himself enough to see over the highest box, Jason peered to the left, then right, then turned to inspect his rear. He was just about to give himself an "all clear" when . . .

An eye, widened to a full circle, stared back at him from the minimal confines of a woman's compact mirror. It was the brown-skinned hottie in the manager's booth. Apparently, she had been checking her make-up when she saw him.

Startled to a flushed hue by what she saw down in aisle thirteen, the brown-skinned hottie dropped her compact, spun around, and backed all the way into the opposite wall.

His reaction delayed by fear, it wasn't until she picked up the phone that Jason thought to drop out of sight.

A frigid embrace began to claim him as the thought of facing the police again, who were surely out for blood now, gestated. He couldn't hear the sirens over all the jingles and holographic spokesmen.

They must be close now, he thought.

Suddenly, the pillar of boxes on either side felt as if they were closing in. He remembered . . . he remembered that he was claustrophobic as well.

From the ass-end of the aisle just below the manager's booth, the screech of rusty wheels finally brought Jason to the balls of his feet and off in the opposite direction.

The mouth of the isle jumped from side to side as he ran. The brighter light at the end beckoned, illuminating the talking magazine and tabloid covers and flashing candy bar wrappers that were strategically placed to snag the dormant majority as they waited to check out. More importantly, he focused on the automatic doors that lay just beyond the checkout counters, to the left of the large windows that stretched along the entire front wall.

Jason focused on the checkout directly in his path, the one with the empty shopping cart wedged between it and the next. He was confident that he could clear it in one dive and roll, but decided to simply plant his hands on the counter and throw his legs over the cart at the last minute. He fully expected to nip it with his foot; he didn't expect that his ankle would momentarily lodge.

Landing awkwardly, Jason turned to run out the double doors. They were conveniently blocked by a man he hadn't noticed before, a stout serial-killer type who had bent over to retrieve the groceries that had just fallen through the bottom of his paper bag. He nearly jumped out of his shoes when he saw Jason.

Thinking quickly, Jason opted for the window. Pushing the serial-killer type aside might have been easier in theory, but Jason was afraid of what might happen to the man if he should retaliate. Besides, what were a few shards of broken glass compared to another death on his hands?

Against the backdrop of night, Jason's reflection stood out like a black Republican. He was about to stop when he saw it move out of sync. And there was something else . . . something distinctly solid moving behind his two-dimensional doppelganger, growing larger as . . . as it approached from the parking lot. It was a man. Someone he had seen before. He was carrying a shotgun, this man, one of those new, lightweight, heat-seeking jobbers. In fact, he was pointing it right at Jason.

BLAM!!!!!!!BLAM!!!!!!!!!BLAM!!!!!!!!! Exploding glass chased Jason along the wall of windows. In his wake, stalactites of glass refused to fall from the top of the giant frames until they could hang on no longer. Projectile shards nipping at his back, Jason dove to the floor at the mouth of the L-shaped vestibule. The burly, serial-killer type sprung from his hiding spot between two vending machines when Jason slid to a stop near him. The man stepped right into the path of a bullet with Jason's name on it. He never knew what hit him.

From the parking lot came a passionate yell, faint, affected by less restricting acoustics as it had come from outside, and delivered with a certain authoritarian zeal.

"Freeze, or I'll blow your ass...!"

Jason didn't wait for him to finish. Had he allowed the voice that advised him "We can take him" to dominate his thoughts as it had been trying to do, then he would have most likely had another dead cop on his hands (and his conscience).

Running as fast as he could—through the checkout lane, into the main area, and up aisle nine, which was empty—Jason just missed being struck by rippled potato-chip fragments traveling at high velocity from the shotgun blast that destroyed an entire display of snacks.

Detective Philip Makane (Kane to his friends) was beside himself with guilt that he didn't make it to the bus station before the police. By all accounts, Jason Williamson was a good kid who just happened to be at the wrong place at the wrong time, and now he would have to kill him too. There was no other way. Though he had only spoken to him briefly in the aftermath of the St. Salacious incident, Kane had been smitten by Jason's quick wit and by the glow of wisdom that swirled beneath those big brown eyes. He remembered thinking that, if given the chance, this kid was going places . . . well, maybe not now, but in a perfect world. Too often, the bad examples seemed to make the most noise, finding empowerment and pride, or something resembling pride, but owing more to rage and insecurity, in the belligerent attitudes that victimization begat. Jason was different: intelligent, charismatic, and street-smart. And look what had become of him. Somehow, it just wasn't fair.

Deep in his subconscious, Kane looked to redirect blame, pointing the finger at Jason's poor judgment in the people with which he associated. Meleeza Duncan, his late girlfriend, certainly was attractive, and seemed nice enough, but for a girl of only seventeen, she came with a lot of baggage, most of all that wack-job mother of hers.

Jogging toward the shattered front window with his shotgun held at the ready, Kane filed his guilt away and concentrated on stealth as he traversed the moat of crystalline shards, climbed in through the empty frame, and crouched behind the checkout counter.

With his back against the filthy bag-bin at the end of the lane, Kane looked to his right, at the mess of red flannel that blocked the entrance. He quietly apologized to the burly man (serial-killer type) who lay bloodied on the floor (feet facing into the store, arms stretched up over his head, automatic doors chewing on him). Kane swallowed his disgust. It never would've gotten this far had he not been bickering with Allison, his partner and occasional fuck-buddy.

Peeking over the lane to develop a visual layout of the store, Kane waved the scattered bystanders who were jockeying for his attention back into hiding. As big as the place was, Jason could've been anywhere.

He was such a good kid. Such a good kid . . .

Kane had thought it was a joke when he first heard Sgt. Stern mention the name Boring. His colleagues were notorious practical jokers. But how on earth would they have known? He never told anyone about Boring, the talking pterodactyl with large human eyes and a long, devious smile that would fly in his window every night when he was ten and berate him for hiding under the covers. Kane never actually saw Boring, so he could've looked like anything; if he had, he might've saved himself from the horrors that his imagination conjured up over the years. It had haunted him ever since, this imaginary friend who, despite Kane's skepticism, he knew in his gut to have been real. Could it be that they were one and the same, that *his* Boring had resurfaced twenty-five years later?

. . . or . . .

Maybe this was just some hyper-contagious virus. All three hosts (Gus Rollins, Meleeza Duncan, and now Jason) had come into close contact with each other. Rollins had taken Meleeza hostage before he was killed by police during his shooting spree at the Springfield Mall, and Meleeza died in Jason's arms after running naked from St Salacious Episcopal a week and a half later and having the shit knocked out of her by a fast-moving SUV.

But then, why the games, why the stab at poignancy with Jason, in his bullet-down guise, representing some twisted metaphor on urban violence? Maybe he was wrong, but that's how Kane saw it.

"Jason!" The voice cut into his concentration with the subtlety of a dull blade slicing through gamey beef as he hid in the frozen meats and seafood area at the back, near his original entrance. "This is Detective Philip Makane. We spoke at the scene of Meleeza's accident a week ago."

"Don't listen to him," the voice inside Jason's head demanded just as he was rounding the corner to recognition.

"I know that you're a good kid, Jason, and that you're being forced to do these things."

"He doesn't know shit. He'll say anything to get you to come out."

"The police will be here any minute, and I'm sure you know how they feel about cop killers. To put it bluntly, I'm the only hope you've got. Now, come out with your hands up, and I'll do my best to see that you get some help."

"Fuck him! Make that piglet work for it."

Jason had yelled out to Kane, whom he now remembered vividly as someone he could trust, only his voice never left his mouth, and even there it was but a mumble trapped beneath figurative meaty palms that stunk of sulfur and ass.

"Don't you fight me, boy. I'll rape your insignificant little ass from the inside out."

Working within the limitations of his cerebral lock-down, Jason searched his mental database for something to distract him from the present: his mother's smile, his dog Emit jumping up to greet him, Meleeza purring in his arms.

"God-dammit!" Kane growled, watching uniformed officers pour hastily from four cars out in the parking lot. Two more stayed at the entrance to assist the rent-a-cops, who had lost one of their men to the zombies.

Warmth fled Jason's body as he marinated in what ifs: what if their bullets, laced with tangible scorn, somehow hurt more; what if he went out looking like some run-of-the-mill thug with a supernatural upgrade. He hated being lumped into the same group with the corner jockeys, who warmed the steps outside liquor stores in his neighborhood, taunting average-looking women and intimidating those whom they envied.

"Relax, boy. You ain't just in here by yourself now. And I don't intend to make it easy for those pigs this time."

"Maybe you didn't hear me, Jason," Kane yelled louder this time to compensate for the sirens outside. "Do you hear *that*, then? They're right out front. Do yourself a favor and come out now, before it's too late."

"Save your breath, pig!" the voice spoke via Jason's mouth. "You might need it to scream bloody murder when all those teeth are ripping into your flesh."

Kane gave the threat little merit as he, realizing that he *was* going to have to kill Jason, tried to find something that might comfort the boy.

"For what it's worth, Jason, I'm sorry."

If anyone was going to kill that kid, it was going to be him. That way he could at least ensure that Jason wouldn't suffer anymore than he already had.

"Where are you, you bastard?" Kane whispered. His eyes rolled from left to right, tracking the sound of Jason's voice via recall, and ignoring, for the moment, the frightened shoppers who were starting to make tentative movements toward the front to greet their rescuers.

A loud crash from the lot spun Kane around.

Kane's POV: The guard-tower and fencing along the front of the lot lay flat, dead rent-a-cops entangled in the broken scaffolding. Chain links bounced beneath slipshod feet shuffling away the weakened electric tentacles that reached up and danced around their legs before fizzling out. Hundreds of full-blown zombies staggered into the Megamart parking lot and immediately went after the escorts, stumbling over and trampling each other along the way. Something resembling enthusiasm grew in their deadened eyes as they reached the escorts and either lunged right through them, or snapped their jaws together with such force that cracked or shattered teeth. Still, they tried and tried. The rest followed the general flow of undead husks toward the store like a tidal wave of molasses rolling both slow and fast toward the cops who stopped, turned, and opened fire.

With all their firepower, the cops probably didn't expect to be overcome as quickly as they were, caught in the undertow of grasping hands and dragged beneath the surface. Jolts of light popping with brilliant yet brief life-spans provided a "you are here"-style position marker as some of the cops tried in vain to shoot their way out of the swarm while others punched, clawed, and scratched the anonymous hands and teeth that tugged their flesh and pinched it away from the bone.

There was a certain pitch of scream that seemed specific to being eaten alive. It was an awful sound, one that came as close as possible to translating the experience, especially the first and last bite.

Kane turned away and repeatedly cleared his throat to block out the sound.

"You were saying about the police?" The voice resonated with maniacal glee. "The question now is . . . is it too late for you to help yourself and the rest of these sheep who you've sworn to protect?"

While the words hit him square in the ear, Kane was busy measuring the parking lot left between him and the zombies. Most of them were on their last legs, so they were slow (he'd seen some first-stagers run as fast as a low-level sprinter for short distances) and basically easy to maneuver around, but it took a certain kind of person to remain calm enough to work out a path through the maze of bad meat, open wounds, and funky stenches. He had no idea what kinds of people he was dealing with here in the store. Nine times out of ten, they weren't the right kind. And with Jason running around to boot, their composure was most definitely stretched thin.

Fuckers are worse than roaches, Kane thought.

The lead zombies already had Kane focused in their sights. When he saw the carnal anticipation bulging from their clouded eyes, as if they knew that his flesh was somehow tastier than the norm, he looked down at his body, almost expecting to see a big red bull's eye painted on his chest. *This fucking place* . . . flat and rectangular, with sickening hospital-white light pouring from the large fanged opening in the front of the building as if to advertise all the edible goodies inside.

These people would surely take his effort for granted, even though he'd be putting his life on the line, *again*, and would lump him into the general slop of authority figures the next time they had a gripe. It made him think twice about wasting his time to come up with a solution rather than just going for broke and hunting down Jason.

Decisions . . . decisions. . . .

As it was close enough to present the possibility of danger, the slap of flat, heavy feet wrapped in hard-soled shoes and traveling at a living stride from his immediate left-rear, bitch-slapped Kane back into action-mode.

Leading with his shotgun, Kane spun around too late to stop the obese black woman from running out the door with her son Darius in tow.

Kane's arm check-beckoned, his lips curling around the words "Stop! Wait!" in silence as he realized just how much momentum she had gained and just how hard it would be to stop her without hurting her. *What is she thinking?* The cops were dead, all but the one whose severed torso was being torn between a cluster of zombies.

"Sweet Jesus!" The obese woman cried out when the burly husk that blocked the doorway (serial-killer type) reached out and grabbed Darius' ankle as he attempted to step over him.

Trapped in a tug of war, Darius shrieked at the top of his lungs.

By the time Kane came within reach of the burly zombie's feet, the obese woman had fallen out of the doorway onto the parking lot. Darius, who snapped like a whip out of the zombie's grip, fell on her, then bounced off. The automatic doors closed behind them, rejoicing with a hiss, trapping Kane's echoed footsteps in the L-shaped vestibule.

The burly zombie whipped around on his hands and knees and flashed a dripping red snarl. Between his teeth dangled a ripped swatch of blood-soaked fabric. It looked like denim.

In the parking lot, the obese woman examined Darius' ankle as he whined at her twisting and turning. There was a large chunk missing from both his jeans and the back of his ankle at the hemline.

The obese woman held Darius close to her enormous bosom and rocked back and forth. She appeared to whisper something in his ear, but Kane was both too far away and too diverted to hear it.

The tidal wave of rotting flesh and raspy moans grew deafening as the zombies approached with greater purpose now that the obese woman and Darius had stumbled onto the scene.

She pulled Darius away, grasped his face in both hands, and ordered him to stand on his injured leg. "Try dammit, try harder than you've ever tried before!" Darius simply cried louder and louder as he watched the zombies close on them.

Maybe you'd be able to carry him if—Kane stopped himself. He had a *thing* about obese people, especially the ones who sported fake satisfaction in their size. "God gave me food to eat," was their credo. The obese woman definitely fit the description, but now was not the time to judge.

As he watched the zombies draw closer, eyes bulging, mouths opening wide, yellow, red, and black-stained teeth clacking in expectant glee, there was no doubt in his mind that the obese woman and Darius were as good as dead, and there wasn't much he could do about it save for dying in their place. Without looking, Kane kicked the burly zombie backward onto his ass, then raised his shotgun and calmly blew off all his limbs.

For a moment, the zombies outside looked up, distracted by the gunplay.

Kane looked down past his shotgun at the limbless zombie that still struggled to reach him, slamming its face into the floor and using it to inch himself closer and closer like a caterpillar. This was once a man, a beer-swilling, chain-smoking, white-trash malaise, but a man nonetheless.

Lifting his shotgun in disgust, Kane aimed down at the burly zombie who, upon reaching him, pushed with his forehead against the end of the barrel. Stiffening his hold, Kane held him at a distance, then at the last minute took a few steps back and whipped towards the screams of "Lord help us!" coming from the parking lot. He could barely hear it over the zombies' collective voice, over the muzak that poured from the overhead speakers, the overlapping jingles, and holographic pitchmen and pitch-women.

Thumbing a button next to the scope, Kane zoomed in his view of the obese woman and Darius as the zombies began to encircle them and reach down. There were only seconds to decide whom to shoot first.

Kane cringed at his options.

Darius was facing away, so at least Kane wouldn't have to see the look on his face should he take the mother out first.

He pulled the trigger in mid-thought. In his haste, he forgot to close his eyes, and he didn't even look away when he lifted his foot, stomped on the limbless, burly zombie's head, and pinned him to the floor.

Gore was nothing new to Kane; however, every nuance of the shotgun's devastating punch into the obese woman's face reso-nated with nauseating discomfort: the way her fat body seized and jiggled, fingers curling into a claw; the way her legs kicked; the sound that rushed out of her mouth along with the blood and brain matter that landed all over Darius, herself, and the first tier of zombies, some of whom recoiled due to residual flickers of instinct.

Worst of all, the obese woman was still clinging to life.

Wobbling on her knees, she made an attempt to reach Darius, who fell on his ass after she dropped him. Confused and overcome by fear, Darius crawled backwards away from his mother, right into the arms of the famished undead.

Her head turning jerkily, loose meat bobbing and spitting, the obese woman spotted Kane and, with one eye left, begged him to put Darius out of his misery. A second later, she was completely surrounded by dead folks who began to feast with impunity.

Kane, who was still watching through the scope, turned the gun on Darius as hundreds of ravenous hands yanked at him. Darius was a crying heap, balling tighter as his clothes were torn from his body and his naked flesh touched first by the chill of night, then by skin hardened to edges, protruding bone ripping like talons, and finally by teeth meeting teeth.

Zeroing in on Darius' head, Kane tried to keep a steady hand. He promised himself a direct hit this time. Darius managed to escape their grasp only to be recaptured again and again, as there was nowhere for him to run.

"MommmmMeeeeeeee!"

Once he was certain that he had Darius in his sights, Kane closed his eyes and pulled the trigger.

CLICK!

The gun was empty.

"No! No! No!" Kane inspected the empty chamber as if he expected a round of ammunition to magically appear.

Thankfully, Darius' screaming was short-lived, though memorable in its bubbly-pitched urgency. It ended in a gurgle, suggesting that Darius' throat was torn out. Kane had already looked away, so he couldn't be sure.

Now there were only zombies. Hundreds of them, thousands counting the lone roamers that began to arrive from deep within the neighborhoods that bordered the Megamart plaza. Fat, thin, old, young, recently deceased, and long dead, they approached with dumbed-down determination that made their primal desire seem all the more frightening. Lazy yet eager, their feet dragged and slid as if a normal gait was foreign to them anymore, foreign as the tear that crawled down Kane's cheek.

A curious blur exploded from the ass-end of aisle seven. Without hesitation, Kane lifted his shotgun, thrust off the balls of his feet, and pulled the trigger in mid-stride. CLICK!

"God-dammit!" Energized by the sudden activity, he forgot that he was out of bullets.

Kane's knee-jerk decision (to hunt Jason down) was probably the wrong one. The zombies were more of an immediate threat to these people, who seemed to forget about Jason for the time being. However, he continued on his path, reminding himself that there was probably ammo back in Sporting Goods.

He . . . *they* were headed for the manager's booth. Jason knew that much. Although he had a good idea why (fuck it, he was positive: to fuck the brown-skinned hottie, probably kill her too, maybe kill her, then fuck her), the image that that cued up set the wheels of shock in motion and he, the limited, new Jason who lurked deep inside the overthrown shell, couldn't afford the extra baggage if he was to maintain the cursory hold on bits and pieces of his inner self. Boring liked to irritate him by making him suddenly wake from his trance-stupor feeling as if he had only been dreaming. Then—BAM! It came back with a vengeance, affecting him like it did the first time he realized that someone . . . something else was inside him.

He . . . *they* were on their way up the short, narrow stairway to the manager's booth, climbing them with purpose, leaden feet lingering with each step to allow the shockwaves of impact to travel up from the floor to the fire in their loins. If there was an upside to being possessed, this was it. The sting of lust was like nothing he'd ever felt, and he had done his share of experimenting. His dick was as hard as a rock. It felt good, damn good: so good, in fact, that he greeted the zombie feeding frenzy that he passed with the same indifference that he showed to the random acts of violence he occasionally walked up on while cruising through the 'hood high as fuck. When their eyes met (his and Kane's), Jason flashed a detached smile, looked away, and continued on, his mind tripping on lust that dripped from his penis, his eyes zeroing in on the brown-skinned hottie through the booth windows.

At the time, Kane was up to his waist in zombies, thrashing the chainsaw with the "Clearance" tag dangling from its handle from right to left, jagged teeth biting deep into and through flesh and bone and muscle. Like some badass zombie-killing machine, Kane swung with all his strength, teeth mashed together, lips curled into a snarl. Behind him, two collegiate types with aluminum tee-ball bats took out the stragglers and the ones smart enough to attempt a sneak attack from the rear.

As a result of his symbiotic sickness, Jason's interpretation of events was beginning to filter through a haze that made things drag and skip and mold to fit some unappeased adolescent fantasy scenario.

80s Teenage Fantasy

An arm, pock-marked with day-old bullet-hits, reaches into the frame, fingers spread, opened palm easing into contact with the black door marked, Manager's Booth. Employees Only Beyond This Point.

The door swings open, the room inside falling upon our eyes gradually. Inside, a portable MP3 boom box cues up *Broken Wings* by Mister Mister.

Her back is to us. Peeking out from beneath her white sheer blouse knotted at her sternum, the nape of her back, smooth and tight as can be, begs for attention. She is wearing tight jeans, the kind the white trash girls liked to sport. Kane called them camel-toe jeans. As she squats, fumbling with something on the lowest shelf of a dented metal bookcase, the pants formed a second skin against the meaty "W" of her hips and ass. Her legs are slightly thick, just enough to make the rebound jiggle of her apple-shaped ass linger against the scrotum after each thrust. She knows that she is being watched. If it wasn't evident before, it is now as she stands with a serpentine sway, leaving her ass to jut out at the end of her hypnotic rise.

Her thick, raven locks flop and slide across her back as she pivots her head from side to side, then turns to face Jason.

The music swells!

A gust of wind lifts her hair from her shoulders, where it whips horizontally two feet behind her, snapping like a flag in the wind. Her eyes light up as if she'd been expecting him, longing for his specific touch. They creep down to his crotch, and back up with a naughty glint. Against her glistening brown hue, a white lace bra screams at us as she loosens the knot in her shirt and lets it slide from her arms, her erect nipples making a strong case for freedom from underneath. Her breasts spill out from the top while below, her waist and the suggestion of a finely tuned abdominal wall lure our eyes in pursuit of her dexterous fingers as they unsnap her jeans and drag the zipper down. The V-shaped opening gives us a preview of what lies beneath.

She glides toward Jason as if on wheels. They embrace.

As they kiss, Jason, too, succumbs to the cinematic wind, and an overall feeling of flight, the song's pop antics, merged with easy-listening sedative qualities, lulls his brain into a cloudy bliss.

When he opens his eyes to reassure himself that this is really happening, we see via Jason's point of view that the three rectangular windows set high on the right side of the room project a scene of fast-moving clouds.

CUT TO:

They are naked on the floor, the brown-skinned hottie on her stomach, Jason thrusting away on top, watching her plump ass bounce to the rhythm. Her face, turned sideways, enough so that she can occasionally seek out his eyes to truly understand his hang-jawed rapture, rests on her folded forearms. Looking down upon her, Jason uses her reaction to fuel his stamina while at the same time fighting to stifle the cum that crawls slowly toward the light.

CUT TO:

We find them in missionary position. It seems like hours have passed, but judging from the song, which is only half-over, it has only been a few minutes. Lifting his torso off hers, Jason arches his back to thrust deeper, and, bracing himself with his right hand, he reaches down and manipulates her breast, circling her nipple with his fingertips, pinching and pulling it taut before letting it snap back into place. Her perfect face is alive with ecstasy. For the tenth time at least, Jason establishes the fact that he never would've gotten a girl like this on his own. In a moment of genuine emotional connection, he caresses her face, cradling the side of it in his palm. He lets his hand slide down to her neck and around.

The music begins to distort. . . .

CUT TO:

This time it was different, waking to reality, or something close to it. His fantasy girl had suddenly hulked-out on him, thrashing violently beneath him, once beautiful beyond words, now wrought with bruises about her face and upper chest, and gulping open-mouthed as Jason tightened his grip around her throat. Instead of the usual symbiotic sucker-punch that kept Jason disconnected, the detached haze that currently separated him from reality was from shock, then horror, then shame, each coming right on the heels of the other. Jason had no time to react, to brace himself for whatever might come next. He expected that it would be the same old shit. Boring and his fucking tricks. . . . However, it had been a full five minutes (the moments of clarity usually lasted a minute at most), and in that time, things had melted to extra sharpness: the abrupt wave of pain as the brown-skinned hottie wrapped her thick legs around his waist and squeezed, the volume at which her twisted, ugly expression screamed utter contempt, the sting of her palm as she slapped him across the face again and again, the burning sensation as she clawed him and dragged her hand down his cheek, neck and chest, or the fact that her naked body no longer incited a sexual response. Worse yet, it made him feel sick.

On the radio, an advert for tea, distinctly AM because of its lack of texture. The sterile whine of an old-fashioned teakettle cut through the kinetic stillness in the manager's booth. The surgical brightness intensified to a white-hot glow that sizzled.

"SOMEBODEEEEE HELP MEEEEEEE!" she screamed, thrusting her face up at him as if she intended to somehow stun him with the weight of her audible wrath.

He hadn't figured her for an around-the-way girl, but he knew that accent well. It was one that he ran from until he found himself. Based on the way she doctored her moaning to sound more innocent (or maybe that was his mind's doing), he pictured her being more soft-spoken, all breathy and sweet. It was clear now that she was running from the same thing that he used to. She probably worked around mostly white people, which, by the looks of her (she was all that, and then some), she saw as a haven from the catcalls that always reached her physically, their sen-similia-soaked words like hands tugging at her belt, fingers sliding across her ass and digging in for an ample chunk to squeeze. They called her names like "shawtee," or "thick legs," or "bitch" if she didn't respond. Sometimes, they even followed her for a block or two, looming over her with their primal funk, arms spread as if they were about to wrap them around her and snatch her up at any moment. This was where she could take off the mask of bastardized masculinity that she, and other girls like her, wore as a result.

Her name was LaToya. Her nametag had been pinned to her shirt the whole time, but Jason only just noticed it as she slid backward on her hands and ass, reaching for her clothes along the way and trying her best to cover herself, first with her arm, then with the shirt.

Jason sprung to his feet and attempted to follow her, arm extended, hand upturned to translate peaceful intentions, his flaccid penis dangling, pubic region encrusted with blood and vagina secretions. He stopped to pull up his pants and underwear from around his ankles.

If he fell on his ass, LaToya might get back at him, she might run out the door, right into the hands of the . . .

The zombies. . . . Jason hurried over to the rectangular windows that looked down into the aisles.

There were two people left: Kane and a younger man in his late teens or early twenties, surrounded behind the four glass bins that encased the deli area by a contingent of zombies. Even the slow-shuffling dead situated farthest from the deli counter acknowledged in some way (a look, body language, a grunt) their stake on the last three warm bodies. Some of them had stopped on their way to fixate on familiar things (cereal boxes with funny characters, brand names they preferred in life, flashing tabloid magazine covers, clothing, stereo equipment, jewelry), hanging onto something similar to memory that, for a millisecond, sparked to life.

These were real people, these mothers, fathers, sons and daughters, brothers and sisters, and nasty little secrets reduced to chewed-upon pieces and fought over with deadfuck zeal. The lucky ones hoarded prime cuts, whole arms and legs and pulled-apart torsos, and large, unidentifiable chunks, and swatted at opportunistic hands hungry for more than just scraps. Jason had seen many of these people alive only minutes ago.

ALIVE. . . .

ALIVE?

The word climbed up Jason's spine and sunk its venomous fangs into his brain-anesthetizing warmth, from his core to the external personal space that his aura claimed. Beneath the layers of noise—shotgun blasts, an authoritarian voice (Kane) yelling profanities, the background moan, the fucking electronic ads attacking from every direction, and the old Beastie Boys song, "So What'cha Want," that spilled from the overhead speakers—Jason could actually hear the dead folks chewing.

Three quarters of Megamart's inventory lay smashed and broken on the floor. Food and liquids coated whole aisles both sticky and slick, and stole some of the zombies' feet from under them.

Jason felt a breeze blow past him.

LaToya. . . .

By the time he turned, she was already out the door and calling to God as she tumbled headfirst down the narrow steps just outside the booth. This time her nudity frightened him.

Standing dumbstruck, paralyzed by the magnitude of evil he had helped wrought so far (and on top of everything else, he expected at any moment to be snatched away from this reality again), a fire ignited in Jason's arm, an unnatural warmth that he was now able to control, his mind charting a path up to his shoulders, his head, and down to the rest of him until the bullets in his flesh began to fidget.

"This is it, kid." Spine-tingling honesty spiked Kane's tone and made the younger man, Doug Springsteen, start to out-and-out cry. "Close your eyes and turn away. I'll try to make this as painless as possible."

Kane turned the shotgun on him and motioned with a matter-of-fact jerk of the barrel for him to turn.

"No! No, wait. . . ." Doug pleaded. "There must . . . there must be an—"

"What? Another way? Sure there is."

Kane looked to his right at . . .

. . . hundreds, no, *thousands* of dead-ass humans looking back at them, all with the same "I'm gonna eat your ass" expression.

Kane pivoted with the shotgun, ready to pick off anything that attempted to climb over. "I'm gonna do myself right after if it makes you feel any better," he told Doug.

He was down to ten bullets (the box of ammo that he found in Sporting Goods was nearly empty when he got it), and he knew it wouldn't be long before the *bang* of the shotgun, which still seemed to half-startle them momentarily, was too old a memory to keep them at bay.

"Whatever you decide, you'd better make it quick."

The zombies were starting to climb over the counter. Kane followed the first one up with his shotgun and blew it back into the four or five who intended to follow.

"Fuck!" Kane backed toward the absolute middle of the deli and right into Doug, who was whimpering noisily. "This is pointless, kid. If you don't give me an answer by the time I'm down to two, I'm going to decide for you."

The pressure squeezed a warm stream of piss from Doug's bladder. Lying too thick and moist inside his lower jaw, his tongue wouldn't let him answer.

Kane slid Doug one last glance as four, five, six zombies made their way over the counter. Kane shook his head and placed the barrel beneath his own chin. He closed his eyes and curled his finger around the trigger.

"Suit yourself, kid."

"Wait . . . look. . . ."

Up on the stairs, a mess of a man (Jason) invoked a Jesus Christ pose and shook violently, flesh undulating, eyes on their way up and back. So far, Kane had only seen the aftermath of the bullet-swarm, and he'd heard the officers who survived the bus station trying to figure out just how Jason took so many rounds without falling. Experienced cop eyes told them that Jason wasn't a zombie. Zombies had their own specific hue. They figured him more for an addict.

"Must be some good shit," one of them quipped as Jason wobbled on his feet after they unloaded full clips into him. There were fifteen cops at the scene, twelve of them who'd participated in the gunplay, each locked and loaded with full twenty-two-shot clips. That equaled 264 rounds, and still he refused to fall. Overkill, maybe, but Jason had just killed a cop . . . a rent-a-cop to be specific, but that was close enough.

"Good shit indeed," replied another. "Where can I get my hands on—"

A bullet ripped through his throat, stealing his last word. On his way down, he saw what looked like a circle of blue-men dancing around another, who stood with his arms extended, recycled rounds jumping from his body like an organic turret.

Based on what he knew, the look on Jason's face told Kane to . . .

"Getthafuckdown!" Kane said. "Everybody, getthafuck-down!" Less than an hour ago, he was addressing a group of people, and his mind had yet to fully acclimate to the drastic reduction.

Doug blacked out when his head hit the floor, bounced, and smacked again under Kane's weight. He opened his eyes and almost lost it at the sight of Kane's face, larger than life, and so close to his; then the extra pressure on his lungs and stomach indicated that someone was on top of him. A man. He could smell old coffee on his breath, and feel stubble when their faces touched. Oh God, what had they talked him into? He must not have locked the door to his dorm. But wait, he didn't remember drinking last night. . . .

"Snap out of it, kid!" Doug heard the man say, as if he knew him.

Did he know him?

Doug remembered seeing Kane's thick arm coming at him, and the feeling of hurried descent, but not the actual impact.

Had he been shot?

His body seized. He reached up and felt the back of his head. Nothing.

Smack!—Kane's hand lagged in the baby-fat when it struck Doug's cheek, turning his head to the side and finally knocking some sense back into him. He looked into Kane's eyes. "Please don't kill me!"

"Just stay down and don't move!" Kane yelled over the din that had eluded Doug's ears thus far. Kane squeezed his eyes shut and pressed himself into Doug.

As he listened, Doug broke the noise down: open hands slapping raw meat (that's what it sounded like anyway), bone cracking and splintering into calcium-flecks, electric pops and buzzes, and that familiar moan, its continuity robbed by repeated impact and challenged by the overbearing roar of a large-caliber machine gun perpetually spitting.

He felt the tap-tapping of fragmented "things" hitting his arms and legs, and something damp that was seeping through his clothes and bespeckling his forearm.

Kane glared down at Doug, squinting at the debris. "You still with me, kid?"

Doug shook his head. To his left and right, everything under the sun bounced to the floor and rolled close enough to him to cause his eyes to flutter. Feet, both naked and clothed, followed haphazard patterns; knees buckled and gave out or exploded into pieces.

Kane was mumbling something about Jason, or to Jason, something along the lines of "That's right. . . . Make those fuckers pay." His head was positioned in a way that finally allowed Doug a good look at what was going on above them.

It reminded him of a nightclub; lights flashing, bodies intoxicated by music (in this case it was something slow and throbbing) and trying their best to translate their own personal sonic euphoria into movement, but instead looking like a roomful of sardonic comedians going for the easy laugh by pulling out their best rhythmless white-guy impressions and literally coming apart at the seams. All around them sparks flew, and glass and paper and plastic fell to the ground. The air was littered with a glowing crisscross of heat like scratches on film that marked the paths of too many bullets to count, ripping in and out of zombified trunks and sending appendages sailing, many of them cut down to mere fibers before they hit the ground, as were the bodies from which they escaped. Without raising his head, Doug traced the glowing bullet-wash that chirped by. Eventually, they led him to Jason, who stood at the top of the steps, stuck in organic turret mode. *Ok, first Jesus . . . then Jesus, then the rain, the zombies and now this?* Doug wondered what else such a short life thus far could possibly have in store for him.

* * *

The atmosphere inside the S11 Police Bulldog (a van-sized quadruped with a short, bulky reinforced shell and loaded with state of the art weaponry) was somber, yet the commentary always seemed to turn to playful insults. Triumphant gestures accompanied by calls of "Yee-Ha!" and derogatory phrases leveled at the zombies (one joked that they had become the new niggers) laced the distinctly masculine conversations. With no source of ventilation, their voices had nowhere to go, ramrodding into Kane's quiet dementia like radio-friendly hip-hop bogarting quaint suburban ecosystems from pimped-out lemons, bass threatening to shake them to pieces.

Bandaged up and reclined on the built-in gurney in the back, Kane felt like a zombie himself, nullified from feeling both emotional and physical by what had happened tonight inside the Megamart. Though he sat back away from the small reinforced window in the back door of the vehicle, Kane could still see the Megamart shrinking in the distance.

Was it over? Had he finally put a stop to Boring? His gut told him no. However, hope was the only method of satiating the ugly images that were already haunting him: blood everywhere, trumped only by barely recognizable remnants of former people; Jason, on his knees, completely spent from maintaining the bullet-swarm for so long; the way he looked up at Kane, his eyes filled with remorse and fear and semi-satisfaction before Kane blew his head apart; the guilt he felt for not feeling guilty enough anymore; the immediate anxiety that chewed him up and spit him out when he realized that, to be sure Boring hadn't jumped again, he'd have to kill Doug too, probably even himself.

At least Doug had gone out on a high note. He had been in the middle of celebrating his survival. Kane waited until he turned his back. Out of bullets, he was forced to do it the old-fashioned way: with an aluminum tee-ball bat. Strange that it felt good almost to kill at this point. The survivors he happened upon in the storage room as he walked out . . . now that was a different story. He had to chase them down, three in all.

"Hey," DeWitt, the big black one, said as he peered out the back window, "I know that chick. Fat bitch used to live in my old neighborhood. Always braggin' about her designer bullshit and lettin' her stank-ass kids run around all hours of the night."

It was Darius' mother. Apparently, she had gotten away before the zombies finished her off, and now she was one of them.

Kane could see her just outside the window, shambling away from the Megamart. Her stomach was torn open, and inside, an upside-down fetus curled into classic position, except for an arm that protruded and dangled from the open wound.

"Man, that's just sick," commented another man who hurried over to get a look.

"I say good riddance, man," DeWitt groaned. "We've got enough ig'nant-ass-mutherfuckas like her spoiling shit for everybody else. It's people like her who make us look bad in the eyes of people like you, Keith."

"Fuck off," Keith replied. He was still feeling salty from the verbal beat-down he took from DeWitt in response to using the "N" word a few moments ago. If DeWitt wasn't so fucking big, Keith would've slugged him when he had walked up face to face and had stared him down.

Kane wanted to tell him that he agreed completely, but experience taught him that guys like DeWitt often jumped sensitive when someone from outside their race pointed out a flaw.

"Y'ever wonder how we must taste to them," a voice from up front interjected, "I mean just fer curiosity's sake?"

Kane grimaced. "Probably like chicken to those deadfucks."

AFTERWORD

Brian Keene

Zombies. You know you love them. Otherwise, you wouldn't have bought this book. You would have purchased one of those horrible *Chicken Soup for the Soul* books, and then I would have had to hunt you down and slap you.

Wonder if they've made a *Chicken Soup for the Undead Soul* book yet? Maybe I should write it.

See, I'm lucky enough to make a living writing horror novels. It's a good gig. I have no complaints. The pay is decent. The commute is unbeatable. And I get to be my own boss. My first two novels, *The Rising* and *City of the Dead*, were zombie novels. I tried to reinvent the mythos. Tried to do something different and fresh. Hopefully, I succeeded. I think I did. Readers loved them. So did most of the critics. And so did Hollywood, because the film rights were snatched up quicker than a fast zombie in *28 Days Later*.

Since then, I've written a number of horror novels; giant, carnivorous earthworms; horny, murderous Satyrs; demon possessed bank robbers; serial killers with homicidal pet tapeworms; ghouls and ghosts; etc. etc. et-fucking-cetera.

And after all of those books, you know what my readers keep asking me? Not, "Will you write another ghost novel?" or "Will there be a sequel to *Terminal*?" Huh-uh. They say, "That was cool, but when are you going to do another zombie novel?"

And I'm okay with that, because I love zombies, too. It was the original *Dawn of the Dead* that screwed me up for life and put me on the path to doing what I now do for a living. (To be fair, it was also *Phantasm* and *Jaws*, but they weren't zombie movies and this isn't an anthology of stories about devilish funeral home directors or rampaging Great White sharks.)

It's very clear that the authors who contributed to this anthology also love zombies, and it did my heart good to read these stories—kudos to all involved for a job well done. There are some valuable new entries into the undead mythos between these pages. They aren't the first, and won't be the last. Zombies are hot again, and it seems like everybody wants to take a stab at them lately.

That's a good thing.

Zombies are the new vampires. Remember, just a few short years ago, when, if you stood in the horror section of your favorite bookstore and closed your eyes, your

finger landed on a vampire novel? I do. It sucked. You couldn't find a fucking zombie novel to save your life, but there were twenty million new vampire books every month. Vampires suck. They used to be cool, but now, vampires are no longer mean and nasty. These days, they are nymphomaniac detectives or morose creatures in desperate need of a suntan, dressed in black that smoke clove cigarettes and listen to too much Bauhaus.

Not exactly scary, are they?

But zombies—oh man, even after all this time, zombies can still scare the shit out of you. Maybe it's because they speak to our deepest shared anxiety—what happens after we die. We don't know. And that rocks us at our spiritual core—that maybe there's nothing after death, nothing except getting back up and munching on the living. Or maybe it's just because they're like undead Energizer bunnies—they keep coming and coming and coming.

Now there's resurging zombie popularity. Zombies are cool again. It started with *28 Days Later* and my own novel, *The Rising*. It continued in both film (*Shaun of the Dead, Resident Evil 2, Return of the Living Dead 4*, the *Dawn of the Dead* remake, and *Land of the Dead*, just to name a few) and in literature (with over a dozen new zombie books published in the last year, including *Xombies, The Zombie Survival Guide, Risen, We Now Pause For Station Identification, Zombie Love, The Walking Dead, Cold Flesh*, Stephen King's upcoming *Cell*, and this book that you hold in your hands, among others). And there are more zombie films and books on the way, along with a slew of new video games. Zombies have invaded pop-culture; everywhere from episodes of *Aqua Teen Hunger Force* to clothing lines at Hot Topic and role-playing games like *All Flesh Must Be*

Eaten. As I write this, I've just come from a children's movie—Tim Burton's *Corpse Bride*. The corpse in question is a zombie.

But even as these reliable old corpses shamble towards their place in the spotlight again, something becomes apparent; these aren't your father's zombies. These fuckers don't lurch around. They run. And forget about just humanity being affected. We've reached the point where we've got zombie squids (as in this anthology's wonderful opening story.)

What comes next? Well, like everything else in the genre, these things are cyclical. This new zombie craze will continue for a little while longer. Then, the market will get flooded with too much of a good thing, and people will move on to other monsters. Werewolves or ghosts or even vampires again (shudders at the thought.) But that doesn't mean that the zombie sub-genre will die. Nope. You can shoot it in the head, but I guarantee you it will come back again. It always does. Sooner or later, the undead rise once more from the grave.

And take a bite out of you, like chicken for dead fucks (if I can toss a subtle nod to this book's closing story.)

Zombies are undead. Un-dead, meaning, they can't die.

And let's all be thankful for that...

Brian Keene
Journey's End, Pennsylvania
September, 2005

About the Authors

Travis Adkins, age 26 years, has been missing since the zombie outbreak began in northern West Virginia. He was the author of *A Time for Every Purpose Under Heaven* and *Twilight of the Dead*. When he wasn't writing, he enjoyed playing video games, shooting pool, and chugging Jager Bombs. He is dearly missed by his two cats, Phantom and Spike, and by all the future ex-girlfriends he certainly would have had. His family still holds the hope that he will be found in a horizontal position, not upright and wandering around the neighborhood. Memorial service pending.

Eric S. Brown is the author of the paperback collections *Space Stations and Graveyards*, *Dying Days*, *Portals of Terror*, *Madmen's Dreams*, and *Waking Nightmares*. His chapbooks include *Zombies the War Stories*, *Still Dead*, *Flashes of Death*, and *As We All Breakdown* to name only a few. His first novel *Cobble* is slated for release in October 2005 from Mundania. Eric lives in North Carolina with his loving wife Shanna where they await the birth of their first child.

Vince Churchill is a life-long fan of horror, space opera and dark fiction. Churchill is the author of two novels *The Dead Shall Inherit the Earth* (2002) and *The Blackest Heart* (2004). Happily married and settled in L.A., he is working on a variety of horror projects. Close to completion is the sequel to *The Blackest Heart*, titled *Pandora*. And his next horror novel—a full blown zombie extravaganza—is slated for completion in 06-07. Visit him online at www.vincechurchill.com.

Kevin L. Donihe is the author of *Shall We Gather At The Garden* (Eraserhead Press) and *Ocean of Lard* (Eraserhead Press) with co-author Carlton Mellick III. His short fiction has been accepted into over 140 publications in ten countries. Visit him online at users.chartertn.net/mbs/kldwriter.

Dave Dunwoody is a Texas native currently residing in Utah. He writes reviews and short stories for independent horror magazine *The Hacker's Source* (www.eveblaackpub.com). Most recently he co-wrote the short film *Snuff* to be released by Timberwolf Entertainment. Dave lives with his wife and two cats who may or may not be dead.

Andre Duza is author of the cult horror novel, *Dead Bitch Army*, which is currently being adapted to graphic novel format by Indie Gods Publishing for an early 2006 release. His second novel, *Jesus Freaks (jē'zəs frēks), n. see ZOMBIE*, an epic zombie tale from which "Like Chicken for Deadfucks" is taken, will be released in fall 2005 by Deadite Press. At this very moment, Andre is somewhere in Philly working on his next four novels, tentatively titled, *U4riac, Dancing and Stabbing, Dirt Dogs* and *UV Junkies*.. Feel free to visit Andre at his website, The House of Duza (www.houseofduza.com).

Derek Gunn lives in the seaside suburb of Clontarf in Dublin, Ireland with his wife, three children and his dog. The normal world constantly tries to get in the way but despite this he manages to create stories of mystery and horror, usually late at night when everyone else is asleep. His first published novel, *Vampire Apocalypse*, is due out autumn 2005 from Black Death Books. Further short stories are available in *The Blackest Death Volume 2* (Black Death Books) and *Chimera World 2* (Cyberpulp), both of which are on sale now. You can find a full list of his writing, sample chapters and news of upcoming works on his website www.derekgunn.com.

John Hubbard is a vaguely known author and poet from Georgia. He creates his moody writing on the NW fringe of Atlanta in an uncomfortable chair. In 2005 alone, his writing has been accepted by: Bare Bone, The Dream People, Permuted Press, Dark Legacy, Southern Gothic, Nocturne, Cyber Pulp, Seasons in the Night, G.A.I.N., The Lightning Journal, Mount Zion Speculative Fiction Review, Horror Carousel, Escaping Elsewhere, Carnifex Press, and more.

Meghan Jurado is an internationally published author and world traveler with a particular fondness for the horror genre, particularly short stories. When not hard at work churning out tales of terror and woe, she can be seen walking her dogs or catching a zombie flick.

Brian Keene is the Bram Stoker Award-winning author of *The Rising*, *Fear of Gravity*, and *City of the Dead*, among other titles. Suspect was last spotted on the border of Pennsylvania, Maryland, and insanity. He has a criminal record but has never robbed a bank—that we know of. Suspect is considered armed and dangerous. Approach with caution. Report all sightings to www.briankeene.com.

Rebecca Lloyd is a horror, fantasy and suspense writer whose first short story was published in 1994. She lives in the San Francisco Bay Area with her fiancé, two cats and a great big bunch of rescued rats, and is working on her first novel.

David Moody is the author of the acclaimed *Autumn* living dead novels. A writer sick of square-jawed, all-American heroes and contrived happy endings, his books are unique and individual. Tried and tested horror and science-fiction themes are twisted and given a fresh perspective by this British author. Moody's characters are ordinary people forced to survive the most extraordinary of conditions and situations. Join more than 100,000 other readers and download the original *Autumn* novel for free from www.theinfected.co.uk or www.djmoody.co.uk.

Robert Morganbesser was born in Brooklyn, New York, and currently lives in Staten Island. When he's not writing, he's working for the City of New York. Robert has been writing since he was about six—science fiction, history and horror being his main interests. Other than writing Rob loves reading and going to the movies. He has a somewhat bizarre sense of humor which sometimes finds its way into what he writes.

Pasquale J. Morrone is known to his friends and family as Pat. He makes his home in Breezy Point, Maryland with his wife, Kathleen. Pat's first novel was *Spook Rock*, which took place in upstate New York. He has many short stories on the web and in print.

E.W. Norton began his current round of material existence in the fairly well known city of Los Angeles, CA. Since that time his travels have brought him through Minnesota, Tennessee, Illinois, and finally to the boreal regions of Northern Maine. It is there that he resides to this day. In this place he engages in various pursuits of disrepute and general inadvisability. In addition to finding sustenance via the manipulation of artificial encephalons, he formulates eldritch tales and euphemisms of dubious worth, contemplates the hidden mechanisms of reality, watches for the omens of the eschaton, and attempts to avoid further confrontations with torch-wielding mobs.

Eric Pape grew up in the in Mojave Desert region of California and currently resides in San Francisco. As a lifelong scholar of zombies, he is delighted to appear in *The Undead*. He spends his time sharing his appreciation of various dark things with his college students, motorcycle riding through the San Francisco fog, and going to goth and fetish clubs. His fiction has appeared previously in *City Slab*, *ChiZine* and *Camp Horror* and his poetry is published widely in the horror field.

James Reilly is a writer, artist, musician, and film critic, but does none of these things particularly well, nor does he earn a living from any of them. He wasted much of his adult life touring around the country in a punk rock band, but recently realized that he'd gotten old, and run out of things to complain about. Now he has shifted his focus to writing full-time, often cranking out as many as several words a day, in between bouts of online gaming and scouring for convincing fake nudes of various celebrity women. Reilly is also the founder and webmaster of Horrorview.com. He currently resides in Massachusetts with his wife, two poodles, and a morbidly obese cat.

Cavan Scott is a professional writer and editor based in the UK. He lives in Bristol with his wife Clare. His work includes official audio plays based on the BBC TV series Doctor Who, 2000AD's Judge Dredd and The Tomorrow People. Cavan's short stories have appeared in a number of small press anthologies, The Judge Dredd Megazine and the BBC Cult Vampire Magazine while his first novel, *Project: Valhalla*, co-written with Mark Wright, was published in September by Big Finish. Visit Cavan's website at www.cavanscott.co.uk.

Eric Shapiro's wide array of fiction and nonfiction pieces have appeared in over 75 publications, in print and on the World Wide Web, including *The Elastic Book of Numbers* (Elastic Press) and *Daikaiju!* (Agog! Press). Eric's two books, *Short of a Picnic* (Be-Mused Publications) and *It's Only Temporary* (Permuted Press), both enjoyed critical success. You can order *It's Only Temporary* now at www.itsonlytemporary.com.

C.M. Shevlin has had stories published in "Thirteen", "Dark Tales" and been shortlisted for the 2004 Brian Moore Short Story Competition. Formerly of Ireland, she has recently relocated to Australia to work for a year in a hospital there. You might think that living beside the beach in one of the most idyllic places in the world would make it hard to find inspiration for zombie stories but so far that doesn't seem to be the case.

D.L. Snell feeds pulp fiction to man-eating corpses. The entrails of his recent offering, "Limbless Bodies Swaying," can be found in *Cold Flesh*, a zombie-infested anthology from Hellbound Books. If you wish to gnaw on a scrap of Snell's next feast, or if you wish to find a slab on which to lay your own cadaverous fiction, visit Snell's website, Exit66.net.

Mike Watt is from Pittsburgh, PA, the zombie capital of the world. While he started out hoping to be a world-famous novelist, he was often side-tracked by the need to eat, and turned his attention towards journalism, writing for such publications as "Cinefantastique", "Femme Fatales", "Draculina", "The Dark Side", "Film Threat", "Pretty-Scary" and "Sirens of Cinema" (of which he is now the editor). Mike's true love is for movies and he has written several screenplays including a script for George Romero's son, G. Cameron Romero, tentatively titled "24 Frames Per Slaughter". You can check out some of this stuff through Mike's company's website at www.happycloudpictures.com.

David Wellington was born in Pittsburgh, Pennsylvania, where George Romero shot his classic zombie films. He attended Syracuse University and Penn State and is currently working towards a degree in Library Science at the Pratt Institute. Mr. Wellington is most famous for his free online serialized zombie novels, the *Monster Island* trilogy. They can be read in their entirety at www.monsternovel.com. He lives in New York City with his wife who, in her wedding vows, promised to "kick serious zombie ass" for him.

Brent Zirnheld has work upcoming in anthologies by Cemetery Dance and Wild Roses Productions as well as two novels, *Fugue* and *Mercy Kills*, also published by WRP. His story "Auteur in Flames" was recently published in Hellbound Books' *Deathgrip3: It Came From the Cinema*. You can visit his website at http://www.lynchville5150.com.

D.L. SNELL

Hourglass

A single father braves dank mines, train tunnels and carnivorous forests, in search of the last hourglass tree, the only hope of saving his son from the deadly sting of an arachnid wasp.

"Tightens like a noose."
~C.D. Phillips, editor, *eye-rhyme*

Exit66.net/indexbooks.htm

Anthology Appearances

- ☠ **Cold Flesh,** Hellbound Books
- ☠ **The Undead,** Permuted Press
- ☠ **Monsters Ink,** Cyber Pulp
- ☠ **Mind Scraps,** Cyber Pulp

Ghostwriter

An evil priest sicks his congregation on a best-selling novelist, who relies on an un-identified entity to write his books.

"Frightful. I couldn't put it down."
~Nora Weston, author of @hell

Exit66.net/indexbooks.htm

If you enjoyed the stories in this anthology, you may also enjoy

TWILIGHT of the DEAD

by Travis Adkins

Courtney Colvin was nearing the end of her teenage years when the undead apocalypse began. She survived, forsaking her youth and innocence, and five years later she continues to exist —albeit lonely —in the fortified town of Eastpointe. Nightmares and the unwelcome advances of Leon Wolfe are the worst things she's dealing with now in her otherwise mundane life.

But when a newcomer arrives in town and claims to know the location of the antidote to the zombie plague, it sends Eastpointe into an uproar. To retrieve this antidote, she and a group of other survivors must venture outside the relative safety of the compound's walls and into a world ruled and dominated by the flesh-eating undead.

Twilight of the Dead puts a new spin on the zombie genre, yet remains true to the classic rules that have already been set forth. A sure-fire reading pleasure for anyone who loves character-driven horror.

Available on Amazon, Barnes & Noble,
and all other online bookstores
or call **888-280-7715** to order

ISBN 1-4208-5324-4

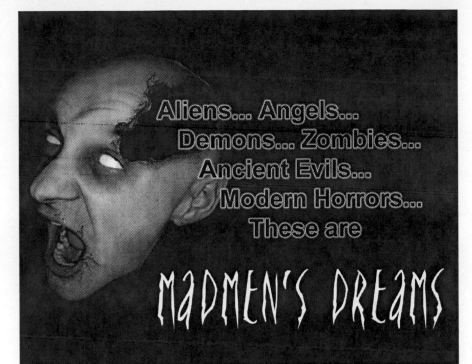

Printed in the United States
209327BV00001B/118-825/A